I0760855

GAIA

KINGDOM OF FAIRYTALES
SEASON SEVEN

You all know the story of your favorite fairytale, but did you ever wonder what happened after the fairytale ending? Well we know. Not all afters end up happily, sometimes the real adventure starts much later...

Following famous fairytale characters, eighteen years after their happily ever after, the Kingdom of Fairytales offers an edge of the seat thrill ride in an all new and sensational way to read.

Lighting-fast reads you won't be able to put down

Fantasy has never been so epic!

KINGDOM OF FAIRYTALES
URBIS PRISON
BADALAH
DRACONIS
DESERT
KISBU
ZHORE
SHIPLEY
THE VALE
AZREN
ELDER
MOSA
ABORIA
URBIS
AZURE
ENCHANTIA
AIRE
SKYLA
EMERALD CITY
OZ
FLORIS
TULIS
THE FORGE
ARCADIA
RENAIS
MELFALL
ATLANTICE
ANTLA
W
E
S

ISBN: 978-1-989997-29-1
Enchanted Quill Press

Contaact the author at www.enchantedquillpress.com
Cover by Enchanted Quilll Press
Interior Formatting by Enchanted Quill Press
Editing by Rose Lipscomb

QUEEN OF THE SUN

17TH JUNE

The man didn't know who he was dealing with. He obviously didn't know I was the princess. I'd hidden my face and hair well with my shawl. I guessed he also didn't know that I wasn't going to stand for being stolen from by a common thief. The light of the crescent moon was just enough for me to see which direction he'd taken after he'd so rudely pulled my bracelet from my wrist. I took off after him, chasing him down the empty streets. Streets I knew, well thanks to my nightly walks through the city.

The thief ran through the empty bazaar, twisting this way and that through the narrow alleys of covered spice stalls. He came to a stop ahead, and I could see he was debating his next move. If he turned left, he would get away. He was quicker than me, and his clothes were much better suited to running than mine. He turned right, exactly where I wanted him to go. I followed, quickly ending up in a dead-end. I could almost feel the panic rolling off of him as he realized he was cornered, but when he turned around and saw I was only a girl, well, his panic shifted into bravado. Big mistake! This "only a girl" was going to kick his butt!

"Come back to give me that pretty necklace of yours?" he sneered. "It will go nicely with the bracelet."

I didn't move. I didn't need to. I knew thieves well. Some stole to put food on their tables. Over the years, this type of crime had fallen greatly, thanks to my parents' generosity and many policies to help the homeless and hungry. Some thieves, like this one, stole for the sheer greed of it

"Come and get it," I asserted. These kinds of thieves were cowards above all else, stealing from those they thought were weaker. This guy was no different.

He hesitated a little, but then moved forward, puffing his chest out and spreading his arms wide.

I held my breath and waited as he walked toward me. His confidence was now in full throttle. It would be his downfall. I slowly pulled my shawl lower. One look at my eyes, even in the dim light of the moon, would give me away as the princess.

When he was two steps away, his hand already outstretched to grab my necklace, I pulled a knife from my belt and pushed him against the nearest wall. Holding the knife to his throat, I pulled his bag from his shoulder.

"Heavy! I guess I'm not your first victim tonight."

His eyes widened, surprised, no doubt that he'd found himself in such a situation, but then they narrowed to mean slits as I took his bag of loot.

The bag jangled as I slipped it over my own shoulder. "I'm taking my bracelet, but I think I'll take the rest too. The Kisbu police would probably like to take a look at what's inside." I pushed the knife further so it marked his skin. "If you are foolish enough to have identification in this bag, I'll keep it to myself, but if I so much as hear that anyone else has been pick-pocketed by an ugly balding man on these streets, I'll make sure the police get that too. Do you comprehend?"

He wasn't so tough now. He nodded quickly, and when I let him go, he took off into the darkness.

As I headed back through the streets of Kisbu, I pondered my evening. It hadn't been the first like this, and no doubt, it wouldn't be the last. That's why I'd taken to carrying a knife around with me. The beautiful city was just outside of the harsh desert in my parent's kingdom of Badalah, and it was an imperfect kingdom. A kingdom that had become infinitely better since the reign of my father, Aladdin, but still had a way to go.

Once a month, my mother, the Sultana Jawahir hosted a huge feast in the gardens of the palace to which the people of the city of Kisbu were all invited. Sometimes thousands of the hungriest families turned up. For many of them, it was the only decent meal they would eat that month. My parents had also opened up many trade routes throughout Badalah, bringing in much-needed food from the other kingdoms. As our land was mostly barren, we imported the majority of our food in exchange for the spices and coffee that did thrive in our hot climate. It was fair to say that my parents had turned Badalah into a kingdom that any person would be proud to live in. We were thriving, or at least we had been until a few months ago. Something had changed. Our feasts were more popular than ever as the people of Kisbu were struggling more and more. At the last one, for the first time ever, we ran out of food before we were able to feed everyone. Thieves like the one tonight were growing ife.

There was definitely a change in the atmosphere, something that no one but me seemed to have noticed, so I'd taken to walking through the streets of Kisbu at night to try to find clues as to what. So far, I'd come up empty.

Giving it up as a bad job, I headed back to the palace, pulling my shawl further over my head so as not to be spotted. Going out alone was not only forbidden, it could be dangerous. Tonight, the thief ran. I might not always be so lucky. I was the princess and heir to the Badalah throne, not some kind of street vigilante. After sneaking through the back gate and running along a hidden pathway through the palace grounds, I climbed the vines outside my window and stepped onto my private terrace, smoothing my clothes as I walked. My Phoenix watched me attentively from his perch on a potted fig tree.

I moved closer to pet my gorgeous majestic bird, catching a glimpse of the gold rings around my hazel eyes in the reflection of his.

"Oh, come on, Asher." I said, firmly stroking the bright red feathers on his back, watching as he closed his eyes. "You know how I hate being cooped up in here. How would you like it if you couldn't stretch your wings every night? You'd be pretty upset, I would imagine."

Asher gave my finger an affectionate nip and tucked his head under his wing to sleep.

My bed had already been turned down. The chambermaids had made it up, expecting that I'd go to sleep earlier. I chuckled, wondering if they knew I rarely climbed into bed until after midnight.

After pulling my bracelet from the thief's bag and placing it back on my wrist, I looked through the bag to see what else he'd stolen. As I expected, there were a number of purses and some jewelry. I'd give the bag to one of the more discrete guards the next day to take to the police. I pulled the bed sheet half over me and quickly fell into a peaceful slumber until I was awakened by my squawking Phoenix the following morning.

"What in Badalah, Asher? What could possibly possess you..." I stopped, following his line of vision. "Mother!" I said with a startle, pulling myself up in bed. "What are you doing here so early?"

Sultana Jawahir smiled. "You, my dear, need to get moving. Your father received word late last night that a very important Sheik, his son, and his envoy are traveling here. They should be arriving in the early afternoon," she said as she disappeared into my closet. That was my cue to jump out of bed. The last thing I wanted was for my mom to pick out my outfit, even less did I want her to find the thief's bag of stolen goods I'd stashed there last night.

"Why does that matter to me? I'm sure you and father will host an elaborate dinner in the guests' honor." The comment came out more contentious than I'd wanted. My parents did their best to help the less fortunate, but as Kisbu was growing at a faster rate than we had jobs available, the wealthier families of the kingdom were taking advantage of the situation and paying their help barely enough to keep a roof over their heads.

I lowered my eyes, "I'm sorry. I'm just frustrated, that's all."

"Is everything all right, Gaia?" My mother asked,

looking at me through eyes that were nothing like mine. Like most of the people in Badalah, her eyes were a deep brown. As an adopted child, I looked nothing like most of the people in Badalah, and my golden ringed irises were what set me apart more than anything else.

Sultana Jawahir was beautiful by all standards, and even though I might not be blood-related to her, I saw a lot of me in her.

I smiled, "Yes, I'm fine. I probably didn't get enough sleep. I'll pick something nice to wear."

"Very well," my mother nodded. "I'll leave you to find an outfit. Breakfast will be brought to you shortly." She turned to leave.

"Please make sure the papers..."

"We all know!" She hollered back at me with a chuckle.

The newspapers of all the kingdoms were my morning reading material. I'd been getting them since I'd started reading at the age of two. Knowing what was going on in the other kingdoms was important to diplomatic affairs, and as the heir to the Badalah throne, it was my duty to keep up to date. The Badalah Beacon kept me abreast of things in my own kingdom; the others gave me a worldview.

I picked a suitable dress from the closet. The wrap-front attached with straps, giving way to three tiers of long layers of sheer fabric while soft ruffles adorned the neckline. I pulled my hair into a smart ponytail and grabbed a pair of heart-shaped earrings that would go well with the dress.

A knock at the door alerted me to my chambermaid's arrival. She quickly moved toward my side table, placing a tray down with a thick pile of papers folded upon it.

"Thank you, Freya."

"Princess Gaia, good morning. Your mother asked me to draw a bath for you. I'll add the rose oils if you don't mind?"

"The rose oils? Why, whatever for? Those are for special occasions, or for when my parents are presenting a possible suitor."

No sooner had those words left my mouth when I realized exactly what was happening.

I looked Freya straight in the eyes. "Are they presenting a suitor?"

Freya quivered, "I do not know, Your Highness."

I sighed. The sheik and his son. I should have known. My mother wouldn't expect me to meet them if she didn't have an ulterior motive. My parents didn't expect me to marry someone they picked out for me. I was free to marry who I wanted, but the problem was, at least in my mother's eyes, that I didn't want to get married at all. In fact, her pushing me to get a boyfriend was more of an attempt to get me out of Genie's library and to socialize like any normal eighteen-year-old. Pointing out that I wasn't a normal eighteen-year-old did nothing to sway her.

It hadn't always been like this. In fact, my parents had always made it quite clear that they wanted me to carve my own path, but just like the kingdom, something had changed with them. In the past few weeks, they'd been paying more attention to the hundreds of marriage proposals I received daily. Three weeks ago, they started bringing potential suitors to the palace to meet me. All unofficial, according to my mother, but the sudden change disconcerted me. I'd not changed, and neither had my opinion on the subject.

I sat down to enjoy my fruit and tea and start reading my newspapers while Freya ran the bath.

The newspapers only added to the general feeling of unease that had been burdening me for months. It seemed that one by one, all the kingdoms were experiencing problems. Not just small problems either—threats of war, kidnappings, magical abnormalities. When I'd brought it up with my parents, they had dismissed me, saying that Badalah was fine. And, apart from the poverty becoming more obvious and the petty thieving, it *was* fine. We were still a great nation, but it was as if something was coming, something that I couldn't foresee and something that I couldn't put a stop to.

I pushed the papers aside and stepped into my bath to ruminate over everything I'd read. Nothing particular had happened overnight, but the Queen of Atlantice was still a mermaid, and the Queen of our neighboring kingdom Draconis, was still asleep. It had been months now, and they were no closer to finding out why. Every single morning, the news agitated me, and every morning, I let it sit like undigested food in my stomach. I needed to speak to my father about it again.

"Gaia, my dear child. I think you are reading a bit too much into all of this," my father, Aladdin, said when I brought it up later.

He paced around his office, one arm behind his back as was his way. He was a good looking man and youthful for his age with only a touch of grey in his black hair, and as he spoke, he gesticulated with his free hand, a habit I'd always known him to have. He ran the kingdom of Badalah with exuberance rather than training.

But despite his words, I wasn't about to be silenced over something that I truly felt was off-kilter. "So, you are saying I'm overreacting?"

He let out a boisterous laugh. "Well, since you've put it that way. Yes. Yes, I do believe you are overreacting. Look, you are of age now. You're a beautiful young lady and extremely intelligent, sometimes to a fault. Regardless of what you've read, you should be exploring other things in life right now. Not occupying yourself with matters that simply don't concern you."

His words rubbed me wrong. "Let me get this straight. You'd rather I busy myself with shopping and fawning over boys? Spending my time on useless pastimes, which are of no benefit or interest to me?" I put my hands on my hips. "Explain to me exactly how that's supposed to prepare me for my role as the future sultana of this kingdom?"

"Gaia..."

"You've seen the papers," I interrupted him, pointing to today's stack of papers. "Something is wrong. It's happening all over, and I can feel it here."

I didn't mention the sudden increase in crime I'd noticed and the need to carry a knife with me when I left the palace. I didn't think he'd take kindly to me roaming the streets after dark. Only Asher knew about that, and that was how I wanted it to stay. Once upon a time, I would have told my father. He'd grown up on the streets himself after all, but he'd changed recently. Up until a few months ago, he encouraged my learning and inquisitiveness. Now he dismissed everything I said.

"I don't know what you want me to do, Gaia. I've read the papers, and I continue to monitor them daily. So some of the other kingdoms are facing difficulties. It happens."

"But that's just it," I continued. "It's not just difficulties. The problems all seem to be magical in nature."

"Well then, we don't have a problem here. There's been little to no magic in Badalah since The Vizier was overthrown, and the genie became human. All of that happened before you were born. I really see no cause for concern."

"What about Elder?"

My father shrugged his shoulders. "What about Elder?"

"They don't have much magic either, but they are struggling with a curse."

"I don't know where you've heard that nonsense, but it's not a curse. It's an illness, a plague even, but it only affects wolves. I believe the Red has it all in hand. I spoke to her advisors recently."

I groaned in frustration. My father had done well because of his optimistic attitude, but in times like this, it didn't help matters. Elder didn't have a newspaper. It was the advisors that I'd heard the news from too. I'd been listening at the door when they visited my father. He had taken the news in his stride, but there was something about it that had struck me. I had a feeling that the people from Elder were playing the problems they were having down a little...or a lot.

"Don't you think it's weird that the kingdoms are all having difficulties this year? I can't remember there ever being problems like this in any of the kingdoms before now."

"It's coincidental, yes, but things can't always be perfect. I think some of the kingdoms were due a bit of bad luck, to be honest. We've had peace throughout all the kingdoms for years."

"Bad luck?" I huffed. "You think this is all bad luck?"

He didn't say a word. He didn't need to. It was written all over his face. My father, the sultan, was burying his head in the sand.

My blood was boiling. Still, I wasn't going to make a scene. I walked away, considering he'd suddenly gone mute, to find the one person who I knew would listen to me. Genie.

"What's with the sullen pout?" Genie asked as I walked into his chambers and sat down on the long chaise next to his bookshelves. He gazed upon me with a twinkle in his hazel eyes and a hint of humor on his face. Most people wouldn't think of Genie as a handsome man. He didn't have the same cute appeal that my father had, but there was something commanding about him, something majestic and regal that even my father could never hope to possess. He also knew everything about everything and had a wit and wisdom I'd never found matched in any other man. He had a whole suite in the palace to himself, and this room was my favorite in the whole palace. I'd lost count of the hours I'd sat here, reading Genie's extensive collection of books and discussing everything and anything with him. The outer chamber where I was now, he referred to as his office, but I thought of it as a library. A door led to his inner suite with his bedroom and bathroom and a living area. I'd never been through that door.

"I've helped my parents rule this kingdom by creating policies that work," I whined as I slouched on the chaise.

Genie listened intently to what I said, taking in my words, weighing everything carefully as he usually did.

"I've rolled up my sleeves and gotten to work when asked. Now suddenly, my father wants me to back off and be more of a traditional young lady. He'd…no, they'd rather I find a good suitor to *help* me rule."

I drummed my fingers on the arm of the chaise and waited for Genie to respond.

Genie's mouth pulled at the edges, giving a hint of dimples. I ignored the tugging in my stomach at the small change in his expression. I was mad. I needed to stay that way.

For the longest time, he'd been like an uncle to me, a mentor of sorts, but in the last few months, I'd noticed things about him I'd not picked up on before, such as his pale eyes framed by long dark lashes and his strong jawline and how fit he was. And the way he gazed at me with such intensity when I told him something he had to think on.

Genie held his hand out to me. "Come, let's take a walk in the palace gardens. I think we can both do with some fresh air."

I took his hand, ignoring the tingle running up my arm, the same tingle I'd been ignoring for weeks now, the same one that was threatening to turn into a veritable earthquake if I wasn't careful. Genie was thousands of years old, but he could pass for a man in his mid-thirties. I needed to remind myself of that fact. The age difference between us was insurmountable… It was beyond that, it was ridiculous. We weren't May to December; we were May to…well, the next millennia. Eighteen years ago, my father had saved him from his prison of a magic lamp, and it was only then that he started to age the way humans do. He told me once that he'd been trapped in the lamp at seventeen years old, which was why now, eighteen years later, he only looked thirty-five. I sneaked a quick look at him as I stood. He stood well over six feet, with broad shoulders and long black hair that usually trailed down his back, but today, he'd tied it back in a plain gold band.

I took a deep breath as the fresh scent of jasmine hit me as we walked outside.

"I think the Sultan simply wants you to relax and smell the flowers once in a while," he said, picking one of the sweet flowers and handing it to me.

I smiled and tucked the flower behind my ear. "However much I enjoy being given flowers, I need to speak to you about something that's been playing on my mind for a while now."

"Something other than your parents trying to hook you up with the first available man that happens to pass these parts?"

I gave him a playful shove, ignoring the electricity building up inside me at his touch. Electricity that he didn't notice, let alone share. "Yes. I've noticed some oddities across the kingdoms. I can't pinpoint anything specific that's wrong, more that it's lots of things happening at the same time. There is something ominous happening, but I don't know what exactly."

He rubbed at his chin. A habit I'd noticed of his when he was thinking. His skin was impossibly flawless, and I found myself wanting to reach out and touch him.

"You've picked up on this from reading your newspapers?"

I nodded, shaking the thought of his skin from my mind. I was here to have an important conversation with him, nothing more. As a veritable bank of worldly knowledge, he was the one person that I indulged my love of intelligent conversation with. My girlfriends only ever filled their heads with fashion and boys, and lately, boys were all my parents talked about too. With Genie, I experienced the world without having to leave the palace.

"Hmm."

The wheels in his head were spinning. I could sense that much. He wouldn't fob me off as my father had done. He would actually think about what I'd said.

Before he had time to answer me, one of the guards came calling. "Princess Gaia, Genie; the sultan and sultana request your presence in the throne room for the sheik's arrival."

Damn! I'd forgotten about the sheik.

I sighed, and Genie took my arm in his sending another rush of adrenaline through me. It was the sweetest torture having him so close to me. Taboo and yet so normal. My emotions tormented me as we walked through the palace.

The throne room was heavily decorated in gold and white, with massive crystal chandeliers hanging from the ceiling. Velvet chairs had been arranged in a circle, something my parents liked to do when entertaining guests. My father thought it put people more at ease than having them sit facing the royal thrones that were set to one side.

"Gaia!" My mother said, looking up at me. "You look beautiful, my daughter. Truly amazing. Come, let me get a good look at you."

Genie released my arm so I could go to my parents' side. Genie elected to stand in the shadows. That was just what he was like, preferring to watch from the sidelines and take everything in before making his presence known.

I gave my parents a quick bow then sat in my designated seat. A second later, a guard entered the room "Your Majesties, Your Royal Highness, may I present Sheik Ahmadullah and his son, Yama."

They both wore pristine white robes, each with a golden belt around the middle.

The son's robe was more modern with a mock stiff collar, giving him an edge of sophistication and class. He smiled brightly, revealing two rows of pearly white, straight teeth.

They reached our inner circle and bowed.

"Sheik Ahmadullah, we welcome you and your son to our palace." My mother said, standing to welcome him.

"Such a pleasure to have you with us. I do hope you stay for a while," my father added.

The sheik smiled, establishing eye to eye contact with my mother. "Sultana Jawahir, Sultan Aladdin, thank you. It is our honor and privilege to be here, among our most beloved rulers."

As they introduced themselves to each other, I took the opportunity to size up the son. He was handsome in a bland kind of way. A little too perfect for my liking, and his eyebrows were too thick. They almost met in the middle. He caught me looking and gave me a wink causing me to blush. A thief wanting to rip my heart out of my body I could cope with, but a pretty boy wannabe prince winking at me had me unraveled. A couple of months ago, it wouldn't have, but now I felt Genie's eyes on me as he watched from the sidelines.

"This is our daughter, Princess Gaia." My mother said pointedly as I vainly fought to keep the redness out of my cheeks. Out of the corner of my eye, I could see Genie chuckling at my predicament. He never missed a trick much to my chagrin.

I stepped forward, allowing the sheik and his people a moment to bow to me, as was the custom.

The sheik turned to his son, "and this is my son and

only heir, Yama."

We all slightly inclined our heads in Yama's direction, acknowledging his presence.

He stepped toward me and took my hand in his, bringing it up to his lips. So much for keeping my blush under control. I needed to get a grip. I hated it when men thought they could kiss my hand. I pretty much hated any kind of contact with boys. Dating was something that held no interest for me whatsoever, and a pretty face wasn't going to change that. And gods, I knew that the blush had less to do with the man giving the kiss than the man watching it.

"Please, let us sit and take tea. Your people will be shown to their rooms, and your luggage will be put away in your suites," my mom said as she gave one of her handmaids a signal to get moving.

I carefully observed my mother's every move, knowing that someday, I too would be in her shoes, ruling over Badalah. I knew Badalah's laws and policies like the back of my hand, but etiquette was something I never felt I got right. Want to know the right way to invade a kingdom? I was your girl. Want to know which fork to use during which dinner course? You were on your own.

"Sheik Ahmadullah, how are your lands?" my father inquisitively asked.

The sheik looked down to his clasped hands, and there was a moment of grief which he quickly brushed off. "They've seen better days. I'm considering visiting the Kingdom of Floris, with Her Majesty's permission, that is." He paused as he looked kindly at my mother. "They've done such amazing things with their flowers that I feel they might have some wisdom to share or trade to help my soil. The spices aren't growing as they once were, and the coffee crop is looking particularly poor this year."

My father tilted his head to one side, carefully placing a forefinger on his temple, lost deep in thought. I, however, sat up and began to take notice. The spice and coffee crops had never failed us before. This was another symptom of whatever it was that was laying plague to the other kingdoms. I was sure of it.

"Floris is the kingdom to go to in matters of plants," the sheik continued. "They can grow anything."

"Their crops have been abysmal this year also. They've had the worst yield in years. Some might say it's a plague," I said, looking pointedly at my father, who shook his head at me.

The sultana was quick to offer words of advice. "Perhaps it would be wise to take a carriage into Atlantice. They've been known to harvest a special variety of kelp. It's said that the values of this type are wondrous for growing vegetables, even in sandy soil."

The sheik perked up. "I hadn't heard of this. I'll certainly consider crossing over to the Kingdom of Atlantice. Thank you, my sultana. I'll send someone first thing to find me a carriage to make the journey."

"We have carriages that can easily and quickly make the journey. I'll send word to have one prepared for your trip. We all have a vested interest in seeing if this kelp truly is key in helping the soils."

"Indeed." The sheik responded then turned to me. "Princess Gaia looks bored with our conversation."

I sat taller in my seat. "I assure you, sir, that I am not. I take a high interest in everything happening in our kingdom. What concerns our citizens also concerns me."

Yama took the chance to enter the conversation.

"Does Her Highness plan on attending university?"

"University? No. I have the best scholars attending to my educational needs here in the palace," I said, shifting in my seat. I didn't like to be the center of attention when I was the subject matter. I'd have preferred to carry on talking about soil.

"What does the Princess do for fun?" he continued quizzing me.

"Fun?" I laughed. "I highly enjoy assisting my parents in overseeing our kingdom. I take great pride and pleasure as we work tirelessly to combat the injustices our most disadvantaged citizens face. Why, just the other day, I attended the judicial court to speak on behalf of a few of our men who were taken into custody, unjustly, for stealing food for their young families. Food!" I said with emphasis. That reminded me, I still had the bag of trinkets from the thief last night stashed in my closet.

"How very kind of you," he said with a hint of mockery. He didn't get the answer he expected, and it showed plainly on his face.

I heard both my parents sigh. I knew what they wanted me to say, how they wanted me to reply. They wanted me to conform to the boy's expectations and tell him I liked picking flowers and reciting poetry and doing other activities more suited to a princess.

I stood in one motion. "Kindness, while good, isn't what our people need. Our people need champions who are willing to lay it all on the line to see that everyone in our kingdom, at minimum, is clothed, fed, and has a roof over their head. Now, if you all will excuse me, I have a previous engagement," I said, not waiting for a response.

My parents would be angry at me later for my

rudeness, but I saw no value in pretending to be someone I was not, nor did I see the point in being interested in the sheik's son. It would only upset him further down the line. Best nip it in the bud while I could.

I slid through the door, purposely not looking at Genie as I went. Behind me, I could still hear the conversation.

"Our daughter is very passionate about our people. We truly are thankful for her support in running the kingdom." I overheard my mother say.

"Yes, but she'll soon need a suitor. It is important we find someone worthy of her and the position of sultan when the time comes," my father added, no doubt trying to placate the sheik after my little outburst. Suitor, pah! He'd always told me he'd never force me to marry, and yet, here they both were, trying to set me up with some stranger. Well, they had another think coming if they thought I'd end up with the sheik's son

"Perhaps there is no better time than the present, then, Your Majesties. It is no secret that my household is one of the wealthiest in the kingdom. I also run a viable and sustainable trade business, which has taken us throughout the kingdoms. All of this has allowed me to give my son and only heir, Yama, the best education money can buy. Look at him," he paused, for effect, I presumed. "He's very handsome."

There was a moment of silence before the sheik continued. "I believe Her Royal Highness, Princess Gaia, and my son, Yama, would make a great match for marriage."

I stormed down the passageway, not wanting to hear another word of the nonsense being spoken in the throne room.

When I finally reached my bedroom, I slammed the

door behind me, startling Asher in the process.

"I'm sorry, Asher," I said as I made my way out to the terrace. I reached my hand over to pet him, but he flinched at my touch.

I turned to him and looked him in the eyes. He seemed rather sickly. "Asher, what is the matter?"

He gave me a sorry stare. Knowing he was a highly magical creature, I wondered if some of what I'd been reading about across several of the kingdoms was connected to him, but he'd never shown an ounce of the magic he was supposed to possess.

I returned indoors to retrieve the daily papers of the kingdoms.

Surely, I missed something, I thought to myself as I spent the next hour scanning every page, line by line and waiting for either of my parents to come to my room to demand my presence again.

A subtle knock alerted me of a visitor, and I let out a breath.

"Yes?" I called out, willing it not to be my parents, or worse, Yama himself.

The door opened.

My heart leapt into my throat as I saw who it was. "Genie! Thank goodness it's you," I said, eager to get back to what I was trying to tell him earlier. "I've been scouring the papers again. I don't know, Genie; something is terribly off. I've gone through every kingdom's paper of the last few weeks. There is something definitely odd; it's as if there is a magical undoing. Like whatever order was put in place is coming undone. It is something to do with magic, I'm sure of it."

Genie flinched. Once, the most magical being in all the kingdoms, he'd shunned any mention of it since becoming human. He feared it. It was the only thing he feared.

He looked past my shoulders out onto the terrace. “Where’s Asher?”

I immediately turned on my heels. “I don’t know,” I said, rushing out only to find Asher sitting on the outdoor table. “Oh, buddy, you really aren’t feeling well, are you?” I said as I cooed over him for a bit, gently petting him.

“Look, I understand what you are saying. I, too, have wondered what the slight shift in our realms has meant. The wolves of Elder and the unicorn incidents in The Vale, the merfolk of Atlantice... I can keep going. Something is happening, but I just don’t know how serious it truly is. Why don’t you follow me?”

I gave Asher a reassuring smile and followed Genie through the palace and to the arboretum, where light music was playing, and my parents were dancing in each other’s arms. At least, they weren’t harboring any grudges against me after my rudeness to our guests earlier.

“You see, Princess Gaia,” Genie started. “Not even magic can undo what is truly meant to be. Aladdin and Jawahir, they possess one of the purest loves I’ve ever witnessed,” he said with a smile.

“Okay, I get it. I suppose some things just happen. Can we get out of here now? I feel like a peeping tom. I really don’t want to continue standing here and watching my parents act like fools.”

“Fools?” Genie asked, scrunching his eyebrows.

“Genie, it’s no secret that I don’t subscribe to the whole notion of love.”

“Princess Gaia, perhaps that’s because you have yet to find the right person.”

I covered my mouth to muffle my loud laugh. After

a few moments of getting control of myself, I finally addressed him. "I have you. Who else can I possibly need?" As soon as the words had escaped my lips, what I'd meant as a flippant remark, felt all too real. I didn't want love, precisely because of Genie.

He smiled, "Oh, but I'm a mere servant and much too old for you. Sooner or later, you'll have to find a match. The more open you are to the process, the better off you'll be."

I wondered if he knew how much his words cut me. He wasn't a servant. That was the whole point of my father freeing him. He'd never been treated as a servant by either of my parents or by me. He was more than that. He was the brother I never had, the friend when I needed someone to talk to, the counselor when I needed advice. He was everything, and yet to him, I was just a young princess who needed to be married off at the first chance.

"Thank you, Genie," I said, carefully shielding my eyes and the tears that fell down my cheeks as I turned to walk away.

18TH JUNE

I was woken by a dream about my parents. One I'd had many times over the years and one I knew intimately. It was a dream about how I'd come to live in the palace as a newborn. I couldn't remember it, of course, but I'd been told the story so many times by my mother that I felt that I knew every detail. Just over eighteen years ago, an older and younger woman showed up at the palace gates and handed me to the sultana and the sultan. Genie was present as were a few members of the palace staff.

After carefully inquiring around Kisbu, it was as if I'd appeared out of thin air. No signs of either women or of my possible beginnings. Therefore, my parents adopted me. It wasn't a secret that I wasn't their natural-born child. However, they had loved me so, and the entire people of Badalah always accepted me as such.

As a child, curiosity had gotten the better of me. Like a jigsaw puzzle, I'd tried desperately to piece together where I'd come from, trying to glean information from the older guards who had worked at the palace at the time, but the attempts were fruitless.

I'd questioned my parents numerous times about how they could simply take in a baby, no questions asked. But, of course, love was always their response. They loved me from the first moment they laid eyes on me. Which, to me, sounded highly implausible. I was sick of hearing stories of love conquering all. What about knowledge? I'd rather they had asked for a name of my birth parents or something rather than falling in love with me the second they saw me and taking me in blindly. And yet, they'd brought me up as though I was their own and loved me and cherished me and given me everything my heart desired. That had happened eighteen years ago. Eighteen and a half years ago, to be precise. Eighteen and a half years ago when the kingdoms found peace and unity until... I pulled the other papers I'd been saving from under my bed and picked up the top one. The Draconis Sentinel dated early January. Just after my eighteenth birthday. Just after the birthday of the princess there, Princess Azia. She'd gone missing about a month after her mother got sick, and the royals of Draconis were being tight-lipped as to where she was. They didn't seem particularly upset by her just disappearing into thin air, so I supposed they must know where she was, but it was strange. She used to be seen so much in royal life, and since January, there were only photos in the papers of her father and brothers.

It was all very strange. But in the papers, I saw patterns and clues which to most people wouldn't seem to have any correlation, except I did see it. This all started around the time of my birthday. It was hard to pinpoint the exact date of my birthday, but I was very young when I'd been brought to the palace, no more than a week. We celebrated it on 26th December, one day after the winter festival.

I reached under the bed to grab the next batch of newspapers, deciding to go through each of them one by one, all the way back to my birthday. There had to be something concrete I could show my father or Genie.

Fear started finding its way through me as I slowly came to the realization that many of the rulers seemed to be impacted, if only subtly, by the most recent change of events.

It was as if each thread of magic was being pulled back.

First, it was the queen of Draconis, then the queen of Atlantice, followed by the Red of Elder. Elder didn't have a newspaper as such, but there were ways to find out information. It didn't take a lot of effort to find out that Elder was having problems with a sickness among wolves. It was like something was taking each kingdom down, one by one, starting at the head of every kingdom. Whatever it was worked indiscriminately, and the pattern I'd found didn't extend to location. As far as I could tell, there had been problems in Draconis, Atlantice, Elder, Floris, The Vale, and, most recently, Arboria. The other kingdoms didn't seem to have any problems yet, but I had a feeling it was only a matter of time. I thought back to my parents dancing together the day before. Whatever it was, it hadn't gotten to us...yet. Or had it, and I hadn't noticed because it had started small. The low yields on crops, the increase in petty theft, my parents' sudden interest in finding me a husband. It all could be linked, or I could be seeing things that weren't even there.

I continued leafing through the papers. *Something.* There had to be some clue that linked everything together. I needed Genie here to go through the papers with me. He would spot the pattern in a second. His brain just worked that way, but I was still upset with him for brushing me aside.

Throwing the papers to one side, I dragged myself out of bed.

Asher made a horrible squawking sound taking me from my thoughts.

"Oh no, Asher! What is the matter with you?" His limp body was barely staying upright on his beautifully hand-carved wooden perch. His beak was as pale as grey ash. I petted him ever so gently, unsure of what to do. His head rested on the back of my hand. "Please, Asher. What do I need to do?" My words trembled as they came out. Asher couldn't be sick, not now. Aside from Genie, he was the only one who actually listened to me.

Genie! He would know how to help Asher.

I ran out of my room to find him, almost crashing into Freya on the way. "Your Highness, please slow down before you hurt yourself."

"I need Genie, something is wrong with Asher. He's sick."

Freya's brows furrowed. "I'm so sorry, Your Highness. I was on my way to speak with you. Your father has been taken ill. The Genie is with him now."

Her words hit me like a punch to the gut. I'd been waiting for some such tragedy to befall our kingdom, and here it was. First Asher, now my father. My knees barely kept me standing as I reached for the wall. Could it be? Could my own father now be affected by whatever seemed to be spreading across the kingdoms?

Pulling myself together, I gathered inner strength. My mother had trained me well in how to keep my composure. Yet something happened in that moment of despair. It was as if I'd been ignited from within. Heat traveled through my veins, making me dizzy.

"Come with me to the Sultan's room!"

Shocked by my cold and commanding voice, I arranged my robe and followed the chambermaid. Her short but nimble legs carried her lightly toward my parent's wing of the palace. All the way, I wondered what was wrong with him. The Queen of Draconis had fallen asleep and never woken up, just like the curse she had suffered before I was born. The Queen of Atlantice had gone back to her original state of being a mermaid. Were the kings and queens of all the kingdoms destined to go back to how they used to be? But my father had never been under a curse, and he'd never been anything other than what he was now. Sure, he was poor as a youth, but poverty wasn't an illness.

I found my mother in the corridor outside her bedroom, talking to one of the butlers.

"Mother, what is it? What is wrong with Father?"

She dismissed the butler then turned to me. "It's nothing, Gaia. Why do you look so worried? He's just been feeling a little fuzzy-headed of late. Genie is making sure he's alright."

"Fuzzy-headed?"

"Yes. I ordered him to take a nap. I think he's been overdoing things, what with trying to keep the kingdom together and the additional pressure yesterday of entertaining our guests."

Guests? Oh, she meant the sheik and his son. So they were still here.

"But he's ok?" I pressed.

"Of course, he's ok. He'll be right as rain after his nap."

I wouldn't be completely reassured until after I saw my father, but my mother didn't seem too bothered by the state of affairs. "Is there anything I can help with?"

"I'll need you to attend to our guests. They were expecting to have lunch with us, but as you can see, your father isn't quite up to it."

The thought of spending a meal talking to that idiot didn't sound like my idea of fun, but it was the least I could do after my huff with them the day before "Yes, I can do that."

She wore a bright, infectious smile. "Thank you."

"Oh! Before I forget. Asher. He doesn't look too good. I think he's sick too."

Her hand went to my hair, and she brushed her long slender fingers through it. "He'll be fine. He's a Phoenix. Phoenix are magical birds. If you like, I'll ask Genie to go and take a look at him once he's finished with your father. Now go and get yourself dressed and then head down for lunch."

I nodded in understanding and returned to my room.

I'd barely noticed I'd been walking around the palace in only my pajamas and robe, but now that my mother had pointed it out, I needed to go and get dressed.

I went into my closet and looked for a dress to wear for lunch.

My hand automatically went to the teal outfit I wore on many occasions, but something stopped me. Instead, I picked out a dress I'd never worn before. The rich burgundy and gold were the perfect color for my taupe skin tone, and I had plenty of gold jewelry to match it.

"That's one beautiful gown," Freya beamed as she walked through the door. "I'll go draw you another bath, and while you are bathing, I'll put together some jewelry to match."

"Why are you so excited?" I asked suspiciously, narrowing my eyes.

"I've just seen the sheik's son," she babbled. "He is absolutely to die for. And, well, he's rich. You two will make a beautiful couple."

The words she spoke were probably the talk throughout the palace. It was as if the entire Kingdom of Badalah wanted to marry me off already. At eighteen!

"I'm sure he'll be a great catch for someone else. I'm really not interested."

Freya's face dropped. She looked at me as though I'd broken her heart.

"Please, don't pout. I'm too young for marriage. There is a whole world of knowledge out there to be explored before I settle down."

"But that's so boring," she sighed. "You know what's interesting? Weddings. Royal weddings," she added pointedly. "And royal babies. Oh, the sheik's son would give you such beautiful babies."

Now it was my turn to frown. I'd gone from dating to marriage to babies in a heartbeat. It reminded me how different I was from other girls my age. I didn't want everything she talked about, and there was no way I could muster up even a tiny percent of the excitement she felt about the whole matter.

"You'll change your mind once you get to know him," she said before heading into my bathroom to run my bath.

Anger flowed through me at her words. I liked Freya, I truly did, but she was so vapid. Why was it that I was expected to want marriage and babies? I'd be happier locking myself in a library and spending my life reading books. I didn't need a man, and I certainly didn't want one. Genie's face popped into my mind, but I pushed it away.

"I don't need him either!" I huffed to myself.

"What was that, Your Highness?" Freya called from the bathroom.

"Nothing!" I shouted back. I didn't want to get into a conversation on my feelings about Genie. Not when I didn't even know what those feelings were myself.

My anger grew stronger. So strong that I didn't even know who I was the maddest at: My parents for wanting me to marry, Asher for being sick, Freya for thinking everything would be fine if only I had a wedding, or Genie for...well for not really seeing me.

My anger grew, like a knot in my stomach until it turned to heat. I felt a strand of something move through my core and up my chest, snake-like.

The feeling was warm, expanding quickly.

My stomach ignited, and I quickly moved toward the floor-to-ceiling, three-way mirrors in my closet, afraid of what might be inside of me, fighting to escape.

There, I watched as a light glow emanated from my skin like a halo but all over my body. I dropped my robe to the ground, which only seemed to make the glow brighter.

What the actual... I stopped myself.

I'm glowing!

I stumbled back toward the doorway.

"Your Royal Highness!" Freya said loudly, bringing her hand up to her chest. "Quick," she continued as she ushered me back into my closet, closing the door behind us. "You must not be seen like this. We shall wait here while your magic wears down." There was a faint smile forming at the edges of her lips.

"Magic?!" I screamed. "I'm on fire!"

"You are not on fire," she assured me. It was easy for her to say. She wasn't the one glowing like a torch. "You are magic!"

My throat tightened as I swallowed back a retort. *What on earth was happening?*

Just as the question escaped my thoughts, a strand of light...fiery light, exited my fingertips as I put my hand before me, mesmerized by what I was witnessing.

"What were you saying?" I asked incredulously, trying to keep from having a complete meltdown—both figuratively and literally.

Freya nodded her head as though this was the most normal thing in the world. "Fire and light, it would seem."

I glanced back toward the mirror. "Yes, it would seem," I echoed weakly.

"Princess Gaia. Did you not know?"

I shook my head. I was pretty sure I would have noticed if the ends of my fingers had erupted into flames before. The question was, why was it happening now? I took a couple of deep breaths, trying to gather my thoughts. I felt hot, but despite the illusion of flames, I wasn't burning. At least, that was something. The flames licking my fingertips were not damaging my skin.

I looked back in the mirror and waved my hand, watching as the trail of light followed me like the ribbon of a rhythmic gymnast.

"It truly is beautiful," Freya marveled. "It makes

sense why the Phoenix took to you. It must've sensed your magic from afar. Phoenix are birds of fire after all."

"Asher?"

"Yes."

"Oh, Asher." I was reminded of how sickly my bird had been. "He's not well."

"He's getting ready for a rebirth," she said knowledgeably. "That's probably why you are like this." She danced on the spot as though she'd just figured something important out. Maybe I'd judged her too harshly, after all.

"What?" I knew that when phoenix die, they are reborn in the ashes. I just didn't expect to be going along with him for the ride.

"Umm hmm. Because your magics are akin. As you are coming into your magic, Asher's is dying. He will soon be reborn, and you and he will be paired for life."

She lit up, sharing the tidbit of information with me.

"How do you know all of this?" It seemed awfully strange that she was so well informed about magic and my bird.

"I studied magic at school. One of our seminars was the pairing of magical beings with magical animals."

"But I'm not magic," I asserted.

She grinned then flicked her eyes to my mirror image. "Your reflection suggests otherwise."

I looked at myself. The glow was diminishing now, and my fingers were no longer alight.

The revelation immediately made me wonder just how many more people within the city were of magic.

No, I wasn't ignorant to the fact that magic existed. It simply wasn't something that was common, anymore. At least, not in the Kingdom of Badalah.

Immediately, my thoughts returned to my recent

research of the kingdoms and the sudden shifts toward chaos.

Magic.

It all went back to the magic that seemed to hold together peace in the kingdoms. Peace that had come about around the time of my birth. In every kingdom. Every. Single. Kingdom. And now that peace was falling apart.

And then there was me. Now that I was glowing and apparently had magic, specifically a fire affinity, I needed to figure out how it was entwined with the current happenings.

I looked back at Freya, who seemed to be lost in thought herself. "Did you come across any other magic people in your seminars?"

She shook her head. "No. I guess here in Badalah, magic folk keep to themselves. There isn't a lot of it about. Since Genie lost his magic, and your grandfather's vizier tried taking over the kingdom with it, it's kind of fallen out of favor here. People fear it."

I contemplated her response. How could this be? After all, Genie was the very Genie of the Magic Lamp. His name literally meant magic person, and he was pretty famous for beating my grandfather's advisor all those years ago. So, how could the people of the kingdom fear it?

But then, I remembered how Genie had flinched when I'd mentioned it the other day.

"Your Highness, look..." Freya said, pointing at my eyes in the mirror.

I turned back to my reflection. The gold outer part of my iris was glowing even though the rest of me had stopped.

"What is going on?"

She took a few steps back. “I don’t know anything about that. In all the lessons I took, no one ever mentioned glowing eyes.”

I wasn’t sure if she was afraid, or if she was simply caught off guard. Either way, her body language told me she wanted to put a lot of distance between us.

“I’m sorry. I need to step out and get some fresh air. Please excuse me, Your Royal Highness.” She scrambled quickly out of my closet, closing the door behind her.

I turned back and stared at my reflection. My eyes were glowing golden. How was I supposed to leave my room and host an elaborate dinner with the sheik and his son without anyone asking questions?

A knock at my bedroom door had my heart hammering. I concentrated on not glowing, which was difficult seeing as I didn’t really know how or why my eyes were glowing in the first place and headed out into my bedroom and to my bedroom door.

“Who is it?” I asked.

“I’ll see you at lunch,” I said, barely opening the door to find Genie. My eyes were somewhat back to normal. Other than being glossed over with tears which had come about due to shock rather than sadness, it didn’t seem anything had severely affected me on the outside.

The inside? That was another story.

“Gaia, I am not going anywhere until you let me in.”

“I’m fine. Just let me be alone…” I didn’t want him to see me like this. I’d never cried in front of him. I never cried in front of anyone.

He pushed on the door strongly enough to move me out of the way.

“What has gotten into you?” he said as he made his way in, closing the door behind him. “I was coming to check on Asher, but when I ran into your chambermaid in the hallway and asked her about you, she moved so quickly I knew something was amiss. So, what is it?"

"Nothing. I told you, I'm fine."

He studied me for a second, his face taking on a quizzical expression like he could see into the depths of my soul. I'd always felt attracted to his beautiful eyes, but now I wanted to look away in case he could somehow guess what was wrong. I wasn't ready to tell him yet. He loathed any mention of magic. How could I have him look at me in disgust if I told him? I couldn't bear it.

He broke eye contact and walked toward my terrace to look at Asher. "He doesn't look too good. Hopefully, he'll transition rather quickly. This phase really doesn't suit him."

"So, you think he's near the end?" I asked, taking a place next to Asher's perch and glad that Genie's attention was not on me.

"Or the beginning," Genie said, stroking Asher's once bright plumage. "I guess it depends on which way you look at it."

I bit my lip as I tried to word my next question. "Why did you buy me a phoenix?" I asked. Asher had been presented to me on my fifth birthday as a gift from Genie. I'd never wondered why he'd picked such a pet instead of a dog or cat. "I mean, it's such a magical bird."

"You were such a free spirit with a fiery temperament as a child. The phoenix seemed to suit you."

"Is that all? My fiery spirit?"

He turned to me and wiped away a stray tear with his thumb. The gesture, if coming from anyone else, would have been sweet. Coming from Genie, it made my heart race and my breath catch in my throat.

"This isn't about Asher, is it?"
Slowly I shook my head and told him everything.

19TH JUNE

My long braid whipped behind me like an angered rattlesnake, as I turned to face my mother. "Another?" I said in disbelief, watching as she soaked in every moment of my anger.

Her smile seemed insincere, at least to me. "Gaia, you are eighteen. It is only natural to have more suitors coming to call on you. Besides, it's no secret that you are stunning...and eligible. "

"Mother, do you even hear yourself? Eighteen, mother. *Eighteen!* Do you really want me to be married at eighteen?"

Her soft, delicate hand caressed my face. "I'm not saying you should get married. I'm asking you to consider the possibility of a suitor. You get so many proposals; it's all we can do to keep up. I honestly thought Yama was a nice boy, but after you missed lunch with him yesterday, he and his father got the message."

My body jerked away from her as I paced toward an open archway that looked out over Kisbu.

"What was this? The third one this week? Are we to entertain all offers?" I said with discontent.

"When I was your age, I'm sure it was the same."

"You said to consider the suitors. But what they are coming to you with is an actual marriage proposal. Have times not changed enough to want to consider my feelings in this at all? Or what, shall I just sit there quietly and obediently as if I have no say in the matter? Is that what you want for me? Because it surely isn't what you wanted for yourself. You got to marry the man you loved, despite his circumstance in life."

"Gaia," she paused. "I'm only asking you to consider. That is all. You have men falling at your feet. The people are beginning to wonder why you haven't found anyone yet. I'm not asking you to marry them. Just go on a date or two. You never know. You might actually have some fun."

I rolled my eyes without a thought, knowing all too well that there was no way I would even consider what she was asking me to do. She left me alone as I stared out over Kisbu. It wasn't perfect, but the people were worth believing in. And I knew that sooner or later, I'd have to consider my position and the future of the kingdom. I wasn't dense. My mother wanted to secure an heir to the throne, and although she didn't think she was pushing marriage on me, she was certainly shuffling me in that direction.

I took my frustration to the one person I knew who would listen. I'd talked with Genie for hours in my room yesterday, hence me missing both lunch and dinner with the sheik and Yama. Even though I'd told him about my magic, or curse, or whatever it was, he'd not looked upon me with disgust as I had feared. He'd done what he always did and listened, before discussing the situation rationally. We'd not come up with any kind of reasonable answers, but just the debate was enough to calm me down.

I knocked on his door and let myself in. He sat behind his desk, looking at some documents.

I perched myself on the edge of his desk and told him about my frustrations.

Genie, as usual, listened to everything I had to say before speaking himself. "I know you know that your mother only wants what is best for you. Besides, settling down isn't such a bad thing."

"Do you know how many marriage proposals I had before I turned eighteen?" I whined to Genie.

"No," he replied, although I knew he was secretly keeping score. Nothing got past Genie.

"Two-hundred and thirty-seven! Not one of them thought to ask me first. They all asked my parents. And now that I'm eighteen, it's worse. I'm getting five or six a week!"

"You are young and beautiful."

I cut him off. "And rich. Don't forget to add rich to my resume. Oh, and while you're at it, tack on the heir to the throne of Badalah. I mean, why not? Right? For kicks and giggles."

"Princess Gaia, they are captivated by you. I've seen photos of some of these men. They're not all that bad. In fact, I might dare to say that some are quite good-looking."

I moved closer toward him. "I have no desire for the looks of the whole lot of them. I only desire one man whose mind is so beautiful that no other human being equals it."

I held my breath. It was no secret who I was talking about. "I desire knowledge, and you have thousands of years of it."

Genie stepped away from me, his face masked of any emotion.

"I'm your father's closest friend and confidant. I can be no more."

His words hurt me more than I cared to admit. I was laying my soul on the line. Me, the girl who didn't believe in love, and he was acting as though this was a casual conversation. I'd hoped in the deepest part of my heart that our conversation last night would have sparked something in him, but he remained as impassive as always.

Later, in a secluded part of my terrace, I tried to recreate the magic that had shocked me so much yesterday. The pulse of magic rolled through my skin as I outstretched my dominant right arm. I focused on a small side table on the terrace. Upon contact, the magic erupted over the wooden furniture, engulfing it in flames. Asher squawked, batting his wings as he moved away from the flames in a geriatric manner.

"Oh, come on, Asher. You can do better than that."

I lifted him from the back of the chair he'd been resting on. Where soft feathers once lay, his shriveled skin showed through. "I love you, Asher," I whispered as I gently pressed him to my chest, listening as he took in labored breaths.

I carefully placed him upon the fig tree, his favorite

spot to rest and returned indoors.

There was a small knock on the door, and for a second, my pulse raced in the hope it was Genie.

"Come in."

Freya entered with a tray of newspapers and a glass of juice, and with her, my heart plummeted. I'd been using my new found magic, attempting to control it, as a way to get Genie from my mind, but it was impossible. However much I didn't want to admit it to myself, Genie was becoming more than a mentor in my eyes. Much more.

"Shall I attempt to feed Asher, Your Royal Highness?" Freya asked, laying the tray on the bedside cabinet. Her eyes turned to my bird that looked ever so sorry for itself. The poor thing was looking so forlorn that I almost wished he would die, just to get it over with. According to legend, he'd come back better than ever.

"Yes, if you don't mind. Although, I doubt he'll eat much. I'll be back later. Thank you, Freya."

I left Asher in her capable hands. I'd been so caught up with Asher and my own pathetic state of affairs, i.e., mooning over Genie, that I'd forgotten to ask after my father. My mother had assured me there was nothing really wrong with him, but he'd not shown up to breakfast that morning.

Two guards at his door stood to attention as I stopped in front of them. "I need to see the sultan, please."

"Your Royal Highness, we have strict orders from Sultana Jawahir to not allow anyone in." One of the guards asserted.

"Really? Did the Sultana specifically say not to let *me* in?"

I waited as the two guards looked to each other for confirmation, and from the looks of it, neither had the answer. Which worked to my advantage. “I didn’t think so. Excuse me, gentleman.” I pushed one of their staffs away and let myself into my parents’ room.

“Father?” I said carefully, walking through the spacious sitting area to announce myself, just in case he was indisposed. “Father?” I said more loudly.

The sound of a throat clearing reached me from the terrace. I found him out there, staring out onto the city. “Dad, how are you feeling?”

He didn’t reply. In fact, he didn’t even bother to look at me. His gaze was fixed across the city toward a large clock tower by the town square. I knew it had meaning to him. He’d shared stories with me about how, when he was much younger, he’d climb up to the tower and look upon the palace, a place he never imagined he’d once live. Yet, in that very moment, I sensed the reverse was happening. He was staring at the clock tower as if he yearned to be there.

“Father...Dad, are you ok?”

His focus slowly turned from the clock tower to me, but his eyes were glazed.

It was like he was looking right through me.

“Daddy?” I waved my hand in front of his eyes, and finally, he came out of his weird trance.

“Gaia...sorry. I was lost in a memory for a second.”

“The clock tower?” I asked.

“The world was mine when I had nothing. When you have nothing, you have nothing...”

“To lose,” I finished for him with a grin. He spoke a lot about his youth and how wonderful it was to be free. Of course, he’d fallen in love with my mother and ended up defeating my grandfather’s chief advisor, who had been threatening to take over the palace through force and magic. But he often wove tales about the adventures he got into before his days in the palace. I guess that's why I often sneaked out and walked around the city at night. I wanted to share his adventures with him. Not that I'd ever tell him where I went. No one but Asher knew of my night time escapades. Asher was the only one who wouldn't stop me.

I would have happily sat with my father for the rest of the day, listening to his stories about his youth, but a knock on the door put a stop to that idea. A quick glance at my father told me he'd drifted off into his trance-like state again. He most certainly wasn't well, despite what my mother said.

I walked through the bedroom and my parents' private sitting room to open the door. To my surprise, it was Freya on the other side.

"Is it Asher?" I asked, noting her worried expression.

She shook her head. "Asher was fine when I left him, Your Highness," she said as she stopped for air. She gave a nervous glance at one of the guards then looked back at me. "My apologies, miss. I've been sent to find you and tell you that you are needed in the throne room."

"Who needs me in the throne room?" I asked, suddenly worried myself.

"I don't know, Your Highness, but I was asked to accompany you at once."

The last request seemed rather strange. Since when did my chambermaid need to accompany me to the throne room?

We walked through the palace in silence, and when we got there, the room was empty.

"Are you sure I was to come here?" I whispered to Freya. She responded by shrugging her shoulders.

"Gaia, there you are," Genie said, strolling in through

the main doors. I could barely look his way after our talk this morning, though it hadn't seemed to have affected him at all. "Her Majesty, the sultana, is on her way. Just a heads up, she is not in the best of moods, and there is a handsome young man in her company."

I rolled my eyes. This was an intervention of the worst kind.

"So now you are bringing men straight to the palace for me?" I said, leveling my finger at Genie. "I'm not a fat cow to be bred with every bull that happens to come along. Just because I told you I had feelings for you, doesn't mean you have to sell me off to the highest bidder just to get rid of me."

My heart pounded, and bile rose in my throat at how embarrassing this all was. I knew love was a crock of crap, and now I'd just proven it. I should have kept my feelings to myself.

Genie held his hands up and took a step back. It was the first time I'd ever seen him quail under anyone's stare. He was usually so strong. Well, it served him right.

"I had nothing to do with this, Gaia. I never thought of you as a fat cow for breeding. And as for your feelings for me..."

"My dear daughter, Princess Gaia."

My mom walked through the main doors with a man at her side. My cheeks flamed as I wondered how much she'd heard.

"I'll speak to you later, Gaia," Genie whispered, and, after a quick nod to my mother and the man, he waltzed out the door.

The young man in tow was truly handsome. Genie wasn't lying about that, but all I could think about was the scene I'd just made.

"Jamal, please meet Princess Gaia. Gaia, this is Jamal. He is the grandson of one of my father's oldest and dearest friends."

He stepped in my direction, bowing without taking his eyes off me, then reached for my hand to kiss.

"It is a great honor and pleasure to make Her Royal Highness's acquaintance."

"Likewise," I responded, quickly retracting my hand. "So, what brings you to the palace?" As if I didn't know.

He smiled before looking at my mother. "I had business in Kisbu. I figured I'd gamble at my chances to stop by and become acquainted with the royal family. After all the wonderful stories I'd heard of this place, I could hardly pass up the opportunity. Thankfully, Her Majesty Sultana Jawahir was gracious to accept me as a guest for the day."

I'll bet she was. I glanced her way, and she had the audacity to give me the thumbs up as though she'd found me a beautiful treasure.

And he was. Beautiful, that is. Strikingly so. Deep dimples formed on each cheek, and I could have sworn there was a bright twinkle in his eyes. His light brown hair stood out as most of the people of Badalah had deep dark silky hair.

"What sort of business is it that you have?" I asked, playing along. The business of asking princesses to marry him then sitting around doing nothing for the rest of this life, I wondered.

"Trade," he said. "I make fine rugs and tapestries, among other things, with wool."

"So, you're a sheep farmer?"

"That I am, fifth-generation, Your Highness. I was born a humble shepherd, but I've built the family business into a thriving company that trades with the other kingdoms. Last year we turned over half a million Rubees."

I was intrigued. He was not the lay-about I thought him to be...if he was telling me the truth. I decided to give him the benefit of the doubt. He was unutterably beautiful, but his hands were rough—the sign of someone who worked hard.

Out of the corner of my eye, I caught my mother smiling. Of course, she was. I was playing her game, and after my horrible morning with Genie, she might just win.

"Jamal's grandfather was a regular visitor to the palace back in the day, He provided the wool for our clothes and furnishings," she said.

"How long will you be in Kisbu?" I asked Jamal.

"I haven't really decided on a return date. You see, I don't make it to this part of the kingdom very often. So, I'd kind of planned to do a bit of everything."

"Yes," my mother interceded, "which is why I called for you and your maid. I know how you've been dying to get out into the city more. I figured Jamal's visit is just that opportunity. You can show him around. Freya can accompany you, along with a few guards."

Oh, she was a sly one. I'd been complaining for months about how I never got to leave the palace save for royal occasions, and here she was, using it as a way to get me on a date. It worked too.

I threw my arms around her, ignoring all royal etiquette. "Just because I'm going on a date, doesn't mean I'm marrying him," I whispered in her ear.

She grinned back at me and mouthed the words, "We'll see."

"Jamal, you'll be guest of the palace," she said, ever efficient. "A hand attendant will come to find you here shortly to show you to one of our guest rooms. I'll see you both after dinner, in the drawing room for a light dessert and drinks."

"Are you not joining us for dinner, mother?"

"I'm afraid not. Genie and I have business to tend to."

My stomach turned at the thought of Genie. A date with a gorgeous guy would be exactly what I needed, and I wasn't going on a date to make him jealous...not at all.

When I looked at Freya, I could see the glow on her face. Of course, I'd noticed. My mother had not so subtly given her a promotion. It wasn't just in title, but it would be in status and pay. Freya was no longer just my chambermaid. She was my Lady in Waiting. My first and only Lady.

I smiled in acknowledgment. "Freya, why don't you go find me a chambermaid and see to it that we are set to venture into Kisbu tomorrow."

She understood the request. I'd essentially tasked her to find her replacement.

Freya curtsied and excused herself, leaving Jamal and I by ourselves.

"Would you like to take a stroll in the gardens, Jamal?"

"If that is what the Princess desires."

"My desires, I'm afraid are much more complicated than that. But I've found I do my best thinking when I am walking in nature."

We made our way outdoors into the gardens, past the door for Genie's room. My heart thudded as we passed, and I made a note to speak more loudly as we did. It was childish and pathetic and beneath me, but I couldn't help myself. Genie had hurt my feelings, and in a small...or not so small way, I wanted to hurt his. Actually, that wasn't it at all. I never wanted to hurt him; I just wanted him to understand that I could be lost to him. He probably didn't even care.

"My father died when I was a child," Jamal said as we stepped out into the sunshine. "My mother moved back home with her father, who'd been widowed when she was a child. Sadly, we didn't have her with us for very long. She became sickly and died. So, he was faced with raising yet another child on his own. I'd like to say he did great, but the jury is still out on that." He laughed, once again, revealing his entrancing dimples.

We walked on the path under the tree cover. "He passed away before my sixteenth birthday. But he'd already shown me everything he knew. I suppose it didn't hurt that I was an eager pupil. I mean, when you lose the ones you love, I guess it forces you to mature in ways you didn't even know were possible." He paused and looked around, spreading his arms. "This is all wonderful."

I nodded in agreement, eager for him to continue.

"By the time I'd turned eighteen, I'd established meaningful trade relationships within other kingdoms. I grew the business more than my grandfather could have ever dreamed of, and now, happily employ over one hundred people, fulltime, not including the household help."

His story amazed me. He'd lost both his parents and then his grandfather, striking out on his own when he was sixteen. I studied his face. He looked to be in his mid-twenties. What he'd achieved was nothing short of a miracle.

We walked through the gardens as he told me of the expansion of his business, and I listened intently to his stories of trips to other kingdoms. Maybe my mother had chosen wisely, after all.

I was surprised at how easy Jamal was to talk to. Although I'd only just met him, I felt comfortable in his presence. And despite my initial reluctance, I wanted to get to know him more.

Maybe it was because everything he had, he'd earned. Unlike the sheik's son, he'd not had everything handed to him on a plate.

I ignored my feelings about Genie all afternoon, pushing them down deep in my belly as I talked to Jamal. The man had it all. Looks, charm, intelligence. If I'd written down everything I wanted on paper, he would be my perfect man, and yet it wasn't perfection I craved. I wanted perfectly imperfect.

Later, after a delightful afternoon, I retreated to my room. A small squawk greeted me as I closed the door behind me. Looking to his perch, I saw that Asher looked even worse than he had before

I passed him a seed, which he ignored. My magic dimmed as my hope dimmed.

I was going to lose him. I'd lost Genie in a way, and now I was going to lose my best friend too. I remembered Genie's promise to speak with me later, but I no longer had the energy. He'd made himself clear. I was going on a date with someone else. It was about time I concentrated on that.

"I don't need Genie," I said to Asher. He ruffled what was left of his feathers and then tucked his head under his wing, ignoring me completely. I couldn't blame him.

20TH JUNE

Freya came to my room early at the request of my mother that she help me prepare for my date.

"The sultana requests you wear something benefiting a princess on a date," she said as she opened my closet doors and walked in.

"You pick something," I called to her as I dragged myself out of bed. I didn't really care what I wore. Clothes were not something I really cared about. Asher, on the other hand, I did care about. While Freya was picking out my outfit for the day, I did what I could for the phoenix. He'd molted more feathers in the night and was now almost completely bald. He was a shell of his former self. He looked up at me with doleful eyes.

"I'm sorry, Asher."

"How about this, Your Highness?" Freya asked, bringing out a thin pink outfit with gold trim.

"It's fine, thank you. What time is Jamal expecting me?" I asked, taking the outfit from her.

"He's taking breakfast with your mother at the moment. I think they are expecting you to join them."

I glanced down at my watch. My mother usually had her breakfast at nine, and it was only eight-thirty, which meant she must have ordered it early, especially for Jamal. It also meant I had half an hour to go and speak to Genie.

I'd spent half the night, tossing and turning, trying to decide whether to see him or not. My heart was already in tatters, and I wasn't sure if it would take another beating, but I had to know how he really felt about me. I needed to hear it said explicitly.

I threw on the outfit and pulled my hair into a quick braid, before dashing out of my room.

I ran down the corridors in bare feet, not wanting to draw attention to myself. As I rounded the corner to Genie's suite, I ran straight into my father.

"I'm sorry, my dear girl," he said. "I wasn't looking where I was going."

"Father, are you ok?" he was dressed in a very peculiar outfit of gardener's pants and a purple waistcoat with no shirt underneath. "Have you just been to see Genie?"

My father's eyebrows knotted together. "Who?"

I raised my hand to his forehead. He didn't feel hot, but there was something definitely wrong with him. I took a deep breath and asked him a question. "Do you know who I am, father?"

He narrowed his eyes as if he was trying to place me.

"It's Gaia, your daughter," I prompted. All of a sudden, comprehension dawned on his features.

"Of course I know who you are, Gaia. What a silly question. Are you quite alright? You look like you've seen a ghost."

Just like that, he was back, but the last few minutes had scared me. "Have the doctors been to see you?"

"Doctors? Whatever for? I'm in the prime of health."

"I think I should take you back to your room to rest, just in case," I said, taking his arm in mine.

I monitored him closely as we walked through the palace back to his room. He spoke normally the whole way and answered any question I threw at him. By the time we'd gotten back to his room, I'd begun to wonder if I was worrying for nothing.

"Where were you heading earlier?" I asked him as I helped him into bed.

"Like you said, I was speaking to Genie. I wish you wouldn't fuss so. I'm perfectly fine."

I left him in his room by himself, but once I'd left, I instructed one of his door guards to fetch the palace physician. A quick look at my watch told me it was too late to go and see Genie now. Perhaps it was for the best, after all.

I found Jamal and my mother having breakfast in the dining room.

"There you are," my mother said. "I rather thought you'd be down here earlier. I expected Freya to bring you."

"I was on my way down here when I ran into Father. He's not well. I had to help him back to his room."

My mother stood up, wiping her mouth on a napkin. "If you'll both excuse me. I should go and see how he is."

I felt much better knowing my mother was going to be with him. With any luck, the palace physician would already be up there and would know what was wrong with him.

"I'm sorry to hear that the sultan is unwell. My visit, it seems, was an untimely one."

I looked toward Jamal. He was as good looking as I remembered, and even though his presence didn't make my heart leap the way Genie's did, he was still a very welcome sight.

"Not at all. It is a pleasure to have you here. I'm sure my father will be better soon."

"I'm glad to hear it's nothing serious. May I be so bold to compliment you on your beauty this morning?"

I'd heard all the compliments, and this one was my least favorite. I was called beautiful all the time. By the papers, by the royal subjects, by the myriad of men that turned up on the doorstep, asking me to marry them on a whim. It was all rather boring.

I lowered my head into a nod, wondering if I'd made a mistake about him after all.

"You don't like being called beautiful, do you?"

I glanced his way, intrigued by his comment.

"What makes you think that?"

"It is such an obvious thing to say. Your beauty is so obvious that I almost think you yawned when I mentioned it. And yet I saw beauty in the way you spoke to your mother about your father. Your eyes showed such compassion. I saw how beautifully composed you were when yet another stranger was introduced to you. I know I'm not the first man here, and yet you listened to what I had to say and didn't dismiss me. I found beauty in the way the light danced off your skin in the garden yesterday, but more than that, how you seemed to glow from it. The way you stopped to inhale every flower we passed, the way you spoke kindly to your staff, the way you knew so much about the wool trade despite not being in it. All of that I found beauty in, though none of it diminishes the beauty of your features and your grace."

Typically, I was aloof to the comments on my looks. They always felt insincere. Yet Jamal's was like a breath of fresh air as if hearing it for the first time.

"Why, thank you."

He smiled back at me, his achingly beautiful face split into a grin that showed his dimples to great effect. "I've heard wonderful things about the Kisbu spice market. I'd love to visit it."

"Then we shall," I said with a smile. "Just as soon as I've finished my breakfast."

After I had eaten, I went to find my mother before I went on my date. I found her, or rather she found me along the corridor to my parents' suites.

"Gaia. I thought you would have gone by now. If you are worried about your father, he's fine. The doctor is with him. A little rest and he'll be back to normal."

I thought back to how he was this morning. He'd not known who I was. I wasn't sure any amount of rest would help that, but I had to believe the physician knew what she was doing.

"I'm glad we are finally out of the palace. It's been a while since I've had the pleasure to venture the streets of Kisbu." I said later to Jamal as we walked through the palace gates flanked by four palace guards with Freya walking in front. It was a little white lie, but my night time adventures didn't count. Not really.

"Your Royal Highness, do you not get out of the palace often?" Jamal quizzed.

"Not as often as I would like, and when I do, it's typically by order of Their Majesties." Due to my nocturnal outings, I knew these streets like the back of my hand in the dark when only night dwellers walked them. During the day, with all the hustle and bustle, they were as much a mystery to me as they were to Jamal.

We continued walking in silence as the street goers opened their arms wide and bowed in my presence. Freya walked a couple of steps behind us, and the guards my mother had ordered kept back further still.

Our presence didn't go unnoticed. As the princess, I was hardly difficult to spot, especially with the armed guards, but I noticed that after the people looked at me, their eyes quickly fell on Jamal where they stayed. Especially among the women.

I couldn't hear everything said, but caught the words *hot* and *gorgeous* enough to know they weren't talking about me. More and more people came out to see the mysterious man at my side. I was under no illusion that I wasn't the one everyone wanted to see. The women we passed positively gawked at Jamal, and the longer we walked, the more whispers I overheard. Jamal really was the man of the moment.

Jamal was not deaf to the talk and gossip all around us.

"Would you feel better if we were to head back to the palace?" he asked.

I put my arm in his, which only started more excited chatter among the people. "Not a chance. We've not been to the spice market yet."

He gave me a grin, and for the first time, I felt tiny flutters. Despite everything going on, I was beginning to enjoy myself.

When we finally reached the spice market, the dust-coveredd streets were swarming with people. The guards pushed everyone back just so we could enter.

I turned to Jamal and whispered in his ear. "You know, I really am not allowed to touch a man until I'm married. Public shows of affection are deemed inappropriate, especially for someone of the royal household, but this is all rather fun."

"I thought all that changed when Sultana Jawahir became the ruler?"

I nodded. "Yes. But there is still protocol. Their Majesties like to keep things traditional."

"I'll let go if you are worried?"

I looked down at my arm and his intertwined. "Don't even think about it," I answered him with a smile. I was having so much fun. Who knew that Kisbu was even more interesting in the daytime than it was in the night?

I was no stranger to the delicious aromas of the spice market after walking through it many times, but now, in the daytime, I could actually see all the spices I'd smelled so often. A myriad of colors added to the heady mix making everything so vibrant, so wonderful.

Every stallholder we passed came to the front of their stall to offer us samples of their wares. Thankfully Freya had brought a purse of Rubees with her because I'd have felt guilty sampling so much without buying anything. Jamal and I tried so many delicious pastries, sweets, and aromatic teas that by the time we'd made our way through to the other side, I was sure I'd never want to eat again.

"My father lived on the streets not far from here when he was a young boy," I remarked to Jamal.

"His past is legendary," Jamal answered, passing me a piece of cake that smelled of coffee. "He is the reason I work so hard. He came from nothing and ended up the sultan of the whole kingdom. A true rags to riches story."

"No more than your own," I replied as he passed a handful of Rubees to the stall owner and asked her to fill a bag with more of the delicious cakes.

"If I eat any more, I shall pop," I said as he handed the bag to one of the guards.

"The cakes aren't for you," he said cryptically as we exited the market.

People still followed us as we walked through the streets with no aim in direction. I was just happy to be free of the palace for a while, as was Jamal, judging by the way everything held his interest. It didn't take long before the reason behind his purchase of cakes was made evident. A small girl, no more than four of five, came up to us. Her face was dirty, and her poor little body was emaciated. Jamal took the bag from the guard and handed her a cake. When she saw the size of it, her eyes went wide. She licked her lips in anticipation then ran off quickly with the cake before we changed our minds. Once the street urchins saw what was happening, they all ran forwards, and soon we were surrounded by children. There were so many of them, the guards couldn't keep them away. Behind us, the adults of Kisbu were still following, and now they watched as Jamal and I gave out cakes. The street was packed as more and more people joined us.

Out of the corner of my eye, I noticed one of the palace staff cut through the people and speak to the guards. The guard nodded, then pushed the children out of the way to get to me.

"We have to leave, Your Highness."

"We can't leave," I said, gesturing to the hungry children around me. "We still have plenty of cakes to give out."

"Her Majesty's orders. She got word of the number of people crowding around you and asked that you go home immediately."

"But she was the one who insisted I go on this date in the first place. What did she think would happen?" I kept my voice down, aware that hundreds of eyes were upon me, but I was livid. I'd done as she asked. No one was getting hurt, and yet now, she was demanding I go home. The guard only shrugged.

I nodded to the messenger. "Send word back to the palace that I'll be back when I'm ready."

"I'm afraid I can't do that. I'm sorry, Your Highness, but you'll have to come with me."

Jamal was nonplussed by being made to go back to the palace, but I was angry. So much so that my newfound magic was beginning to burn in my stomach, and it took everything I had to keep it from erupting out of me.

"Where's the sultana?" I demanded, forcing my way through her offices once we were back at the palace. Two guards stood at the door, blocking my path.

What on Badalah was going on?

"Her Majesty is currently unavailable," one of them said. "You'll have to schedule a time to meet with her, per orders of the sultana."

"Since when do I have to schedule an appointment with my mother? Let me past."

The two guards gave each other a look, seemingly unsure on how to proceed, but they pulled back their staffs and let me through.

My mother wasn't in her office, so I carried on through until I got to her private parlor.

I found her laid out on a chaise with a cloth over her

forehead. “Gaia, my dear. How was your date?”

“It was fine up until the point you ordered me home,” I shouted, feeling the anger growing again.

“Please keep your voice down. I’m not feeling too well. I only asked the guards to bring you home because word had got back to the palace that you were being swamped. I was only worried about your safety. I take it from your angry outburst that you were enjoying yourself before I so rudely interrupted?”

She sat up, and the damp cloth fell into her lap. The way she looked at me with one eyebrow raised made me laugh. I couldn’t be angry at her when all she was doing was looking after my own wellbeing.

“I was, actually,” I replied nonchalantly, taking a seat next to her on the chaise.

“I knew you’d like him. As soon as he came to the palace, I knew he wasn’t like the other men you’ve turned away.”

“Most of the men, you’ve turned away,” I pointed out.

“Only because you asked me to,” she countered. It was true. I had so many proposals of marriage, most of which were from men I’d never met or worse still, men whose parents had written letters to my parents. At least Jamal had the guts to actually come to the palace.

“I like him,” I admitted.

“I knew you would,” she answered with a smile. “Tell me what you think.”

“He’s smart,” I started, thinking back to everything he’d told me about his business. It wasn’t just bluster. He was widely versed on the Badalah trading routes. “He’s kind, he’s interesting, he’s...”

“Not too bad on the eye,” my mother added.

“Yes, he’s very good-looking,” I admitted. “The

townswomen were practically drooling over him. I rather got the impression they thought I was a very lucky woman to be with him."

My mother put her hand to the side of my face. "They are wrong. He is the lucky one. Do you think you'll go on a second date?"

"I think I'll have to as you ended the first one so abruptly," I said with a smirk.

"You can take more guards next time, or you can go somewhere not quite so public. It might be nice to spend some private time with him."

I blushed at her words. "We'll see."

It was all I could say. I'd had a wonderful date, but I barely knew Jamal. "I'm not going to rush into anything, just because everyone else thinks he's hot."

"If everyone else thinks he's hot, you might not want to wait around. Let me tell you. Men like Jamal don't come by very often. You have to take your chance while you can before some Kisbu girl snags him right from under you."

"Weren't you just telling me that he's the lucky one to be with me and not the other way around?"

"And so he is, but I still wouldn't keep him waiting. What really is it you are waiting for?"

A picture of Genie flashed in my mind. I still hadn't spoken to him after what he'd said to me the day before. Maybe I didn't need to. My mother was right. Jamal was a great catch. What did I even need Genie for?

"Nothing," I said. "In fact, I was going to have dinner with him tonight in the gardens."

"That's nice," she said, picking up the cloth and putting it back on her forehead. She laid back and let the cloth slip over her eyes. "I'll join you if this headache ever lets up."

"Headache? Are you alright?"

She waved her hand, dismissing my worry. "I'm fine. Just a small headache. The summer heat always gets to me."

Badalah was a hot kingdom, especially in the summer months. I'd never known the heat give her a headache before.

"Is father ok still? I haven't had time to go see him since this morning."

"Who?"

"Father. He was acting strange this morning. What did the physician say?"

"I don't know what you mean, Gaia."

I furrowed my eyebrows and pulled the cloth from her face so she'd have to look at me.

"Father was ill," I said slowly. The same puzzled expression I'd seen on my father only that morning was now in the eyes of my mother. "I'm asking you if he is alright."

"Oh," she said, coming round. "Your father. For a second there, I thought you were talking about my father."

My grandfather had been dead for over ten years. How could I have been talking about him? There was something going on in the palace that was much worse than stress and heat. Both my parents were acting weird now. I left my mother and went straight to the one person that should know why.

"I don't know what to tell you," The physician said when I cornered her in her office. "It's just a touch of stress. He's the sultan. He's bound to be stressed."

"And my mother?" I countered. "Is she stressed too?"

"She could be. If she was worried about your father, it could manifest itself in a little forgetfulness."

"A little forgetfulness? She forgot who my father was and this morning he forgot who I was. He was looking right at me at the time. I don't think this is stress."

The physician sat up straight in her chair. "If they are not better tomorrow, I'll request an audience with them both. You have to remember my position. They are the sultan and sultana. I can't demand they see me."

"Then please request it," I said.

The physician had no more idea of what was happening than I did. I'd been waiting for something to happen for a while. After everything I'd seen happening in the other kingdoms, especially to the other royal families, it seemed inevitable that whatever it was would find its way here.

Aside from Asher, who had enough problems of his own and couldn't help me even if he wanted to, there was only one other person I could speak to about what was happening.

My nerves almost got the better of me as I made my way to Genie's suite. I'd never been nervous in his presence before, but things had changed and not for the better. My feelings for him had changed in the past few months and had grown to the point where they were unbearable. His dismissal of them the other day should have been the slap in the face I needed to wake up and smell the Jamal-flavored coffee, but it wasn't Jamal I needed to see in the middle of a crisis.

I knocked quietly on his door, half-hoping he wouldn't answer. When he did, I found I didn't know what to say to him.

"Gaia. I was hoping you'd come and see me. Please, come in."

I followed him into his office. It was as neat as

always with thousands of books lining the shelves of his bookcases. I'd spent so many hours here as a child reading those books. Some of my happiest memories were in this room.

"I'm an old man," he began before I'd even sat down.

"You're not old," I interrupted. It was a lie. He was so old, he couldn't even remember how many years he'd spent trapped in the lamp. Hundreds, possibly thousands of years, had passed before my father had freed him over eighteen years ago. "You can't count the years you were in the lamp."

He gave me a soft smile and sat in his chair. The way he looked at me almost broke my heart, and I suddenly found I didn't want to hear what he had to say.

"It doesn't matter anyway. That's not why I'm here. I'm here about my parents."

He was silent for a minute, studying me. I hated it when he did that. It felt like he could see right through me. If he truly could see through me, he'd see the pain, just being near him caused.

"What about your parents?"

"They are behaving oddly."

"I know. Your mother told me she wasn't feeling well earlier. I told her to rest. I don't think it's anything to worry about. Just a headache."

I shook my head, feeling frustration building up inside me. It was a damn sight better than the pain I'd been feeling before, but it was still an unwelcome emotion.

"So people keep telling me. It's just a headache, it's just the heat. It's just stress. She's forgetting things. I spoke with her today, and her eyes glazed over as though I wasn't there. I think it's something to do with magic."

Genie shuddered at the word. "You think this has something to do with what's been happening in the other kingdoms?"

I nodded my head. "It's all a bit coincidental. My parents becoming ill in the very same week I find out I can conjure fire. The queen of Draconis was fine one day, and then she was asleep the next. The same with the queen of Atlantice. She'd shown no signs of being a mermaid before she turned into one."

"It's hardly the same as having a headache and forgetting a few things," Genie pointed out, ever the voice of reason.

"She didn't just forget a few things," I said softly. "She forgot the sultan."

"The sultan of where?"

I looked at him incredulously. "*The* sultan. My father. My mother's husband."

He knotted his eyebrows together. "Gaia, are you feeling ok?"

"Yes, I'm fine, why?"

"Because your mother was never married. There hasn't been a sultan since your grandfather died ten years ago."

21ST JUNE

Sleep didn't come. How could it? Everyone in the palace was losing their minds, and yet, I felt perfectly fine. My mind was as sharp as ever. After an agonizing night of tossing and turning, I decided to head to Genie's office area to study neurological diseases in his vast library of books.

Genie wasn't there, so I found a couple of books that looked like they had something to do with the brain and sat down in my usual spot.

There were so many things that could go wrong with the human brain and so many things that affected memories, but in none of the books I looked at could I find anything about group hallucinations, for this was almost certainly what it was. My mother and father were usually inseparable, and Genie was my father's best friend. The trio was together every day, so how was it possible that both Genie and my mother had forgotten my father? And father himself. He was the first to come down with memory loss, but he'd seemed to have forgotten everything. Genie's library had never failed me before, but it had failed me twice in the past week. This was the second time. The first time it failed me without my even trying. I had wanted to look up magic, or at least why I'd suddenly come down with the ability to produce fire, but I knew Genie's loathing of anything to do with magic would extend to books.

In the end, I gave up and decided to go and see how my father was doing. He might have been forgotten by two out of the three people that loved him the most, but he still had me, and I was going to make damn sure he was recognized in his own home.

The guards were no longer at the door, which I took to be a good sign. Maybe this had all blown over, and everything could go back to normal. A quick glance outside the window told me it was dawn. I'd been awake all night, and yet I didn't feel tired.

"Father," I called, knocking lightly at his door. When he didn't answer, I knocked again and opened the door.

A feeling of foreboding hit me hard as I walked through the suite to his bedroom. He wasn't there. Not in his room, nor on his terrace. My mother wasn't there either, but she was always an early riser. My father, not so much.

"Father," I called out, panic filling my every word. Normally, my father not being in their suite would mean nothing, but what with the way he had been, the way everyone had been recently, his disappearance was a cause for concern.

I ran through the palace, looking in all the usual

places, his office, the throne room, the gardens. He was nowhere to be seen.

After scouring the palace and coming up with nothing, I ended my search in the dining room. I didn't find him there, but I did find my mother eating breakfast as though she didn't have a care in the world.

"Mother, Father has gone. I can't find him anywhere."

She cocked her head to the side slightly and knitted her eyebrows together. I knew what she was going to say before she opened her mouth, but it was still a punch to the gut when she spoke.

"Are you alright, Gaia, dear? You know you don't have a father. I adopted you as a child. I suppose you must have a real father out there somewhere, but I never met him. It was two women that brought you to the palace as a babe."

Frustration bubbled up in me. Only a few days ago, they'd been completely in love, dancing in the gardens. Now, it was as though my father had ceased to exist completely. But he hadn't. I knew him. I remembered him.

"I'm not talking about my real father. I'm talking about the sultan, Aladdin."

"Who?"

"Never mind," I snapped back and ran out of the dining room. There was no point going to see Genie. He didn't remember my father any more than my mother did. I ran through the palace, asking every member of the staff I could find if they knew where he was, but the response was the same. No one knew who he was, let alone where he was. Whatever had happed to my parents was now affecting everyone but me.

I jogged my memory for the stories my father had once told me. The orphanage came up as the place I could start searching. He'd spent a number of years there before moving on to the streets. Climbing out down the trellis I usually took at night was easy. The stale warm air pressed against my face as I moved quickly through the streets until arriving at the children's orphanage. It was highly secure, an important detail my father had seen to. Along with a huge renovation. I knew the place just as I knew the palace, having spent a lot of my volunteer time there.

My grandfather had been a wonderful man, but he was wholly unprepared to rule a kingdom, despite being brought up in the palace and destined for the job. Ironically, my father, a street rat, an urchin with no formal education, had done something that centuries of sultans before him had not been able to do. He'd unified Badalah. His upbringing, if anyone could call it that made him the hero, and since he'd come to the palace, he'd changed Badalah for the better. He was the first sultan to implement social housing, food banks, and clothes drives. He donated vast amounts of wealth to orphanages throughout Badalah and especially in Kisbu where he grew up hungry. There was a reason my father was loved by his people, and it wasn't just because his story inspired people. It was because he was a great man and a wonderful leader. The rich loved him because he championed business, the poor loved him because he provided safety and food and warmth. There were still people sleeping rough on Kisbu's streets, but only by choice. There were enough beds in the city to house everyone, even those who didn't have a Rubee to their names.

Yes, my father was the best leader Badalah had ever seen, which made it all the more awful that no one remembered him.

The large gates of the orphanage loomed up ahead. Once they had been a necessary precaution to keep thieves out and the children in and, as my father had told me, been kept locked most of the time. We lived in a different era now, and though the wrought iron gates were closed, I knew I'd find them unlocked. The orphanage was a happy place now, where the children were well cared for and had enough food, clothing, and beds to go round. The palace was the biggest donor of money, giving thousands of Rubees a year to the mistress of the orphanage to keep it running.

At least, the gate had always been unlocked before, but as I went to push it, I found a large padlock linking the two gates together.

Beside me, the breeze ruffled the leaves of the bushes, giving me a startle. What was going on? Never once had I known this gate to be locked. Not in the daytime. Calming my nerves, I continued my trek around the fence to the servants' entrance. The small gate around the back opened with a creak, pulling my nerves tighter, though I didn't really know why. I'd been here hundreds of times. I knew the mistress well. I had no reason to feel panic, and yet stabs of fear needled me. Something felt off, but apart from the lock on the gates, I couldn't see what.

I walked around the building to the front door, determined to get some answers.

A dim light showed through the window. I sneaked a peek through the glass, noticing the light came from the study. The headmistress was in there, looking over books from what I could see. But she wasn't alone. One of the palace guards was there. I should have walked past the window to the main entrance, but something about the expression on the guard's face made me pause. I pulled back so they couldn't see me and continued to watch through the window, which was open a crack.

"I'm not a fool, mistress. I know you have a purse in the orphanage." The guard said.

She sighed. "For the last time, sir. I do not. I've allowed you to see our books. Everything we need for the facility is done on good credit once the palace approves the budget. The palace handles all of our bills. There is absolutely no need for me to keep money on site."

He grunted. "And what of your purse? Hmm? I'm sure the sultana compensates you handsomely. Are you going to share some of those spoils with me? Or am I going to have to force these out of you?"

My breath caught in my throat. The guard was threatening the mistress. I knew him. He was one of my father's most trusted guards. What did he think he was playing at? Ducking down, I crept past the window and ran to the orphanage entrance.

The large oak door opened silently, and I crept in. Keeping to the carpet to not make any noise, I stopped outside the study door.

"Sir! What is it that you are trying to accomplish? Surely your earnings are far more than my own. Why is it that you feel the need to come here and attempt a shakedown of a woman who has hardly a Rubee to her name?"

There was a great sense of fear in her tone, along with pain. I needed to do something; I just wasn't sure of what.

"Oh, please, woman! I know the palace has always been quite generous to the orphanage. Now, give me all the money you have, or I'll find a way to make your life a living hell..."

She cut him off. "A living hell? What do you think

we do here? We take children from their own living hell and give them a home."

"Just give me what I ask for. Or maybe I'll take more than just money."

I didn't like where his implication was going, and I could feel the fire burning at my core as the energy built up quickly, sending my hands a glowing.

I ran toward the office, hands blazing in front of me, kicking the door all the way open.

The flames hid my face as I yelled at the guard, "Leave, or you'll be sorry!"

The man had no fear. He stood, taking a few steps in my direction, testing me. "And who are you?"

I sidestepped, avoiding any chance he got to get a look at my face. "Leave!" I demanded.

Still, he stepped a few more steps closer. "I'll do no such thing, little girl." He drew his sword, and I reactively sent a blast of hot smoke in his direction, sending him hurtling to the ground in a coughing fit.

"How dare you!" he said, slamming his fist onto the floor.

Quickly, I sent another blast of hot smoke. This time, I allowed my mind to connect with the smoke, as if an extension of myself, I wielded it to encircle the guard like an anaconda, tightening around him until he could no longer breathe.

"That's enough!" he finally said, gasping for air. "I'll go." He crawled toward the door, pulling himself up with the help of the door frame until he could walk on his own. I waited, making the flames go out as I heard the front door click.

I turned, expecting the mistress to be happy to see the back of him, but her expression showed only fear. Fear, not of the guard, but of me.

"Miss! You need to leave. I cannot be associated with your evil sorcery," she said, panicked.

"Sorcery? What? No! I'm not a sorceress..." I protested, but she cut me off too soon.

"Please. I don't want any trouble for the orphanage. For the children. I beg of you. Please, leave."

"I'll leave," I said, defeated. "But first, I must look around. I need to find the Sultan. Aladdin."

"Who?"

It made sense she didn't know who he was, If my father's own wife and best friend couldn't remember him, why should she, but I'd hoped the sickness had been confined to the palace. It obviously hadn't

"The sultan. My father," I said again, losing hope.

She eyed me coolly. "The sultana is unwed. She never took a husband. You are mistaken."

"My father is Aladdin, and he's the sultan, husband of Sultana Jawahir."

The mistress stood motionless, as if unsure what to do next.

It was clear to me that not only did she not know who my father was, she also didn't recognize me. I'd stood beside her at so many events at the palace where we'd given food out to the poor, and here she was looking at me as though I was a deranged stranger.

"My name is Gaia. I'm the daughter of the Sultana Jawahir."

Her eyes remained wide as she shook her head.

"I'm sorry," I continued, seeing that I was making things all the worse. "I was brought up here. I was adopted out at a very young age and wanted to see where I spent my youngest days. I lied to you about the sultana. I guess it's what we adoptees do, pretend our parents are royalty."

It was an outrageous lie, but the truth was weirder, and it was the only thing I could think of to say to her to be able to look around. Even as I spoke, I knew I wouldn't find my father here, but it was the only link I had to my father's past. If he wasn't here, I didn't know where else to look.

"Very well. I'll accompany you. But as soon as we've finished, you must leave and never return." She hesitated as though she'd not finished speaking her mind.

"Please. Speak freely," I said.

"What you did with fire. That is not normal, nor is it something people in the kingdom are very welcoming about. You helped me. So, I'll give you the benefit of the doubt, but I do not want any sorcery in front of the children."

"Understood."

We walked through the orphanage. I knew the place well, but there was something different. Whereas the children had once been happy, they were all sullen and miserable. What had happened here? There was no mistreatment as far as I could see, but the atmosphere was markedly different from the last time I visited.

As I suspected, my father wasn't there, and I left the orphanage with a feeling of despair. It was as if my father had completely vanished, not only from Kisbu but from existence. And now I was going the same way.

I walked around town with my headscarf wrapped around half of my face, to avoid anyone recognizing me. Just because the mistress didn't, didn't mean no one else would. I needed to find my father, just so I knew I wasn't going insane.

I spent all morning under the scorching sun, taking one street at a time, leaving nothing unsearched, until exhaustion found me, and my body couldn't push further.

After buying a small meal from a street vendor, I sat down on the side of the street feeling completely despondent.

That's when I saw the newspaper stand and made my way to it.

If this sickness was happening in Kisbu, I wondered if it was happening elsewhere. Where did the sickness stop?

A group of people gathered around the stand. Ice invaded my chest as I took in the headline

SULTANA JAWAHIR INCREASES TAXES AND CANCELS TRADE DEALS WITH NEIGHBORING KINGDOMS

I lifted my hand to my mouth as I read the paper. Badalah needed trade. My mother had set up many of the trade deals herself. Both she and my father had made Badalah as prosperous as it was, largely due to trade. We needed it. Badalah land was arid, and not much grew here. We needed to trade just so we had enough food. Without food from other kingdoms, the people of Badalah would starve. There were a few farms between Kisbu and the neighboring town of Khoha, which supplied a lot of Kisbu's food, but the rest of the kingdom didn't have the right kind of land to farm anything. And increasing the taxes! Why?

"That woman is pure evil," a small woman to the side of me said to her friend. "She'd do well to abdicate and give us a true government."

All around me, people bobbed their heads in agreement. Not once in my life had I heard a bad word against her, and yet it seemed that everyone hated her.

"Perhaps she needs to finally get married," someone

else said.

Others exploded in laughter.

"Imagine that. Sultana Jawahir married? Who could possibly tolerate such a foolish hag? Sure, she might still hold some of that beauty of her youth, but her soul is evil to the core. It radiates from her like something putrid."

The mumblings spread as I distanced myself, bumping into someone as I ran.

"My apologies," I said, holding my headscarf in place.

"Princess Gaia? Is that you?"

My heart leapt as I heard my name and title. I wasn't going completely mad, after all. "Jamal. You remember me?"

He stared at me, confused. "Remember you? We spent much of yesterday together. We gave out cakes to the poor, not far from here. Princess, are you all right?"

Tears rolled down my face. I wanted desperately not to cry, except it was too late. I couldn't stop. I didn't even care that I'd thrown myself into his arms for comfort. "I... I think I'm losing my mind. Nothing makes sense."

He squinted his eyes. "I've noticed something strange happening, but I'm not sure you are the one with the problem. The sultana is behaving quite bizarrely. I left the palace early because..." he paused. "Well, it seems your mother has taken a liking to me. She has it stuck in her head that I am here to court her."

"What?" I jumped back, feeling as if a stampede of camels were crossing my chest.

"Yes, exactly. And then there is the situation with your father. It's as if everyone in the palace has forgotten about him. Your lady servant remembers him, but I fear she is the only one."

"Something terrible is happening, Jamal. I can feel

it. Truth be told. I've been out here since the wee hours looking for my father. I haven't been able to find him. And I was just reading the kingdom's paper. They are speaking ill of my mother! She's making decisions going against everything she and my father spent eighteen years building up. Not only doesn't she remember my father; she's actively trying to cancel out all the good he did."

"I don't mean to pry, but were there problems in your parent's marriage?"

I thought back to how they'd been dancing together only days ago. They only had eyes for each other."

I shook my head. "I've never met a couple more in love than those two. This isn't a problem marriage, it's a sickness. A group hallucination..." I broke down completely. "I don't know what it is."

Jamal looked over toward the paper stand and watched the people. "Something is definitely strange. But we'll get to the bottom of it."

"Don't you think it is strange that you and Freya are not affected by this?" I asked. The whole world had gone mad, and yet, having two people believe me made it easier. At least, it wasn't I that had gone insane.

"Come with me," he said, taking my hand. "I'll share our theories."

"You and Freya have been talking?"

"Yes, all morning. She noticed you were gone and came straight to me. You see, she knows I too am of magic."

I stopped in my tracks. "Of magic? But..."

"Now is not the time for this. Let's keep moving. I'll explain it all as soon as we are in a safe place."

"We aren't going back to the palace?" I asked, noticing we were heading in the opposite direction.

“Freya came with me to look for you. Kisbu is a big town. We split up to look but agreed to meet up in an hour. She wrote an address for me.” He fished out a folded piece of paper and handed it to me. On it, in neat handwriting was an address I didn’t recognize.

“It’s in the old part of town apparently,” Jamal said, whisking me through the crowds of market-goers. “I think it’s best to keep your scarf covering you until we get to where we are going. The world is crazy, and I don’t know how safe you are.”

“I’m pretty sure most people don’t know who I am anymore,” I countered. “I think I’m safer now than I usually am.”

He didn’t answer, and I kept my scarf on as he’d asked.

We walked quickly through the winding streets of the old part of Kisbu until we reached one of the original older neighborhoods of the less fortunate.

Jamal asked a couple of people if they knew the address until one pointed us to an old door in a run-down building.

He tapped on it, and a woman that had to be my mother’s age opened it. Her hair was covered with a scarf, but wisps of silver hair escaped it.

“Mrs. Shan.” He acknowledged her with a slight nod.

She simply gave him a slight bow of the head and gestured for us to enter. Her sharp eyes took me in as I entered the house.

“Freya will be here shortly. She’s sent word that I should expect the two of you here. I guess she wasn’t wrong.”

She closed the door and returned to the modest space that served as her kitchen and sitting room. “Have a seat. I’m preparing lunch. I’m sure the two of you can do with some food. Jamal, you can sit here, and Your Highness, you may take the head of the table."

"Wait? You recognize me?"

"Yes. Where do you think Freya gets her magic blood from? If you haven't already gathered, I'm Freya's mother."

"Freya is magic?"

"Indeed. Although, she doesn't understand it and probably will never be strong enough to wield it."

"She told me she learned about magic at university."

"Magic is not something to be proud of in these parts. Since The Vizier tried taking Badalah using magic, it has fallen out of favor. She was only protecting herself. Please don't punish her lie."

"I wouldn't," I assured her. No wonder Freya figured out I was magic before I did. "Why do people not like magic here anymore?" I asked. "It can't all be to do with The Vizier."

"He was a very bad man. Evil ran through his pores. I wonder if this isn't his magic." She said, gesturing the air around her. She shuffled back to her cooking, leaving me confused.

"My grandfather's vizier is long gone. He's not been seen since my parents married. My father told me that he became trapped in the very same lamp that Genie spent most of his life in. It was taken to the desert and was buried."

"Things that are buried have ways of becoming unburied," she said cryptically. "Besides, no lamp could hold The Vizier. I doubt that's where he has been all these years. He might have been trapped there for a while...I don't know."

The thought of someone as wicked as The Vizier being around terrified me. He'd used his own brand of evil magic to try and take over Badalah. My father had stopped him. The story was legendary. No stories of The Vizier had surfaced since I was born. He was well and truly gone.

"What makes you think this is the work of The Vizier?" I asked her.

She shrugged her shoulders and turned to look at me. "It feels the same. Before your father became the sultan, Badalah was a miserable place. You won't remember it, but crime was rife and people starved. I saw the Badalah Beacon this morning. I don't think your mother would suspend trade if she was in her right mind. The Vizier wanted to suspend trade. This smacks of him."

I felt a chill creep into my bones. The Vizier had been a powerful and evil man. "Why did he want to suspend trade?"

"He wanted to be the only one who could trade with the other kingdoms. He didn't care about the people of Badalah, only about lining his own pockets."

"You don't think my mother wants to do that?"

Mrs. Shan came over to me and took my hand. "Your mother and father are the best rulers Badalah has ever seen. I know your father is lost. Freya told me. I think your mother is just as lost. Her father, the sultan before Aladdin, also acted strangely in his time. It turned out The Vizier was hypnotizing him. I don't know how anyone would be able to hypnotize a whole kingdom, but it feels that way."

"And only people with magic can see through that?"

She let go of my hands and nodded her head. "I believe that to be the case."

"But what about Genie? He can't remember father either."

"But he is no longer magic, is he? He lost his magic at the same time The Vizier left. It makes me wonder if The Vizier somehow got the genie's magic when he was sent into the lamp. The lamp was the only thing able to contain such powerful magic."

Bile caught in my throat. If The Vizier had escaped, no one would be able to stop him. Not even Genie. I turned to Jamal.

"Tell me, Jamal. What is your magic?"

He paced the room. "Earth. But like Freya, I cannot wield it. That is something I've never been able to do. I don't know anyone who is capable of using their magic in the way you do. Not from Badalah anyway. I can only sense it."

"It is extremely uncommon, that is for sure," Mrs. Shan added. "Freya tells me you came upon this magic recently. Do you think it is connected to everything that is happening in Badalah?"

"It seems likely, though I cannot say how. I've never met anyone who knows magic outside of Badalah." The palace had hosted parties with dignitaries from other kingdoms, some of which had magic. The people of Enchantia especially were known for their magic, but that was all. "My magic only came to me within the last week, and now this. I don't know what the connection is, though."

"We should think about asking around to see if anyone else has noticed their magic becoming strong," she said, nodding to herself. "But first, you eat."

Mrs. Shan placed in front of us a modest lunch of beans and bread.

The door swung open and in popped Freya, short of breath.

"Oh dear, are you all right?" her mother asked,

rushing to her daughter's side.

"I am. I just ran all the way here." She let out a big laugh and joined us on the cushions for her lunch. "I'm glad Jamal found you in one piece. Where'd you go? Don't answer that. You went to find your father, didn't you?"

I nodded.

"You went to the orphanage?"

I nodded again as Mrs. Shan placed a plate of food in front of her daughter.

"Yeah, I didn't think you would find him there."

"And why is that?" I countered.

She dipped a piece of bread in the sauce and shoved it in her mouth.

"Because I know where he's at."

"Where do you think he is?" I asked Freya.

She waited to finish chewing. "I think he's in the bell tower. I asked around after someone matching your father's description was seen acting strangely. Someone told me he saw someone break into the bell tower last night."

Of course! He'd mentioned how he'd sometimes find refuge there when he was living on the streets. He always spoke of the place fondly. I stood up to go find him, but Mrs. Shan pushed me back in my seat.

"Finish your food before you leave. You'll not get very far on an empty stomach."

She was right, but the thought of my father out there alone made me feel sick to my stomach.

"He lived on the streets for years without your help. He can do it again for another half-hour or so."

She was right. He'd grown up out here.

"We could do with finding out what all this magic nonsense is about," Mrs. Shan said, sitting down at the table with her own food. “Magic just doesn’t appear like...well, magic. Especially magic like this. Something has happened.”

I put down my spoon. “I’ve been following the news from the other kingdoms. I’ve been expecting something like this for quite a while.”

“What do you mean?” Freya asked, looking right at me.

“You know I read the papers. I’ve noticed a kind of pattern. As far as I can tell, it started in Draconis. At the beginning of the year, their queen fell asleep, and so far hasn’t woken up.”

“It’s a terrible business,” Mrs. Shan interjected.

“But it didn’t end there. In Atlantice, the queen there reverted back to being a mermaid.”

“She was cursed too?” Jamal asked, the interest in the subject evident in his eyes.

“Actually, no. According to reports that came out later, she was a mermaid to begin with. She used magic to get her legs and then pretended to the entire kingdom that she was human for years.”

“So her magic didn’t appear; it did the opposite? It disappeared.”

I nodded. “I guess so, but it’s been happening in other kingdoms. As far as I can tell, eighteen years ago, something happened that spewed magic out into the world. That magic calmed the years of war and depression.”

“I remember it well,” Mrs. Shan said, leveling a spoon in my direction. “It was as though peace occurred overnight. Of course, that was because your father became sultan. Badalah sorely needed a fresh perspective.”

“It wasn’t just my father. All over the kingdoms,

the royal families came into luck. They married their sweethearts, they took over the rule. It was as if everything magically was set right."

Freya looked at me with excitement. "So, you think a spell has been broken?"

"No." Jamal shook his head. "I might not know much magic, but I know of it. I've traveled a lot for business. No spell is that powerful. No person, not even the mages of Enchantia, could produce a spell that would cover all of the twelve kingdoms."

I ruminated on his words. He was right. No one person was that powerful. I didn't know much about magic, but I knew enough to know there were limits to it. I sighed. Maybe I was looking at this all wrong.

"I'll have to do some research," I concluded, finishing up my lunch. I sat back and patted my full stomach. "So, now what?" I asked, glancing at the others.

"We are going to get back into the city and find your father. Then, we'll figure it out from there."

Freya looked at me with such determination. She was right. My father was my number one priority. Finding out the cause of all the sudden magic would have to wait for another day.

Freya led the way to the bell tower near the center of the huge walled city. I was surprised to see it was part of another building. The front door was open. The three of us stepped inside.

"How can I help you?" a small woman with a messy bun and a tea stain on her dress said. Looking around the room, I saw leaflets about Badalah's tourist attractions. The camel tours of the desert, walking tours of the Badalah Mountains, and spice market tours. This was a tourist information place. At the end of the room was a set of stairs winding upward. The bell tower.

"Has anyone broken into the tower recently?" I asked, pointing to the stairs.

The small woman shook her head. "Not to my knowledge. The doors were locked when I came in this morning. Nothing's been stolen. Why do you ask?"

I looked to Freya, who shrugged.

"Has anyone been up there today? Could anyone have slept up there?"

The woman laughed. "No one sleeps up there. I've had one tour up there this morning, but I think they all came down. Feel free to go and have a look for yourself."

I thanked her and raced up the stairs. The bell part was closed to the public, but there was one window that looked out toward the palace. Was this the view my father had looked out over in his youth.

Jamal tried the door that led to the bell above us, but it was locked.

"Does the room to the bell get opened often?" I asked the woman when we came down.

"Only in emergencies and when the palace asks for it to be rung on special occasions. Each peal of the bell has a different meaning, you see. It's not been unlocked for weeks."

"Did the sultan ask you to unlock it?"

She scrunched her face "Who?"

I thanked her and stepped outside.

"What now?" Jamal asked.

Freya wiped her brow. "We keep looking!"

By the time the sun set in the sky, we were no closer to finding him and had no leads.

Freya invited me back to her house. There was no reason for me not to go back to the palace to sleep, but the fear of my mother and Genie not recognizing me kept me away.

Mrs. Shan gave Jamal and me a blanket each, and we both took a sofa to sleep on. Freya stayed up with us chatting, but after a while, I turned over and threw the blanket over me. Tuning them out, I closed my eyes and fell asleep.

22ND JUNE

The brazen sun pounded on our backs as we moved carefully through Kisbu.

The clock tower had been a bust as had many other places in Kisbu. We trudged through the city, checking out all the places where a man with nothing might hide.

"We need to get to the highest place," I said, trying to remember the things my father had told me about his youth. "He liked to look upon the palace and daydream."

Eventually, we came upon a cafe that boasted a rooftop terrace. It cost us the price of a coffee and cake each, but it was worth it. The city of Kisbu laid before us in all its glory.

"Do you see what I see?" Jamal said as we gazed out.

My heart leapt as I took in the sight. "There's another bell tower!" I exclaimed. The one I'd always imagined my father to have been talking about dominated the skyline, but now as I looked at it, I realized how new it looked compared to many of the other buildings. The other, smaller bell tower blended in more with its surroundings.

After rushing the coffee, I slipped the cake into my pocket, and the three of us ran back onto the streets.

Twenty minutes later, we stood at the entrance to the tower. The dilapidated building had seen better days, and the one entrance had a door with peeling paint that was probably red at one point, but now was a faded, dull brown.

The door opened easily. Once upon a time, it would have housed a huge bell. Maybe it still did, but it was the new clock tower that signaled a threat to Badalah now. I pushed forward, nimbly skipping two steps at a time.

When we reached the top, I heard a thumping noise. Jamal and Freya motioned for me to go ahead.

And that's when I found him. My father. Aladdin. The sultan. The street rat. He was curled up on a pile of old newspapers. When he saw me enter, he sat up and pulled back. The fear in his eyes almost broke my heart.

"Aladdin," I said softly.

He squinted, studying me carefully.

"Do you remember me?" I continued.

In a swift move, he was on his feet.

It had only been two days since he was last at the palace and about three since I'd seen him. Yet, his facial hair was grown out, and the hair on his head was a mess, as were the clothes he wore. Nothing about him resembled anything from royalty.

"Who are you?" he asked gruffly, keeping me at bay.

"You don't remember me?" Again, I asked.

He shook his head, looking past me.

"They're with me."

"Your friends?"

"Yes, and yours. My name is Gaia. I'm..." I stopped myself. Perhaps telling him I was his daughter wasn't the best idea. At least, not until I could be sure he wouldn't freak out. "We are here to help you."

"I don't need your help. So please, leave me be."

Jamal moved in closer. "Sir, if I may. There seems to be something strange happening in the kingdom. Many people will suffer if you don't come with us." He moved closer, his hands up showing Aladdin there was nothing there to hurt him with. "We can explain everything if you just please come with us. I promise no harm will come to you."

In a split second, my father turned and leapt from the bell tower, causing me to lose my footing, tripping forward into the heap of papers scattered about. Jamal tried to help me up instead. I screamed for him to save my father. I was sure he was injured, or worse.

Freya was at the ledge when I found my footing. "What is it?" I demanded.

"Your Highness, it seems the sultan escaped. See for yourself," she said, stepping away.

When I looked over the ledge, I could see just how my father had used the carved stones in the architectural detail of the tower to rappel to the lower outlook.

"Quick! Follow him!" I shouted, running toward the stairs, Jamal and Freya followed.

We pressed down the stairs. Jamal ran ahead,

thankfully. If anyone had a chance of catching up to my father, it was he.

Freya and I finally caught up to him at the bottom.

"He's gone," Jamal said, and as I looked past him into the bustling streets, I knew he was right. We would be extremely lucky to find him again.

"What am I going to do?" I asked, collapsing onto a bench in the middle of the city square. The sun was starting to go down, but the benches still held the heat. It seeped through my linen frock, igniting my magic.

Not now. I whispered to myself, carefully pulling my hands to my center, focusing the energy elsewhere.

"Perhaps we should head back to my mother's place," Freya suggested.

"We have to continue looking," I said, standing to look around. Surely, we were missing something. Yet, no matter how much I jogged my memory, I couldn't figure out where my father could possibly have gone. "Actually, why don't the two of you return to the palace? We need eyes and ears on the inside. It's getting late, and soon, we won't be able to see much without looking suspicious."

"What of you, Princess?" Freya said, looking to me with sadness and concern.

"I'm going to head back to the bell tower. Who knows, he might just turn up there."

Jamal took hold of my hand. "I can't let you wander the streets alone. You are the princess."

"I was the princess," I said sadly. "I don't even know if anyone even recognizes me anymore. I could be anyone."

"People still know you. I saw the stares as we walked through the city. They were wondering what the princess was doing wandering around."

"Not everyone. There used to be a time when I couldn't set foot outside the palace gates without the media showing up and hordes of people trying to catch a glimpse of me. You saw what it was like the other day. Today we've walked around freely."

"That may be, but you haven't completely been forgotten. Not that your title makes any difference. I wouldn't want to leave a young lady wandering around the streets of Kisbu no matter who she was."

I bit my lip, knowing I was going to let him into my biggest secret. One I'd never told anyone. "I come out here at night a lot. I've been sneaking out of the palace for a couple of years now. I always go alone, and I never find trouble."

Jamal's eyes widened, and then his mouth pulled up at the corners. "I don't doubt it. I bet you know how to handle yourself even if you do find trouble, don't you?"

"I do."

"I wondered why your clothes were always dirty in the mornings," Freya exclaimed. "I should have guessed."

I gave her a smile.

Jamal pulled on my hand.

"Wait. What are you doing? I said I was going back to the bell tower."

"I believe that you know these streets and you believe that you will be ok, but I would never forgive myself if you got hurt. I cannot leave you. We'll go back to the palace, speak to the guards, and get them to come and look for your father. He'll be fine for a few more hours."

I pulled my hand from his. "And how do you expect them to do that? They don't remember what he looks like. And how would we explain it to them? We can't. I'm going to look for my father, and as your princess, I demand you let me go."

I narrowed my eyes at him, willing him to dare to try to stop me, but he didn't.

He turned and began to walk away without saying another word. Freya looked at me nervously, stuck in the middle. I waved my hand to tell her to leave. Unlike Jamal, she didn't fight my decision. Soon I was alone.

It felt freeing.

I ran through the streets feeling more normal than I had in days. This was normal to me. The dark streets were now devoid of life. It was almost like coming home. I knew then why my father was so eager to come back. No pressures of royalty, no parties, or government issues. Just me and the streets. Aladdin's daughter.

I was so caught up in my own thoughts that I missed the broken paving slab and tripped, falling onto my hands. As I pulled myself up, I noticed blood dripping from a scrape.

"You should get that cleaned up." A familiar voice said from behind me.

"D..." I stopped myself. "Aladdin, sir," I said, trying desperately not to cry. "Yes, I should. Except, I'm not too familiar with where I can go?"

My magic pulsed at my innards, desperately trying to surface. It churned continuously, causing me to feel heat where there was none.

"What is it?" he asked as I furtively looked around at the change of atmosphere

"I'm not sure... Danger, I think. We need to move."

"Move?"

"Yes. Now!" I demanded as I looked around, carefully surveying the area, yet again. There was something sinister in the air. I could feel it. My magic was on alert. "Where can we go that is safe?"

He looked back as he took the lead. "The palace. There are several places we can hide."

"The palace?" I carefully said, trying not to sound too excited. "Why the palace?"

"It's the last place people look."

I wanted to laugh. He was taking me home, and he didn't even know it. My father's memories were still in there somewhere.

"Very well. Hurry."

We moved hastily along the darker streets. Whatever was in pursuit of us seemed to have fallen behind, and I wondered if it had been nothing but my imagination.

We reached the back of the palace wall. "Where now?" I asked, curious about where he would take me. I knew the back way in through the palace walls. I used it most nights, but I was keen to see if he knew it. If he remembered it. Most of the citizens of Kisbu didn't know of the small entryway. It was one of three ways into the palace grounds. The imposing golden gates at the front and the less ostentatious staff entrance were the other two. He beckoned me forward, keeping the wall to his right. He was taking me away from the back entrance, which meant he was planning on going in through the front entrance. Something about that made me happy. If he planned to go in past the guards, it meant he knew that he could. It meant he remembered who he was. Except he stopped long before we cornered the palace.

He lifted his hand at some of the bougainvillea that crept up the wall and pushed it aside, exposing a small crack in the wall, just big enough for a man to squeeze through. I gasped as he ducked through. Did the guards know about this lapse in security? I doubted it. But my father obviously knew, and he'd never told anyone to guard it, and not once in his reign had he had it filled in. I followed him into the palace grounds and to a covered hole that I knew led to the cellar. Aladdin pulled the cover off and jumped down.

I followed him in and watched as he found a pile of dirty blankets.

"We can hide here," he whispered. "No one ever comes down here."

He settled on the blankets and closed his eyes.

I waited for him to fall asleep then crept upstairs to the main part of the palace. Ironically, he was probably safer here than anywhere else. He'd found home even if he didn't know it.

"Gaia! What happened to you?" Jamal blurted out as I stepped into the entrance hall. His eyes fell to the graze on my arm and hand. It was clear that he'd been waiting for me to come back. I noticed one of the palace guards eyeing us with curiosity from his position at the main door. Taking Jamal's arm, I pulled him away from the guard and into a corridor.

"I..." I stopped myself, choosing to leave my father out of it. "I couldn't get back into the bell tower. I fell," I said, lifting my hand. "I cut myself. I had to find my way back into the palace to get cleaned up. The last thing I need is a mean infection on my hand."

"Would you like me to help?"

I looked at Jamal, wishing I wanted him near me, but I didn't. I wanted to be alone.

"I'm sorry," I said, shaking my head. "I need to go check on Asher for now."

"As you wish," Jamal said, moving back so I could pass him. As I walked up the stairs to my room, I thought about going to see Genie. I missed him. I didn't even know if he remembered me, or how I'd deal with it if he didn't. Deciding that I couldn't take him looking at me blankly after everything we'd been through together, I did what I told Jamal I was going to do and headed back to my room.

"Asher!" I shouted, rushing out onto the terrace. "Oh, buddy."

I carefully took him into my arms. His frail, decrepit body seemed like it would fall apart if I handled him too tightly.

He raised a watery eye to me and hung his limp head on my shoulder.

My tears finally breached, flowing down my face, some falling onto my balding dying bird.

"I'm sorry," I whispered to him as I brought him inside. I shouldn't have left him alone for so long. He was close to death, and with that thought, I let my tears finally flow freely.

23RD JUNE

A loud squawk woke me up in the early hours. I'd crept to bed the night before without speaking to anyone and fallen into bed. I'd expected not to be able to sleep, but due to the hours of pounding the streets in the summer heat the day before, exhaustion had taken over, and I'd slept like a baby. Rubbing my eyes, I glanced over to the fig tree on the terrace. My heart lurched when I couldn't see Asher's outline in the dim morning light.

"No!" I hissed as I stumbled out of bed. Not Asher, not now. I rushed to the tree where Asher liked to sleep, but all that was left of him was a pile of black ash at the base of the tree. At some point in the night, he'd died, giving up his life in a puff of smoke.

"Asher," I screamed, frantically searching through

the ash, sending small particles of black into the air. My finger caught on something in the ash, and at the moment of contact, something strange happened to my body. Flames erupted all around me, surrounding me in a tornado of heat. I could barely see through the swirling mass of red and yellow flames that licked my body. Despite being swallowed by flames, I felt no pain, only energy that flowed through my veins. My skin began to peel away from my flesh, but again, I felt no pain. I also felt no fear. Whatever was happening to me was coming from within. I brought my hands up to see what I'd touched and found a beautiful baby phoenix. It stretched its wings out wide and let out another squawk. My entire body fell away until there was only flame. I was made entirely of flames and fire. A true daughter of the sun.

I sucked in a breath, and the flames stopped as suddenly as they had started. Looking down at my arms, the skin was still there, but now with a healthy glow to it. I felt refreshed. I felt reborn.

"Asher?" I said breathlessly to the tiny bird. It nodded cheerfully.

I took him over to the mirror and looked at my reflection. I was still me, but somehow better. My skin was flush with the aftereffects of the heat. My hair shone with a luster it had never had before and my eyes. The rings around the irises were lit up like stars on a clear night.

I was new. I also felt new on the inside, more powerful, somehow healthier.

"Was I reborn with you, Asher?" I asked the bird, who'd hopped up onto my shoulder. Far from being bald and ugly like most newborn birds, he was stunningly beautiful. We both were.

Asher nodded his head then gave me an affectionate nip of my ear. If I was worried that the new phoenix wouldn't really be Asher, I could feel better now. I was still me. I had all my memories, and apart from a shine that made me look like I'd spent hours in a beauty salon, I was still the same old Gaia.

I popped him back on the fig tree and dressed quickly, wanting to see if my father was still in the palace. If he was, I was going to bring him up to my mother. If she saw him, she'd know who he was immediately. She had to. He was the love of her life.

Taking a route through the palace that was as far away from Genie's room as possible, I moved stealthily, not wanting to be seen. Unfortunately, luck was not on my side. I was collared by a guard long before I got to the cellar door.

"Her Majesty has been looking for you. She's in the dining room."

"You know who I am?" I asked the guard pointlessly. Obviously, he did, or he wouldn't be telling me my mother was looking for me.

He tipped his head to the side. "Ma'am?"

I ignored him and went straight to the dining room. My mother remembered me. I'd been worried she wouldn't.

"Daughter, where have you been?" My mother asked with quizzical eyes as she took a sip of juice from the gold-trimmed stemware.

"Asher. He's transitioning. He had me worried, so I didn't want to leave him alone."

Well, it was kind of true.

"You are looking beautiful today. What's your secret?"

"A good night's sleep," I lied.

"It's done you a world of good."

I fidgeted in my chair, not enjoying the small talk. There had been a time not so long ago when I could talk to her about anything, but now, there were so many secrets I was keeping. My magic, my father, hiding in the cellar. My worry that Genie would forget who I was.

I stood up to leave.

"Where are you going?" she asked, narrowing her eyes at me. "I thought we'd have breakfast together."

"I thought I'd go out for a bit."

"Out?"

I braced myself for her to tell me I couldn't, but she didn't. "Take some guards with you. The streets of Kisbu are not as safe as they once were."

"You remember that?" I asked, hope rising in my chest. "You remember that things were pretty safe in Kisbu until this year?"

She studied me curiously. "Of course, I remember. One cannot be too careful these days."

"No, they can't," I agreed, heading out of the room. She was not herself at all. I wanted to ask her why she had canceled trade, but I had a feeling she didn't know herself.

Down in the cellar, my fears came to fruition. My father was gone.

I sat on the blankets feeling bereft. I'd lost my father, but he was the one who'd lost everyone else. No one remembered him.

There was one person who would know the answers, even if he didn't like talking about it. In all the time I'd known Genie, he'd shunned away from talk of magic, and I'd let him. Before now, I'd had no more than a passing interest in it myself.

I raced up to his rooms and knocked on his door for

the very first time. Usually, I just walked in, but now I didn't even know if he knew who I was.

Butterflies raced in my stomach as I waited for the door to open.

"Gaia," he said when he opened the door. "I've been hoping for a while that you'd come to see me. I wanted to come to you, but in my position..."

"What position is that?" I asked, waltzing past him and taking my familiar place on the chaise. The pattern on it had worn away long ago, thanks to the hours I'd spent there reading books and discussing life with Genie.

Genie didn't answer my question, and I wasn't sure that he could. Now that my father no longer existed to him, he had no reason to put up a barrier between us.

"You look different."

"Asher was reborn today," I said, not particularly wanting to talk about Asher. I cast a quick glance at the bookshelves beside me, wishing he wasn't so afraid of magic. The answer to all this could be on his shelves if he wasn't so against it.

"You were reborn with him? I've heard such things happen."

"I didn't come here to talk about my bird," I said, ignoring the feeling in the pit of my stomach. I stood and walked over to where he'd perched himself on the edge of his desk. I was at his exact eye level.

"Why did you come here?" he asked quietly. I saw something in his eyes, something I'd not seen before. Longing. His breathing deepened as I reached out and touched his cheek. Maybe I had seen the look in his eyes before and not believed it, or maybe I knew more after my rebirth. His lips parted slightly, and I could feel the beat of his heart quicken. Something had changed me that morning. It wasn't Genie that was different; it was I.

"Do you want me?" I whispered.

The familiar expression came over him as though he was reaching into his depths. I could almost see the cogs whirring in his mind, but what I was asking him was beyond reasoning. He either wanted me, or he didn't.

In the back of my mind, I knew I should be out looking for my father, for a cure or for a solution, but I knew in my heart that if only Genie truly wanted me, then the rest would fall into place. He'd always been my champion in the past. Now I wanted him to be more.

My own breathing quickened, matching his. His stare penetrated my eyes as though he was searching my soul for something.

"I've wanted you for a long time," I said to him when he didn't speak. I moved my fingers slowly down his cheek, feeling his warm skin beneath my own. He reached up and clasped my wrist.

"Stop!"

One word, but it sent my whole world crashing down around me. I'd lost my father, my mother wasn't herself, and now I was losing Genie too.

"I can't," he said, slipping out between me and the desk.

"Why can't you?"

"I just can't. You are young. I am old."

"I'm eighteen. I'm old enough."

He ran his fingers over his head, causing some of his hair to come loose from the gold tie holding it in place.

"It's not just that. You are forbidden to me."

I moved forward toward him, and he held out his hands to stop me. "Please stop." He turned from me and placed his hands against the wall, lowering his head.

"I'm forbidden? Why? I'm of legal age. I want you. There is nothing forbidden about this."

He turned, and this time I saw something else in his eyes. Not quite rage, not quite confusion, but a mix of the two.

"You come in here, looking as beautiful as you do, which is bad enough, but then you blow me away. Constantly. You always have, with the power of your mind. With your questioning. With the way you speak. Do you have any idea how hard it is to watch you leave after we've talked for hours? Do you not think I want you to stay? Do you think I've not thought what it would be like to have you in my bed?"

My heart pounded at his words. I'd not imagined it. He did want me, so what was the problem?

"I'm here. You can have me. All of me. My body, my mind. It's all yours. It's always been yours."

"But I can't have it!" he said, his voice rising an octave.

"Why not?" I bellowed back at him.

"Because you are Aladdin's daughter," he screamed. "Because you are my best friend's daughter. I cannot do that to him."

"You remember? You remember my father?"

"I..." He ran his fingers through his hair again, and this time, the gold tie fell to the floor, and his long black hair came loose around his shoulders.

"I think you should leave," he said, throwing the door open. Hot tears flooded my eyes and spilled out down my cheeks.

"I can't leave now. Who is my father, Genie?"

A crazed look came over his face. "I don't know," he screamed. "I don't know who your father is." He pushed me out of the door and slammed it shut behind me. I heard the key turn in the lock for the first time ever.

"You ok?"

I turned to see Jamal running down the corridor to me. "I heard what Genie said. It was foolish to even try. You know he doesn't remember."

"He did remember. For a second."

I fell into his arms and sobbed onto his shoulder. If he wanted to think I was crying because Genie didn't remember my father, I wasn't going to dispel him of the notion.

Genie had hinted that nothing could happen between him and me before, but he'd never shouted at me. He'd never before told me he wanted me. Somehow, it made it all the worse. If he'd just told me he didn't think of me that way, it would have broken my heart, but the crushing pain settling in my chest eclipsed mere heartbreak. I felt like all of me was broken.

"Do you want to go and look for your father again? I'm guessing you didn't catch up with him last night."

I got my sobbing under control and nodded my head. Part of me wanted to head back to my room and hide under the blankets, but what good would that do? I needed to be proactive.

"Come on, let's go."

I took his hand and let him lead me out of the palace. Freya came along with us as before, but whereas she had once been my servant, she had become more of a friend. She was one of only two people I was wading through the muck of this curse with.

We combed the streets in much the same way we had done the day before, but this time, I had no heart left in it. My father didn't want to be found, and if I did find him, what was I going to do with him? He didn't even know who I was. If he was truly back to being a street rat, he would stay out of everyone's way, and that meant mine. I was under no illusions that my nightly prowls around the streets meant I knew Kisbu better than he did. He'd survived a long time on the streets before. There was no reason to think he wouldn't again.

"We should stop," I said, feeling the weight of defeat on my shoulders.

"We can't give up," Freya protested.

"I don't mean give up entirely. I meant give up looking for my father and start looking for a solution instead. There is a reason that this is happening."

I gestured to the streets around us. Rubbish was piled up along the edges of the street, and no one was bothering to pick it up. In the distance, a couple of men fought over what looked to be a sandwich.

A few weeks ago, they would have simply gone to the palace, and my parents would have fed them. Now, no one dared go close. We'd shut our gates. I'd not asked my mother outright if she was still planning to do this month's feast for the hungry, but it didn't look likely. My mother had gone back to the way things were run before my father became sultan. It wasn't just the memory of him that had gone, but all the good that he had brought to Badalah. It, too, was being erased.

"Where would we even start looking for a solution?" Freya asked.

"Your mother said that my grandfather's vizier hypnotized people. He put them in trances. Don't the people all look like they are in a trance to you?"

She looked around the street. People were going about their daily business as they always did, but they did it with blank looks on their faces.

"They do look hypnotized," Freya agreed. "But it's

impossible to hypnotize a whole kingdom. No one is that powerful."

"Not even The Vizier?"

"Not even The Vizier," Freya said, "but it doesn't matter. He is long gone."

I shook my head. "I don't think so. I think he's back, and what's more, I think he's more powerful than he ever was before."

HEIRESS OF SHADOWS

24TH JUNE

The whole kingdom had forgotten Aladdin, or so it seemed.

My whole world had descended into chaos, and the shifting of magic within me swirled, churning in my stomach, distracting me from everything. I clicked my fingers and watched as they lit up, sending shadows dancing around my bedroom's walls. Asher squawked appreciatively, then flew across the room and landed on my fingers, extinguishing the flames.

"You like that, don't you?" I said, patting him on the head. At least, something was going well. Since Asher's rebirth, he was now flying again, something I'd not seen him do in the days leading up to his disintegration into ash. I lifted my hand, and he took off, his brand new feathers giving him lift as he flew around my room before settling back on his perch. I'd noticed he was attracted to the heat and light of the flames I produced, so I'd been producing them more frequently. It also helped dispel some of the energy the magic produced, which meant I was less likely to spontaneously combust in front of people.

After getting dressed, I headed downstairs. I found Jamal eating breakfast with my mother. I was about to join them when I saw my mother lean forward and hand Jamal a piece of toast, except she didn't put it on his plate, but fed it to him. I'd seen her do that before. Both she and my father fed each other from their own plates. I'd never seen her do it with anyone else. Fire churned in me, but I took a couple of deep breaths to quell it. It wasn't her fault. She wasn't herself anymore. At least, Jamal looked uncomfortable with her flirting with him because that's exactly what she was doing. His cheeks were a cherry red, and he didn't know where to put his eyes.

"Ah, Gaia!" he said, standing to greet me as I made my presence known. "Please, join us....please!" He hissed the last word quietly and swiped a side-eye at my mother.

My mother didn't speak as I sat at the table, but the way she looked at me caused me to shudder. She looked at me the way any woman would do if I was about to steal her man. But Jamal didn't belong to my mother any more than he belonged to me. I wondered if she even knew who I was. I watched as she scooped sugar into her tea blankly. She usually took it without.

"It's a nice day," I said airily, grabbing some meat. Jamal raised his eyebrows, but I only shrugged in response. What else was I supposed to say? Ask my mother if she knew who I was? Ask when her wedding to Jamal would be? The weather seemed like the safest option.

"Hmm," my mother murmured noncommittally.

"I think we should go for a walk," Jamal said, tugging at my hand and nodding at my mother. She didn't even look up from her tea.

I grabbed a piece of bread to put with the meat I'd already taken and made a quick sandwich before following Jamal out into the corridor.

When he was certain we were out of earshot of both my mother and the guards, he spoke. "Your mother asked me to come to her rooms after breakfast, and I don't think she had a discussion of the weather in mind if you know what I mean."

I almost spit my sandwich out as I took in his words. A nervous giggle erupted from my throat. The idea of my mother, seducing Jamal was preposterous.

"You think it's funny? She was running her leg up and down mine before you walked in."

"I'm sorry. I'm only laughing because it's so unreal. I'm nervous and scared, and my body seems to be betraying me. Before I walked in, I almost ignited. I don't seem to have control over anything anymore."

"I promise, I would never..."

"I don't believe for a second you would take advantage. I'm not mad at you. I'm upset and confused. My mother shouldn't be by herself." I made to head back to the dining room, but Jamal stopped me.

"I don't think you should go back in there. Get your court physician to see her if you must, but I think it would be better for both of you if you had a little time apart."

"She's my mother, Jamal." I tapped my toe on the

floor, a nervous habit I seemed to have just picked up. It was better than setting myself on fire, I supposed.

"I know she is, but I'm not sure she knows that anymore. I just don't want you getting hurt. Why don't we find Freya and go out and do another search for your father? Your mother is in no danger here in the palace."

"My father doesn't want to be found," I said, but then, I realized I wasn't ready for the time when my own mother didn't recognize me. If I could put it off just one more day... "Ok, come on, let's go out."

Freya jumped at the chance to join us, although she didn't think we had much chance of finding my father any more than I did.

We walked through the town easily. Even with no guards by our sides, no one stopped us, nor paid us any attention. It was a marked difference from a week or so ago when people had come out of their houses to gawk at us. I wasn't looking out for my father. I knew he would be alright wherever he was, but I wanted to see a spark of recognition in my subjects. I'd been on the front cover of the Badalah Beacon so many times that everyone should know my face, but even as I caught the eyes of many, none gave me a second glance. It was almost as if I were invisible. I was a complete nobody in my own town. It was both liberating and terrifying in equal measure. I was becoming as forgotten as my father.

We'd not gone very far when I heard someone shouting. I turned to see a couple of older teenage girls staring at me. After feeling invisible, I should have been happy that someone recognized me, but the look in their eyes told me that they weren't too happy to see their princess strolling through the streets.

"There's that spoiled-rotten brat!"

The first one hollered from across the street.

"She and the Sultana, and all of the aristocrats, for that matter, simply want to see us all in their servitude forever," the other said loudly enough that I could hear them all the way across the dusty street.

My body tightened at the abuse being hurled at me, and my breathing came faster.

The girls laughed. "She's not even of true royal blood. There's no way she'll ascend to Sultana."

A group of onlookers joined in the laughter.

"We should afford her the same as she and her palace afford us!"

A boy of about sixteen in the group that had been laughing picked up a stone from the street and hurled it in my direction. It hit me just above the stomach. I felt a sharp painful sensation, and I found myself paralyzed in fear.

Soon, more stones followed as the group began to pelt me with whatever they had at hand. I'd wanted to be recognized, but not like this. This was worse than the feeling of invisibility. They knew me, but they didn't know me. They knew I was the princess, but they had forgotten how much I'd fought for their rights for years. I was many things, but a spoiled rotten brat was not one of them.

Jamal jumped in front of me, shielding me from the onslaught, while Freya sprang into action. Inside, I felt the fire of magic begin to kindle. I didn't know how to control it yet. If they carried on, I was going to go up in flames. I took a few deep breaths to steady myself as Freya strode toward the congregated group.

"Enough!" she hollered with her hands upright towards the perpetrators. "What is it that you think to achieve by stoning the Princess? Huh? Are you all asking for a death sentence? A quick execution?"

The sound of rocks dropping to the ground alerted me that many from all directions had intended harm to my person. The nervous energy continued to burn within me.

"Go, you cowards!" Jamal added, standing tall, still protecting me.

I felt so small. Insignificant. Terrified of what I might do if they didn't leave me alone. And for the first time, I truly feared the people of Badalah.

"And who are you to tell us what to do? Another handler of the Sultana?" someone said in a menacing voice.

"You really don't want to know," Jamal said with a cold, unrecognizable edge in his words.

Freya once again stepped in. "Leave. The Princess's private guards have already alerted the palace."

It was a lie, and everyone knew it. We had no guard with us.

Someone laughed. "Look at that one trying to yank our chain."

Their eyes widened as my skin began to smolder. I could actually see smoke rising from the parts of me that were bare.

Jamal grabbed my hand and began to pull me in the opposite direction. Freya ran alongside us as we sprinted back to the palace, back to safety.

"You need to learn to control that," Jamal said, once we were away from the people.

"I know, but I'm so angry!" I made sure no one was looking, then let flames dance on my fingers to diffuse the anger within me. When it was slightly more manageable, I headed back to the palace with Jamal and Freya.

Enraged with anger and defeat, I stormed the palace doors, hollering for my mother.

"What are you doing?" whispered Jamal.

"My mother needs to understand what's happening. Her illness, or whatever it is, has caused her to make some really bad decisions these past few days. She needs to see the consequences of those decisions. Please leave me to speak to her."

Jamal looked like he didn't want to go anywhere, but Freya took his hand and led him away. I was surprised to see that he acquiesced so easily to her.

"What is this behavior?" My mother asked, rounding a corner with two advisors and her lady's maid.

"Mother. I must speak to you at once." I said without hesitation. "In private," I added, eyeing the advisors.

Both men bowed to leave. She waited, then whispered something to her lady's maid, who quickly disappeared as well.

"Now, please explain yourself!"

I took a deep breath, finally an opportunity to get it off my chest.

"Something is terribly the matter. There seems to be a shroud of forgetfulness covering the kingdom, and no one else is picking up on it. Even you, Mother, you don't even realize what you've forgotten. Your memory is coming and going."

She found an ornate backless bench near one of the floor-to-ceiling-windows that overlooked the gardens, and took it, patting the empty space next to her.

"Gaia, my sweet girl, what are you talking about?"

I took a seat next to her, desperately wanting to curl up in her arms the way I used to do as a child. She knew who I was again, and unlike this morning at breakfast, she seemed back to her normal self. A part of me wanted to forget this whole thing was happening.

"I went into town this morning, and people threw stones at me."

"You went without guards?" she asked, bringing me into a hug. "What were you thinking?"

"Yes, I deliberately disobeyed you. I'm sorry, Mother. Jamal and Freya were with me. Please, allow me to show you exactly what I'm talking about."

"I'm aware of the problems in town. It seems there is some restlessness happening just outside the walls of Kibsu also. Some of our outlying villages have taken up arms and are trying to breach the walls with farm tools and what have you. I was just speaking to my advisors about it. They tell me that the country folk are quite insane over the whole thing. Most of them don't even know what they used to trade in the first place. I've had to order the gates to the city closed until all this madness is over."

She held her hand to her head and sighed. "It's just one thing after another."

I'd thought this was confined to Kisbu, but it looked like it extended past the reach of the capital city. My heart fell with the monumental task we faced. If it wasn't bad enough that everyone was hypnotized, they were also mad because of my mother's poor decisions. "That's what I'm trying to tell you. The people are losing their memories."

My mother stared blankly at me.

"What are their demands?" I said with a sigh.

"They are demanding more food, it would seem. Honestly, I really don't understand. Most of the people from outside of the walls either have their own lands to farm or work for wealthy families. That they suddenly claim to be going hungry is outrageous."

My mother had ceased trade to all kingdoms and increased taxes a few days ago. It was no wonder they were angry. Added to the fact that most of them probably didn't know what they were doing or should be doing, it was a disaster of epic proportions.

I fidgeted with my headscarf, wondering when the magic had started to grow outside of the city. Maybe I was wrong, and the magic was radiating inwards. I'd not heard anything until now about trouble outside the city, but it was possible that this had been going on in Badalah longer than I thought. I already knew it was happening in other kingdoms outside of Badalah.

"Mother, do you believe in magic?"

She smiled and looked away. "Perhaps I did once upon a time. But I've been so busy ruling a kingdom that I cannot allow myself such musings."

"What of Genie?"

Her brows furrowed. "Genie?" She paused, "Like the genie of the lamp?"

I nodded.

She smoothed out her skirt, trying to hold back a laugh, from what I could see.

"Oh, dear Gaia. Genies are the things of fairytales. They are not real. My goodness, young lady. Who's been filling your head with such nonsense?"

I pulled back from her embrace. Wishing she was back to normal didn't make it so. I could shout at her all I liked, but she was in no fit state to make any changes to the kingdom. A few weeks ago, she was the strongest, most compassionate woman I knew. Everything I was, I owed to her, but now she was a shell of her former self. I no longer recognized her.

"I'm sorry, Mother. If you need help with anything,

let me know." She kissed my forehead as she had done countless times before, but when she pulled back, the blank stare was back on her face. Before she asked me who I was, I stood and wandered to the only place in the palace, I felt truly safe anymore, my bedroom.

Asher greeted me with a squawk as he always did when I entered.

"At least, you remember me," I whispered, choking back the tears. The last few moments had made me realize just how much I missed my mother. The real her, not this weird version of her that seemed to flitter in and out of comprehension. I realized with a thump in my chest that this weirdness was probably the cause of her wanting to find me a husband. A few weeks ago, they'd shown no interest in having me married off. My mother had playfully enquired if I had my eye on anyone a couple of times, but we'd both giggled over the ridiculous amount of marriage proposals I received week after week.

It was little consolation. My mother, as I knew her, was gone. Even though I realized that all of her bizarre policy changes and her sudden interest in marrying me off were probably a result of the spell she was under, I didn't know how to bring her back.

A knock at the door made me jump. As safe as I thought my bedroom to be, the truth was, it didn't have a lock on it. Not that I thought my physical safety was in jeopardy, but what with everything else going on, I wasn't too sure how long that would last. My mental wellbeing was already shot, thanks to being forgotten by almost everyone.

The only people that truly remembered me within the palace walls were Freya and Jamal. As Freya tended to walk in without waiting for me to answer, I expected

Jamal to be on the other side of the door. When I saw Genie standing there, so many emotions hit me at once. The last time I'd seen him, he'd told me he thought about me being in his bed. I' tried to forget it, but it was hard when I thought about him constantly.

"Genie...I..."

"May I come in?" he asked, glancing quickly down the corridor as though he didn't want to be seen coming into my room. I opened the door and let him in, quickly shutting the door behind me.

If I'd hoped he was here to kiss me, to tell me he loved me and wanted me, I was sorely disappointed. He pushed me onto my bed, alright, but he sat down next to me with a respectable distance between us. I waited for him to speak.

"I've been thinking about what you said to me the other day," he began, his words measured.

This didn't look like it was about to be a declaration of love, but at least, he was acknowledging it.

"You said you wanted me in your bed..."I said my voice barely above a whisper. Genie cocked his head to one side, his eyebrows knotted in the middle.

He didn't remember. It was plain as the nose on his face. I felt my heart pounding and a flush rise to my face.

"I'm talking about your magic, Gaia, what are you talking about?"

I swallowed back the tears that were threatening. He'd forgotten our conversation. I'd thought of barely anything other than what he'd said, but his words were now lost in the ether to him.

"My magic?" I replied with a sigh.

"I know I've not wanted to talk about it. I've made it no secret what I think of magic, but the truth is that you have it."

"I don't want it. This whole problem has to do with magic and seeing as I didn't have any a couple of weeks ago, I figure it's connected somehow, I just don't know how."

Genie shifted on the bed, looking as uncomfortable as I felt about the situation. "Nor do I. The connection isn't the issue. What is the issue is how you wield your magic and what you do with it."

I snapped my fingers and lit the tips of my fingers without even thinking about it. Genie flinched as I waved the small flames in front of me.

He composed himself quickly. "You have this gift for a reason."

I looked at him. How much did he remember? He knew who I was, and he remembered our talk when I'd cried in his arms.

"Do you know who my mother is?" I asked him, blowing the light out with a quick puff of breath. I watched his reaction. It was like he was searching his mind for something.

"The Sultana Jawahir," he said eventually. It took too long for him to answer. Normally he could remember obscure facts about almost anything with barely a thought.

"And my father?"

"That I do not know. You know you were adopted. Your father's name was never given."

That had come easily to him. He didn't even think about my father, just jumped to the conclusion that I was talking about my birth father.

"Why do you think I need to learn how to wield my magic?" I asked, changing the subject.

"Is that not obvious?" he said. It was obvious to me.

The whole kingdom was going insane, but I needed to know what it meant to Genie.

"Tell me."

"People are revolting against us," he explained. I guess he'd either been talking to my mother and she'd forgotten, or he'd found out from some other source. "We need to be ready to fight. I remember when I was magic. I know how it feels. I can teach you."

"Fight our own people?" I asked, fear welling up inside me. He'd never talked like this before. He never hurt anyone.

"Yes. The palace guards might not be enough."

I closed my eyes. If I wasn't careful, we were going to end up in a civil war. Just as I'd lost my mother, I was losing Genie. It wasn't just their memories that were taken from them, but the very essence of who they were. I'd been so angry at the people who'd thrown stones at me, but maybe they weren't the people they used to be either. It made my head and my heart hurt just thinking about it.

"Thank you, Genie," I said, moving close to him. "I'll think on what you said. We do need to be prepared."

I moved closer still until my mouth was next to his ear. "Never forget that I love you." I whispered it so softly, I wasn't sure if he heard me. He stood up and left my room, leaving me more bereft than I'd felt before.

Later, I sought out Jamal. I'd left both him and Freya in a hurry when I'd marched back into the palace. I found him in the gardens, sitting on a bench deep in thought.

"Not disturbing you, am I?"

Jamal looked up and shook his head, "Not at all. I'm glad you are here. I have something to tell you. Sultana Jawahir has sought my counsel to assist her with the impending revolt just outside the city walls."

My stomach churned, "She told me about it earlier. Do you know how bad it is?"

Jamal stood up. "It's not good news. She's managed to set up a meeting with them as soon as the guards can assure her safety."

"You don't think she's safe?"

Jamal took my hand in his. "I don't think any of us are safe in the palace. You saw what happened to you out in the town this morning. People are angry; they are hurt and hungry."

"They don't know what they are doing," I said. "Some people remember; some don't. Most are making up their own memories based on the last week."

"I don't know what to tell you, Gaia. None of this makes sense, but I do know that we need to be cautious."

"Genie told me the same thing in my room."

Jamal suddenly looked perturbed. "Genie was in your room? Are you alright?"

My heart was shattered into millions of pieces, but I could hardly tell Jamal that.

"I'm fine. Genie would never hurt me."

Jamal didn't look convinced.

"He wouldn't!" I reiterated. "He wanted me to learn to wield my magic in case we are attacked."

Jamal sat back down beside me, a little closer than he'd been sitting before. "I think he might be right. I hate to say it, but if your magic is the only thing that can keep you safe, you should learn how to use it."

I closed my eyes. When had life gotten so complicated? I felt Jamal take my hand again. I pulled back and stood up, opening my eyes. "You are right. I should go to him."

Jamal suddenly seemed smaller on the bench.

"Hey, I wondered where you two were."

I turned and smiled at Freya, grateful at her opportune timing.

"I was just going to find Genie." I turned to Jamal. "Why don't you get Freya up to speed with what my mother intends to do, and I'll meet you both for dinner later."

I thought I saw Jamal's eyes light up when I mentioned dinner, but they quickly faded again as I said goodbye and walked away.

~

"I want you to teach me magic," I said, as Genie opened his door.

He nodded briefly, then took my hand. At first, I thought he was going to pull me into his room, but instead, he began a quick march down the corridor.

"Not here," he hissed, picking up the pace. I ran alongside him, trying to keep up, aware that we were holding hands...or at least, he was holding mine. I was just along for the ride, it seemed.

We ended up in the palace cellars, not too far from where my father had slept a few nights ago.

He stopped, pulling me in front of him. In the dim light cast by the small dirty windows that never got cleaned as the maids never came down here, I wanted nothing more than to kiss him. No one knew we were down here. No one would see us. I almost leaned forward, but Genie caught my wrists.

"Show me what you can do," he demanded.

I held my hands in front of him and set every finger alight, a dancing flame atop every one of them.

"I think there is more," he said, letting go of my wrists.

I closed my eyes and focused on the pain of him not wanting me, or at least, forgetting he wanted me. I pulled in the pain of my mother forgetting my father, and of my father forgetting me until a ball of burning hot rage swirled in my belly. I let it go, radiating the heat outward.

White-hot flames danced in front of my eyes as my body was engulfed in fire. When it faded less than a minute later, I was exhausted. My breath came quickly as though I'd just run the entire length of the palace.

"Did that hurt you?" Genie said, stepping forward and taking hold of my arm. He ran his hand up it, pulling my sleeve up to examine my skin. The heat hadn't caused me pain, but his touch did. Emotional pain that ate my very soul. I prayed he wouldn't stop.

I shook my head slowly, desperate for his hand to continue its journey upwards. He let me go, then brought out a match.

"I wonder?"

He struck it against the box then held the small flame to my hand. I pulled my hand back sharply as the sting of the flame touched my hand.

Ow!

"I am sorry," he said, blowing the match out and throwing it to the floor. He picked up my hand once more and kissed the area that had burned. If only he knew how much more that affected me than the match had.

"Fire hurts you, but not your own. Create a flame again."

I held my hand out and let a small flame dance in my palm. Genie reached out to it, but before he touched it, he pulled back.

"I feel the heat from you."

I could feel the heat too, but it had nothing to do with the flame in my hand.

My breathing came fast and hard as the flame died out.

"I'm going to attack you," Genie said after a while. "I want you to fight back."

My mouth fell open as I took in what he was asking me to do.

"You want us to fight? Physically fight?"

"I won't hurt you, Gaia."

His words were sincere. My heart pounded at them. Why couldn't he remember wanting me as much as I wanted him?

"I have something to tell you," he said. "Something I've been keeping to myself. I've not told a soul until now."

"What is it?" I asked my voice barely more than a whisper.

His face contorted into something resembling pain. Whatever he was about to tell me was not something that was making him happy. "My magic has been coming back. I didn't want it, and I didn't ask for it, but in the past few days, I've noticed the sensations returning."

"This is a good thing!" I said, suddenly feeling a lot more optimistic. "You were the most powerful being in Badalah at one point. You can use your power to stop this."

He shook his head. "I don't want that kind of power again. I was a slave to it, Gaia, just as you will be if people find out about your gift. And I use the term gift lightly. Don't think that being magic makes things easier. It doesn't. It makes everything much more difficult. Before your father saved me from the lamp, I was at the mercy of other people's whims. I had no control over what they asked for and had to provide it for them, no matter how materialistic and shallow their requests. I do not want this, but there it is. I can fight your magic with mine. I will not do anything that will really hurt."

It was a lot of information to get in a short period of time, but one thing did stick out to me.

He'd remembered my father.

"You remember Aladdin again!" I said.

The blank look fell over his features. "Who?"

"Never mind," I said, feeling despondent. "Let's get this over with. Attack me, and I'll fight back."

At least, I had enough misery to convert into magical energy if things got a little overheated.

Before I'd managed to ready myself, a blast of cold air struck me, sending me skidding backward with the force of it. It had come from Genie. He was fighting fire with air! Didn't he know how dangerous that was? He left me no time to think about it because his arms were extended to attack again.

I felt my magic ignite in my core as I threw my hands in the air to respond to Genie's attack.

A quick blast of fire spat from my palm toward the ceiling.

"Focus!" Genie hollered.

Anger rose in me. He didn't have to yell.

Again, I shot in his direction, missing him completely. Then he shot back with a burst of air. I threw my arms up to protect myself, causing a blazing shield to manifest.

"What the?" I said, completely mesmerized by what I'd created.

"Yes!" He clamored. "That's exactly right. Allow your instincts to take over."

It sort of made sense. But no sooner had I allowed myself a moment of victory than he attacked me again, slamming me to the ground with a twisting wind.

My back crashed hard, taking most of the impact, while I fought to keep my head from smashing against the stone.

The wind was knocked out of me, but Genie did not rescind. He prepared for another attack. However, this time I was ready, quickly rolling over until I was out of his path. I jumped to my feet, recognizing my robe was going to be an issue. Still, I needed to not look for excuses.

Without a second thought, I shot back, both palms facing him. A strong stream of fire erupted from me and shot him directly in the chest. For a moment, I panicked, unable to see anything but a huge ball of combustion until I heard his gravelly laughter.

"Very good, Gaia." The fire whirled around him in a tornado effect then petered out. "That is exactly what is needed. Now that you've learned just how powerful your magic can be, you must learn to focus it and wield it in different manners," he said, dusting off his sleeves. "Fire magic is one of the finest weapons."

I calmed my breathing, not having realized just how much energy calling upon my magic had taken. Looking up, I caught a smirk on Genie's face. My lips twitched at the edges, and I found myself laughing.

"Your Highness, that was impressive." a voice said.

I stopped laughing and turned to the stairs to find

both Freya and Jamal watching. How long had they been there?

Where Freya's eyes were wide with wonder, by contrast, Jamal looked irked by the whole thing.

"Your eyes..." she stuttered, "They are... golden." Freya's words were barely a whisper.

"What do you mean?"

Jamal moved in closer, taking my hands in his. "The ring of your eyes is shining brightly," he said, a smile slowly forming on his lips. "I believe that is your magic."

Genie interrupted. "Yes. It would seem so."

Jamal shot him a look, then turned back to me. "I was hoping you'd come for a walk on the terrace with me this evening after dinner."

I was about to say that I was having too much fun with Genie when Genie spoke for me.

"I think that's a marvelous idea," he said. "We have finished here anyway."

"But we've only started!" I protested.

"I'll find you early tomorrow morning so we may do more training. I'll fetch you before the sun rises. Be ready."

He didn't give me an opportunity to respond as he walked past us and headed upstairs.

My excitement waned. I wanted him so badly that I'd made the last half hour into something it was not.

I wanted to run after him, to ask him to continue practicing with me, but Jamal still had hold of my hands.

"You were magnificent," he said, his eyes shining. I'd never felt less so.

~

"Are you ok, Gaia?" Jamal asked during dinner. "You've hardly said a word all evening."

"Lost in thought," I replied, picking at my food.

"Freya was just telling us that her grandparents used to teach magic here in Kisbu. Isn't that fascinating?"

I looked up to see a gleam in Freya's eyes and a grin on her face.

She'd followed me around, almost like a subservient puppy for days, and I'd barely spoken to her.

"Tell me about them," I said, smiling back at her.

"Before The Vizier came to work at the palace, magic was abundant in Badalah. My mother told me that the markets used to sell all kinds of things for potions before they became spice markets. Badalah was once almost as magic as Enchantia."

"It seems so strange. No one here is magic anymore."

"You are," Jamal pointed out. He raised his eyebrows and gave me a grin as he speared asparagus onto his fork.

"Isn't it awful, though?" Freya continued, her black hair bobbing around her ears. I'd never seen her wear it down before. She was usually dressed in uniform, but tonight she'd worn a pretty dress. She was even wearing makeup. "I hate that magic has become a dirty word around here. There must be others in Kisbu who are magic. I know I've felt magical vibrations before when I've walked through the streets. Not as much as this," she gestured around her. "But I know there is magic out there."

"Did you know I was magic before...?"

"Before you went up in flames in your closet? No. I was shocked, to be honest. People are either magic or not. I've never known someone to spontaneously become magic."

I returned her grin. "Or spontaneously combust, either?"

"Enough talk. Have you finished, Gaia?"

He looked down at my plate, where I'd picked at my food, barely touching it.

"I think so."

He stood and held his hand out to me. "Come, let's take that walk on the terrace."

"Please excuse us, Freya," I said, taking Jamal's hand. She gave me a quick nod and then turned back to her food.

The terrace had always been a romantic spot. It was no surprise that my parents danced there every night... or used to. Torches lit the pathways, and the sound of crickets filled the warm air. Fireflies danced around us and somewhere music played.

"Is that a violin?" I asked, looking out over the city. The terrace was raised, and so at parts of it, such as this one afforded an amazing view.

"I hope so. I asked one of the court musicians to play for us."

I gripped the balustrade and inhaled the jasmine.

"Are you alright, Gaia?" Jamal asked. "You've been so distant lately. I wonder if you want me here at all."

I turned to face him. He was so beautiful in the evening light.

"Of course, I want you here."

His face brightened, and his eyes crinkled at the edges as he smiled. "I hoped you'd say that. I like you, Gaia. I like you a lot."

He took my hand and gazed into my eyes, then leaned forward and kissed me lightly on the lips. I didn't move, unsure of what to do. He was the most beautiful man I'd ever seen, but when he leaned in again to kiss me a second time, I pulled back.

He licked his lips and gave me a small nod. Then he kissed the back of my hand. “Goodnight, Gaia.”

“Goodnight,” I replied weakly as he turned and walked away.

25TH JUNE

I didn't sleep much. Thoughts of once again heading out into the streets consumed me, but Badalah wasn't the place I knew anymore. In only a short week, things had changed. Most people would argue that a princess sneaking out of the palace in the middle of the night was never safe, but for the first time, I felt it wasn't safe myself. That thought led me to tossing and turning and fretting instead. And above everything else, I couldn't escape the thoughts of Genie that plagued me nor the kiss from Jamal that still burned on my lips.

The fake fight we'd had in the basement was the only physical thing Genie and I had ever done together. Our bodies hadn't even touched, and yet our energy had. It was quite the most exciting thing that had ever happened to me, and yet, it was nothing. To him, at least. He was preparing me for war, but my body was distracted by the attraction I'd felt throughout. I wasn't supposed to feel attracted to him. Empowered maybe. Scared even, but not the burning desire I had felt.

And then there was Jamal. Jamal, who had made it very clear that he liked me. He'd said it right before kissing me as if kissing me wasn't enough.

I punched my pillow and forced myself to think of something else until sleep finally came.

Breakfast was a similar affair to the day before, with my mother staring blankly at her food. She didn't even look up or greet me when I entered. Jamal came in just after I did and took his place at the table.

"I'm glad you came down early today," he whispered in my ear. "I waited until you showed up so your mother wouldn't try to seduce me over her scrambled eggs."

I almost spat my coffee across the table at his words. "Idiot!" I whispered back as good-naturedly as I could. It broke the tension. I'd been so nervous about seeing him after last night, but he seemed jovial enough. He gave me a grin and then said 'Hi' to my mother.

She finally looked up and spoke, adopting a soppy expression, which I'd most certainly not seen on her before. "Hi, lover." She gave him a wink and went back to staring at her plate.

This time, I really did lose my coffee.

"See!" Jamal whispered with a shrug.

Freya walked in and gave a small curtsey. She was dressed in her usual palace uniform with her hair tied back. Behind her, strode the Palace's chief guard. He came to a stop, stomped his foot, and saluted. The blank stare left my mother.

"Your Majesty, I've been tasked to let you know that the gates to the city have been breached. The people of

Badalah are demanding an audience with you."

"No!" I said loudly. The guard didn't flinch, but my mother's eyes widened at my outburst.

"Gaia! That is no way to speak to our staff."

"I'm sorry, Mother, but you aren't well. The people are angry. I'm scared for your safety."

"Don't be ridiculous. I am the Sultana. The people have a right to request an audience with me. I had planned for this yesterday. I hoped they would give me some time, but as they didn't..."

She stood up, trailing off her sentence, and swished her dress out behind her.

"Then, please take the guards with you."

The irony was not lost on me that our roles had reversed. It was usually her telling me to take guards into Kisbu.

She gave me a smile before turning to the chief guard. "Assemble a dozen guards and have a messenger head out into the town and deliver word that I will come out and visit with the people. There is a platform in the central district reserved for theatre and announcements. I'll be there when the hour is up."

The guard saluted again, then turned purposefully and left the room.

"I should get ready," my mother announced and glided out of the room.

"I'm sorry," Freya said once my mother had left. "I knew this was coming. I saw them coming in when I was on the way back to the palace from visiting my mother. I'd hoped to get here in time to warn you."

"How bad is it?" Jamal asked.

Freya screwed her face up. "Not good. There are a lot of people. The town is overrun with farmers and country folk."

I ran to the window and pulled back the curtain slightly. Hundreds of people stood outside, some shouting angrily, some waving pitchforks. As I watched, I felt Jamal come up behind me and put his arm around my waist. I knew he was doing it to comfort me, but my body tensed under his touch. Outside, a messenger ran out and blew a horn, quieting the crowd. I couldn't hear what he said to them, but I assumed he was directing them to the stage in town that my mother had mentioned since they soon began to drift away.

"I can't let her go alone," I said, turning around. I found myself eye to eye with Jamal, still in the confines of his arms. He gave me a small smile, making his beautiful eyes crinkle up slightly at the corner. He lifted a hand and moved a lock of my hair behind my ear. It was such an intimate move.

"I'll go along too. I have a feeling she'll need all the help she can get."

I knew he was trying to make me feel better.

"Thank you," I said, pushing him slightly to get out of his grip. I didn't see the look of disappointment in his eyes, but I knew it was there.

Less than ten minutes later, Jamal, Freya, my mother, myself, and the guards were heading through town. On formal occasions, my parents used a palanquin or a carriage to move through the streets. Now, however, we walked, surrounded by much more than the requested dozen guards.

In the town square, Freya led us toward the back of the stage through a walkway reserved for actors. It meant we could get to the stage itself without having to push through the angry crowd.

"Excuse me, good sir," Freya said, leaning into a middle-aged man standing square in front of the steps to the back of the platform.

She whispered something into his ear and no sooner had she finished speaking, than he was looking over Freya's shoulder toward my mother. He looked around and signaled another man who joined us.

"Sultana Jawahir. What an honor to meet you." The arriving man said. "Thank you for coming here. I am the curator of the stage. My name is Malik." He gave a small bow and raised the hat from his head.

My mother stepped forward with conviction. "Thank you, Malik. I'm here to speak to everyone. Would you kindly get their attention so I may address the crowds?"

"Of course," the man replied, motioning to the other to get everyone's attention. He then took the stage. "Ladies and gentlemen, may I please have your attention." He paused, waiting for the onlookers to focus quietly on him. "We have the honor to welcome our leader, Sultana Jawahir. Please, I ask that we all give her respect, and engage accordingly."

Murmurings spread across the people as my mother took the stage alongside Malik. The angry rumbles I'd heard among them had subsided a little. Maybe they genuinely wanted to hear what she had to say. I watched on from the back of the stage.

Jamal took my hand in his. It was so natural that we could have been dating, but we weren't...or were we? I'd never been on a date in my life. I had no clue what we were doing. I certainly had no clue as to how I felt about what we were doing. I hazarded a quick glance his way. He was watching my mother with something I could only describe as pride. He caught me looking and gave my hand a quick squeeze.

"My loyal subjects," my mother began. "I come to you today in hopes of gathering a better understanding of what is happening among Badalah's communities that would have you traveling here. Please, speak one by one, so I may hear you and address each as best as possible."

She spoke with such eloquence, yet there was an authority in her voice that could not be mistaken. She was the Sultana, ruler of Badalah, and one of the most powerful individuals throughout the land. This was the woman I knew as my mother, not the dazed woman who winked at Jamal over breakfast. The ebbs and flows of this strange magical condition were more heartbreaking than if I'd lost her for good. It was at times like this that I remembered exactly who she was and, at the same time, had the crushing fear that she'd drift back into what she was becoming.

"Your Royal Highness, Sultana Jawahir, we are starving. Your trade bans have made it impossible for us to do our jobs. If we can't do our jobs, how do you expect us to buy the things we need?"

"Trade bans?" My mother asked.

My stomach lurched. She was not prepared for this. How could she be? She'd forgotten everything she'd put in place only last week.

"And the taxes are ridiculous," someone else shouted. The crowd nodded and jeered.

My mother suddenly looked scared. She opened her mouth to speak, but nothing came out.

"Let me pass!" I shouted to Malik.

Jamal caught my arm. "What are you doing?"

"I can't leave her up there. You can see what's happening. They are going to storm the stage!"

He licked his lips. "You can't go up. The people remember Jawahir. Half of them don't remember you. You'll only add to the confusion."

"But..."

"What do you think is going to happen when you go up? They'll wonder who you are. When you tell them you are the Sultana's daughter, most won't believe you. Do you trust me?"

He relaxed his grip on my arm and looked right into my eyes.

"Do you trust me, Gaia?" he repeated.

I nodded my head. Seconds later, he'd pushed past Malik and joined my mother on the stage.

"My name is Jamal. I'm an advisor to the Sultana. I know you are all hungry and scared. We are going through unprecedented times. The Sultana has been working tirelessly to get us through these past few weeks despite not feeling well herself."

A white lie. My mother had barely done anything these past weeks, and the things she had done had caused this mess in the first place.

"The tax raise and the trade restrictions were a mistake," Jamal continued. "I had proposed it for consideration for the future, but somehow the memo got leaked. It was never meant for public eyes. The tax raises, if they should happen, will only come when things are better in Badalah, and they will be nowhere near the amount on the memo. As for trade, the ban is lifted from immediate effect."

I let out a breath I hadn't known I was holding. He'd gone up there and lied to the people. And they were cheering him. He'd even said that taxes would be raised at some point. The man was a genius.

"He's great at this, isn't he?" Freya said, grabbing my arm.

I flicked my eyes to my mother to see how she was taking this. The blank stare I'd come to recognize was still on her face. Jamal took her hand in his, and she seemed to snap out of it.

"But we're still hungry," someone shouted. "We've not been able to sell our wares for two weeks."

"I couldn't collect a shipment from Draconis last week!" another said.

"My children are starving!" yet another said. "Our crops are failing."

In a loud, determined voice, my mother stepped forward and spoke.

"I've heard enough. At my direction, the people of the palace will be setting up food banks for each of you to take what you need and bring it back to your homes to tide you over. In the meantime, you are all welcome into the palace where I'll make sure food is laid out for all of you."

I almost laughed. This is what we did all the time before the curse hit Kisbu. She'd just forgotten.

I felt hope that maybe she was starting to get better, starting to remember.

Back in the palace, we all set to work, organizing the kitchens, and getting everything ready for the people. My heart was full as I did what I loved best, helping the staff to prepare for one of the Palace Parties, as they were known.

Maybe, just maybe if my mother was beginning to remember, maybe my father would too, and this weird... whatever it was would go as quickly as it had come.

Jamal buttered slices of bread, tossing them to me with a grin, which I then filled with meat and passed to Freya to add salad.

It wasn't the same without my father, nor without Genie, but it was a step in the right direction.

Genie! He used to love this. "I need to tell Genie," I

said, breaking off.

"Really?" Jamal said. "I'm sure he wouldn't want to be bothered with something as menial as this."

"Actually, he always helped before. I think he should know what is happening."

Jamal nodded curtly then kissed my cheek. "If you must." He turned to Freya. "It looks like it's just you and me on sandwich duty."

My heart felt light as I skipped down the corridor to Genie's room.

"Genie! There you are. I've got some good news." I enthused, opening the outer door. When I saw him, I stopped. Something was wrong. He was sitting, gazing out of the window in much the same way my father had done at the beginning of his illness.

My throat constricted. As my mother was getting better, was Genie getting worse?

He turned to me with a weird expression. His eyes were red and held a pained expression

"What's the matter?" I whispered.

Genie lifted his arms, and over his wrists were two bronze cuffs.

"Genie..." I whispered, rushing to his side. The veins in his strong hands looked as if they were about to pop. I reached for one of his hands and carefully touched the cuff.

"It's happening again," he said.

"What do you mean?"

"I mean the magic. The wish. It is all fading away."

The reality of what he was saying hit me like a punch to the gut. He was a free man because of my father. My father had saved him from a life of slavery by using a wish to do so. A wish that belonged to my father, one of three.

“What does that mean?” I asked my voice barely more than a choked sob.

“I don’t know for sure, but these cuffs are the mark of a genie. If they are back, it must mean the lamp is back.”

“It can’t be! My father threw it out into the desert. It hasn’t been seen for over eighteen years.”

I remembered what Freya’s mother had told me when I’d first met her. She said it was unlikely that The Vizier was still in it. Maybe when he escaped, it paved the way for Genie to turn back to what he once was. It kind of made sense. My father’s other two wishes were also disappearing. He’d wished to be the sultan, and he’d wished for my mother to fall in love with him. Genie couldn’t produce love, so he’d produced a magical night with flowers and music and moonlight. My mother had fallen in love with my father all on her own. Now, my father was living on the streets, and my mother had forgotten he existed. His last wish of three was to free Genie.

He looked at me through watery eyes.

“Neither had these,” he replied sadly, holding his wrists up.

“No! I will not allow that. Do you hear me? I won’t allow you to go back to being someone’s slave. There must be something I can do. What about the wishes? If you are a genie again, you owe wishes, right? You gave my father three? Well, I wish...”

Genie stopped me with a finger to my lips. “Don’t do it.”

He held his hand out to mine. The coldness of the metal on his wrists grazed my fingertips.

“Owning wishes is not for people like you. Only the greedy covet the riches I can bring them. Even those who don't start greedy turn that way when they find out what they can do. If you make the first wish, I will be bound to you for three wishes. I will become your slave."

Tears sprang to my eyes. "Finding out you are a genie again is one thing. Finding out that's what you think of me is another entirely." I looked directly at him. "Is that really what you think of me? That I'll use the wishes for my own gain. Don't you know me at all?"

"I'm sorry, Gaia. I barely know myself anymore. There are gaps in my memory. And there are things I remember that I don't even know if they really happened."

I'd never seen him look so helpless. In fact, I'd never seen him look helpless at all before now. I leaned forward and touched my lips to his. He didn't flinch or pull away. He closed his eyes as I pulled back.

"Do you remember that?" I whispered. "Do you remember me now?"

"Gaia," he said his voice soft and warm.

"I will use my first wish to free you as my father did," I said, holding his wrists and running my thumb over the metal. That's all I want. I don't care about anything else."

His lips tightened, and I could see he was trying to hold his emotions back.

"What about your father? The curse spreading through our kingdom. You've talked about nothing but the strange magic for weeks. What about that?"

He remembered my father again. Just like with my mother, the magic came and went. "Can you cure it?"

"Even with these on my wrists, I don't understand the magic. I feel it, but my wishes are not powerful enough to stop it."

"You were the most powerful in all the kingdom."

Genie dropped his head. "In the kingdom, yes. In most of the kingdoms, but there were others that were more powerful than me. The gods..."

"Gods? I don't believe in gods."

"Hmm."

I waited for him to say something else, but he didn't. All I could think about was the taste of his lips on mine, but I had to concentrate on more pressing matters. The kingdom was depending on me, even if they didn't know it.

I thought of all the things I could ask for. For my father to be home, for him to remember me, for the people to have enough food. There were so many things that battled for prominence in my mind.

In the end, the solution was clear. The million things I could ask for I already had a couple of weeks ago. I wanted everything to go back to normal.

"Can you send me back in time? Maybe if I go back a few weeks, I can stop this. Then you won't become a genie again."

Genie gave me a sad smile. "You had an inkling that something was going to happen, but you didn't know what. Knowing what you know now, what do you propose you'll do to stop it?"

"I'll..." I didn't know. This wasn't a single thing I could touch or see, it was a myriad of problems created by a magical force. A magical force I didn't know how to stop now any more than I did then. I didn't even know where it had come from. I didn't believe it was a thing of the gods. I doubted Genie believed that either. This had something to do with me. My magic started when this started in Badalah.

"Take me back to my birth."

"You want to go back to when your parents were

young? You know that time travel will take you out of this timeline to put you in another. You'll cease to exist here. What would I tell your mother?"

"Can you send me back long enough to see where I came from and then bring me back?"

"I can. It will take you two of your three wishes. One for each way. If you just want to see what happened, I can show you without you leaving the palace. That will take one wish. You'll stay exactly where you are."

"Do it!" I said, standing up. "Show me everything you can around my birth. And when you are done, I'll wish for your freedom."

"I don't even know this will work without the lamp."

"Neither of us will know without trying."

"You have to say the words," he said with a sigh. He'd known me better than myself. He'd known I would make a wish, but it wasn't a frivolous wish. I was doing this for him as well as for me. I was doing this for all of us.

He looked at me as though he was hoping I wouldn't. But I had no choice. If I wanted my father back, my mother well, and Genie to be free, I needed to find out how this all started.

I took his hands in mine. "Genie. I wish for you to show me my own birth."

The hairs on my arm stood on end, sending a chill down my spine as his magical energy spun around us.

It peeled away and formed a spinning orb of light.

Genie let go of me and nodded to the light.

"In there, is what you seek. It will appear to you that you are somewhere else, but in reality, you'll not leave my office."

The light was cold, making me shiver as I stepped through it.

A dense fog rolled in, and with it, a scream pierced the air. Not mine, not Genie.

A hazy image appeared before me.

A younger woman on a bed, screaming. But I couldn't do anything. There was some invisible shield between us. It wasn't real, it was a memory.

Then an older woman came into view. She was at the end of the bed.

She held a baby in her arms. A newborn still tethered to its mother.

The old woman cleaned it up and cut the cord. The golden rings around its irises were unmistakable. I was looking at myself.

It was the most bizarre feeling. I felt a strange sensation in my stomach as the older lady passed the baby to the mother...my mother. As she passed it, I noticed something else about the child. I'd been so caught up in its eyes, that I'd not paid attention to the rest of it. It wasn't me, after all. It was a baby boy.

Disappointment filled me. Genie was wrong. This wasn't about me. This was someone else. The look of love on the mother as she gazed down at her new son was unmistakable.

She was an extraordinarily beautiful woman, with long dark hair that clung to her face with sweat, but I imagined it hung beautifully straight on normal days. Her features contorted, and she screamed again. The older woman took the babe and disappeared from view, returning a few seconds later without the child. For a second, I was confused. What was happening? But as the older woman took her place at the foot of the bed, I understood. Twins.

I watched in awe as the young woman bore down and pushed another child into the world. It came out quickly, almost falling into the older woman's hands.

"A girl!" she announced. She proceeded to clean her up in the same way she had with the boy. The mother was flushed with exhaustion, but the same look of love I'd seen moments earlier came back to her face as the baby was swaddled and handed to her.

I'd asked to see my birth, and here it was. I had a brother. A twin brother. Of all the things I'd wondered about where I'd come from, I'd never expected to see another child. If I had a twin, where was he? Why didn't the women want to keep us together?

"What will you do with the babes?" The old woman asked, gazing down at the small child.

I looked at the baby myself, willing myself closer. She had the golden rings around her eyes. Other than that, she could have been anyone.

We both watched on as she carefully caressed the little girl's cheeks, cuddling her into her bosom.

The younger woman finally looked up to the older one and spoke. "My father will kill them if he finds out. I've hidden the pregnancy. I can't hide the babies."

It suddenly made sense. She was young. There was no man in the room, so probably no father was in the picture, and she'd kept it from her own father. I wanted to reach out and hug her, but before my eyes, the scene shifted.

The women were seated at a table in what looked to be a kitchen. I could hear the babies crying, but I couldn't see them. The fog around the edges of the picture was thick, and I knew if I tried to walk into it, I'd only find myself out of the picture altogether and back in Genie's office.

The young woman was in tears, but the older woman was speaking. "You must have noticed the magic that came into the world when the babies were born."

"I don't want to give them away. I love them."

"I know you do, but this is bigger than you. Look at this." she pushed a newspaper toward the younger woman. I leaned forward and read the headline. *A hundred years of sleep comes to an end. Draconis celebrates.*

Below it was a picture of a young woman looking at a man adoringly. I recognized them as the king and queen of Draconis.

The young woman barely looked at the paper before pushing it away.

"You can't ignore it," the old one said. "All the bad in the world. It's gone. You made something beautiful. The babies are special, but you know they aren't safe. If your father finds out about them and kills them to make up for your sins, all this good will be over. Did you see the marriage announcement of the young prince in Atlantice? It's not the only one. The kingdoms are protected from evil. For the first time in a long time, people are happy."

"I'm not happy," the younger one said, wiping her eyes with the back of her hand "Why must their happiness take precedence over mine?"

The older woman reached across the table and patted the younger woman's hand. "You know why. We are talking about everyone in all the kingdoms. That's millions of people. Besides, will you be happy if your father kills them? No, you won't. I'm afraid your happiness is not possible, but your children's might be. You want them to be happy, don't you?"

Tears flowed down her face, but she nodded.

"The magic won't last forever," the young woman said assertively. "When they turn eighteen, this burst will fade. It is about then that they will come into their own powers. I just need to hide them until they are adults."

With a heavy sigh, the old woman spoke up again. "I will help you. I have an idea..."

The fog rolled out, and the haze was gone. Suddenly, I was back in Genie's office.

My head hurt with everything I'd just witnessed, but I was soon brought back to the present when Genie fell to the floor in front of me.

"Genie, are you all right?" I asked, running toward him. I crouched down and wrapped my arm around his back.

He smiled weakly, "I forgot how exhausting magic can be. I'm not the man...the genie I once was. I'm an old man now."

"You aren't old," I said, ignoring the fact that he was generations old. He didn't look it. What he did look was tired.

"Come on, let's get you up onto the couch."

I already had my arm around him, and with the other, I grabbed his arm and helped him to his feet.

"Not the couch," he huffed. His face was sheet white with the exertion of standing. "My bed."

Not once in my whole life had I gone through the doors from his office to his private quarters. He was usually so private. Asking me to help him to bed was a huge deal.

Using my foot, I carefully opened the doors. Inside was a small living area with a couch and yet more books in bookshelves along the far wall. Normally, I'd have made a quip about him keeping the best books to himself, but he was sick. He nodded to a door on the opposite side. We shuffled across slowly with me holding most of his weight. Opening the door, I found myself in Genie's bedroom. The white walls were the same at the rest of the palace, but instead of the thick heavy curtains that hung everywhere else, his full-length windows were covered by a flimsy white gauzy material that flapped in the light breeze. His bed was the only color in the room, covered as it was with a colorful bedspread of pinks, purples, and turquoise.

I helped him down, making sure his head was on the pillow.

He looked at me in such a way that almost broke me. I'd never seen him look at me like that before, with such intensity as though he was seeing me for the first time.

"I wish I could see what was going on in your head," I said lightly.

He smiled, and the Genie that I knew came back. There was a tear in the corner of his eye, and sweat covered his forehead.

"Is that a real wish?"

"Just a turn of phrase," I said, smiling back. I turned to leave, but he caught my hand.

"Stay," he murmured.

My heart sped up at his words.

"What?" I'd heard him, I just wasn't sure I believed my own ears.

The tear began to make its way down the side of his head.

"Stay with me."

I swallowed back a response and climbed onto the bed next to him. He moved over enough to let me on, but his body remained next to mine. I could barely breathe with the intensity of my heart pounding as it was.

He snaked his arm under my head, pulling me

toward him so that my head ended up on his chest. With my free hand, I conjured up a flame, partly for something to quiet my racing heart and partly to dispel some of the magical energy burning through me.

We both watched the flames, dancing on my fingertips, but I was more aware of Genie's fingers as he traced swirls on my temple and ran his fingers through my hair.

My entire body was burning with desire, and with magic, the two things seemingly linked, swirling around inside me, so much so that it was hard to keep control of the flame I was producing.

I watched the flame until I could bear it no longer. Letting the flame extinguish, I turned to Genie. His eyes were closed, and his chest was rising and falling rhythmically in sleep.

I kissed him lightly on the cheek and smiled as I closed my own eyes and let myself fall into blissful sleep next to him.

26TH JUNE

When I awoke, the sun was much higher in the sky that it had been when I'd fallen asleep. I'd spent the night in Genie's arms. My arm had gone numb from being in one position for so long, but everything felt so right, so perfect that I was loathe to move.

Genie still slept soundly, his braided hair curled out at his other side. I moved slightly, sending a shot of pain up my arm. Gritting my teeth against it, I shuffled my body until I was close enough to kiss him. His lips were warm, delicious. My heart was pounding so loudly that I was sure it would wake him. As it was, the touch of my lips to his was what caused his eyelids to flutter open.

"Good morning," I whispered, pulling back slightly

and ignoring the pain in my arm as the blood was draining back into it.

He seemed surprised to see me. Not the reaction I wanted. Sitting up in bed, he pulled the covers aside.

"I'm sorry. I shouldn't have taken advantage."

My heart fell as he twisted his legs out of bed.

"You didn't take advantage. I wanted to be here."

"That's the problem," he said, standing up and pulling a robe over his clothes. "I know you did. I should have been stronger."

I stepped out of bed. "It's not like we did anything," I pouted, ignoring the way I'd woken him up, not moments before.

"I acted badly. Come, let's go to my office and you can tell me what you saw in the memory. Was it what you expected to see?"

And just like that, we were mentor and mentee again. The closeness we'd shared had been in my own head. With a heavy heart, I followed him out of the bedroom, through the living area and back to his office where I'd spent many hours.

"Gaia... What happened last night..."

I nodded.

"That can never happen again. I am grateful for your friendship and care, but I have nothing else to offer you. Besides, your father is my best friend, and well, you've got a lot more you need to deal with, like finding out exactly what is happening across the kingdoms."

At least, he remembered my father again. It was little consolation in the circumstances.

"It doesn't matter," I said.

He didn't buy it, but what could we do. I wanted something he wasn't able to give me, not with all the wishes in the world.

"Tell me what you saw last night. I couldn't see what you saw. The magic was only for you."

"I saw my mother. I saw myself as a baby. Genie, I have a twin brother."

Genie's eyes widened at the confession.

"I was there when you were brought to the palace. There was only you. The women mentioned no other child."

I sighed. "Tell me about the night I was brought to the palace."

I needed to get my mind on something else rather than how beautiful he looked and how much I wished I was still in his bed with him. I needed to concentrate on what was important.

"I was called from my room. It was late. Very late. Your parents didn't like to disturb me in the night, so I knew it was important. I found them in the entrance hall. Your mother was holding you. Your father stood at the door, talking to an older woman. I remember him almost begging her for details."

"What kind of details?"

"I think he wanted to know everything, but the old woman refused to answer his questions. She looked desperate to get away if I remember correctly."

"I saw her in the vision. What about a younger woman with long black hair."

"I only got a glimpse of her. She stood behind the older one. She didn't say a word. She did walk into the palace as your father was demanding answers from the older one and kissed your cheek. I saw the heartbreak on her face. She never said a word, though.

As she walked back to the door, your father asked the older woman what your name was. That's when the younger woman spoke. She only said one word. 'Gaia.'"

I'd seen the pain on her face myself. She hadn't wanted to give me away. She'd done it to save my life and that of my brother's.

"In the vision, she said that her father would kill us if he ever found out. What kind of man would kill a newborn baby?"

Genie shook his head slowly. "There are all kinds of people out there. They are not all as good as you."

"I'm not good enough for you, though, right?"

Genie sighed, sucking in his cheek.

"Gaia. We've been through this. There are too many reasons for us not to be together. Look at me." He held up the cuffs on his wrists. "I am a slave. I am destined to spend my life as a slave. It is not that you are not good enough for me. It is I that is not good enough." There was sincere pain in his eyes. "I will not drag you into what I've become and what I will continue to become. I will not take your freedom from you."

Every word he said was like a dagger to my chest, but the worst part about it was that I understood his reasoning. He was turning back into a genie. At some point in the near future, he'd become trapped in his lamp again. The same lamp my father threw out into the desert. I didn't even know where it was. No one did.

"I should go and see my mother. She'll be wondering where I am."

I walked past him, not daring to look him in the eyes and headed out into the corridor and set off toward my mother's chambers.

"Gaia! Oh, my dear girl. Where have you been?" My mother demanded. There was a sincere sense of relief in her tone and her embrace when I found her in her chambers. Freya was sitting with her, which I was thankful for.

"I'm so sorry, mother. Genie and I were trying to figure something out, and next thing we knew, we got to talking and fell asleep. I think all of the stress and exhaustion finally caught up to me."

Freya's eyes widened at this, and she gave me a knowing look, but my mother took it in her stride.

"You missed the party yesterday." She turned to Freya. "Freya, my dear. Will you please send word to Jamal via the guards?"

"Yes, Your Majesty," she said, disappearing through the antechamber.

"Jamal has been looking for me?"

"I told him you'd be fine. To be honest, I thought you were sleeping in your own chambers. Jamal was worried when you didn't show up this morning, so I let him search the palace for you."

I wasn't sure what I thought of that. While I should have told everyone where I was going last night, I was eighteen years old. Old enough to go somewhere in my own palace without anyone searching for me.

Just then, Freya and Jamal returned. Both bowing to my mother, waiting for her to give them to the command to proceed. Even in those trying times, everyone but me seemed to be sticking with customs.

"Princess. I'm so glad you are all right." Jamal said, bowing to me. I narrowed my eyes, surprised by his sudden need to treat me like I was above him. He usually called me Gaia.

"Freya tells me you were with the Genie."

Behind him, Freya gave me a sorry look and shrugged her shoulders.

"I was. I needed to ask him something. It was important."

"What was so important that you needed to speak to

him all night about it?"

I sucked up a breath, not daring myself to speak. What business was it of his where I spent my evenings? Luckily, my mother stepped in before I had the chance to answer.

"Jamal, darling," she said, putting her arm around his shoulder. "Gaia is a big girl. I was wondering if you'll talk to me about the party yesterday. I'd like your input on where we can do a better job next time."

Jamal looked increasingly uncomfortable, but I used it as an excuse to leave. I was in no mood to have a discussion about Genie. I didn't even know how I felt about everything yet. I had a feeling that Jamal didn't want to know what my feelings toward Genie were anyway.

Freya followed me out of my mother's chambers. Once we were in the clear, Freya leaned in. "So, what were you doing, really?"

Something about the way she said it moved me to the core. I had tried to brush off Genie's words. But I wasn't really all right.

"I'll tell you in my room," I said, pulling at her faster, feeling as if my emotions were about to breach a damn.

When we made it to my room, I threw myself on my bed, while Freya disappeared to get my bath started. As soon as she resurfaced, she went through my wardrobe and pulled a clean change of clothes out for me.

"Can't have you wearing the same clothes as yesterday. People will talk," she winked.

I closed my eyes. If she'd noticed, so would Jamal. No wonder he was snippy with me.

"I swear I went to Genie's room to..." I had to think back. So much had happened since then. "To tell him about the party."

I held my hands up and placed the word party in finger quotes.

"He loved helping feed the poor as much as my parents did. How did it go anyway? I'm sorry I wasn't there."

"Oh, no, you don't, lady!" she said, sitting next to me on the bed.

"It's as plain as the nose on your face that you are in love with him. I want the juicy details. I can tell you about feeding the poor later."

I covered my eyes with my hand. "It's that obvious, huh?"

"I'm not sure it is to everyone else, but I can feel the difference in your energy when you are around him. I can feel it when you just mention his name."

"Do you think Jamal can feel it too?"

"Probably. He's one of the few that isn't affected by this magic going around. I'm not sure he needs to feel it to know it, though. Your eyes light up when anyone mentions Genie's name."

"Urgh!" I let my head fall into my hands. "I feel so bad. Jamal thinks we are dating, and I've never really dispelled him of the notion. I've handled everything so badly."

"Jamal will get over it. Besides, he had your mother hanging off his every word yesterday. I think they are going to announce their engagement any day now." She laughed at her joke, but I didn't want to think about it. My mother's flirting was just another thing in a long line of things I could quite happily not hear about again.

"I have something to tell you about last night..." I started. "No, it isn't juicy. Well, not what you are thinking anyway. I fell asleep with Genie, that's all. I'm going to tell you what happened before that."

She pulled herself up on the bed and crossed her legs, watching me with a rapt expression. “Tell me everything!”

I rolled my eyes at her. “Genie is starting to become a Genie again. He has cuffs on his wrists.”

Her eyes widened. She wasn’t expecting that. She was going to be blown away when she heard the rest of what I was about to tell her.

I took a deep breath and began to speak. I told her about how I’d seen my mother and that I had a twin out there somewhere. She sat in awed silence as I told her everything.

“This is great!” she said when I’d finished. “We know that your birth somehow triggered this.” She waved her hands about. “What are you going to do about it?”

“Do? I wasn’t going to do anything. What can I do? I don’t know why or how. Nothing from what I saw told me why my birth prompted this. The woman…my mother, was beautiful, but she didn’t look particularly powerful. There’s no way to tell if she was a witch or a mage… She wasn’t fae,” I added. “Her ears weren’t pointed. I don’t know what happened to my twin. I don’t even know if he’s still alive. I can think of no reason why my real mother would separate us.”

“Forget your brother for a second. Did you recognize the place? There has to be a clue in there somewhere.”

I jogged my memory back to that hazy scene. I looked beyond the women and the babies. What was I missing?

“Oh!” I said with a startle. “I think I have a clue.”

Freya immediately perked up. “What is it?”

I stood to pace, biting down on my lower lip. A nervous habit I’d picked up from my mom.

“The room. There was a window. I saw a white steeple. I think I’ve seen ones like it before. I saw a street sign too."

"Where? Somewhere in Badalah?"

"No," I shook my head. "They weren't in Badalah. I think they were in Urbis. The buildings outside were made from brick, but in the distance, I saw white stone. I've only ever seen buildings like that in Urbis when I went for a royal tour."

"That's interesting," Freya said, turning her attention toward the terrace. She then got up and walked out there. I followed.

We both stared out into the horizon. It was impossible to see Urbis from here, but if I looked southeast, it was over the horizon.

"What will you do?" she asked again.

"I need to know if I'm causing this. If I am, maybe I can stop it."

It sounded preposterous that I could have done anything as a newborn, even to my own ears, but that's what the old woman had said.

"I don't think you are causing the problems in the kingdom. I think maybe your birth stopped the problems that were already there. You are like a shield, stopping the problems of Badalah, but as you've aged, the shield has broken, letting the problems back in again."

It was an interesting way of thinking about it. "But these problems didn't begin in Badalah. I've got so many newspapers telling me of problems in other kingdoms too."

"Maybe your magic is so powerful that you saved all the kingdoms?"

I laughed. "I doubt it. All I can do is turn my body into an inferno. Not exactly helpful."

"Not now, maybe, but one day it might be. Do you think you'll go to Urbis?"

"I don't think I have any choice. Not if I want to figure out what is happening."

Freya nodded, "I agree. How soon will you leave?"

"I don't know. I don't even know if I should."

"Of course you should," Freya gesticulated wildly, her face full of excitement. "There is something about you that I can't quite put my finger on. Your magic is...weird. I can't think of a single group of people that have the magic you do. If you did put a stop to all the darkness in the world as a newborn, you are something really special."

"Yeah, but what?"

"That, my friend, I cannot answer."

A commotion broke out down below. We both ran to the edge of the terrace and leaned over to see what was going on. The people on the streets were stoning the palace walls, chanting angrily.

"What now?" I asked, rushing past Freya, through my bedroom and out into the corridor. The palace guards ran past me toward the palace entrance.

"What's happening?" I mumbled, catching Jamal in the entrance hall looking flustered.

"It's the people of Kisbu. They are angry that Sultana Jawahir entertained the outsiders and completely ignored them."

"But she didn't ignore them," I argued. "We made sure that food was sent out to those in need within the city walls, as well as outside."

"They know that. And still, they want what they perceive to be fair. They want a feast on the palace grounds."

"Are you serious?" I said, rolling my eyes. "Everyone was invited to it. It wasn't like we were stopping anyone coming in..." I became aware that I wasn't even there. I was busy sleeping in Genie's bed. "Were we?"

He shrugged his shoulders, letting out a deep sigh. "No. Anyone who wanted to come was allowed in, but it wasn't set up exclusively for them, and now, they want one that is just for them."

"We've put these things on most weekends for years!" I cried in frustration.

"I never said anyone was acting rationally. I've asked your mother to go to her rooms and gathered the guards together to put a stop to it."

"You really are amazing, you know that, right? What can I do to help?"

His cheeks colored, and he gave me a quick bow.

Before he could answer, Freya caught up with us. "Agreed. He's the best, but you don't have time to deal with all this. You need to decide how you're getting to Urbis."

"You are going to Urbis?" Jamal asked, narrowing his eyes.

"I think so."

He looked like he wanted to ask why, but one of the guards was calling for his attention.

He reluctantly left Freya and me and headed outside.

"He'd make a great leader," I remarked.

"Hmm," Freya agreed. "He'll also miss you when you are gone.""I don't know, Gaia," Genie said later when I approached him with my plan. "I didn't show you your birth for you to go gallivanting off on your own to another kingdom."

"It's not technically a kingdom," I pointed out. "It's a governmental district belonging to and overseeing all the twelve kingdoms."

"Don't be facetious, Gaia. I know full well what it is, and you know full well what I meant."

"You don't want me to go?"

Hope rose in my chest that he'd fall to his knees and beg me to stay.

"No, I don't. I don't think it's safe to travel alone in these trying times. I cannot go with you. These cuffs bind me. I don't know where the lamp is, but I can only assume it is near because I feel its pull."

"I have to go," I said, trying to sound defiant while every fiber in my being wanted Genie to stop me. To tell me he couldn't live without me.

He sighed. "Then, so be it. How will you get there? Carriage?"

"I was thinking of taking the Urbis Express. It's much quicker. I'll be there within a day if I travel that way."

He nodded. "There is one leaving for Urbis today. In a few hours, in fact. I can arrange for you to get a seat. For your own safety, I think you should change your clothes."

I looked down at the dress Freya had picked out for me earlier. It was one of my favorites, yellow with pink and orange silk.

"You'll stand out a mile in Urbis. They don't dress like us. If you want to find out about your mother, go incognito. Your beauty will be your downfall."

He thought I was beautiful. It was a bittersweet admission. What was the point of my beauty if he didn't want me?

I left him and went back to my room to change. I chose to wear pants and a wrap in earthen tones. I tightened the suede laces around my distressed long, brown, leather boots and picked up a backpack with enough clothes for a couple of days.

Freya handed me a poncho-like shawl with a head

cover. I took it, knowing that regardless of what I thought, Genie was right; I needed to conceal my identity. And the hood was large enough to allow me to see while remaining covert.

“You look ready,” Freya said, examining me from all angles. “Are you?”

“I am,” I responded.

A knock on the door told me Genie was back. He’d promised to come to the station with me.

The three of us walked through the palace to the staff entrance.

As far as I was aware, there were still problems by the main entrance, and I didn’t need to get caught up in them. I also didn’t want Jamal to know where I was going. He’d only try and stop me. Freya could tell him when she got back from the station.

No one paid us any attention as we walked through the streets to the Urbis Express station. The huge airship was already docked and accepting passengers. I watched as they bustled aboard and handed their tickets to a conductor at the door.

“I’ll get your ticket,” Genie said, leaving Freya and me to watch as he strode over to the ticket booth. I noticed he kept his cuffs hidden under long sleeves. He came back a minute later with a ticket.

“I could have bought you a royal ticket to get you your own compartment, but I figured you’d prefer to travel in the main compartment with everyone else.” He handed me the ticket. “Keep it safe.”

Freya cleared her throat, “We really don’t have time for chit chat. They are boarding. Be safe, please,” she said, giving me a hug.

“I will. I promise. And please, take care of my mom,” I said, waving back at them as I boarded the airship, making sure my hood was covering as much of my face as possible.

There didn't seem to be assigned seating, so I found one next to a window.

A woman and her young child sat across from me. She looked sad, as did the young child. I tried to offer a warm smile, but she turned away.

The airship filled quickly, and before long, we lifted off with a lurch. I watched my beloved city of Kisbu fall beneath me as we climbed higher in the sky. I waved at Genie and Freya, watching them until they turned to head back to the palace. The palace itself dominated the skyline, it's white and gold domes glinting in the evening sun.

Leaving Genie was harder than I could ever have imagined. I'd spent the last year or more roaming the streets of Kisbu after darkness fell, but going to Urbis without my parents, without the posse of guards, was something else entirely.

This was the craziest thing I'd ever done. I wasn't one for rebellion. I'd never had reason to run away from home, but the world was crazy, and I was heading away from everything I loved to find a way to bring it back to normal.

27TH JUNE

My eyes flew open as the airship began to lower in the sky. Quickly, I sat up and glanced out of the window. The morning sky was filled with a myriad of pink and orange hues. The city of Urbis loomed up ahead. Surrounded by stone walls, the massive city was quite the spectacle. A few inner-city parks dotted the landscape, and trees lined the streets of the more affluent parts, but the majority of the giant metropolis was grey stone. In the inner parts where the government buildings were located and where the most affluent members of society lived, the houses and buildings were white. Coming in from above, it reminded me of a giant target. We drifted down slowly, and I took the time to straighten my clothes and pull up my hood. No one in Urbis knew I was coming, and I didn't know anyone who lived there save for a number of dignitaries who had visited the Badalah palace. But I wasn't close to any of them, and I didn't know where in Urbis they lived. I was happy to keep my trip as private as possible. I had work to do.

The conductor came around with a bag for us to put our garbage in as we began our final descent into Urbis. I tossed the sandwich wrapper from the tuna sub I'd bought from him the night before. On the other side of the aisle, the woman with the child threw a whole heap of wrappers in the bag. The child slept, his head on her knee and chocolate from last night's chocolate fest around his mouth.

I smiled, this time to myself, and turned my attention back to Urbis. Now that we were closer, I could see the city more clearly, the details, the people. A huge area was empty, reserved for the airship to land. We docked with a thump, and the little boy finally woke up.

My first job was to find the steeple I'd seen in the vision, but now that the whole city was laid out before me, I found that there were many steeples. Hundreds of spires, steeples, and chimneys were dotted around the vast city.

The doors opened, and I let the mother and child get out before me. The little boy stuck his tongue out as he passed, so I gave him a grin and stuck my tongue out back. It lifted my spirits, the simple act of communicating with another person, even if that person was three years old and covered in chocolate.

Pulling myself together and pulling my hood further over my face, I walked the few steps to the door and then down the steps to the cobbled streets of Urbis.

The immediate area around the massive airship was quiet except for the Urbis Express workers and those like me, who were getting off. I walked quickly away, not wanting to get caught up in the throng of people meeting their loved ones. At the far end of the square where it was quiet, I stopped and took a deep breath, trying to get a bearing on my surroundings. I'd up and left Badalah in such a hurry that I'd forgotten to bring a map with me. I'd brought enough money to see me through a couple of days and to buy a ticket back to Badalah, but not much more. Money wasn't something I ever had to worry about. One of the perks of being a princess was I didn't have to know the cost of anything, but the downside to that was that I didn't actually know the cost of anything. If someone were to ask me the price of a cup of coffee in Urbis, I wouldn't even be able to guess.

It didn't help that all the money I'd brought with me was in Rubees and not Urbis dollars. I needed to find a currency exchange quickly so I could buy myself a map and one of those coffees I didn't know the cost of.

Tall buildings surrounded the massive square that housed the airship station. Cafes took up most of the ground floors with seating set out outside where people sat and drank their coffee and ate cake. My stomach grumbled as I took it all in. I needed to find a currency exchange and fast.

A sudden gust of coldness hit me, making me turn on the spot to find the source of the breeze, but as I looked around, no one else had noticed the creeping coldness that had come in from nowhere. It reminded me of the time it had happened last week in Badalah when I was with my father.

I shrugged it off and glanced around at the number of side streets that radiated out from the square.

I took the one that looked most promising. The wide

street was one of the few that allowed vehicles. Most of Urbis was reserved for pedestrians, but some of the major roads allowed carriages and the steam vehicles from The Forge. The first time I'd come to Urbis, I'd been fascinated with the steam bikes that filled the streets, but now, I found them noisy and distracting, not to mention, dirty. The street was filled with people going about their business and flanked on either side by shops selling mostly clothing.

I could tell by the clothes displayed that this was neither the slums of Urbis on the outskirts, nor was it the exclusive boutiques that could be found nearer the center. The fashions of Urbis were so different from those of Kisbu and presented an eclectic range from the twelve kingdoms.

Ignoring the clothing stores, I hurried down the street, keeping my head down, only looking up long enough to find what I was looking for. Soon enough, I came upon a currency exchange where I swapped my Rubees for Urbis Dollars. After finding a place that sold maps, I headed to a cafe to grab myself breakfast and that coffee I'd been thinking about.

As I waited for my breakfast sandwich, I sipped on my coffee and spread the map out in front of me. It filled the table and hung over all four sides. I picked up the coffee cup and held it in my hand to allow the map to lie flat. I'd known, in a vague way, that Urbis was huge, but I'd not counted on just how massive it was. Nor had I counted on the sheer number of steeples that were marked on the map. I was on a fool's errand.

Downing the coffee, I rubbed my temples, wondering if I'd made a mistake. Small details were coming back to me about the night of my birth. The style of houses out of the window was not like the ones in this part of the city. I also remembered the run-down street and a partial street sign. The word I'd seen on the sign hit me when the waitress brought my sandwich and another coffee, which she put right on the map.

"Maple!" I said out loud as I remembered the word on the sign I'd seen.

"You want maple syrup?" the waitress asked, raising an eyebrow.

"Oh, no, thank you. I was talking to myself. Do you know any streets in Urbis that begin with Maple? Maple Street? Maple Lane?"

The waitress shrugged. "I don't know of any personally, but I reckon there will be quite a few what with all the maple trees we have."

She gestured to the cafe window and to the line of trees outside. They were maple trees. I'd not recognized them, but now that I looked closely, it was unmistakable what they were.

"Do maple trees only grow in this part of town?"

The waitress shook her head. "No, they are all over Urbis."

My heart dropped.

"Thanks," I said with a sigh, rubbing my finger on the handle of the coffee cup she'd brought out. The coldness I'd felt earlier had not left me despite the blazing June sun.

The waitress shrugged again and left me to get the order of a couple at the next table.

I looked back at the map, noting all the tiny streets, each with their name in minute writing. Finding the right Maple Street or Maple Lane or whatever it was would take me ages. I chewed on my sandwich as I perused the map, hoping the right name would jump out at me. With my eyes closed, I tried to picture the sign

I'd seen in the memory. It hadn't been the full sign. Only the word Maple could be seen within the foggy confines of Genie's magic. The dilapidated houses opposite the house I'd been born were tatty, with peeling paint and broken windows, some of which had been boarded up. The white steeple in the background didn't make sense. It wasn't in keeping with the grey stone buildings in the foreground. I massaged my temples and sipped at my coffee, trying to rid myself of the cloying coldness that seemed to be following me.

Something flashed, causing me to look up and away from the map. My heart sank as a man with a camera took another photo. I pulled my hood back up, but it was too late. I'd been in Urbis only a couple of hours, and already, I'd been spotted. There was no doubt in my mind that the man was a member of the Urbis paparazzi. He had the look of one. I'd certainly seen enough in my time. He wore jeans and a wrinkled jacket over a t-shirt with some graphic I didn't recognize on the front, and his stubble told me he hadn't shaved for a couple of days. On his head, he wore a blue cap. Thousand dollar camera, five-dollar outfit. Yep, he was definitely planning to sell my photo to the press.

The waitress and the lady at the currency exchange hadn't recognized me, but once word got out that there was a princess in town, I'd be mobbed. I folded the map, drank the coffee back quickly, and grabbed my half-eaten sandwich. My hope was that I could reason with the man with the camera, but when I got outside, he'd already disappeared into the throng of shoppers.

Pulling my hood further up, I hurried down the street. My priority now was finding somewhere to stay. Looking for a steeple near a street called Maple would have to wait.

I ran down the street, feeling lost in the scores of people, not knowing which way to go. I looked desperately for a hotel, but it was apparent that this was a street for fashion, not lodging.

I stopped to catch my breath. On the other side of the street, I saw someone pointing at me. It was the man with the camera from earlier, but now, he was with another man. When they saw me, they ran across the road in my direction. I turned and fled, taking one of the small pedestrian side streets. The buildings were much closer together here, with narrow cobbled pavements. Because the buildings were so high, they blocked the sun, leaving the street much colder and darker than the main street I'd just left. There were still shops here, but fewer and far between. I ran aimlessly, turning left and right, losing myself in the maze of back alleys.

Behind me, I could hear the footsteps of the men following. I'd fled because I didn't want my photo in the paper, not out of fear for my safety, but now that I was away from the hustle and bustle of the main street, I felt real fear. The weird coldness that I'd felt since landing in Urbis was still with me, but now, without the sun on my skin, I realized it was different from a normal cold. I could feel both. The normal temperature of the day on my skin and the creeping cold inside me, a force like nothing I'd encountered before. My street smarts, acquired on the streets of Badalah, had left me. I didn't know this place. I was quite literally lost. I turned a corner, only to find myself trapped. Fear gripped me until I pulled myself together. Only a couple of weeks ago, I'd stopped a thief in Badalah. I could handle a couple of reporters. I took a deep breath and felt for my knife.

My throat constricted as I realized that in my hurry

to get packed, I'd forgotten to bring it.

I had nothing except... the heat of magic swirled within me, fueled by my fear, burning through the bitter cold. I wasn't completely unarmed. I was my own weapon. I twirled around on the spot and pulled myself up to my full height as they rounded the corner.

"Yes, gentlemen," I said, pulling my hood down. "Can I help you? You seem to be following me."

The one without a camera, a short, pudgy man with ruddy cheeks and a balding head with tufts of straw-colored hair elbowed the taller one.

"You're right. It's 'er." He had a thick Urbis accent, drawling and skipping letters. "You're 'er, right?"

I sighed. These idiots weren't going to hurt me. At least, not now. Putting my picture in the paper would hurt my plans, though.

"Who do you think I am?" I asked, hoping they'd mistaken me for someone else.

"You're that princess, Gala something."

They couldn't even get my name right.

"What is it you want?"

The shorter of the two whipped out a notebook and pen. "Are you here on official duty?"

"I'm here for some peace and quiet. I'd like it if it could remain that way."

Behind them, I noticed a sign saying Hotel. I walked past them pointedly, trying not to freak out. They followed me into the hotel reception, taking photographs.

"Hi," I said to the young clerk behind the reception desk. "I'm Princess Gaia of Badalah. I'd like a room for the night, but before you give me a key, could you kindly show these gentlemen out. They are following me and taking photos. I'd like to not be disturbed."

Once the clerk had gotten over his shock at having

a princess come into his establishment, he did exactly as I asked him.

"Gentlemen, you heard Her Highness," he said, stepping out from behind the desk and shooing them as if they were unpleasant vermin. "Unless you have a room here, you are not welcome."

"We'd like a room!" the shorter one said quickly, elbowing the taller one who nodded in agreement.

"Not today, gentlemen. We're fully booked. I'd advise you to reserve your room ahead of time in the future."

"But you're letting her have one," the shorter man grumbled as the clerk shut and locked the doors with the two men on the outside.

"Thank you for that," I said, giving him an appreciative look. "And sorry to have caused you so much trouble."

"No trouble at all, Your Highness. It's my pleasure to serve. I'm afraid our penthouse suites are taken, but I do have a nice room on the fifth floor. It is likely not up to your standards, but it has a nice view."

"It sounds perfect. Thank you, er..."

"Alex, Your Highness."

His voice was fast and slightly high pitched, but he bubbled over in enthusiasm. I liked him immediately. I followed him up the stairs, grateful I only had a small bag to carry and gave him a tip as he opened the door to room 509 and handed me the keys.

Despite being located on a back street, the room was pleasant enough and, as the clerk had said, had a great view of the city over the roofs of the nearby buildings.

After throwing my bag down on the bed, I headed to the window to get a better view. I stepped out onto a small balcony. In the far distance, I could just about make out the tower of Urbis. It was one of the major landmarks of Urbis, situated in the central business district, right in the middle of the bullseye I'd seen earlier from up above. It looked so tiny from this distance even though I knew it to be the tallest building in the whole of Urbis, perhaps of all the kingdoms. I'd climbed it once with my father on a royal visit. Thousands of buildings stood between me and the tower. I counted the steeples. Almost a dozen, and those were just the ones between here and Inner Urbis.

Urbis was laid out in three distinctive districts. Inner Urbis was the place I knew best, having visited it a number of times on royal visits. This was where the elite lived and where all the laws were passed. The center of the bull's-eye was the most affluent district anywhere in the twelve kingdoms, and the people that ran it were, in a way, more important than the royals of each kingdom. The kings, queens, presidents, and prime ministers of each kingdom could make up any laws they wanted, but all of them had to be passed through the Urbis government. Inner Urbis was sophistication at its finest with the buildings there made of brilliant white stone and marble. The next circle outward and the largest of the Urbis areas was Middle Urbis. This is where I was now. Hundreds of thousands of people lived here, all going about their daily business. I heard a staggering statistic once. Most of the people living in Urbis never left the giant walls that surrounded it. Seeing the mass of humanity sprawled out in front of me, the dirty streets, the shops, the apartment buildings, it made me feel sad that the people that lived here missed out on so much. The magnificent mountains of Draconis, the beautiful flowered fields of Floris, the magical sky islands of Skyla. And of course, the sands of Badalah. I couldn't imagine spending my whole life within the confines of a walled city, even one as big as Urbis.

In the opposite direction to Inner Urbis was outer Urbis. I couldn't see it from where I was standing on the small balcony, but it was there, behind me somewhere. The derelict houses, the slums, my birthplace. As I looked out over miles of urban landscape, it hit home just how much of a job I had ahead of me.

28TH JUNE

Alex sent a complimentary breakfast to my room, along with a note saying he was available for anything I might need. I'd asked him the day before for solitude, and he'd been great about leaving me alone. Now, I needed answers. The map I'd bought was way too huge to sift through the thousands of street names. I needed help.

Down at the front desk, Alex bowed when he saw me.

"Your Highness, I trust you had a restful night?" His face was lit up with a thousand-watt smile, and he stood to attention, ready for whatever I was about to ask him.

"Perfectly. Thank you for the breakfast. I was

wondering if you'd be able to help me?"

His eyes shifted to the door of the hotel. I followed his line of sight to find a crowd of people, most of whom had cameras.

"I'm sorry to say that we haven't been successful in keeping the reporters away. I could send a messenger to grab you a carriage, and you could leave through the back door if you want to."

I sighed. Finding my birthplace was going to be hard enough as it was without a mass of reporters on my heels.

"It wasn't quite what I wanted, but I wonder, would you be able to come up to my room to aid me with something?"

I'd planned to show him the map right there on the counter, but I didn't want a posse of reporters gawking at my every move.

Alex raised his eyebrows but nodded. After telling some unseen person in the back office that he was running an errand and asking them to watch the reception desk, he followed me back to the room.

"I'm sorry to ask you to come up here," I said, rolling the giant map out on the low coffee table in the middle of the suite. "I need help with this. I wonder. Are you from Urbis? Do you know the streets well?"

"Born and raised, Your Highness," he said, sitting next to me on one of the low couches. "I know some of the areas pretty well. This is where we are now." He pointed to an area about halfway between the giant outer wall of Urbis and the bullseye of Inner Urbis.

"Where is it that you are looking for?"

"A street with the word maple in it. I don't know if it's Maple Street, Maple Avenue, Maple Crescent, or what."

He looked at me strangely, but let me continue

talking. “The houses on the street are made of brick. They aren’t kept very well. The wooden frames on the windows have peeling paint. There’s a steeple in the distance.”

“Ok. It sounds like you are thinking of one of the streets around the outer edge, before the wall. The older districts have rows of houses made out of brick. The problem you have is that we are talking miles and miles of houses. Urbis is much bigger than any other city. It’s almost a kingdom in its own right.”

“I can see that,” I said with a sigh. The map not only covered the table but hung down off the sides of the coffee table and draped onto the floor. “Do you know any Maple Streets?”

He shrugged but then offered me a good-natured grin. “No, but I can help you look. My break is in fifteen minutes, and the assistant manager can watch the reception until then.”

We each took a side of the map and scoured the tiny street names, looking for anything that mentioned the word Maple.

The minutes passed, turning into hours. Alex left when his break was over, coming back on his lunch hour with a coffee and a sandwich for each of us.

“Any luck?”

“Not really,” I said as he passed me the sandwich. “The street names are so small I can barely read them, and there are thousands of them.”

I took a bite of the sandwich, keeping my eyes on the map. “What about you? Is it madness down there? I've not dared look out of the window.”

“It’s not good,” Alex admitted. “I think every reporter in town has wind of you being here. I can’t get them to leave as they aren’t on the property, but they are stopping the guests from coming and going. I've dealt with four complaints this morning already."

I glanced up at him, ready with a sorry on my lips, but he gave me a smile, which I returned.

"Can you think of anything else at all that might help us?" he said, dripping some sauce from his sandwich onto the outer edge of the map and hurriedly wiping it off with his thumb.

"Nothing I can think of. Just the white steeple and the brick..."

"White steeple? It was white? You sure?"

I thought back to the magical memory Genie had conjured.

"Yes, I think so."

The clerk stood. "If you'll permit me, please follow me." He held his hand out for me."

He led me out of the room and down to the end of the corridor. A vase of flowers sat on a windowsill at the end. Alex pulled the gauzy curtain back a crack.

"Did it look like that?" he said, pointing to the far right.

In the distance, I saw a number of steeples, but only one was white. The others were grey or brown.

"It could be, but surely there are a great many steeples in Urbis that are white."

"That's true," the clerk said, closing the curtains again before any reporters noticed us. "Many of the places of worship of the gods in the central district have white steeples to match the other white buildings, but that steeple you saw wasn't in the inner district, it was in Outer Urbis. That is the only white steeple I know of in that area. It's also the only steeple I know of that isn't for a place of worship."

"It's not?"

"No," he said as we walked back to my room. "It's a nightclub. It used to be a church, but about twenty years or so ago, it was sold. The developer who bought it turned it into a nightclub. It's actually quite well known. People from all over Urbis go to it."

I ran back to my room and the map. "Can you point it out for me?"

He sat down and ran his finger over the map. I watched with bated breath as his finger finally stopped.

"There!"

I circled around the table to where he was sitting on the floor and looked at the small symbol that depicted a steeple. A circle with a cross on the top.

"It's still showing as an actual church on this map."

I barely looked at where he was pointing. Instead, my eyes scoured the map of the area nearby.

Finally, I saw it a short distance away. "Look!" I said, my voice brimming with excitement. "Maplechase Park!"

The clerk slapped a hand to his forehead. "I know that park. Why didn't I think of it? There's a Maplechase Crescent nearby too. A friend of mine used to live in that area before I moved here."

I looked down again. In the area, I found a Maplechase Road, a Maplechase Lane, and a Maplechase Drive. The writing was so tiny, and the streets so narrow that there could have been more, but at least, I was in the right area.

I stood up.

"Shall I hire you a carriage?" Alex asked, his eyes brimming with excitement. "It's a long way to travel. It will take you days on foot."

My own excitement waned. Days! I didn't want to be here for days. I needed to find out the information and get back to Badalah.

"How long will it take in a carriage?"

The clerk shrugged his shoulders. "If you set off straight away, you might get there very early tomorrow morning."

My face fell. It still wasn't quick enough. I didn't want to spend all night traveling. I'd already been gone two nights.

"You could take the train," Alex suggested. "It's maybe a couple of hours away. The trains are fairly frequent, and there is a station just around the corner from here."

I followed the tiny train line on the map and saw that one of the lines went to the area I needed to be.

"Thank you!" I said, folding the map and slipping it into my bag. "I'll do that. Please hold my room. I'll probably be back late."

"My pleasure. Come on. I'll take you out of the hotel's back entrance. No point in letting the media know where you are going."

I pulled on my coat, and the pair of us dashed down the stairs to the hotel kitchens. The chefs working there looked up in confusion as I ran through with Alex.

At the back door, he pointed to a small stone building up the street.

"If you run, you might be able to catch the half-past one train. If not, there'll be one at two-thirty."

I thanked him again and dashed up the cobbled alley.

The train station wasn't like the broad white buildings I remembered from my trips here in the past with scores of train lines snaking through them, the arteries of Urbis. This station had just two tracks and a small ticket office. As I got to the office, the sound of a train approaching filled the air. I looked down at my watch, a gift from my parents on my last birthday, to see that it was twenty-nine minutes past one.

"A ticket to here please," I said, pointing to the district on the map that I'd just unfolded. I didn't even know the name of it.

He gave me a bored look and gave me a ticket from his machine.

"Three dollars," he said, holding his hand out.

"Can I buy a return?" I asked as a great steam train pulled into the station. He gave a sigh and pressed a button on his machine.

"Six dollars."

I fished in my bag for my purse and handed over the money. People began to file past me as I stepped away from the ticket office. Most were heading down the platform away from the train, but some, like me, were waiting until we could board. When the last person headed past, I stepped up the small step onto the train.

Along one side, a long corridor ran the entire length of the carriage with compartments taking up the other side. I opened the door to one, relieved to find it empty. The ticket collector hadn't recognized me, but that didn't mean no one else would. It seemed that the troubles of my own kingdom had not reached here yet, and I didn't want to gamble on being followed. As I let the thought go round in my mind, the platform outside the train filled with people. I ducked down, but it was too late. I recognized some of the reporters from the hotel. Somehow they'd found me. I willed the train to move off quickly before any of them could get tickets, but it felt like a painfully long time before the train began to rumble, and we pulled out of the station.

I sat, waiting for the inevitable rush of reporters to

my compartment, but after ten minutes had gone by, I relaxed. Maybe they hadn't seen me at all, or maybe they hadn't been able to purchase a ticket in time. I sat up straight in my chair and watched the streets of Urbis whizzing by.

I saw an Urbis I'd never seen before, and I wished I had time to stop and explore. Every so often we'd stop at a station and people would get on and off, but no one ever tried to come into my compartment. Every time we stopped, I looked up the name of the station on the map, following the tiny train line drawn on it and counting down the stations until my stop. Two and a quarter hours after I'd started my journey, the train pulled into the station I'd memorized as being the closest to the area with the streets named Maplechase.

I stepped off the train, hoping to get some fresh air, but one deep breath and a lungful of sooty air later, I had to step away from the train. The streets in this area were nothing like the posh streets in Inner Urbis, but they were also a far cry from the shopping area where I'd spent the last night. There were shops here too, but nothing like the boutiques that lined the main street near the hotel. These were a cobbled-together mishmash of buildings, none of which looked like it would stand up to a strong gust of wind. Still, a thrill of anticipation ran through me. The buildings were made of brick. Pulling out the map, I found the station I'd just come from and traced a line to the first of the Maplechases.

Behind me, I heard my name being shouted.

"Princess Gaia!"

I turned to find a dozen flashes, nearly blinding me. The reporters and photographers had been on the train after all. They'd just waited to see where I'd get off before announcing themselves.

I turned away from them and ran. Yes, I could have stood up to them, but they'd never leave me alone. Running was my only option. I took off down a back street, glad that I was wearing jeans and not my traditional dress. I'd had no idea just how much my dress hampered me until now. Behind me, the paparazzi chased me as I ran through the unfamiliar streets, ducking and weaving around the evening shoppers and various animals that seemed to be everywhere. Dogs, cats, even chickens, sheep, and goats. The streets were even narrower here than they were in the mid-part of Urbis and the buildings were taller, blocking out most of the light. I turned corners, keeping my speed up, getting lost, and all the while they followed, keeping up with me despite me running as fast as I could. The further I ran into the winding maze of streets, the darker it became until I could barely see anything in front of me despite it being the afternoon. The coldness I'd felt the other day crept up on me again, but this time I kept it at bay with the heat of my magic. I turned, anger burning me up. The reporters stopped short when they saw me watching them. Some of the people with cameras brought them up, ready to take another shot of me, but I was too quick. Pulling all my magical energy into my core, I shot it out. A huge ball of fire hurtled at the men, causing them to run away from me. I was a fire woman! I turned back to my original direction and carried on running, this time only stopping when I was sure they wouldn't be able to find me. I dropped to the ground, and sat with my back to a shop wall, out of breath as a shopkeeper opposite me gave me a quick nod then shut his door, turning the open sign to closed.

Exhaustion filled me, partly from the running and

partly from the expending of energy the ball of fire had caused. Now that I didn't have the heat of magic to keep me warm, the strange coldness surrounded me, turning my breath to vapor. I lowered my head, bringing it to my knees and pulled my jacket more tightly around myself, all the while wishing I'd never left the comfort of my home and started on this ridiculous journey. I wasn't helping the people of Badalah; I was on a wild goose chase. I missed Genie. I missed my mother and father. I missed my own bed.

Something landed on my shoulder with a soft thump, and the coldness drifted away. Pulling my head up quickly, I saw it was Asher.

"Asher! How did you find me?"

Asher whistled and nuzzled his feathery head against my cheek. I reached up and stroked his head, never more glad for the company.

"You flew all this way and found me."

Genie had said there was a magical connection between Asher and me. I hadn't really understood what he meant before now. Asher had flown hundreds of miles and known exactly where I was.

"Come on, Ash," I said, getting to my feet. "Let's go find my birth mother."

Asher took off from my shoulder and flew upward, landing on a street sign. Not any old street sign, a street sign saying Maplechase Lane. I'd inadvertently run away from the reporters to exactly the place I needed to be. But this street was wrong. I couldn't see the white steeple from here, and even though the houses were similar to the ones in the magical memory, none of them were exactly right. Still, if I was on Maplechase Lane, it meant the other Maplechases were nearby. The streets were dimly lit by lamps as the sun continued its journey down in the sky. I walked the streets, following the map as best I could in the dim light. Every time I found a Maplechase, I walked the street slowly, but it wasn't until I hit Maplechase Drive that everything suddenly fell into place.

"This is it, Asher," I whispered. The street was empty, and there was no need for me to whisper, but I felt that if I spoke out loud, I might jinx myself.

One side of the street had the same multi-story blocks of apartments that I'd come to expect in this area, but the other side had a row of single-story houses. Peeking above them in the distance, the white steeple of the nightclub showed above.

I'd expected something more interesting, something better than this, but the ramshackle houses were a far cry from the palace I was brought up in. "My mother wanted better for me," I whispered to Asher as I knocked on the door that looked the closest to the correct area.

A man in his thirties with a beard and glasses opened the door.

"Hi," I said. "I know this is going to sound strange, but I'm looking for someone who used to live on this street about eighteen years ago. Two women, a younger one with long dark hair and an older lady with grey hair in a bun."

Even as I spoke, I knew it was a long shot. This guy would have been a kid eighteen years ago, and the description I gave him wasn't particularly useful.

"I've lived in this house my whole life, and my mother was a blonde before her hair turned gray," the guy said, dashing my hopes, "but there was an old lady that lived next door. Jean. She died late last year."

"Did she have a daughter?"

The man shrugged. "Not that I know of. I'm sorry I

couldn't be more help."

I thanked him, and he closed the door.

When I knocked on the door of the house next to his, a woman with a toddler on her hip answered. It wasn't the woman from my dream, but the kitchen behind her looked awfully familiar. My heart sped up as I took in the details of the kitchen. It had been updated a little, but the range cooker was the same as the memory. Somewhere in this building, two babies were born. Myself and my twin.

"Hi. I'm sorry to intrude, but I think I was born in this house. I'm looking for my birth mother."

The woman's eyes widened, and she gave me a smile. "I just bought this house with my husband a few months ago. There was an elderly lady living here before us. I'm afraid I didn't know her."

"Do you happen to know if she had a daughter?" I asked, feeling ridiculous. "I've come a long way to find her."

She regarded me with almost pity. "Why don't you come inside for a cup of tea? You look exhausted. I'll tell you everything I know about the house. I'm not sure it will be enough to help you."

"Any information you have will help," I said, accepting her offer. The toddler gazed in wonder at Asher as her mother boiled a kettle of water on the stove.

I sat in the exact place my mother had sat in the memory. The kitchen table and chairs were different, and the kitchen walls had been updated, but I knew this was where I was born. I could feel it. Somewhere in a room upstairs, my mother had pushed myself and my brother into the world. The older woman had died, but if she had been related to me, and I found out her name, I might find out who my mother was. Maybe the old lady was my grandmother or aunt.

"This place was a bit of a mess when we moved in," the woman said. "I'm Kate, by the way. This is Elise." She pointed to the baby who was gazing at Asher with a rapt expression.

"Gaia. The beauty flying around over our heads is Asher. He's a phoenix." It was clear she didn't recognize me as the princess of Badalah, which made me feel a little better. At least, I wouldn't have to worry about her rushing to the press the second I left.

"A rare bird," Kate smiled.

"What do you know about the lady that lived here before you? Do you know if she had a daughter?" I asked again.

Kate took a deep breath then blew on her tea. "I only know what the agent who sold me the house told me. The lady lived on her own. She had no relatives as far as I'm aware. At least, this house wasn't passed down to any of them. It was taken by the government when no one came forward as a relative. We got the place pretty cheap as it needed a lot of work."

"I don't suppose she left anything behind, did she? Any scrapbooks, newspaper clippings, anything?"

Kate shook her head. "It was empty when we bought it. Some of the furniture was left behind, but a lot of it was old. We threw most of it away and bought new when we renovated. I'm so sorry that I can't be of more help to you. What makes you think that you were born here?"

"It's a long story," I said, finishing my tea and standing up. I felt magic in this place. It mingled with my own, but it felt like it was faded like the wallpaper in the memory. "I'm sorry to take up your time."

She stood and rifled through a drawer. When she

came back, she handed me a photo. My heart thumped as I recognized the old woman. "This is the only thing left behind that I kept," Kate said. "I was holding on to it in case any of her relatives did come to find out about her. I should have thrown it away months ago. You can keep it."

"Thank you," I said, tucking it into my pocket. I'd already known I was born here, but the photograph was proof.

Asher flew through the front door when Kate opened it.

She seemed nice enough, and Elise was a peach, but I'd come a long way for nothing. I thanked her for her time and began the long trek back to the train station.

The next-door neighbor peeked his head out as I passed.

"I remembered something that might help you," he said.

"Oh?"

"Jean's death. It was weird."

I walked closer to him, suddenly wondering if I'd not made a mistake in coming here after all.

"What was weird about it?"

"It might be nothing. She was old after all, but the day before she died, she was visited by a tall woman wearing a long black and purple cloak."

"And?" I prompted, hoping that wasn't the extent of what he was going to tell me.

"I saw the woman walk past through my window. She reminded me of a witch. There was something creepy about her."

"Maybe it was a friend of Jean's?"

"I doubt it. I'd never seen her before. Anyway, about five minutes after she arrived, there was a bit of commotion next door. A bang. Then I saw the tall woman walking past my door again, heading out in the opposite direction. I didn't think that much of it, but a couple of days later, I saw the police there. They'd found her body."

"You think she was murdered?" I asked my heart racing at the thought of it.

The guy shrugged his shoulders and leaned in closer to me.

"I can't say for sure. The police said that she'd died of natural causes, but I hadn't seen her since that tall woman had visited and she usually walked past my window and waved if she saw me. She must have died around the time that woman was there or not much later."

"Did you tell the police?"

"I did, but they weren't interested. Nobody cares about people in this part of town. Especially old retired midwives."

"She was a midwife?" Well, that explained why she was at my birth. She wasn't related to me at all.

"Until she retired, yes. She retired a few years ago now."

"When exactly did she die?"

The man screwed his face up in concentration. "It was late last year some time...or early this year. It was after the Winter Festival sometime."

I thanked him and set back off on my way with Asher flying above me. The train station was almost empty, and the reporters were nowhere to be seen. I hopped on the next train and thought about the tall woman, the witch that the neighbor had spoken of. It didn't help me find my mother, but it was interesting that Jean had died at around the time of my eighteenth birthday.

I thought back to the memory. My mother had said she wanted to keep me safe for eighteen years because of her father. Was the witch-like woman that the neighbor spoke of something to do with my own grandfather? If the neighbor was right and she had killed Jean, she'd have no second thoughts about killing me too.

I'd worried about my safety ever since stepping foot in this part of Urbis, but for the first time, my worries became personal.

If Jean told the witch where she'd taken me as a baby, did that mean she'd go to Badalah to find me?

I was glad when the train pulled into the station in Mid Urbis, and I could get to the hotel and sleep. Tomorrow I'd have to find out what exactly was going on.

29TH JUNE

After my stunt with the fireball the day before, the front of the hotel was swarmed with reporters, all desperate, no doubt to see me conjure fire again. I heard them before I even opened my curtains to look, but as I peeped through the crack in the curtains, I could see that they filled the whole street.

I'd managed to sneak out of the back door yesterday, but as they'd caught up with me at the station, I had to admit to myself that it was an ineffective solution. I needed a way to get rid of them altogether.

Downstairs, Alex ran over to me the second he saw me.

"I'm so sorry!" I said as he ushered me away from the line of sight of the glass doors at the hotel's entrance.

"It's no problem, Your Highness. I was wondering if

you would be leaving the hotel today at all?"

"I was hoping to attend to some business, but the reporters followed me yesterday. I think they must have had someone stationed at your other exit who signaled to the others."

"I have a plan." His eyes widened in glee as he pulled out a garment bag that had been hanging on a hook. He opened it up and held a traditional Badalah dress up in front of me.

"I'm pretty sure I'll not manage to sneak past them in that if I couldn't manage to do it in jeans and a t-shirt," I mused, looking at the bright yellow garment.

"It's not for you. It's for me."

I raised an eyebrow in query.

"I'm not sure yellow is your color," I said.

He smirked. "I put this on. Cover my head with the veil and sneak out the back. As you said, they'll have someone there waiting to signal the others. I'll lead them on a merry little dance around town while you do whatever it is you need to do."

He looked at me with so much expectation that I had to laugh. I had a feeling he was going to enjoy pretending to be a princess for the day.

"Thank you."

Ten minutes later, I was peeking through the tiniest crack in the office door watching the reporters. Alex had left to sneak out around the back just a minute before, dressed as he said he would be in the yellow dress. Sure enough, the crowd of reporters responded to a signal and began to run off. When they'd all left, I stepped out.

"You know he was planning this all day yesterday," the girl on the reception desk said with a grin. "He's planned to visit all of Urbis's landmarks and hit the shops."

"I feel so terrible."

"Don't," she laughed. "I've been trying to get him to take a day off for months. He's going to have a whale of a time. Just make sure you do what you have to and get back here before he makes the big reveal."

"The big reveal?"

"He's planning to climb to the top of the Urbis tower and throw his veil to the wind."

I laughed at the image. The Urbis Tower was a landmark I knew well. It was part of the Urbis governmental building, and one of the few parts of the building opened to the public. If he was going there, he'd have to get the train.

I headed out into the deserted street and whistled for Asher, who'd been waiting on my hotel room balcony for my signal. After pouring over the map last evening, I knew exactly where I needed to go. I also knew I'd have to go to the train station again. I dawdled for half an hour, admiring the fashions in the shop windows before heading to catch a train. The last thing I needed was to bump into any of the reporters who might be still at the station after following Alex.

The train to central Urbis was much more packed than the train I'd caught the day before. Hundreds of commuters squeezed together on the train. This time there were rows of seats rather than compartments, and as these were already full, I had to stand.

I kept my head down and my hood up, hoping that no one would recognize me. It was a stark contrast to a week or so ago when I'd hoped that the public *would* recognize me.

As we pulled into the station at the end of the line, the train car emptied of businessmen and women, who filed out to their executive jobs in the center of Urbis.

The central district of Urbis never failed to amaze me with its beautiful white buildings. The main capital building was the grandest by far, it's majestic columned facade dominating the cobbled square right in the very center of the bullseye. As I stood looking at the main doors, the Urbis library stood to my right, and various government buildings that weren't quite the main building stood to my left. Behind me were apartments in the same style that only the wealthiest of the wealthy could afford, and on a slight hill behind the main government building, the huge Urbis University could be seen. Standing in this square always took my breath away. My father and my mother were the wealthiest people in Badalah, but the combined wealth of the people that lived in a five-mile radius of this square was more than that of all the twelve kingdoms combined. At least that was what I'd been told when I'd last come here for a royal visit. I could believe it. The streets were pristine despite the thousands of feet that walked them daily. I turned to my right and headed to the Library. It was the one place I'd been the most excited to see on my last visit, but we'd been rushed through it by some diplomat eager to talk business with my father. I wasn't going to be able to go inside now either, but I vowed to take a look after doing what I'd come here for. Behind the library was the records building. I stood in awe of it. In my head, I'd expected a mid-sized nondescript building, but this was equally as impressive as the library that stood in front of it. The words Urbis Central Archives dominated the white stone facade above the double doors. I made to open one of the huge wooden doors, wondering how I'd be able to move such a colossal door, but it yielded at the slightest touch, opening up to the place where the birth and adoption records were. If I was born in Urbis, a record of it would be here.

The inside was even more impressive as the outside. The circular building with its domed roof was full of boxes of records spanning the whole history of Urbis and its people.

"Hi," I said to the receptionist behind a large circular desk. Above me, a bunch of papers clipped to a pulley system flew, almost knocking poor Asher out of the air. The whole place was a hive of activity with papers flying left and right on the pulleys' wires. People like me sat in booths to give them privacy while workers in blue uniforms rifled through the boxes, pinning the required papers to the right wire to go to the right person. The scope of the place had me in awe, and I wondered why I'd never been shown here on any of my royal visits. "I'd like to see your birth records."

Her smile widened. "Of course. Is there a particular year you'd like to see?"

I told her the approximate date of my birth and told her a little of my story, keeping out the magic part. She pulled a brass key out from somewhere under her desk.

"Please follow me."

I followed her through the chaos of papers flying about over my head to a room with the year I'd given her engraved on a brass plate on the door.

"If you don't know if you were born in January or December the previous year, you might have to change rooms. A junior archivist will be in shortly to help you."

I'd expected shelves filled with records, but instead, there was a leather-covered table, two chairs, and wooden cabinets lining the walls.

I sat on one of the seats and waited. A couple of minutes passed, and a young man in a blue uniform strode into the room. He had an eager expression on his face, and on his lapel, he had a badge bearing the name Derek.

"I hear you are looking for information about your birth. What do you know?" He opened his arms wide, waiting for me to answer.

"Not much, I'm afraid. My name is Gaia. I was adopted in Badalah, but I was born here."

He licked his lips and suppressed a grin. "You are Princess Gaia, aren't you? I thought so."

I gave him a smile.

"I'd appreciate it if you could keep my search discrete. The people of Badalah know I'm adopted, but they don't know that I'm looking for my birth parents. I'm afraid I don't know the exact date of my birth. It was probably late December, but it could have been early January. I came to my parents in the second week of January."

"Came to your parents? Didn't they adopt you in Badalah? Don't they have the records?"

"I'm afraid not," I said with a rueful grin. "I was kind of left on the doorstep."

"And the king and queen took you in?" Derek asked with amazement.

"It's not as bad as it sounds. My birth mother dropped me at the palace. Anyway. All I know is that I was born in the outer part of Urbis eighteen years ago. My name is Gaia, which was given to me by my birth mother. She never left a surname."

"That's going to be tough," Derek said, clapping his hands together. "But, as luck would have it, I enjoy a puzzle. I can look through the records and see how many Gaia's we had born in that time frame."

"Thank you."

He pulled a key from his pocket. It was attached to his jacket by a small chain. The cabinets were filled with boxes, each labeled with a date.

I was dismayed to find they were not in alphabetical order. It was going to take a significant amount of time to go through all the boxes of the months of December and January.

"Can I help?" I asked, standing up. Derek held his hand out to me. "I'm sorry. It's not permitted. I'll go through and bring you any of the documents I think might fit." He pulled a pair of gloves from his pocket and, after pulling them on his hands, started going through the first box. I was forced to sit still, twiddling my thumbs while he sifted through the first batch.

"Just how many people are born in Urbis every day?" I asked, trying to estimate how long it would take to go through the thirty-one days of December and the thirty-one days of January.

"We have hundreds of births registered here every day. Plus, the other registry offices throughout Urbis bring their birth, marriage, and death registrations to us daily. Don't worry, I've been doing this a long time. I know how to sift information quickly."

He wasn't wrong. His fingers moved so quickly, sorting through the papers that they were almost a blur. From the first box, he pulled one file, which he let me look at as he moved to the second box.

The document held the name of the parents and the name of the Child. Gaia Louise Middleton. Her parents were Janet and Alfred Middleton from Middle Urbis.

There was no mention of a boy born to the same mother.

"If the baby has a twin, would they share a birth certificate?"

Derek stopped what he was doing and eyed me with surprise. "No, but multiple births are mentioned on each of the babies' certificates so we can cross-reference. If there is a mention of it, it will be on the top right with a code or codes to match up the certificates. Are you a twin?"

"I don't know...maybe," I lied. No point making this more complicated than it already was.

I looked at the top right. No code. This Gaia was an only child. She felt wrong. I didn't have a middle name. If my birth mother had given me my first name, surely she'd have mentioned a middle name too? Plus, the father was mentioned. Not once in the memory was he brought up at all. He certainly wasn't at the birth. I had the feeling that he wasn't in the picture at all.

I put it to one side and waited for the next file. After three hours and one room change, I had a stack of thirty-seven Gaia's born within the time frame I'd given to Derek. Not one of them showed a code for a multiple birth.

"Is this all of them?" I asked as I handed Derek the last file back for him to file.

"I've never once in all the time I've been working here failed to find the information requested. Just because you don't have a birth certificate doesn't mean clues about your birth aren't here."

I didn't have a birth certificate. It was like I didn't exist at all.

"What clues could possibly be here?"

"Look around you." Derek said as we walked back through the huge domed part of the main building. As before, it was a hive of activity with files flying around the room by the thousand. Asher sat on my shoulder for fear of being knocked out of the air. "We use the most sophisticated systems from The Forge to get information quickly. A group of mages works in the lower basement dealing with magical information, and we have staff from all the twelve kingdoms, each an expert on their particular kingdom. For example, over in that room there..." he pointed to a closed door, one of many that circled the large room we were in. "There is a collection of Atlantice shells dating back hundreds of years. And in a temperature-controlled vault, we have the seeds of every known plant in all the kingdoms. We have more seeds than Floris. I think if we have all that, we should be able to find out more about where you came from."

However impressive his talk was, I was not a seed from Floris, nor a shell from Atlantice. I was a person without a history.

"Thank you, but I have to go home. I've been away too long." I turned to leave, but he put his hand on my shoulder to stop me. "I'll find something, Your Highness. I've not failed yet. I'll happily post anything I find to the palace in Badalah."

I gave him a smile. I'd met some of the best and some of the worst people on my trip. As I went to thank him, a thought crossed my mind.

"If you send me something, please put it in a yellow envelope."

It was a weird request, but with the hundreds of marriage proposals coming via the post every day, a letter would get lost among them. This way, I could ask the palace staff to bring the envelope straight to me.

He didn't even question me about it. "I sure will. It was a pleasure to help."

Back outside, I treated myself to a stop at a cafe in the cobbled square in front of the library and sat at one of the outdoor tables. I ordered lunch and a coffee to collect my thoughts. The sun shone brightly in the sky, making me think of home where it was almost always sunny. I made to take my coat off, but the freezing cold that had been bothering me for days made a sudden reappearance. I squinted up at the sun, wondering if a cloud had passed in front of it, but there wasn't a cloud to be seen. I pulled my coat around myself as a waitress brought my lunch.

Asher circled overhead, stretching his wings as I ate. Hundreds of people walked through the square, each of them dressed immaculately, going about their business as I mulled over the information or lack of information I had. I knew I'd been born in Urbis, and I knew I had a brother out there somewhere, but neither of us existed on paper. As I ate my sandwich, I watched the men go by, wondering if any of them was my brother.

I'd never really put much thought into having siblings, but now that I knew I had one, my heart ached to meet him. What was he like? Did he look like me?

My skin was significantly darker than that of my mother's, though I'd looked pale at birth too. Now, I looked the same as everyone else in Badalah. All except for my eyes. Somewhere out there, there was a man with eyes like mine.

I was still thinking about him when the cold I'd been feeling turned bitter, like a gust of freezing air that drilled right down to my bones. My magical heat was extinguished inside me. A flash of purple and gold appeared in the corner of my eye, distinctive against the blacks, grays, and blues of the business attire. I turned quickly, feeling a strange pull of cold magic, but when

I looked at the crowds of people, nothing seemed out of place. My heart raced with anticipation, but for what? Dropping my sandwich and leaving a few Urbis dollars as a tip, I called for Asher and began the trip back to the train station, eager to get back to the safety of the hotel. Everyone around me was wearing clothes fit for a summer's day, and yet, the icy temperature had me shivering. This wasn't normal. There was no doubt in my mind that the cold was made by a magical source, affecting no one but me. As soon as the train came in, I jumped aboard, in a hurry to get back to the hotel. The feeling of magic still gripped me, but it was nothing like the magic of Genie or my own magic. This one was cold and evil and had me shivering, desperate to outrun it. As the train began to pull off, I saw a flash of gold and purple. I spun my head around quickly to the people still on the platform.

My blood ran cold when I saw who it was that had been following me. The man in the purple and gold was my grandfather's Vizier. The same sorcerer who'd tried to take the throne before my father saved us all.

He was supposed to be dead. No one had seen him in eighteen years, but as I looked into his eyes, cold and hard, I knew it was him. The evil Vizier was back, and he was following me.

30TH JUNE

I'd spent the night in my room, not daring to come out. The reporters were back and were, in a way, more comforting than the thought of the Vizier. Up here in my room, the coldness had once again receded, but now that I knew where it had come from, the fear of it remained.

I sat on the bed unsure of what to do. The Vizier was back, and it seemed he was after me. He'd not got on the train with me yesterday, but he'd known where I was.

And it was him, I was sure of it. I'd seen photos of him before, shown to me by Genie, who had told me the story about how my father had defeated him so many times it felt as though I'd lived through it myself, despite it happening before I was born.

I'd learned precisely nothing on this trip, and yet, I'd managed to find more danger. I still didn't know who my mother was, just that she'd never registered my birth. It meant that I'd probably never find out who my brother was either.

"It's time to go home," I said to Asher, who peeked out from under his wing and clicked his beak.

I'd set out to make things better, but I'd only made things worse. I missed Genie. I missed home, and however much I hated to admit it, I was scared.

After packing what few things I had, I headed downstairs to the reception desk. Alex gave me a wide smile when he saw me, but his face dropped when he spotted my bag.

"Checking out?"

"Yes, please. I do appreciate all you've done for me."

The flashes from the photographers bounced off his face as they tried to get a shot of me through the glass doors.

"I've enjoyed every minute of it!" he said with a grin. "I'm only sorry that I couldn't get rid of them properly for you. I could try again today."

I pulled out my purse and gave him enough to cover my nights in the hotel and a hefty tip. He deserved every penny. "I doubt they will fall for it a second time," I said wistfully. "Did you manage to get up the Urbis Tower?"

"I did! It was bloody marvelous!"

I smiled at his enthusiasm. "I saw the tower yesterday too, but I left before you got there, I think."

After thanking him, I turned to the photographers and reporters. Their cameras continued to flash even though the pictures would come back with the flash reflected on the windows. I was going to give them what they wanted. What they'd been following me for days to get. I was going to give them an interview. I wasn't going to be honest with them, but I was going to speak to them, nonetheless. Their presence had been nothing but a nuisance, but with the Vizier out there, it was now a comfort. If I was surrounded by people, no matter how annoying, he wouldn't be able to get me.

Let the reporters follow me. Let them walk the main street alongside me and take pictures of me stepping onto the Urbis Express. There was no way I was getting out of Urbis without my picture being on the front page of the Urbis newspapers anyway.

"Gentlemen," I said, stepping out of the front entrance of the hotel, making sure to smile at the cameras. "I'm sure you'd all like to know what I've been up to here in Urbis."

The men, for they were all men, pulled out their pencils and notepads and began to scribble while those with cameras carried on, snapping away.

"I'm here on vacation. I wanted to see the real Urbis, away from the confines of a royal tour. You found me out on my very first day."

"What have you been doing in Urbis?" one of them asked.

"I visited the shops, and just yesterday, I took a train to see the Urbis Library. It is a place I've long wanted to visit alone. I'm sure you know my love of books."

I only hoped none of them had seen me. I didn't think so, and I supposed it didn't matter.

"What about the day before when you visited Outer Urbis?"

I knew they'd ask me and I'd already come up with an answer.

"Outer Urbis was never on the schedule for any of the royal tours, and I wanted to see it for myself. I had a lovely evening looking at the shops there."

"You threw a fireball at us," the guy continued. "How did you do that?"

I laughed, hoping it sounded sincere. "A fireball? Let's not get silly, gentlemen. There was a strange flash of lightning, I grant you, but let's not make it into something it wasn't."

"We saw you conjure it. It came out of your hands. Are you magic?"

I held my hand up to my face. "Of course not. If I was magic, the press of Badalah would have already reported it. If it was a fireball, surely you'd have gotten burned. Are any of you burned, gentlemen?" I looked around them, already knowing their answer. I could have burned them if I'd have chosen to, but I'd thrown them some warning magic with only a hint of heat. The fireball had looked a lot more dangerous than it actually was.

"No, but..."

"Lightning!" I reiterated. "I wish I could do magic. As it is, I can't."

The cold I'd been so fearful off began to creep up on me, wrapping tendrils of ice around my heart.

"If you want to follow me, you'll see I'm heading to the Urbis Express station to make my way home," I said, trying to step through them.

The guy who'd been asking the questions stopped talking, and I thought I might be allowed to leave, but then another one began.

"What's your take on what is happening in Badalah at the moment?"

I gritted my teeth and tried to keep the smile on my face. I did not want to have an in-depth discussion on the state of my kingdom. My eyes darted to each side, but the Vizier had yet to make his appearance known. These men couldn't feel him, but I could. He was close. "I don't quite know what you mean."

"Your father has vanished."

Damn. He knew about that? It meant that outside of Badalah, the people remembered him. It was little comfort. If the press were printing their stories, the mess we were in would spread like wildfire.

"My father is merely doing what I am doing. Taking a break. This is no conspiracy. We are just taking a little time for ourselves. I chose to come here, my father chose to vacation in Badalah." Ok, it wasn't exactly a lie. He *was* in Badalah somewhere. "My mother is perfectly capable of running the kingdom in our absence. Now, if you don't mind, I have an airship to catch."

I started to walk through them forcefully, but something stopped me. The cold intensified. I looked over my shoulder. About fifty feet down the alley, the Vizier stepped out from a side street, his purple and gold cloak flapping in the wind. Asher flew down to my shoulder.

"What about the unrest in Badalah?" the reporter asked, obviously unaware of the interloper. "There's word that your mother is falling apart."

"Excuse me," I said, attempting to push through them. If the Vizier was coming, I didn't want to be here.

A gust of wind hurtled down the narrow alley, blowing Asher from my shoulder and almost knocking me over with its severity. I grabbed hold of the hotel doorhandle as the reporters struggled to stay upright.

My options were limited. I could duck back into the hotel, try to push through the reporters, many of whom had fallen to the ground, or I could try another way.

"Asher!" I yelled as I ran deliberately toward the Vizier

before ducking down a side alley. From memory, this whole place was a warren of alleys and passageways twisting and turning, maze-like to goodness only knew where. Ahead of me, Asher flew, pushing me to run faster. Another bolt of wind flew up the narrow passageway sending Asher spiraling through the air and me falling to the ground.

I turned over and pulled myself into a sitting position with the intention of getting up and running, but it was too late, the Vizier was already almost upon me.

"How did you do it, I wonder?" he said, scratching his goatee beard. "You were but a babe in arms."

"I don't know what you are talking about," I spat, trying to sound more defiant than scared.

"Defeated me. I was the most powerful sorcerer in all of Badalah."

"My father defeated you."

The vizier narrowed his black eyes at me, then threw his head back and began to laugh. "Aladdin? Ha. Aladdin was nothing but a street rat. It was only luck that he became Sultan. It should have been me."

"My father became Sultan because my mother fell in love with him," I said, finally getting to my feet. Asher hovered over my head, ready to guard me. He wouldn't be able to, but I knew he'd try. "She fell in love with him because of all the good he did. Badalah has flourished since you left."

"Not that I've seen. Poverty, thievery. It's still there."

"Maybe, but at least it's not being done by those in charge."

The Vizier's eyes narrowed. "Aladdin might have done some things for Badalah, but he couldn't defeat me."

"Genie helped him."

"Genie. I'd almost forgotten about him. One click of my fingers, and I'll have him back in that atrocious lamp where he belongs. He is insignificant. I spent many, many years wondering how the Genie and a street rat defeated me, but it wasn't them. You did it, or so I've been led to believe. I just don't know how."

"You are insane. I've never met you before."

"Magic is a wondrous thing," he said, stepping closer.

I took a step back, trying to eliminate his coldness with my own magic.

"When you and your siblings were born, I lost my magic. I've been without it for a long time, but now that it's back, I'm going to make amends. No one in Badalah remembers your father. It's about time your mother fell in love again, and this time I won't let you stop me."

He pulled back his arm to lob another round of magic at me, but I was ready. I stood my ground, pulling all the heat I had left and hurtled it in his direction. The fireball lit up the alleyway, giving the grey buildings an orange glow. The Vizier's face also lit up, but with shock. I didn't stick around to see what he'd do next. Whistling to Asher, I turned on my heel and raced through the alleys until I was back on the main road. From there, it was easy enough to find the Urbis Express station. I bought a ticket for the first airship leaving. It meant stopping in Zhore in Draconis first, but with the coldness looming again, I wasn't prepared to hang around for the next Kisbu bound flight.

In the air, I scanned the ground to catch sight of him, but he was nowhere to be seen among the throngs of people. The effects of his magic didn't leave me until we were over the outer wall of Urbis and Flying over Draconis. But it was clear. Whatever was happening with Badalah, the Vizier was part of it.

THRONE OF THE PHOENIX

1ST JULY

The kingdom of Badalah shone like a crown in the desert, and Kisbu was the jewel in the center. The sun glinted off the domes of the palace as we came in to land. The giant airship of the Urbis Express lowered slowly in the sky, finally resting with a slight bump on the ground at the station.

All around the station, people were running, fear etched onto their faces.

"What's happening?" I said to the conductor who merely shrugged. I craned to see what everyone was running away from through the small windows. All I could see were people, all running toward the center of Kisbu. Hesitantly, I stepped down from the airship, and almost immediately, I was swept out into the crowd.

"Go home," I whispered to Asher. "I'll see you there." Asher rose into the sky as I was jostled along, caught up in the tide of fear. It was only as the gates of the palace came into view that it became apparent that these people weren't running from something but to something. They were crowding the palace, banging on the gates, shouting at the guards who stood at the other side of the gates. I pushed through to the front.

"What's happening here?" I shouted through to a guard, but he didn't even acknowledge who I was, let alone respond. Whatever was going on, I wasn't going to get answers here. Nor was I going to be let into the building. Fortunately for me, I'd been sneaking out of the palace at night for a year. It meant I'd also been sneaking into the palace. Pushing through the swathes of people, I heard them chanting for food. They were hungry, starving even. Young children were among them, the elderly. All the people my parents had sworn to protect were now crammed together in anger. The back of the palace wasn't as crowded as the front, but there were enough people there that would see if I climbed the vines I normally used to get over the walls. All it would take was one person to see me, and then they'd all follow. The palace would be swarmed with people. Angry people who were currently muttering threats about my mother.

As I continued on around the perimeter, I remembered another way into the grounds. A way my father had taught me not too long ago. He'd crawled through a gap in the wall, invisible to everyone as it was hidden behind a bush. I picked up my speed, keeping my hood up so no one would recognize me. Not that I knew if they would if I walked through them wearing full ceremonial costume and shouting my name, but I wasn't going to chance it.

When I was sure no one was looking, I dove into the bush and through the gap. Before anyone had the chance to see me, I followed the path my father had shown me down to the underbelly of the palace. From there, it was only a matter of walking into the main cellars and up to the palace. It was eerily quiet, a stark difference to the bedlam outside the walls. Fear gripped me as I wondered if anyone would remember me. My mother flitted in and out of her memory so often, and that was before I'd left for days.

As I walked through the palace, the sound of my shoes echoing off the marble floor was a poignant reminder of my situation. I was alone. The noise of the crowds outside remained, though, a distant chanting getting louder, the closer I walked to the front of the palace. I headed to the one man I needed to see more than anyone. Maybe he wouldn't remember me, but I remembered him. I was halfway down the corridor that housed his suite when someone called my name.

"Jamal!" I said when I saw who it was. I ran to him and almost fell into his arms. Almost, but not quite.

"What's happening?"

He pulled me away from the window that looked out over the front of the palace.

"I don't want them to see you," he said by way of explanation. "They aren't very happy with the monarchy at the moment."

"I can see that. Why? What's happened? Are they still mad that my mother held a party in the name of the out of towners?"

"I wish it was that simple," Jamal replied. He pointed to a set of stairs to the second floor. "Come on, I should show you the extent of the problem before I tell you what the problem is."

The stairwell was dark, and it was only as we began to climb the stairs that I realized why. The curtains covering the windows that opened out onto the royal balcony were closed.

At the top, Jamal pulled them back an inch to give me a view of the people outside. It was much worse than I feared. The balcony had been built for the royals to stand on and wave to the people during special occasions. From it, the view stretched on down Kisbu's busiest street for miles. It had been designed that way to allow as many people as possible to see us. It also meant that from here we could see them...all of them. People by the thousands filled the streets in every direction.

"Everyone in Kisbu is out there!" I exclaimed, stepping back from the curtain.

"Not quite," Jamal added, "but most of them. They are hungry. There's no food."

I ran my hand over the back of my neck, rubbing it to comfort myself. "We fed them a few days ago. Kisbu has plenty of food. They can't all be hungry."

"We fed the poor a few days ago."

"These aren't the poor?" I asked, confused. If they weren't poor, why were they protesting for food?

"You said it yourself. Most of Kisbu is out there—rich, poor, and everyone in between."

"I don't understand."

Jamal took my hands in his. "When you left, there was food in the shops. Now the shops are closing. They cannot buy food from the farmers. People who can afford food cannot get access to it. The whole of Kisbu has shut down. The gates are closed. The people of

Kisbu closed them to stop the out of towners, but now they can't get food in."

"You mean the people did this to themselves? Why doesn't Mother just demand that the gates to the city be opened again?"

Jamal slowly shook his head. "It was your mother that ordered them shut in the first place."

Now I was really confused. "Why would she do that?"

"She's gone, Gaia. Or at least, the memory of who she is has. Completely. Since you left, I've seen none of the woman I once admired. She was sad that you'd gone, but when I asked her about it, she couldn't articulate the cause of her sadness. When I said your name, there was no flicker of recognition."

This was my fault. Talking to my mother wouldn't help. If what Jamal said was true, the only way to bring her back was to solve this whole problem. The problem of the magical curse that was blighting our kingdom. I just wish I knew how to fix it. I sneaked another peek through the gap in the curtains. So many unhappy people. How had we spiraled into this in a matter of weeks? Then I saw something that tore my heart in two. Right near the gates, at the front of the crowd, was a man dressed in rags, not the Sultan's uniform I was used to seeing him in.

"My father is out there!" I said, turning to Jamal.

"Aladdin?"

He joined me at the window, and I pointed out the pathetic looking figure at the front. My father was practically eye-to-eye with one of the guards. The men he had personally hand-picked to serve the royals.

"Do we have food?" I asked.

"You don't need to worry on that score, Gaia. The kitchens are well stocked."

I turned and began to run downstairs.

"Where are you going?"

I paused, turning my head back to face him. "I'm going to open the gates. I'm going to let them all in."

"Are you serious?" Jamal said, chasing me down the stairs. But I was too quick for him. I knew what I was about to do was insanity. We'd be swamped, overrun with people, but I'd made a pledge to serve my kingdom. I might not be the Sultana, but I was the only royal in the palace who hadn't lost their mind.

In the main entrance, a lone figure stood at the doors. Peering through the glass.

"Freya!"

She turned around. Her face lit up immediately when she saw who it was. She ran toward me, but stopped short about five feet from where I stood. Her face lost its excitement, and her expression turned to one of worry. Her eyes darted to the side, just over my left shoulder. When I turned around to see what had gotten her attention, I saw Jamal just behind me shaking his head. When he saw me looking, he stopped.

"What?" I asked.

"You can't open the gates, Gaia. Look at the people out there. They are out for blood."

"They are out for food, and I'm going to give it to them." I turned back to Freya. "Can you go down to the kitchens and tell them to bring everything we have into the main hall?"

"Everything?" she asked quietly, looking more at Jamal than me.

"Everything!" I reiterated. "Jamal, find a guard. Take them to my mother. I'm assuming she is in her room. I want to make sure she is safe if things do turn nasty."

Jamal walked around me to stand between me and

the door. Just behind him, Freya watched on with tears in her eyes.

"Turn? Open your eyes, Gaia. Things are already nasty. If you'd have stayed here to deal with this mess rather than go off gallivanting to Urbis, you'd know how bad it's got."

"I can see for myself how bad it is, but my father is out there."

"Your father doesn't even know who you are!" Jamal shouted.

I stood stock-still, not used to the way he was speaking to me.

"I know who he is," I replied, standing my ground. "Now, please do what I ask you. I'm still in charge here."

He put his hands on his hips, blocking my way.

"Move...now!" I looked into his eyes, which had taken on a hard edge. He was taller than me, so I had to incline my head slightly, but I wasn't going to back down.

When it became apparent he wasn't going to move, I casually walked around him and opened the door to the palace. No one was going hungry while I was in charge, no matter what Jamal said.

The crowd jeered as I walked down the stairs to the gates. The noise rumbled through my ears, making me wonder if I was making the right decision, after all. But then I saw my father. While all those around him were shouting, he was still. He looked at me with such sadness that my heart broke.

"Open the gates!" I said to the nearest guard. At first, I thought he'd forgotten who I was, but then, I realized the look of incredulity he was giving me had more to do with my request than who I was.

Inside the guards' hut, was a horn. It was used to

announce ceremonial affairs to the public. Today was far from a ceremony, but if I could get at least some of the people's attention, then it would have to do. I ducked in, found the horn, and ran back up the stairs to the palace doors. Inside the open door, the entrance hall was empty, which meant either Freya and Jamal had acquiesced to my requests, or they had gone and hidden somewhere. I held the horn to my lips and blew with as much force as I could muster.

Immediately, the crowd quietened.

"People of Kisbu," I shouted. "I know you are hungry. I know you are scared, and I know you are angry. I'm going to open the gates of the palace to feed as many of you as we can. I hope to open the gates to the city too and solve the problems we are having. Until then, I invite you all to come and have a meal on us. I only ask that you line up in an orderly manner and take only what you need. We also have a limited supply of food, and I'd like as many of you to eat as possible. I want you to be assured that I'll be doing everything I can to solve the situation so that none of you go hungry in the future. Guards. Open the gates."

My heart almost stopped as the guards did what was asked of them. Despite my assurances, I wasn't sure how the crowds would react. I was in the doorway of the palace. If they wanted to overrun the palace, I'd be trampled in seconds. But as I watched, the people did exactly as I had asked, shuffling themselves into an orderly line once they were within the palace grounds.

I watched my father take his place at about twenty people back. I gave him a smile that he didn't return. When the man at the front of the line got to me, I ushered him inside.

"This way, ladies and gentlemen. I've asked the

kitchen staff to bring food into the great hall. There are two doors, one at the front and one at the back. I ask that you take your food and move through quickly to the back exit so that others can get food too."

Freya was in the hall with some of the palace staff. Long tables had already been set up, and the kitchen staff was busily bringing food in. It was a long cry from the banquets we usually put on in the grand hall. There were no decorations, no tablecloths or place settings. There were not even chairs for people to sit on, but there was food, and that was all that mattered.

I extended my hand in invitation for the people to go in.

"Freya!" I shouted as the people began to file past me. She turned her head in my direction and placed the platter she was carrying on one of the tables. I beckoned her over.

"Can you go to the other side of the hall and escort the people out once they've got enough food. They can walk the far corridor and out of the staff entrance. That should keep the flow of people going."

"There's not going to be enough food," she whispered. "What will we do when it runs out?"

I looked at the long line of people slowly snaking its way through the door. By some miracle, everyone was being orderly, but Freya's fear was justified. In our grand hall, we could seat and feed over a thousand people for a formal banquet, more for a buffet. We could probably handle as many as two thousand, but there were so many more people than that. I waited until my father came to the front of the line before I ventured into the crowd myself.

"We meet again," I said.

He smiled up at me. "This is a nice thing you are

doing. There are a lot of hungry people. They need someone to take charge. If I was the Sultan, I'd do the same."

I wanted to tell him that he was the sultan and that the only way I knew to do something like this was from following his lead. He'd made it his life's work to make sure that not one person in the kingdom went hungry. This was his legacy. I wanted to tell him all this, but I couldn't. I wanted to hug him, but I couldn't do that either. I had to let him go. To get his food along with all the others. At least, I knew he was alright, and he was eating. It was all I could hope for right now.

The staff was coming and going almost as fast as the people were filing in. They filled the tables up quickly then turned to head back to the kitchen to grab more. They knew the drill. They might not know my father. They might not even know my mother or me, but they knew how to do this.

I helped, collecting platters as they were emptied and passing them to the staff to refill. Freya joined in, helping along with most of the palace staff. I'd been letting people walk through for ten minutes or so when a figure appeared at the other end of the grand hall that made my heart soar.

The line was moving smoothly, so I left my place at the door, ignoring my own empty stomach and bounded through the hall that was filling rapidly.

"What's happening?" Genie asked.

"I opened the doors. I'm feeding them."

I waited for the lecture, but it never came. He gave me a smile. "I've never known anyone quite like you."

"So, you remember me?" I asked. My biggest fear was that he'd forget me again. Apparently, my mother had, and I knew, for a fact, my father only remembered me from our meeting the previous week.

"You are not easy to forget, Gaia. How did it go in Urbis?"

I pulled him out of earshot and told him everything I'd learned. It was only when I'd gotten to the end of my story that I remembered the other problem we had. "The Vizier is back. I saw him with my own eyes. He said it was me that defeated him all those years ago."

A blank look came over his eyes. One I knew only too well. How long would it be before I lost him completely too?

I looked down at his wrists. The cuffs were still there. Not only was he losing his memory, I'd soon lose him to the lamp. The lamp that had been hidden for eighteen years since my father threw it out into the desert.

"May I interrupt?"

I turned to find Jamal behind me. His face was set in stone.

"I thought you were with my mother?"

He raised his eyebrows and pointed to the other side of the room. My mother was helping serve the food to the long line of people. She looked so normal, so happy in her role. I missed her so much that seeing her in these lucid moments made it all the worse.

"When I explained the situation, she demanded that she be down here to help. I couldn't stop her without using force."

"You did a good job. Thank you, Jamal."

I ran to her, pulling her into a hug.

"Gaia! Where have you been, my darling?"

Tears streamed down my face. Jamal was wrong. She wasn't completely lost. There was a part of her in there somewhere still. She stroked my hair as I silently sobbed into her shoulder. I could have stayed by her side all day, but a thought popped into my head. If she remembered me, surely she'd remember my father. I left her side and ran past the line of people snaking through, past Jamal, who was now helping along with Freya, and past Genie, who had stayed at his position near the door where people were leaving. I ran down the corridor, running past people with food in their mouths, in their hands, in their pockets, and goodness only knew where else they had stuffed it. Out through the staff entrance and through the grounds to the street. The person I was looking for was gone, having taken his fill. If I'd have known my mother was going to come to help, I'd have kept my father in the palace. I barely got to speak to him, and now he was gone.

I walked back slowly into the palace. The hall was filling up quickly as more people were coming in than going out.

The staff was valiantly trying to keep up with the demands of the people, bringing up platter after platter of food. My mother took platters from the staff, finding space on the long tables. Freya and Jamal did the same. Guards stood at the main doors to the palace, the doors to the hall, and at the gates to the palace grounds, ensuring order was kept.

A surge of hope flooded me. We were coping. People were doing exactly what they were supposed to. Sure, some were taking more than their share, but it was going much better than I expected it to.

My eyes sought out Genie. He stood in his position at the door, smiling at all the people leaving. To an outsider, they would see him as a guard, but he didn't care if people were taking too much food. He knew as well as I did that people had families to feed as well as themselves. He didn't stop a single person leaving, no matter how full their pockets. When he finally did look my way, I offered him a smile. He returned it, making my heart jump. It was bittersweet. Yeah, he remembered me now, but for how long? The only people I could count on remembering me in all this were Jamal and Freya, and currently, Jamal was mad with me. At least, he was doing a good impression of it, purposely keeping out of my way and casting his eyes in the opposite direction when I did glance his way.

Three hours later, and my feet were almost ready to drop off. I'd run up and down from the kitchen so many times; it felt like I'd climbed a mountain. Dropping of the dirty silver platters in the washing up area, I turned to grab some more full ones, only to find the giant kitchen table empty.

"Where's the food?" I asked one of the nearby kitchen staff, a young girl with pink cheeks and a messy bun with strands of hair falling out.

"It's gone."

"All of it?" I asked, running to the cold room. I flung open the door to find all the shelves emptied. There was nothing left at all.

Back upstairs, I ran to the front doors of the palace. The line of people stretched down Kisbu's mains street as far as the eye could see. So many of them. We'd fed a fraction of them. Dashing back inside, I saw the insanity of my decision. I'd not rationed the food. We'd always had enough when we'd put on our parties before. I'd naively thought we'd be fine, that the kitchen's capacity for making food would be enough, if only for this one day. I was wrong. By a long shot.

"Stop!" I shouted, bustling into the main hall. "Just take enough food for you. Don't put food in your pockets."

Jamal strode over to me. "What's going on?"

"The kitchen is out of food."

He sucked in a breath as he took in the scene before him. So far, everyone had shown decorum, but it would only last as long as the food did, and judging by the platters that were emptying fast, it wouldn't be long.

"We need to close the front gates," Jamal asserted.

"There'll be a revolt!"

"So what do you suggest we do, Gaia? Bring them in and serve them air? What do you think will happen then?"

"I just wish we had more food. Enough to feed everyone."

Suddenly the room began to rumble. I held onto Jamal for fear of falling. My first thought was an earthquake, but when the tables began to fill with food piled high, I realized it was much worse than any earthquake.

Jamal turned toward the mountains of food. "What the...?"

My heart almost stopped when I realized what had happened. "I just did something stupid!" Pulling away from Jamal I ran past the people grabbing for the food and over to Genie. He was slumped on the floor, his face ashen.

"Did you do this?" I asked him.

With a shaky voice, he answered. "Did you wish it?"

"I said I wish, but it was a figure of speech. I didn't mean it."

"But you said the words. You said I wish?"

I nodded. "But I said it to you before, and you asked me if I was sure. I told you it was a figure of speech. Why didn't you ask me this time?"

He shook his head sadly. "I don't have control anymore. I did then."

He held his hands up. The cuffs on his wrists were chained together. He was becoming the slave to magic he once was...And I only had one wish left.

2ND JULY

The first night back in my own bed was fraught with nightmares. The kingdom was now fed, and, for the moment, the people seemed to be happy. But at what cost?

The day, as lovely as it had turned out to be, meant that Genie was down to one wish, and we were once again without food. Not even Genie knew if my wish of food for everyone would cover just the palace and just for that day, or whether the extent of the magic would travel outside of the kingdom, to the people of Kisbu and maybe beyond. We'd postponed the problem, not gotten rid of it. At least, we still had plenty of food left at the palace after yesterday, so none of us would starve, but what would happen when that ran out?

I didn't know. No one did. My mother had had big ideas about speaking to the farmers once again and opening the gates to the city. There'd been so much talk of sustaining and building and doing the right thing by the citizens of Badalah while we were clearing up the platters, but I knew that it wouldn't last. I didn't dare go and visit her this morning. I wanted to keep hold of the wonderful memories we'd made the night before when I could almost believe that things had gone back to normal.

I rolled over in the bed and saw the outline of Asher in the early morning sun. My nighttime rambles had become a thing of the past, but my affinity for my phoenix was unwavering. I walked over to him and gazed out over my terrace as I gave him a quick stroke of his feathers. Looking out over Kisbu, I saw the streets were calm, everything as it should be.

A knock on my door took my attention away.

"Gaia, it's Freya."

She opened the door and stepped in like she had so many times. Helping me get dressed was not her job anymore. She'd been asked by my mother to find her replacement, but what with everything that had happened since then, it had not happened. Not that I cared. I didn't need help to dress anymore.

"Is everything alright?"

She nodded but didn't speak. There was something wrong. "What is it, Freya?"

"My mother came to the palace yesterday."

"I'm sorry I didn't see her. Is she okay?"

Freya brought her hand up to her face and scratched her temple. "She's fine, but she says the magic is strengthening."

I'd felt it myself; I just hadn't wanted to admit it. I'd had to produce flames on my fingers more regularly just to stop from completely going up in an inferno. I'd hoped it was just me, but if Freya's mother was feeling it, it meant others did too.

"The Vizier is back," I said, flopping down on the unmade bed. In all the chaos yesterday, I'd forgotten to tell Freya.

Her hand moved from her temple to cover her mouth. "He can't be back. He's dead. I know you said that you thought he was back before. Are you sure?"

"I saw him in Urbis. He told me that I defeated him all those years ago."

Freya furrowed her brows and cocked her head to the side. "He died when you were tiny...before you were born even."

I shrugged my shoulders and stood back up. "He *disappeared* around the time I was born. My birth had something to do with it, and it has something to do with all this magic that's circling now. I just don't know what."

"Didn't you find anything out in Urbis? Did you find your brother?"

"I didn't. There was no birth certificate, no adoption certificate, nothing. It's like we don't exist. I'm not sure I only have a brother, either."

Freya's eyes widened again. "What do you mean?"

It was something The Vizier said to me. I didn't really pick up on it at the time, but when he was telling me that I defeated him, he said it was me and my siblings, plural.

"Huh. You have a huge family then?"

I gave a wry smile. "I'm not sure of that, but there may be more like me. More people of magic with golden rings around their eyes. I just wish I knew where they were. I wish I'd have found my birth mother too. I have no idea who or where she is. I ran out of clues, and I ran out of time."

"What about the old lady you saw at your birth? Did you find out about her?"

I nodded sadly. "I did. She was a midwife. She isn't really part of my story apart from the very beginning of it. I found the house where I was born. It was nothing special at all. It was in the poorest area of Urbis, and it belonged to the midwife, not my mother. The next-door neighbor told me he thought she was murdered earlier this year."

Freya's eyes widened. "Maybe The Vizier did it! If he was looking for you, it would make sense."

I shook my head. "He said it was a woman. He said she looked like a witch, but what does a witch really look like?"

"Er, dark hair, long black robes, green skin, pointy hat." She held her hands up to her head to mime the hat.

I laughed. "I think you've been reading too many fairy tales."

I walked past her to the door. "I have to go, sorry. Can you check in on my mother this morning? Make sure she is alright?"

"Where are you going?"

"I need to speak to Genie. I accidentally wished last night. That's why we had so much food. The magic nearly killed him. Just don't let my mother make any big decisions about Kisbu or Badalah. I know we need to open the city gates, but it needs to be done strategically. I don't think my mother is in a fit state to make any decisions right now."

"Okay, I'll ask Jamal to help me. He's been spending time with her."

I walked through the palace in my pajamas and

robe, not caring what the guards thought. This wasn't normal times.

I knocked on Genie's suite door and opened it without waiting for him to answer.

His office was the same as always, impeccably neat with the exception of a couple of books left out on his desk.

A noise came from his private quarters. This time, I knocked and waited. It was one thing to walk into his office, quite another to invade his private space.

"Genie, it's me."

The door opened. He stood there, looking wretched. He had dark circles under his eyes, and his skin was pale. The chains clanked around his wrists.

"Can I come in?" I whispered.

He opened the door wider so I could slip past him.

"I'm sorry I made that wish yesterday. I didn't mean it. I did it without thinking."

Genie walked across the room and sat on one of the couches.

"Don't apologize for what you did, Gaia. Don't ever apologize. You used your wish to help others. I've only ever seen one other person do that before you. Your father."

"You remember him?" I asked, surprised.

He nodded. "There are moments I remember who I am. When I remember who you are. I cling to them, but it's like holding on to sand slipping through my fingers. I can only cherish the moments I do have before they are gone forever."

I sat next to him on the sofa.

"I'll always be here," I whispered.

He held his hand up to my cheek, and I felt the cool metal of the chains upon my chin.

"Sorry," he said, pulling away as I flinched against the cold.

"The chains made me jump," I said, taking his hand in mine. "I can't live with you like this. I won't."

Genie smiled sadly, almost breaking my heart in the process. "What choice do we have?"

"Genie," I said with a firm voice. "I wish for you to be fr..."

I couldn't get the last word out. He'd clamped his hand down on my mouth. I looked into his eyes that were filling with tears.

"Don't do it, Gaia. Don't give up your final wish for me. I'm not worth it."

He slowly lifted his hand away from my mouth.

"If I don't do it, you'll end up becoming enslaved to someone else. Either I never wish for anything again, or I wish for your freedom. There is no alternative."

"I've been a genie for a long time. So long that I don't even remember my real name. I have come to accept my status in life."

"No! I don't accept it. You let my father free you. Why won't you let me?"

"His circumstances were different then. He'd already got what he wanted. He'd won the heart of your mother and we'd defeated The Vizier... You could use your last wish to defeat The Vizier now."

I shook my head. The Vizier had told me himself that Genie hadn't been powerful enough to stop him. It had been my magic or my birth that had done it. I didn't know why and perhaps I never would.

I looked into Genie's eyes. He was so heartbreakingly beautiful, even as haunted as he was with his past.

I took a deep breath and spoke slowly. "I wish for you to..."

This time it wasn't his hand on my mouth. He pushed his lips against mine, crushing them, taking away thoughts of wishes and Viziers. I leaned into him, kissing him back. I parted my lips, tasting him, and like an addict, I couldn't stop, not that I wanted to. I wrapped my arms around him, bringing him closer still until I felt his body against mine through my silk pajama top. The chains jangled between us until I was so close the sound stopped. His lips were demanding, setting my soul on fire, but the heat I was feeling had nothing to do with the magic inside me. It was all from the burning need for this to continue. I kept expecting him to pull away, to tell me he was too old or that it was wrong, but he didn't. I had to pull back to breathe, to make my heart pump again, to see if this was real or if I'd accidentally wished for it, and it was only magic taking over the pair of us. But Genie couldn't make people fall in love. He'd told me once. The hungry look in his eyes was real, not a figment of my imagination or a wish. His eyes were almost imploring as I sucked in air, just inches from his face, one of my hands in his flowing hair, the other between his manacled wrists. It was the mark of a slave, but now, the only slave was me. I was a slave to him, and I knew I'd do anything he wanted because I wanted it too.

He gave me a small smile, barely a curling up of his lips at the edges, but I caught it. We'd done the unthinkable, crossed the line. He'd kissed me, and I'd kissed back.

He opened his mouth to speak, but this time, it was I that stopped him.

"Don't say it," I whispered.

"Don't say what?"

"Don't tell me that this is a mistake." I couldn't bear

it.

"If it's a mistake, it's the most beautiful mistake I've ever made." He leaned in again, and this time, I closed my eyes to receive his lips upon mine, but they never came. Instead, his hands rounded my body and tipped it before he pulled me upwards. I opened my eyes to the sounds of the chains clanging beneath me and found that I was in his arms, being carried from the sofa of his living room to the bedroom.

Laying me on the bed was easy, extricating his hands from beneath me less so. The cuffs and the chain tying them together pulled on my pajamas and dug into my skin, so I had to arch my back to let him pull them out. I lay down, staring up at him expectantly, waiting while my burning magic swirled within me, fueled by desire.

He made no move, leaving me confused, unable to interpret what was going on. Then I realized what it was. Any move toward me would have his chains resting on me. I sat up, put my hand on his chest, and pushed slowly until he was lying on his back. He pulled his hands above his head, with the chains going with them. I leaned over and kissed him again, and this time, I let myself fall into what I'd been waiting so long for.

I woke later, a thin sheen of sweat clinging to my naked skin and the warmth of Genie's body against mine. Hours had passed since I'd first come to his room, and the first flush of desire had long since been sated. The only light to touch us was the burning of a torch outside of the room on Genie's terrace, haloing his head, making his hair appear as if it were on fire.

I looked up to find Genie staring down at me. His

eyes were warm, alive. I saw something in them I'd not seen for weeks. I saw hope.

I grinned up at him, unable to feel anything but joy, despite the world we were living in and the problems that came with it.

His grin came back, infectious. "You, lady, are something else."

"Is that good or bad?"

"Oh, so good," he said, leaning in and taking my breath away again.

"You don't feel bad about what we did?" I asked once I'd come back up for air.

He shook his head and stroked the skin on my cheeks. The chains jangled lightly as he moved.

"I thought I would. I thought I'd wake up and feel like I'd done something unspeakable. I thought I'd feel shame. I've known you for a long time. That doesn't sit easily on me."

"Do you feel shame?" I asked, propping my head up on my hand with my elbow on the bed.

"I feel nothing but...I can't even describe it. I was once human. Before my enslavement. I thought that part of me was long gone, taken over by the power of magic, but this, what I feel now is power that is much rawer. More real." He twirled a lock of my hair between his fingers and curled up the edges of his mouth. "More wonderful than anything I could ever have imagined, but more than that. It didn't feel wrong. It doesn't feel wrong now. I thought for a long time that if anything happened between us, I would be taking advantage of you."

I leaned forward. "If I remember correctly, it was I that took advantage of you."

He laughed. A loud braying laugh that warmed my

heart. It had been a long time since I'd seen him happy. "Yes, you did. You can take advantage of me like that any time you like." He lay his head back on his hands and smirked. I hit him with a pillow.

I could have stayed with Genie, lying in his bed, limbs entangled, tasting his lips until the end of time, but time was something we didn't have. The cuffs around his wrists were proof of that.

"We need to talk about The Vizier," I said, hating myself for even thinking it when I was so happy.

"Who?" Genie replied airily.

I turned to look into his eyes. The cloud had descended again. His memories were once again leaving him.

"Look at me," I demanded.

He flicked his eyes my way, and the genie I knew returned in an instant. He pulled me close and kissed me.

"Do you remember who you are? How you came to be here?"

It was exhausting, these fleeting lapses in memory followed by even more fleeting returns to normal.

"I don't really know who I am, but I know who you are, and I know how I feel about you. It's probably the only thing I can hold onto. Everything else is fading."

"I need you to hold onto that," I said, taking his hand in mine. Hold onto that feeling, and I'll always be here. Do you remember Aladdin?"

He shook his head. I guess it was too much to hope for. My father had been lost to us the longest.

"A long time ago, he saved you from the lamp. The Vizier I just mentioned wanted to own you. To control you as he had controlled my grandfather. As he had controlled Badalah through my grandfather."

Genie closed his eyes and sucked in a breath

through his nose. “I remember. At least I remember feeling unhappy, then happy again. The fabric of my mind is being torn apart.”

I kissed him lightly on his temple and whispered. “I know.”

“You told me yesterday that The Vizier was back. This man hurt you?”

“Not yet, but he wants to. He believes that I was the one to defeat him the first time. I don’t understand it at all, but my birth has something to do with it. I have a brother and maybe more brothers and sisters. Our mother was magic...she had to be, or maybe our father was. We are magic too. I have siblings out there who have magic like mine.”

I lit two of my fingers alight and watched the flames flicker in the low light. It diffused some of the pent-up feelings circling inside me. “I think our birth created a burst of magic that defeated all the evil in all the kingdoms. And now it’s back along with my magic. Our magic. I wish I knew who my brother was. I could do with speaking to someone about this.”

“You have me, my love.”

I snuggled up closer to him. “I know I do, but you don’t remember how powerful The Vizier is. He’s trying to enslave you, and I think he’s doing it to get to me.”

Genie pulled back. “If that is the case, then I must leave. I cannot put you in danger. I will not play a part in anything that will hurt you.”

“You can’t leave me. We are bonded with magic, remember? I am the owner of the three wishes, and until I use the last one, you have to be close to me if I want you to be.”

“Damn it, Gaia,” he said, raising his voice. “Stop this. I don’t want to be bound to you because of magic, because I have to be. I want to be bound to you because you want me as much as I want you. I'd use my last breath to keep you safe, but I can't do that if you keep me near you."

He got out of bed and walked backward and forward at the foot of the bed while I sat up and pulled the covers up to my chin.

"I want you. I've always wanted you. What I'm feeling isn't magic. It's so much more than that. Your magic fascinates me, I won't lie, but I loved you before I learned of your magic. I loved you before I knew your magic had returned, and I loved you before I knew of my magic. We are not bonded together because of magic, but because I love you and I hope you love me. But if holding onto that last wish will stop you from doing something stupid, I'll hold onto it. I want you to be free. I've tried wishing it twice now, but both times you've stopped me. I think you did that for a reason. Until I make that last wish or someone finds the lamp, you must always come back to me no matter how far you go."

He sat down on the bed and lowered his head into his hands. "What have I done?"

I moved down the bed, letting the covers fall from my naked body. "Do you love me, Genie?"

He turned his head to the side. "I love you more than I could possibly have imagined. I have spent my entire life not wanting to get close to anyone, but then I fell in love with you. I've tried to fight it. For so long. I love you with everything that I have, which is why you should let me go."

"If you go, I will die. I will have nothing left to live for."

He raised his hands in the air and brought them

down over my head and behind my back, bringing me close to him.

"I can't fight The Vizier alone," I whispered. "You were always the person who knew what to do in a crisis, even when you didn't have magic. I want you to be free, but I can't use the last wish anymore. Not until you tell me you'll stay and help me fight."

He looked up. His eyes were red. "I'll fight, and I'll stay with you."

"That's all I want."

I moved to kiss him again, but he leaned back. "I need you to promise me something."

"What?"

"My memory is fading. I slip in and out of the fog. Promise me that you'll save yourself if you need to. Use the last wish to keep yourself safe. Do not waste it on me."

"If your mind goes completely, I promise, but I'm not going to let that happen."

He gave me a sad smile. "And I need you to stay as safe as possible. I know you don't like being cooped up inside the palace, but for now, until we sort this out, I think you should stay inside."

"I promise to stay by you if you promise to stay by me."

His smile came back. "Deal."

He leaned forward and kissed me. We didn't leave his room for the rest of the day or night.

3RD JULY

Genie slept peacefully as I slipped out of bed and pulled on my pajamas for the first time in 24 hours. I kissed him lightly on the cheek and tiptoed across the floor and out through his private suite and into the corridor. Looking both ways to make sure no one noticed me, I ran all the way back to my room and jumped in the shower.

My magic had become almost incontrollable thanks to the high emotion and the lack of letting it out. Igniting my fingers for a few seconds was not enough to diffuse the swirling energy. I let the fire burn as the cold water of the shower hit me with a hiss. I let myself sizzle until my magic was burned out completely, and only then, did I turn the shower up a little warmer and wash my hair. I'd known for a while that my magic was strengthening. That, in itself, was not a problem. If The Vizier's was growing, then having mine strengthen was a bonus, but I needed to learn to keep it under control. I couldn't run to the shower after moments of extreme emotion because now that I was with Genie, strong emotions were going to be a part of my life. Not to mention the emotions that went along with running a kingdom.

I jumped out of the shower and dried quickly. My wonderful day with Genie yesterday had been perfect, but I'd left my mother alone when she needed me the most. I'd left the whole kingdom alone to indulge in my own pleasure.

I dressed in my most business-like attire and left my room to find my mother.

She wasn't in her room, nor in the breakfast parlor, although breakfast had been laid out ready for her. It wasn't the usual breakfast affair, but some bread, butter, and fruit. I picked up a slice of bread and slathered the butter on it thickly. I'd not ventured from Genie's room the whole day before, so our food supply had been limited to the fruit bowl he kept in his bedroom.

I'd been hiding from the world, I realized as I wolfed down the bread and picked up an apple. I'd been using my time with Genie as an excuse not to have to do anything else.

"Nice of you to show up," Jamal said, grabbing a plate.

"I was looking for my mother. I think we need to come up with a plan of what to do now."

Jamal raised his eyebrows and pursed his lips. "If you'd have not spent the whole day in Genie's room, you would know that we already came up with a plan. Your mother is in her study. I said I'd bring up some food for her."

My cheeks colored. So Jamal knew where I had been. I guessed the rest of the palace did too. I'd never promised Jamal anything, but he'd stayed here in our moment of need for me. I knew that.

"I'm sorry, Jamal."

"Yeah," he said, retreating from the room with the plate of fruit. I ran after him down the corridor.

"What's the plan?"

He didn't stop. If anything, he picked up his pace so that I had to keep running just to keep up with him.

"The gates need to be opened, but tension is high on both sides. Your mother was in talks with people from Kisbu and those from out of the city yesterday."

He turned and began to walk up the main stairwell to the office my mother and father had shared when things were peaceful.

"How did she speak to people from the outside if the gates were closed?" I asked breathlessly.

He finally stopped and turned to face me. "Freya and I took her to the gates yesterday. As the Sultana, she was allowed to pass through. We ventured to the city of Khoha to speak to the mayor there. The mayor agreed to speak to the leaders of the other nearby towns to come up with a plan. I'm surprised you care."

"What do you mean? Of course, I care."

"You didn't seem to care yesterday. I came to find you so you could come along. Freya told me you'd gone to speak to Genie. I assume you stayed there all day because I couldn't find you when I got back either."

There was no point denying it. I wasn't planning to hide my love of Genie. I just hadn't thought I'd have to admit to it so soon. There were so many other things going on that I'd hoped to fly under the radar a little longer.

"I said I was sorry. If you knew I was with Genie, you should have knocked on his door."

"So it's true then? I'd really hoped I was wrong." He moved to turn away from me, but I caught his shoulder.

"You should have come and got me."

"Would you have left his bed for me?"

I was silent. He was right. Nothing beyond the palace being on fire would have dragged me from Genie yesterday.

"I thought so," he said, turning away and walking down the corridor.

My mother was sat in her usual chair in her study. The room only had two chairs. My mother's at one side of a table and my father's at the other. This is the place where they ruled the kingdom together. Freya stood to my mother's side as they both peered down at a piece of paper. They both looked up as Jamal and I entered the room.

"Jamal...and Gaia, darling. It's so lovely to see you. Jamal, what's the matter?"

"Nothing," he said, dropping the plate of fruit onto the table with a thump. An apple rolled out. Freya picked it up and gave me a questioning look.

"Later!" I mouthed at her from behind Jamal's back.

"I think everyone is on the same side," my mother said. "I received this letter from the Mayor of Khoha this morning. She really is a delight. She said that if we open the gates to the city, she will make sure that the farmers bring food. I assured her yesterday that I'll lower my previous tax hike. I don't really know what possessed me to raise taxes in the first place. I've really not been myself these past few weeks."

Jamal rounded the table and sat in my father's

chair. Something about it annoyed me, but I kept my mouth shut. I'd never seen anyone sit in my father's chair besides my father. It made no sense for Jamal to stand though when there was a perfectly good chair to sit in, and it wasn't like my father was going to show up any minute now.

"Don't sit there, Jamal darling," my mother said.

Jamal stood up at her request.

"Why not, Mother?" Did she remember Aladdin?

She looked up at me in confusion. "I don't know." She gave a little shiver. "It just feels wrong."

I leaned across the table and looked her in the eyes. "Why? Why does it feel wrong? What is it about that chair?"

Both Jamal and Freya were silent. They knew what I was doing. My father was still in her memory. I just needed to get it out

Tears formed in her eyes. "I don't know. I don't..."

She stood up and walked past Freya and to the door. "Please excuse me."

She bolted from the room, closing the door behind her.

"Well done," Jamal said, his voice dripping with sarcasm.

"She remembers him," I replied, ignoring his tone. "I know she does. Do you know what this means?"

"What?" Freya asked.

"If I can get my father to somehow come to the castle and meet with my mother, she might know who he is again. I can ask the Genie if he can make them fall in love."

I ran from the room, but not before I saw Jamal roll his eyes. Yeah, he was pissed at me for wanting to go and see Genie, but this time it wasn't about me. It was about my parents.

I found him whistling a tune in his office. After our day together yesterday, something had changed in him for the better. His hair was brushed back and tied neatly, and the pallor in his skin was gone.

"Gaia!" he said, pulling me as best he could into a twirl and ending it with a kiss.

"I didn't come to you for that," I said, laughing. On the way there, I wondered if he'd already forgotten our time together. It seemed he hadn't.

"What did you come to me for? Is something wrong?"

He let me go and turned back into the man I knew and fell in love with. This new happy side of him was all kinds of wonderful, but I fell in love with his serious side, with the part of him that could tell me any fact I asked of him.

"I've been thinking about that last wish."

"The one you said you wouldn't use because you don't want to lose me."

I smiled up at him shyly. "That's the one."

He took my hand and pulled me to the sofa. "I've been thinking about that. I won't leave you. Not ever. But I still don't want you to free me. I'm yours whatever you do, but you might need that wish for something more important than me."

I kissed him slowly, inhaling his spicy scent. "There is nothing more important than you."

His eyes crinkled up at the side. "You are more important than me. Keep the wish until you really need it."

"Actually, the wishes are the reason I'm here. What exactly did my father wish for? You can't make people fall in love right, so what did he do to make mother fall in love with him?"

"You are asking me about your father again? You know I don't remember. I only remember being inside the lamp and then living here, being an aide to your mother."

"My father was a brilliant leader," I prompted.

Genie stroked my hand. "I know. You've told me. I know you want me to remember him, but I can't."

"He was only the leader he was because of my mother. They were an inseparable team. They worked so well together, and they were so in love. Even after eighteen years together. I've never known another couple love each other as much as they did."

"They were very lucky to have found each other. Just as I am lucky to have found their daughter."

My mouth turned up at the corners. I wasn't used to him talking this way. It was sweet but funny at the same time.

"If I asked you how you think I could get someone to fall in love with me using wishes, what would you say?"

"I'd say, be you, but I'm guessing that's not what you are really asking."

"Whatever made my parents fall in love before, I'm going to try and recreate it. My father was at the palace the other day. My mother missed him, but if I found him and introduced them, maybe they'll remember each other. I just want to make it the same as the first time. He was a street rat, she was a princess. How did they even meet?"

"Hmm," Genies said, crossing his legs and stroking his chin. "If you were a street rat and wanted to marry a prince, I'd conjure up new clothes. I'd make you look like a princess."

I thought back to how my father looked the last time I saw him. His clothes were filthy and full of holes, and he hadn't shaved in weeks. "I can do that. I have all his clothes here. I just need to get him to the palace under some pretense and get him cleaned up."

Genie shook his head. "You promised me you wouldn't venture outside."

"I promised I wouldn't venture outside alone."

Genie sighed and pulled me close to him. He rested his chin on my head and sighed loudly. "I knew falling in love with you would keep me on my toes."

I felt the corners of my mouth pulling upward and my heart skipping along quickly with the words he'd just spoken. I pulled my head out from under his and kissed him again. This time quickly and with the grin still on my mouth. "I never promised you otherwise."

"No, you didn't," Genie accepted. "So who will you take out with you? Jamal and Freya?"

I cocked my head to the side, surprised. "You wouldn't mind if I went out with Jamal?"

"Jamal is a good man. He's been working hard to keep this place together and with nothing in it for himself. He doesn't wish to take over, nor to overthrow the palace. He has a good heart and a strong head."

"He's completely in love with me," I pointed out.

"All the more reason I trust him. He'd be a fool not to be in love with you. It's all the other men in this kingdom that aren't in love with you that I don't trust. They are all fools."

I pushed his shoulder playfully and let out a laugh. "You are not supposed to say things like that. You are supposed to be consumed with raving jealousy over any man that looks my way."

He leaned forward and kissed my forehead. "My Gaia. I trust you. That is all there is to it."

I wanted to stay, to repeat our day from yesterday,

but if I kissed him one more time, I wasn't going to leave his room at all, and I needed to. I had a job to do.

"I'll go and find him. I'll come back and let you know how we fared."

I found Jamal and Freya deep in discussion in the garden. They both looked up as I neared them, but it was Jamal that spoke.

"The Sultana is asleep if you are looking for her. The magic came over her, making her forget what we were doing and gave her a migraine. I thought it best to let her sleep today and worry about opening the gates tomorrow. People are getting fractious again, but I think they can wait one more day."

"Actually, that's a good thing. I have a job I need to do, and I was hoping you'd help me with it. Both of you."

Jamal raised an eyebrow as Freya stood up.

"Anything. What do you want us to do?"

I glanced at Jamal, who looked at me with a surly expression. Genie was right about him. He made a fine leader. If only he wasn't so angry with me, then I'd feel a lot more comfortable.

"I want to go find my father."

"Again?" Jamal inquired, his voice full of contempt.

"My mother remembered him this morning."

Jamal stood. "She didn't remember him. She merely didn't want me sitting in his seat."

"Right," I agreed, "but she couldn't articulate why. There was no logical reason she didn't want you sitting there. There was a spare chair and three of us standing. It would have made more sense for her to offer one of us the empty seat."

Jamal sighed. "I have enough things to deal with other than go on another wild goose chase around

Kisbu. Why not ask Genie to take you since you two are now so cozy?"

"Jamal!" Freya admonished.

I hadn't asked Genie, and he hadn't offered, even though he wanted me to be safe. The reason was his chains. The second he left the palace with his chains on display, the people would see what he'd become again. Some of them wouldn't remember him, but those that did would panic. They'd guess the truth, that The Vizier was back. It would set up a major panic throughout Kisbu and Badalah, making the situation even worse than it already was.

"I'm asking for your help. I want to find him because he was a great leader. You are doing an amazing job of leading this kingdom, Jamal. I've watched how you've taken the reins without asking for anything, and you've done everything you needed to do. I have no doubt that this kingdom would have fallen apart these past few weeks without you being here, but I can see how tired you are. I have to deal with The Vizier, and my mother can't help. If my father comes back to the palace and we can convince him to stay, maybe he and my mother will fall in love with each other again. Then you can rest."

Jamal didn't move, but Freya took hold of his arm.

"Come on. We can't let Gaia go alone. It won't be a wild goose chase. We know where he's been sleeping. Besides, Gaia is right. You do need a rest. If Aladdin comes back, we can all have a little time to ourselves."

Jamal's expression softened.

"Fine."

We left the palace through the staff entrance and made our way across town to the old bell tower.

The door at the base of the tower was partially open.

"I'll go," Jamal said, stepping forward, but I held my hand out to stop him.

"I'd rather go up alone."

Jamal looked like he was about to argue, but once again, Freya took his arm.

"Let her go. He's her father. He won't hurt her."

Jamal didn't look particularly happy about it, but I ran past him and up the stairs before he could think of a reason to stop me.

Aladdin dropped the copy of The Badalah Beacon he was reading and made to jump out of the window the way he had before.

"Please don't!" I said. "I'm here to help you. You remember me? From the palace the other day? I'm Princess Gaia, daughter of Sultana Jawahir."

He nodded, and his demeanor relaxed. "I remember you. Why are you here?"

"I'd like you to meet my mother."

His eyebrows shot up, and he backed up a little. His eyes darted to the window.

"I'd like to take you to the palace and give you some clean clothes and a shave and then introduce you to the Sultana."

"Why? Why are you so interested in me? Why won't you leave me alone?"

"I only want to help you."

"I don't need help."

I looked down at the clothes he was wearing. They were filthy and ripped. He was clean, but his clothes weren't. They were the same clothes he'd left the palace in all those weeks ago.

"If you won't come to the palace, at least, let me buy you some food and a clean outfit."

He wavered then spoke. "You have food?"

I didn't. I'd not thought to bring any. "I don't have food now, but I can bring you some tomorrow."

I looked out of the window at the palace. There was no way I was going to be able to get him to the palace without force, and I didn't want to do that. I needed him to be comfortable when he met my mom for the first time...again. My eyes drifted down to a restaurant on the street. It had a sign saying closed like most of the other restaurants in town. Distribution problems due to the city gates being closed had forced most food businesses to shut. Well, I was going to open them, and I was going to make sure my father was there when I did.

"Come to the window," I said, beckoning him over. I pointed down to the restaurant that was rather aptly named The Sultan's Shawarma. "Come to the restaurant tomorrow evening, and I'll make sure you get fed."

He didn't answer, but then I didn't expect him to. He was wasting away, though, and the skin was loosening on his bones. He would come. If he'd come to the palace for free food, he'd go to a restaurant.

Back at the palace, I ran straight up to my parents' room and began to rifle through my father's wardrobe. Pushing his ceremonial clothing to one side, I picked out a pair of simple pants and a shirt. I might not be able to get him to wear them, but I could try. I also found some shoes and bundled them all up into a bag, which I dropped off in my room. My next stop was to see my mother. She was having dinner alone in the dining room. She barely registered me as I took a seat next to her. Before I even spoke, I knew she wasn't herself again. The building and fading of the magic exhausted me more than if my mother had lost her memory for good. It gave me hope then pulled it out from under me.

"How are you feeling?" I asked my mother hesitantly as a member of staff brought me a plate of spicy chicken and couscous.

She looked up from her food and stared right through me.

"The headache gone?"

"Mmmm," she answered, going back to her food.

My plan was starting to feel like a colossal waste of time. My father didn't want to go anywhere, and my mother barely knew what day it was, let alone who my father was. All I could do was talk to her and hope she took some of it in.

"I was thinking of taking you to the city gates tomorrow," I began, taking a bite out of the chicken. "You promised that you'd instruct the guards to open them so that people in Kisbu can eat. I thought we could go down after breakfast and help deliver the food."

My mother played with her couscous, moving it around the plate with her fork and not taking a bite. With all the starving people in Kisbu, it pained me to see my mother voluntarily not eating.

After dinner, I helped her to her room and got her ready for bed. She didn't complain, but neither did she say anything else. She was compliant, letting me pull her nightdress over her head. Our roles were reversed. I was no longer the child. It broke my heart to see her like this. She gave me a small smile as I said goodnight to her, but when I returned it, she'd already closed her eyes for sleep.

The pain I felt over my parents intensified and began to burn under my skin.

Wherever The Vizier was, the magic was definitely intensifying. It made me wonder if he was in Badalah. He knew where I lived, and he'd made it pretty clear to me that he blamed me for his previous downfall.

I'd kept my wits about me while I was out in Kisbu earlier, and nothing had happened, but the pressure was building. I could feel the heat seeping out of my pores. Like a schoolboy around a hot girl, cold showers were fast becoming my best friend. I could release all the heat from my body and then cool down afterward. It was annoying, but it was also a necessity.

As the night crept in, I wandered the palace toward Genie's room. There was no point in hiding where I was sleeping. Half of the staff already knew, and the other half had forgotten who either Genie or I was. It made for interesting conversations with guards, who, most of the time, appeared bewildered.

As I passed the open terrace, I glanced out to see Jamal and Freya together. They were just chatting quietly among themselves, but I sensed an intimacy between them I'd not seen before.

I was surprised by the pang of jealousy that reared up within me. I was with the man I loved, and I'd never had true feelings for Jamal, but watching him with my best friend caught me off guard. It felt like I was being left out. It was my own fault, I knew that, but Jamal and Freya were the only two people in Kisbu who hadn't lost parts of their minds.

I pushed the feeling down and carried on walking to Genie's room.

I didn't need any invitation to stay the night.

4TH JULY

Pain shot through my face as my nose hit the floor. The agony and shock of being hurled out of bed with such force caused my body to erupt, setting the covers on fire.

"What's happening?" I screamed, pulling myself to my feet. On the other side of the room, Genie stared at me as though I were a feral creature invading his room. With blood dripping down my face, I picked up a vase and threw the water, flowers, and all into the inferno that the bed had become. It barely made a dent in the flames.

Genie recovered from his shock at finding a girl he didn't know in his bed because that was what had happened. He'd forgotten me again. I saw it in his eyes as he grabbed the flaming covers and tossed the whole lot out of the window. We both watched from his terrace as the covers blazed, then finally settled to the ground in a blackened heap.

"Why are you in my room?" he said, handing me a handkerchief to stem the bleeding.

He wasn't scared of me, even though he didn't recognize me. His throwing me from the bed had been a reaction to the shock of waking to find a stranger in his bed.

Sadness crept into my very soul. He'd forgotten me before, but I'd hoped that after we'd made love, his memory of me would be fixed. It seemed I was wrong.

"You invited me into your bed."

He shook his head as though trying to find the memories trapped inside it.

I kissed his cheek as tears fell down mine. "I'll see you later."

His face showed a look of confusion that broke me to my core. Whatever this magic was or where it was coming from, I needed to stop it.

I threw on a robe, left his room, and ran to my own in bare feet, feeling torn. I had two main problems to deal with. The cause of the magic, namely, The Vizier, and the effect of it, and the people of Kisbu going hungry. I'd been putting too much energy into the latter, thinking if my mother and father met again, the problems would solve themselves. The bigger issue was The Vizier, but I didn't know how to deal with him. He'd not shown himself since attacking me in Urbis. I didn't even know if he was still there or if he'd made it to Badalah. It certainly felt like he was closer, but there had been no sightings of him as far as I knew. I sat on my bed. Asher flew to my lap.

"I'm sorry, Asher. I've not been a good friend lately,

have I?"

He gave me a whistle then, opened his wings, and took flight. I watched as he crossed the room and picked something up from the desk on which his perch rested before bringing it back over to me.

He dropped the yellow envelope on my lap and flew out onto the terrace to stretch his wings.

I turned the envelope over in my hands. The return address was stamped on the back. Urbis Central Archives. My heart rate increased as I remembered my request to Derek, the Junior Archivist, who had helped me at the archives. I'd asked him to send me information in a yellow envelope.

With mounting excitement, I ran my finger under the wax seal, breaking it.

Inside, wasn't the birth certificate I'd hoped for, but a number of newspaper clippings and a handwritten note.

I moved the clippings to one side and began to read.

Your highness, I hope this letter finds you well. I'm afraid I haven't found any more information out about your siblings, but I did notice something odd. I don't know if it pertains to your particular query, but I think the top article will bring a smile to your face. Yours sincerely, Derek Waterton, Junior Archivist.

I put the letter to one side and picked up the pile of newspaper clippings. As Derek had predicted, the first one did make me smile. It was an old copy of the Badalah Beacon dated January 14th of the year I was born, or possibly the year after if I was born in December.

It was a photo of my mother and father looking so young. In my mother's arms was a tiny baby. Me.

The headline read 'Royal family welcomes new arrival.'

I read the article underneath. It mentioned I was a surprise to the people of Badalah and that I'd been adopted, but where from was very vague. I guessed that was because my parents had been deliberately vague when interviewed for the article. There were quotes from both my parents saying how delighted they were to have me and how much they loved me already.

I set it aside with the intension of showing it to my mother later. If she saw it, she wouldn't be able to deny that my father existed.

I picked up the next one, surprised to see it wasn't from the Beacon, but from the Draconian Sentinel. The article was remarkably similar to the one I'd just read except it was king and queen of Draconis, our neighboring kingdom, who were the ones smiling down at a small child. The article was almost word for word the same as the one I'd just read. It was as though Princess Azia Rose had just appeared at the Draconis castle one night. The article didn't say that's what had happened, but it also didn't say where she'd come from. It didn't take a big leap of faith to see why Derek had picked this article out for me. I lifted my eyes to the top of the page. The date read January 2nd, the same year as mine.

I put it to one side and found a small clipping next. It wasn't the front page like the others, so I couldn't see which paper it came from, but I didn't need to. It mentioned the king and queen of Floris. There was no mysterious adoption here, but a baby had been left on their doorstep, and they'd decided to take it in. It mentioned that the baby was a boy. I thought back to my knowledge of the royal family in Floris. They had one daughter, no sons. Princess Lilian if memory served. The name caught my attention. Before all this mess had started, I'd read something about Princess Lilian of Floris. I pulled out the stack of newspapers I'd hoarded when I first noticed something going on. I sifted through them until I found what I was looking for. A Copy of the Floris Buckle. I'd been tracking the blight that had overcome the flowers in their kingdom, coming seemingly from nowhere. The last copy I'd picked up had a wedding on the cover. Princess Lilian and the palace's head gardener, Deon.

I read the article with interest. I'd read so many articles from so many kingdoms that a lot of them had blurred together in my mind, but this one had stood out. The wedding had started out between Princess Lilian and Duke Remington, and she'd swapped suitors halfway through and married the gardener. It brought a smile to my face now, just as it had the first time I read it. What a scandal it must have been. And yet she looked so happy in the arms of Deon.

I looked at the small scrap of paper that Derek had sent. The little boy that had been left on the king and queen's doorstep. They'd named him Deon.

My body was abuzz with so much excitement that I had to leave the flammable papers and walk out to the terrace to let some of the excitement out in the form of flames from my fingers. I gave a phoenix call. Asher flew through the flames, weaving between them. The fire didn't bother him at all. I pondered the information I'd found out. Was it possible that Azia and Deon were my brother and sister? I'd seen two babies born in the memory, but I'd walked in halfway through. The Vizier had said siblings. A thought occurred to me. I ran back inside and picked up the old copy of the Floris Buckle with the photo of Princess Lilian and Deon. I studied his eyes. It was hard to tell in a black and white photo, but was it possible that he had a golden ring around his iris too? I searched through the old newspapers until I came upon a copy of the Draconian Sentinel. One more recent than the one announcing Princess Azia's adoption. I pulled one out of the stack and stared at the picture on the cover. It was a photo of Azia's brother lying on the ground with his eyes closed. A man with long white hair leaned over him, and at the very edge of the photo, the princess Azia running into the shot. Her head was slightly to the side, so yet again, I couldn't see her eyes. If only newspapers printed pictures in color and I could have my answer. I'd met some of the royals before. My parents often took me on their royal visits, but I'd never paid attention to the eye colors of the young princes and princesses. Why would I have? My own eyes always had the hint of gold around the iris, but it was only in times of high emotion or intense stress that it really shone out, almost lighting up.

I looked at the remaining snippets cut from newspapers. These were birth announcements. One from Atlantice and one from Enchantia. Both from January, eighteen years ago. There was nothing in them about adoption, but it was a strange coincidence. Five kingdoms, each having a child either born to or adopted by the royals. I needed to find out about the other kingdoms, but first, I needed to sort out the more immediate problem.

Folding the newspaper clippings up carefully, I put them with the huge stack of newspapers I'd already amassed, to look at them later. There was something that linked us all; I just wished I knew what it was. Something that went beyond our births. It was insane to think I might have four brothers and sisters out there, quintuplets. It wasn't beyond the realms of possibility, but it was rare. If, of course, I was right. None of it made sense in my mind. I needed to mull it all over. Normally I'd do my best thinking bouncing ideas off Genie in his office, but I wasn't in a hurry to venture back there today. Him not remembering who I was hurt more than I ever imagined it would. Instead, I was going to do what I'd set out to do before getting the letter from Derek.

I dressed quickly and headed to the breakfast room. I was surprised to find Jamal and Freya there talking with my mother. Her eyes were bright, and she was talking with such animation with them. While Genie's memory had faded again, it seemed hers had come back a little. The whole thing was exhausting, but at least, it would make my plan for today much easier to execute.

"Gaia," Jamal said a smile on his face. "We were just talking about heading to the gates." He nodded his head toward my mother.

It was a relief he was talking to me at all.

"We thought we'd all go after breakfast," he added, pulling out a chair for me. I sat next to him with a little trepidation. He'd been so upset with me. What had changed?

My mother passed me a scone and a plate of butter. "This has gone on long enough. We'll open the gates, travel to Khoha, and ask the mayor to tell the farmers to bring the food."

I gave her a smile. The sooner we got food into Kisbu, the sooner the restaurants could open, and the sooner I could introduce my parents to each other, and then they'd fall in love again. In theory, it sounded so easy. In reality, there were a million reasons it could all go wrong.

We headed into town flanked by a dozen guards. I

could sometimes get away with being invisible, but my mother was a different story. People came out of their houses and shops to see what was happening as we walked through the streets to the gates. We could have taken Palanquins or a royal carriage, but my mother insisted we walk among the people. The carriage that would take us to Khoha had been sent ahead of us, to meet us at the gates. I walked a few steps behind her, letting her have all the limelight. The people needed a leader, and she was it. As we walked, our numbers grew and grew, a procession of Kisbu residents following behind us.

The gates of our giant walled city loomed large, making me nervous. I didn't expect food to magically appear at the other side of the gates when they were opened, but the hundreds of people that had followed us were expecting something.

My nerves only increased as my mother ordered the gates open. The whole crowd held a collective breath as the gates were pulled open by four of the wall guards.

A cheer went up among the people as the door creaked to a halt, fully open, exposing the scene on the other side. Almost as many people stood at the other side of the walls as there were on this side, but the difference was, they all carried something. Lines of people, most with carts, some with carriages and the odd one or two with bags strapped to horses and camels, began to walk through the gates.

I turned to one of the guards at the gates. "How long have they been waiting?"

"They started lining up a couple of days ago."

I watched as the farmers and merchants were swamped with people throwing money at them as they began to sell their wares in an impromptu market on both sides of the wall.

All around me, I saw smiling faces as farmers handed over food, and the people of Kisbu gave them money. For a while, it looked like everything was going to be fine after all, but I knew it wouldn't last. The people buying the wares were the people that could afford them. There were plenty that couldn't.

Once the chaos had died down a bit and many of the hundreds of Kisbu residents had gone back to their homes, I climbed a set of steps up to the top of the wall above the open gates. I cleared my throat and shouted down. "Let the farmers be on their way. The gates are open and will remain that way. We need to get food into the shops and restaurants for everyone else."

Okay, it was selfish of me. I needed the Sultan's Shawarma restaurant to open.

The crowd began to disperse as the farmers were allowed through.

"I think this went rather well, don't you?" My mother commented as she handed over a handful of Rubees to a passing pastry cart. "Cakes for the guards, please."

She picked up four of the delicate little cakes and passed them to Freya, Jamal, and me before biting into the last one herself.

The cakes weren't the freshest. Goodness only knew how long they'd been waiting on the cart, but they were better than nothing, and the guards certainly seemed appreciative of them.

We spent the day walking through Kisbu, as we didn't need to make the trip to Khoha anymore. The sun shone down, lighting the smiles on everyone's faces, and for a while, all was well.

It gave me hope that my plan would work. My mother had never looked so beautiful. As the sun began to lower in the sky, I pulled Jamal and Freya to one side. "I need to find my father. I'll be back in ten minutes."

Jamal nodded and began to steer my mother over to The Sultan's Shawarma Restaurant that was, thankfully, open again.

Pulling my bag firmly over my shoulder, I slipped away from my mother when she wasn't looking and headed up to the bell tower.

My heart fell when I saw that my father wasn't there. I'd brought clothes and shoes for him along with a comb and a bottle of water to clean himself up. I'd even brought a pair of scissors with the intention of giving him a quick haircut. I let the bag fall to the floor, leaving it there. What else could I do? I didn't have the energy to track him down again. I could only suggest he go to the restaurant, I couldn't force him.

With a heavy heart, I ambled back down the dusty stairwell and crossed the road to the restaurant. Inside, a fuss was being made over my mother. The Sultan's Shawarma, despite the name, was not the kind of establishment that was used to catering to royalty, and it showed. The decor was faded, with wallpaper peeling in places. The menus were covered in grease, and the whole place looked like it needed a good cleaning. The proprietor, a portly man with thinning hair and a thick mustache, seemed to realize the same thing and hastily ran a cloth over the menus as he passed them to us.

We were shown to what I assumed was the best table near the window overlooking the street, and the four of us sat down. Outside, the guards lined up, conspicuous as they were in their palace uniforms.

I leaned over to Freya, who had taken the seat next to me and whispered in her ear. "Can you get rid of the guards? My father won't come if he sees them."

Freya nodded. A few seconds later, she raised her hand to her head and moaned.

"Are you alright, Freya, dear?" My mother asked, full of concern as Freya closed her eyes.

"I'm fine. I think I have a migraine coming on." She opened her eyes and looked over to Jamal.

"Jamal," my mother said, turning his way. "Would you be a dear and take Freya home. Migraines are truly awful. I've been suffering from them myself recently."

"It would be my pleasure." Jamal stood up and held a hand out to Freya. I saw how easily she took it. I watched them through the window as they walked away from the restaurant along with the guards, and he never let go of her.

"I do wish they'd hurry up and take our order," my mother said, taking me out of my thoughts. "I'm starving. All we've had to eat since breakfast was that little cake from the pastry cart."

My stomach rumbled in answer. As if on cue, the mustachioed man ran over with a bottle of wine and a notebook and pen.

"What can I get you, Your Majesty, Your Highness?"

"I'll have whatever you think is your best dish and lots of it," my mother said, passing him back the menu.

He turned to me to take my order, but then there was a kerfuffle at the door.

"No, no, no," he said to a waitress as she started letting other customers through the door. "The restaurant is closed for a private event," he explained, his eyes darting our way.

We were obviously the private event.

"Don't be silly," my mother shouted over to him. "You've been closed for days. Let them in. The more, the merrier."

The owner wiped the sweat from his brow and ushered them in. The family seemed quite surprised to be eating alongside royalty as they were shown a table near the back of the restaurant.

After I'd ordered, I let my mother dominate the conversation as she talked about how well the day had gone and mulled over ways to carry on the good work. I let her speak. It was nice to hear her thinking again. Every so often, my eyes would dart to the door at the bottom of the bell tower, but by the time our meal arrived, my father hadn't shown.

I started to eat the meal in front of me as my mother talked strategies. I remembered her doing the same thing with my father many times as they debated ways to make Badalah a better place for everyone. It was sad that all their hard work had crashed down in only a few short weeks.

A flash of white took my attention away from my mother. It was my father wearing the shirt I'd brought for him. My heart leapt as he crossed the road and stopped in front of the restaurant. He wavered a little, then when he saw me, he stepped inside.

I jumped up to get him, but he shook his head when he saw me, and his eyes widened. The waitress led him to a table near ours. My plan had been to invite him to our table, but this way was better. He could come over when he was comfortable, and I could think of a way to ease him into the conversation.

"I'll be right back," I said, standing up. "Bathroom break."

My mother nodded and continued to eat as I walked past my father.

"Order what you want," I whispered. "I have it covered."

At the back of the restaurant, I sought out the owner and gave him enough Rubees for my father to have a good meal.

"We never did get to Khoha," my mother said as I sat back down. "I do need to speak to the mayor. The farmers are bringing food in, but it won't last, the way things are. I really could do with having a royal tour, visiting all the main cities in Badalah to turn things around. I just wish I felt better. Every time I make plans, I forget them."

Out of the corner of my eye, I could see my father listening intently to our conversation. Even when the waiter brought food out to him, he kept looking up at my mother. He was rapt with her. I gave him a smile, but he didn't see it, he was too engrossed with my mother, exactly how I wanted him to be.

I waited for him to make a move and come over. It was plain he was interested in what she had to say as much as he was transfixed by her beauty. They might have forgotten each other on the surface, but underneath, he remembered his love for her. Now I needed him to come to the table and for my mother to see him. So far, she'd not even glanced his way. I was just about to stand up and invite him over when he finished up his meal and stood.

I gave him an encouraging grin as he walked slowly toward our table. He stopped. I held my breath, waiting to see what he would say. He reached down quickly, and when he came up, he had my mother's handbag in his hand. I opened my mouth to question what he was doing, but he ran. Quick as a flash, he was out the door and down the street with my mother's bag.

My mother brought her hand to her neck. "That man stole my bag!"

"Yes, he did," I said with a sigh. My father hadn't stolen anything in his whole life. Why did he have to choose today to start?

The restaurant owner gave chase, but he was nowhere near fit enough to catch my father.

He apologized profusely as I handed him enough Rubees to cover our bill.

Walking back to the palace was particularly fraught. It had seemed like a good idea at the time to dismiss the guards, but as we walked through the streets in the dark, I realized how exposed we were. It wasn't the same as my nighttime trips I'd taken alone. Now, I had my mother to worry about, and she was already nervous after the theft of her purse. It didn't help that the pair of us had dressed in our royal attire to stand out, exactly the opposite of what I'd prefer to be wearing. Only half the town's people recognized me these days and then only half the time, but love her or hate her, they all remembered my mother. They seemed to remember me more if I was around her too. Sometimes like this morning, it brought me comfort, but walking through the dark streets, I'd have preferred to be as incognito as possible.

We finally got home safely, and after leaving her at her room, I went back to mine. My heart ached for Genie, but my soul wouldn't stand a repeat of this morning. Instead, I flopped down on my own bed and wondered why people remembered my mother and not my father.

5TH JULY

"You've never forgotten me, have you, Asher?" I asked as the phoenix flew around the room above my head. The newspaper articles were laid out on my bed around me as I tried to piece everything together. I needed Genie's input. He could see things other people could not. There were so many mysteries. Like who killed the midwife that delivered me? It was a woman, according to her neighbor, and yet the only person I could think that might be an enemy to her would be The Vizier. If he somehow blamed her for my birth or wanted to find me, I could understand that. But it wasn't him. As far as I could tell, the midwife had no money. The house she lived in was in a less than desirable part of Urbis. If only I'd found my mother. I still knew nothing about her beyond what I'd seen in the memory. I didn't even know her name. I picked up the adoption announcement of Princess Azia of Draconis and read it again, trying to glean something more from it.

Copies of the Draconian Sentinel were laid out neatly in chronological order starting from January of this year when I'd started collecting them. My bed looked like a chaos of papers, but there was order there. Just no meaning as far as I could see.

A knock on the door took my attention away from the papers. Freya walked in. Her eyes widened at the mess on my bed.

I handed over a photo of Azia I found from a February edition of the Draconian Sentinel. The accompanying article was about how she'd disappeared, but the photo was from an official photoshoot taken sometime the year before.

"Do you think she looks like me?" I asked.

Freya accepted the paper and squinted. "She has different color skin to you," she said, pointing out the obvious.

"Yes. I know. Look beyond that. Do you see any resemblance?" I took the paper back and held the photo next to my own face. Freya's eyes darted between the two.

"Not really. You are both a similar age and both beautiful, but I don't really see much resemblance. Why?"

I moved a stack of papers and sat back down on the bed. "I think she's my sister."

Freya furrowed her eyebrows and took the paper back from me. "What makes you think that?"

"Look at her eyes. I know it's a black and white photo, but don't you think that bit of lightness around the iris might be golden?"

Freya shrugged, unconvinced. "I'm sorry. I don't see it. What is all this?"

I looked at the piles of papers and felt defeated. My kingdom was falling to pieces, my parents were sick, and I was no closer to finding out what was going on in all this. And the only person that might be able to see the connection didn't even know who I was, despite the fact he'd seen me naked.

Some of the kingdoms' royal families also had babies around the time I was born. Some were adopted in weird circumstances. Some were apparently born to the royals.

Freya picked up a copy of The Conch, Atlantice's daily paper, and read the headline to herself.

"Do you think Princess Blaise is related to you, too?" she asked.

I shrugged. "I don't know. I thought so, but she looks even less like me than Azia does."

Freya walked over to my vanity unit, picked up the chair at it, and brought it over to the bed where she sat it down in front of me. "Walk me through this. You think you are related to what...four other royals? Which ones?"

It sounded so stupid to say it out loud. I had no brothers and sisters, and here I was thinking I was one of a set of quintuplets, none of which looked like me.

"Azia from Draconis, Blaise from Atlantice, Deon from Floris, although he wasn't a royal. He married the princess there a couple of months ago. And finally, Kelis from Enchantia. Before you ask, no, none of them look like me, they just all appeared at their palaces and castles in a similar time frame."

"Weird," Freya said, picking up another paper.

"These princes and princesses. Are they in the same kingdoms that have had the problems?"

"Oh, the gods! Freya!" I jumped up and kissed her cheek. "Why did I not think of this?"

I started to rearrange the piles of papers into a makeshift timeline with the photos of the princes and princesses on the top.

"Draconis was first!" I said, pointing to the photo of Azia, my voice full of excitement.

Freya held out a hand. "Wait!" she ran over to my nightstand and brought out a pad of paper and a pen. "Draconis first. What dates?"

I cast my mind back to everything I'd read. "There were problems with the dragons in January. I think it was about that time that the Queen fell asleep, She's not woken up yet."

Freya wrote furiously. "Draconis, Azia, Sleepy Queen, and dragons in January. Then what?"

I looked over at my carefully curated piles of papers. "Princess Blaise of Atlantice. Her mother turned back into a mermaid. That was in late January or early February."

"Blaise, mother a mermaid, Feb. Got it. Next?"

"There was a bit of a gap and then Floris. Now, the princess there is called Lilian, and she's of a similar age, but not quite. It seems the Royals took on a baby boy that year, and he's the one that I think is my brother. His name is Deon."

"Deon. What happened to him?"

"It wasn't just him," I said, picking up a copy of the Floris Buckle with a picture of the royal gardens on the front. All the plants were dead or dying. It was a pitiful sight. "The whole kingdom is a mess. They had a blight on their plants. Everything died."

Freya screwed up her face and wrote some more.

"This was late Feb, early March."

Freya nodded. "Next?"

"The next kingdom I noticed to have problems was The Vale. Then it was..." I checked the pile of papers again. "Arboria."

"And do either of those places have a prince or princess the same age as you?"

I shook my head. "I don't know. The royals from The Vale had a daughter, but I thought she was older than me. She was married and had a baby. The baby was kidnapped."

Freya raised an eyebrow. "You *think* she's older than you?"

I'd never visited The Vale, but I knew the king and queen had a daughter and a granddaughter. They'd endured so much tragedy. First, the husband of the princess had died when the princess was pregnant, and then, the newborn had been kidnapped. My heart hurt just thinking about it. "I don't know. I feel way too young to be married with a child."

"Doesn't mean she is, though, does it? Do you know her name?"

"Eliana."

Freya wrote it down. "Have you noticed that all these names run in alphabetical order starting from A? Azia, Blaise, Deon, Eliana. If you tell me that the prince or princess from Arboria is called Fred or Felicity, then this will be something huge."

"Fallon!" I said, my eyes widening. "And then me."

"Gaia!" Freya mouthed breathily.

We stared at each other open-mouthed as I tried to consider the implications. There weren't just five, there were more.

"The last one I was going to tell you about is Princess Kelis of Enchantia, but nothing has happened there as far as I know. The Enchantia Charm is reporting nothing strange."

Freya picked up a copy of The Charm and read the headline on the cover. It was an article about a mage rescuing a puppy from a burning building.

"Hmmmm. I wonder if the magic hasn't hit Enchantia yet?" she shrugged and threw the newspaper back on the bed. "It's hopping from kingdom to kingdom. Maybe this is more widespread than you think. What if it's happening in all the kingdoms, some of which it hasn't started in yet?"

"So we are missing the letters C, H, I and J...Maybe L, M, N..." she continued. "We are missing the kingdoms Arcadia, Elder, Oz, The Forge, and Skyla. What do you know about the royal families from those places?"

"My knowledge of Elder is limited. They don't have a royal family, and they don't have a newspaper. I know that Skyla is without a royal family too. They kind of live communally, and I'm not even sure who is in charge there."

"What about Arcadia?"

I sat forward. "Arcadia hasn't had any problems as far as I'm aware, and the king and queen are childless."

Freya stood back up. "Maybe we are clutching at straws then, and the names of the royal princes and princesses are just coincidental."

"Maybe," I mused. "But I don't like coincidences. My mother would probably know more about the leaders of Elder and Skyla. I do know the president of the Forge is called Alice. She has two daughters, Ivy and Pearl."

"There's your letter I," Freya pointed out.

I stood up and followed her out onto the terrace.

Asher flew over our heads and out over the streets of Kisbu. I envied him sometimes, the freedom he had to go wherever he pleased. I'd fly to Skyla and Arcadia and all the other places and find out what was going on. If Ivy was part of this, did that mean Pearl was too? If so, where were the other letters of the alphabet? I counted the letters from A to K on my fingers. K was the eleventh letter of the alphabet. Was Kelis the last one, or was Pearl? Eleven children in one go was impossible. I didn't even bother to count to P. Instead of this making sense, it had only thrown more mysteries my way.

I leaned on the balustrade and brought my hand up to my temple. "I feel like my head is spinning."

Beside me, Freya smirked. "I know what you mean. Maybe we should come back to this later. How did it go with your mother and father last night?. Did they meet and fall in love again?"

I almost laughed. "Not quite. My father came to the restaurant and stole my mother's purse."

Freya's eyes widened. "He did what?"

"I was stupid to think that my plan would work. It feels like no matter what I do, it goes wrong. I feel like I'm making everything worse."

"Aladdin isn't a thief. He might have forgotten who he is, but deep down he's still the same person. He wouldn't steal."

I shrugged. "I saw him do it. He might be the same person, but his circumstances have changed. He's living on the streets. He's hungry."

Freya took my hands and turned me to face her. "You were in a restaurant. I'm assuming you paid for his meal. He didn't steal your mother's handbag because he was hungry. I think you should go and find him and ask him what he was doing."

I sighed and headed back inside. Going to find my father was just another job to add to my list.

"I wish I could ask Genie about all this," I said, indicating the papers still strewn all over my bed.

"Actually, that's why I came to see you. I feel like we've not had a proper talk in ages. What's happening with you and Genie?"

"I slept with him."

Freya grinned. "I guessed."

She quickly moved the newspapers away as I sat back down on the bed. I watched as she stacked them all carefully into one big pile and then placed them by the side of the bed.

She joined me on the bed. "What happened? I thought that he said he was too old for you?"

My heart wrenched as I remembered the way he'd looked at me as I last left his room.

"It was magical, beautiful. I love him."

Freya pulled me into a hug as I tried to keep the tears at bay. I'd always felt so confident in every aspect of my life, and now, there wasn't a single part of it that I felt as if I knew what I was doing. My foundations had been pulled out from beneath me.

"Does he not love you back?"

I stood up and headed to my bedroom door. "Sometimes, he does. The last time I saw him, he threw me out of his room because he didn't even know who I was."

Comprehension dawned on Freya's face. "Oh, honey. I'm so sorry."

"It's fine. It's not like I'm not used to it by now. First, my father, then my mother, now Genie."

I opened the door and headed out into the corridor. Freya followed.

"Go and have some breakfast," she ordered. "I'll find Jamal, and we can come up with a plan."

"A plan for what?" I asked. There were so many things going on. I didn't know which to prioritize.

Freya smiled. "Everything. We'll break it all down and tackle one thing at a time."

My mother looked up as I entered the breakfast room.

"Gaia Darling. I was hoping to see you this morning. First reports are in. The townsfolk are behaving. The out of towners are still bringing in their wares. It seems things are back to some normality."

I gave her a smile, wishing that were the case. Normality wasn't going to come back just because we opened the gates. The magic had been coming in waves, ebbing and flowing. She remembered me now, but how long would it last?

"I was thinking of heading into town and seeing if I can find the man who stole your purse yesterday," I said airily, slathering butter on a pastry.

"The man needs locking up. I don't want you going to look for him. There's no telling what he might do to you."

I poured black coffee into a cup and took a sip. "He's not dangerous, Mother."

She pointed a butter knife at me as she talked. "You can't possibly know that. I have enough on my plate to deal with without wondering what happened to my daughter if you don't come home."

"Oh?" I said, taking a bite from the flaky pastry. "What are your plans?"

Letting my mother do anything without supervision these days was much more dangerous than looking for my father in Kisbu. At some point in the past few weeks, I'd become a mother to a bunch of toddlers, or at least, that's what it felt like.

"I was thinking of visiting Khoha. I should have gone there yesterday, but of course, I didn't."

Ten minutes later, Freya and Jamal showed up. I watched my mother as Jamal took a seat next to her, but her eyes didn't even flicker toward him. Maybe she was getting better.

"Freya tells me you wanted to speak to me," Jamal said, filling his plate with meats and cheeses.

I glanced Freya's way.

"I was thinking about the current situation with the townsfolk." She turned to my mother. "Your Majesty. I believe you were thinking of visiting Khoha today? The mayor was expecting a visit."

"Was I?" My mother looked surprised. The blankness had descended over her eyes again. It was as if she'd not just mentioned it to me only moments ago.

"Yes. I was thinking that Jamal and I could go with you and help out. I believe Gaia has things to do here."

Jamal looked my way and narrowed his eyes. "Something to do with Genie, no doubt....ow!" He looked over at Freya, who smiled innocently at him as he bent down to rub his leg.

"Actually, I was planning to go into Kisbu and see if I can find the thief that stole my mother's purse."

Now, Jamal looked confused. Freya obviously hadn't told him what had happened with my father the previous day. My mother continued to stare blankly at her plate. At least, I wouldn't have to worry about her stopping me from going out to find my father.

"I'll tell you all about it later," Freya said, motioning toward my mother with her eyes. "How about we all meet back here later and have a debrief?"

Despite how Jamal felt about me right now, I was blessed to have him and Freya here at the palace. Without the pair of them, the whole of Badalah would have collapsed long before now.

An hour later and I was out on the streets of Kisbu, dressed in the same clothes I wore in Urbis. Today I wanted to be able to walk through the streets unseen. I found my father exactly where I expected to find him, asleep in the top of the old bell tower.

I nudged him with my toe and waited for him to wake. He snorted, then opened his eyes, and pulled himself back into almost an attack stance. When he saw it was me, he relaxed.

"I'm sorry about yesterday," he said, pulling something out from under a pile of newspapers. It was my mother's purse. He held it out at arm's length as if it would bite him.

I took the purse and looked inside. All the Rubees my mother had taken out with her were still there along with everything else she usually carried with her.

"I didn't take the money."

"Why did you steal it?" I asked, sitting on the window ledge.

He licked his lips and sat down. "I don't want your money. I don't need it," he reiterated.

I looked around the messy room where he lived with broken floorboards and old newspapers as a bed. "I beg to differ, but if you weren't planning on using the money, why steal it in the first place?"

He ran his hands through his filthy hair. I noticed that he was still wearing the shirt and pants I'd brought for him to wear. I couldn't see his old clothes anywhere.

"The second I saw her, I felt something. I don't even know what. It sounds crazy. I don't even know her. I guess it's because she's the queen or because she's so beautiful. I wanted to come and talk to her. It was stupid, but I thought if I took the purse, I could come to the palace and use it as an excuse to speak to her."

"So, why didn't you? That's why I invited you to the restaurant in the first place."

He raised an eyebrow and narrowed his eyes. I'd forgotten for a second that I'd told him I'd invited him because I wanted to feed him. I'd not even mentioned my mother being there to him.

"I couldn't. Look at me. I'm a pauper, a nothing. Why would the queen want to speak to someone like me?"

I sighed. "My mother would sit and listen to you talk for hours. There was nothing she liked more than to discuss current affairs with you. She just doesn't remember it, and neither do you. You love her. You've been in love with her from the first moment you laid eyes on her and she with you. I've never known any couple more suited to each other than the pair of you. I can't believe you've forgotten everything you had together."

I was shouting, and I knew it. He stared at me, his eyes wide open.

"She's in love with me? The Sultana of Badalah is in love with me?"

"Yes!" I replied exasperated. "She needs you, and you need her. Badalah needs both of you, and so do I."

He closed his eyes and brought his hands up to his temples. "I remember...I remember my childhood. I lived on these streets. How would I know the Sultana?"

I moved from the windowsill and sat next to him on the floor.

"You found a lamp. Many years ago. It contained a genie. The genie helped you meet her. The genie can't help you anymore, but I can."

"You can introduce me to the Sultana?"

"Ye..." I remembered what my mother had told me that morning at breakfast. The second my father set foot in the palace, my mother would have him arrested for theft. "If you truly want to meet my mother, I'll find a way," I promised him. I kissed his cheek and pulled some Rubees from the purse, which I handed over to him. "Get yourself a haircut and some food. I'll do the rest. I'll come back when I've figured out how to play this. Don't go far."

His eyes drifted to the riches in his hands and then to me in amazement. I'd given him enough money to feed himself for a few days and to get himself cleaned up. To me, it was pennies; to him, it was a great deal of wealth. I wished I could give him more.

Back at the palace, I resisted the urge to go and check on Genie. Instead, I went down to the basement to practice my magic while I waited for Jamal, Freya, and my mother to come back. As the Sultana's daughter, it should have been me heading to Khoha with my mother, but I trusted Jamal and Freya. They understood the importance of keeping relations with our nearest town outside of Kisbu cordial. When this was all over, I'd make sure that Jamal had a place in the palace for as long as he wanted. He deserved it.

The fire began to build up within me, almost shooting out of my fingertips as my mind wandered to The Vizier. I reigned it in and kept control of the swirling mass of hot magic within me. In the far corner of the cellar, stood a seamstress's mannequin that had been brought down here when it was no longer needed. Picturing The Vizier's face on top of the feminine body, I hurled my fire at it, sending it flying into the wall in an inferno. It fell to the floor as flames licked the wall next to it.

I'd started the fire, but could I put it out using magic? I didn't know. Imagining a magical lasso, I wrapped it around the flames and began to pull back. The flames pulled away from the wall and the smoldering mannequin and floated in mid-air toward me in a long line as though an invisible rope was burning.

"Cool!" I whispered, waving my hand and letting go of the magic. With nothing to burn and no magic tethering it to anything, the flames vanished. All that was left were scorch marks on the wall and the blackened mannequin along with the smell of burning.

Later, Freya and Jamal came to find me. The three of us walked out into the gardens away from the guards.

"How did it go?" Freya and I asked simultaneously.

"Your mother forgot who she was," Jamal answered. "We had to leave her in the carriage while we spoke to the Mayor of Khoha."

It broke my heart, but it was no more than I expected, I'd seen the blackness glaze her eyes this morning at breakfast. I'd hoped that once she was out of Kisbu, she'd come back, but it wasn't to be.

"The mayor knows the situation. We told her everything."

"We told her about Aladdin and The Vizier," added Freya

I nodded. No point keeping quiet about it. Not to the mayor, at least. However, I wouldn't like The Vizier's comeback becoming common knowledge.

"And?" I prompted.

"She doesn't remember Aladdin or The Vizier," Jamal said, "but she says that she's noticed a lot of weird things happening. A lot of the people of Khoha have forgotten her too. I think as long as we keep the taxes low for now, she'll do her best. It was all we could ask."

I held my hand out to him. "You did a great job. Thank you." I glanced across at Freya. Her face had taken a sour turn, and I understood why. I'd reached out for Jamal's hand without thinking. I held my other hand toward her, and she brightened up immediately.

"My father stole the purse because he wanted to bring it back to the palace to meet my mother. He wants to meet her as much as I want him to. Unfortunately, I don't think my mother wants to speak to him."

Freya gave an exaggerated yawn. "Maybe we should solve that problem another day?"

I nodded and walked away. When they thought I'd gone, I turned back, and I saw Freya and Jamal kissing. That's why she wanted me to go. She wanted to be alone with Jamal. My lips curled up at the corners as I turned and headed for bed.

6TH JULY

After another night of tossing and turning, I could stand it no more.

My heart ached for Genie. I needed to see him even if he didn't know who I was. My heart pounded as I walked down the corridor that would take me to his suite. As I held my hand up to knock on his door, I hesitated, wondering if I'd be strong enough to have him look at me blankly the way my mother did so often these days. My father remembered me perfectly from all the times I'd visited him since he lost his memories in the first place but nothing from before. My mother's memories flitted in and out, but she seemed to be losing new memories as well as old ones. The magic did not treat people equally. Same with the guards. Some remembered me; some looked at me blankly as

I passed them. I was yet to have one try to throw me out because he or she didn't know who I was, but I knew it could happen. And then, there was Genie. Just like my mother, his memories came and went, and like her, his personality had changed. My mother made bad decisions about what to do with the kingdom. Was Genie making bad decisions about being with me? Was his love for me nothing more than a by-product of the evil magic swirling around all of us? Part of me wanted to think that like too much alcohol, the magic was just bringing out everyone's true self, and Genie loved me all the time, but it didn't ring true for my mother. Her decision to increase taxes had almost crippled Kisbu. I was still pondering such things when the door opened.

My fears vanished when Genie pulled me into his arms and swept me into a kiss.

I clung to him as he pulled me inside, our lips still locked together as he managed to close the door behind us with his foot. I kissed back with such fervor, scared that this would slip away and be pulled out from beneath my feet as everything so often had. I held everything close to me, locking it away in my memory. The way he tasted, the light spice on his skin and the way he held me tightly, the chains around my back. And I left mental fingerprints, everywhere I touched, his skin, his hair, his face, terrified that this might be the last time we did this.

He picked me up and carried me through his living room into his bedroom where we made love. What had started off as something fast and desperate became a long, drawn-out dance of making memories for him and for me.

When it was over, I wouldn't let him sleep for fear that sleep would bring back the blank look in his eyes again.

He stroked the side of my face. "There is something very wrong. I can see it in your eyes."

I blinked and sucked in a breath. "The last time I was in this bed with you, you threw me out of it. You didn't know who I was."

He swallowed, and pain clouded his features.

"I am so sorry, my Gaia. I'd wondered why you hadn't visited me for a few days. I wanted to come to you, but the guards don't recognize me anymore. I had to wait for you to come to me. I can't believe I did such a thing."

"I didn't come to you because I was scared you wouldn't remember me. I didn't think I could bear it."

He pulled me to his chest and stroked my hair.

"I have no control over what is happening to my mind. I hate that it is so. Look at me."

I pulled back and gazed into his eyes. It felt like I was looking into forever.

"If I ever forget you again, look at me like this. Exactly as you are looking at me now. I see so much love in your eyes. I will know it in my heart, even if I don't see it in my mind."

I gave him a small, sad smile. "Your mind is what I fell in love with."

"I will always be here, and I'll always keep you in both my mind and heart. If the darkness comes again, know that like the seasons, it will pass."

I laid my head back on the pillow and stared up at the ceiling. "Will it pass? Really? You can't possibly know that. You don't know what this is any more than I do. Most of your memories of the past are warped or gone completely. Freya and I noticed something weird about the princes and princesses of the other kingdoms, but I don't see how it helps us solve the problems we are having here."

"What did you notice?"

I told him everything Freya and I had talked about the previous day. I wished I had all the newspapers to show him, but getting them would involve leaving his bed, something I wasn't ready to do just yet, even temporarily.

He didn't say a word as I talked, but I noticed he watched my lips. If anyone could make sense of what was happening, it was Genie.

"Siblings seem like a stretch when you take into consideration the numbers of people involved," Genie concluded.

"That's what I thought, too, but I saw my birth."

"You saw your birth?"

"I asked you to show you my birth," I reminded him.

He nodded and pulled his hands up and rested his head on them, the length of chain running under his neck.

"I don't think that what happened eighteen years ago is our main priority, even if it does pertain to what's happening now. Perhaps we should put the why's of this on the back burner and concentrate on our more immediate problems."

"Which one? There are so many problems; I don't know what to deal with first."

"List them."

I thought of all the things that were going wrong. Everything seemed the most immediate problem.

"My mother is losing her mind. The city...the whole kingdom is barely hanging on by a thread. Jamal and Freya are doing a magnificent job, but they are not royalty. I think the only reason that people are accepting them is because everyone's memories are messed up, and no one knows who is who these days."

"Okay, what else?"

"The Vizier. I know he's back because I saw him, but I don't know if he's in Badalah or still in Urbis. He wants to destroy me. He also wants to destroy you, which brings me to problem number three." I pulled on his arm and held up the chain that held his wrists together. "I know how to solve this problem if only you'd let me."

He shook his head. "Not yet. Now is not the time. Is that everything?"

I looked at him incredulously. "Isn't that enough? No one remembers me. You might forget me any second, and I'm scared. What if this becomes permanent, and Jamal, Freya, and I are the only ones that remember anything? What if I lose you, but this time forever? If someone finds the lamp, you'll become theirs. If you forget me, it will be like I don't exist."

"Gaia. You will exist with or without me. Do not base your worth on whether I remember you or not."

"If you don't remember me, I'll have nothing left."

"You've just told me the priority. We need to find a way to make our memories return. Have you looked in my books?"

Genie had thousands of books. His office had bookshelves bursting with them, and there were thousands more I'd not looked at in his living room. We didn't have a library in the palace because we didn't need one. Genie had enough books to fill two libraries, and every single one of them was nonfiction.

"You don't have any books on magic," I reminded him.

He sat up and brought his hands to his lap. "Not everything has to be about magic. While it is true I have no books on spells or the art of magic, there are other ways to bring back memories."

"What do you mean?"

"Potions have been known to do things that spells cannot. I have told you before that I cannot make people fall in love, but love potions exist. I don't know how well they work, but they are bought and sold in some kingdoms. I suggest you look at books on the other kingdoms to see if you can find anything. My personal library in my living room has books that might help. I suggest you start with The Forge."

"What are you going to do?" I asked as I pulled my clothes back on.

A grin split his face, "I'm going to sleep. You've fair worn me out."

I left him to sleep with a grin of my own. If he forgot me when he woke up, I'd do something to remind him who I was.

Second, only to Genie himself, his magnificent library was one reason I loved being in his private suite. I'd never known the existence of it before that first time he brought me in here, but ever since I knew of it, I'd been dying to search the shelves to read everything there was to read. Of course, that would take me weeks, if not months, and I didn't have that kind of time, so I began my search more methodically. It seemed Genie had cultivated an interest in the other kingdoms, and a quick search showed that the books were organized by region rather than alphabetically by author. Thirteen bookcases, twelve kingdoms, and Urbis.

Instead of taking Genie's advice, I first went to the bookcase with books about Badalah.

The entire history of my kingdom was laid out before me. The books on the very top were old, the spines faded by years of sunlight, their bindings falling apart. Lower down were the newer books. Next to a tourist book on the cafes of Badalah was a hand-drawn book, barely more than ten pages long. I pulled it out and flicked through it, my heart swelling with memories. I'd made this book when I was five or six years old and presented it to Genie. It was the story of a princess in the Badalah palace. Not so original, but the cute scribbles and misspelled words brought a smile to my face. He'd kept it all these years, giving it space among the books of Badalah's history.

Putting it back, I moved to books about The Forge. Just like the ones about Badalah, these books were arranged in much the same way with the older ones at the top and the newer ones at the bottom. Apart from that, there seemed to be no particular order. History books were mingled in with tour guides, fashion guides, and the history of the vampires that lived there.

I could have spent many happy hours finding out about The Forge, but I needed to figure out how to solve the problems of Badalah before I did a spot of light reading for pleasure. With great reluctance, I put back the book of weird inventions I'd picked up and searched for a book on potions. My eyes fell on a shelf that just so happened to be full of books about elixirs and potions. The majority of them were beauty-related, which made me chuckle. I pulled out a book titled The Forge: a kingdom of Technology and Alchemy. The thick tome was so heavy that I had to carry it through to Genie's office and set it on his table to read it. Like many of the other books, this one also made mention of beauty, but it read like a guide to The Forge rather than a recipe book. Pages upon pages were filled with the history of the Red Queen, who although cruel with a penchant for chopping people's heads off, was a true groundbreaker when it came to technology. She ruled The Forge from her house in the capital city of Melfall with the help of mechanical playing cards. The cards were monoliths of size and advanced technology and would roam the streets doing her bidding. The whole thing was fascinating, and I found myself sucked into this weird and wonderful world that was so unlike my own kingdom.

It was only when Genie appeared a couple of hours later and kissed my cheek that I realized I'd been so consumed by The Forge that I'd completely forgotten to look for something that might help.

"What are you reading?" Genie asked, passing me an apple from the fruit bowl in his bedroom.

"Did you know that The Forge has guilds for inventors?" I asked, full of enthusiasm.

"There are many guilds in The Forge. Inventing is just one, although all are art or technology based. The Forge is a strange place. They covet beauty over all else. Their currency is based on it, and yet they have some of the most intelligent minds in all the kingdoms. I once thought I'd like to visit there, but I have always been indebted to your father."

"You remember him now?" I asked, glancing up from the book.

He put his hand on my shoulder. "A little. I had a dream about him. I don't think I'd recognize him if I saw him."

"I'm surprised you stayed here out of a sense of duty. You could have visited."

He nodded his head. "I should have. There was always so much to do here."

I turned my whole body his way. "Why don't we go?

Both of us? I could look for someone who could make us a memory potion, and you could finally see the place. We could go to Melfall. It will give me a great excuse to meet Ivy and Pearl, the daughters of President Alice and see if either of them has a gold ring around her irises."

He took my hands in his. "There is nothing I'd like more than to travel with you. Maybe when this is all over, we can travel together and see all the kingdoms, but now..." he shook his head.

"Why not now?"

He held his hands up, reminding me of his bondage to the palace. It wasn't just to me that he was bonded. The second he stepped outside, the people would see him for the slave he was. Many people over the years had looked for the lamp, and none had found it, but it felt like we were closer than ever to someone finding it and using it. Images of The Vizier came into my mind. If anyone found it, I knew it would be him. My father had told me that The Vizier spent years and years looking for it before he'd thrown my father into a mysterious cave in the desert where my father had survived by the skin of his teeth.

"There is one way I know to make these chains go away," I said, wrapping my fingers around the cuffs. I looked up into his eyes, pleading with him. He knew I could wish it all away. If I did it without his permission, he'd still be bound to do what I wished, but to do that, even to free him would hurt him. Not just physically. The actual pain of the magic would pass with a good night's sleep, but to make him do something against his will would put something between us. I wasn't sure if he would ever forgive me, so I had to wait until the stubborn ass changed his mind before I could use my last wish to free him.

"You know I can't let you do that," he said, leaning forward and kissing me lightly on the mouth. My heart skipped a beat at the gentleness of his touch.

"I have lived a thousand lives. You have lived but one, and you are still young. I will not give up your life for my freedom."

The tingle of tears made me blink. "I'm not asking you to save my life. My life isn't in danger right now."

"Gaia..."

He knew the situation enough to know that I was lying to him. My life was in grave danger. Just because that danger hadn't presented itself yet beyond giving me a warning, didn't mean it wouldn't come. The Vizier knew who I was, and he knew where I lived. I was actually surprised he hadn't made himself known here in Badalah yet. I'd instructed the guards to keep an eye out for him, but with half of them not knowing who I was and the other half not remembering who The Vizier was, our protection was at our leanest in years, and that was with a full contingent of guards. The only two people I could trust in all of this were Jamal and Freya. A maid and a farmer, neither of whom had any royal blood, were practically running the whole kingdom. I couldn't expect them to save me from The Vizier, should he decide to appear. They wouldn't be able to. If he did decide to come to kill me, I only had myself and my magic. It would stave him off for a while, but I wasn't powerful enough to keep him away forever. It didn't look good whichever way I looked at it.

"Okay, okay, I know. I won't do it. You know how I feel. I want you to be free. I don't want to accidentally wish for something like I did before and waste it on something stupid. Saying I wish is a turn of phrase that people say all the time."

“I trust you.”

I smiled. He had more faith in me than I did in myself.

“I should go. I’ve left the kingdom to Jamal and Freya long enough. The kingdom needs a leader, and that leader should be me.”

“Don’t be too hard on yourself. The people of the kingdom don’t know what they want anymore. You are doing your best in a strange situation.”

I stood and let go of his hands. “I know, but it feels like no matter what I do, it’s wrong. The kingdom is still failing, I don’t understand what part I have to play in all this, and The Vizier is out there biding his time.”

“He will make himself known when the time is right for him. Until then, we must keep you safe.”

I leaned forward and kissed him, knowing that our kisses were limited. It wasn’t just me in danger; it was Genie too, and if I didn’t figure out how to stop it, the entire kingdom. A knock on the door broke us apart.

“Who is it?”

The voice of one of the guards came through the door. “Your Highness, I was asked to come and find you. Mr. Jamal and Ms. Freya are holding a meeting with the palace advisors. They thought you might like to attend.”

I looked toward Genie, who nodded.

“I’ll read through these books and see if I can find a recipe for memory elixirs. You go and rule the kingdom.”

I followed the guard to the meeting room where Jamal and Freya sat, not quite at the head of the table. My parents’ chairs sat empty.

Despite their seating positions, it was clear that Jamal and Freya were leading the meeting. There was something about them, the calm confidence that made them natural leaders. They were doing a better job than

I was, and it showed.

"Gaia!" Jamal said, standing up and walking around the table. He kissed me quickly on the cheek. "Your mother isn't well. I've had the court physician look at her, but it seems it's just tiredness. She's resting. I thought we should try and get a grip on what's happening in the kingdom and try to put it back in some order. I know you and Freya have had some thoughts on the other kingdoms, but if we don't keep on top of everything here, then none of that will matter. I'm afraid all the seats are taken, but I'm sure your parents won't mind you using their seats."

Something had changed between us. The awkwardness and resentment had gone. It probably had more to do with his and Freya's burgeoning relationship rather than anything I had done, but it was nice. I sat in my mother's chair, leaving my father's empty.

Freya gave me a nod and a smile and stood to address the advisors. There were ten of them altogether. Six women and four men. All of them had been working in the palace for years. Without fear, Freya spoke.

"Ladies and gentlemen, as you know, Badalah is in crisis. The town of Kisbu is at the center of that crisis. The Sultan and Sultana are unable to rule at the moment, so we are going to have to work together and keep the kingdom going until we can solve the whys and wherefores of what is happening."

"There isn't a Sultan," one of the advisors pointed out.

"Who are you to tell us what we should be doing?" another one said. "You are a maid. We aren't here to draw baths and make beds."

I saw Jamal's lip twitch. He made to stand, but I placed my hand on his arm to stop him. Instead, I stood up.

"Freya and Jamal are here because of me. As the Sultana's daughter, you have to listen to me. I've picked Jamal and Freya to help me run this kingdom, and I want you to show them the respect they deserve. Freya was my maid. It's true, but unless you are blind, you'll notice that she has been instrumental in stopping the disaster that befell us when my mother decided to raise taxes. I didn't see any of you helping with the feasts for the people. Freya was at both. Without Freya and Jamal, this kingdom would have fallen weeks ago."

I waited to see the advisors' reactions, but they remained silent. What could they say? Jamal and Freya had done a lot more than any of them had over the past weeks. Not that I could blame them. I recognized the dazed look in their eyes. They probably didn't know who they were, let alone what their jobs were.

Jamal spoke. "We are in the middle of something unlike anything we have seen before. I might have no royal blood running through my veins, but I have something that the majority of the people of Badalah do not. I have immunity to the magic that is polluting the atmosphere. How many of you have experienced disorientation these past weeks? How many of you have forgotten things you shouldn't? How many of you have found yourself talking to people who know you, but you have forgotten them?"

Around the table, the advisors began to raise their hands. First one or two, then all of them.

"This is a magical force that is sweeping through Badalah. It is the source of all our problems. Three weeks ago, Badalah was a flourishing kingdom with few problems. You might not remember, but there was a Sultan as well as the Sultana. My aim isn't to get us back to the state Badalah once was. I believe only Sultan Aladdin and Sultana Jawahir can do that. I am but a farmer and businessman, but I do plan to do my best to keep Badalah going through this mess until a time when both Aladdin and Jawahir recover from this magical madness. I need to know you will help with that to the best of your abilities. We are all on the same side. The fight is ours, not against ourselves, but against the person who brought this magic among us. The former Sultan's Vizier. The same one who tried to bring down the kingdom all those years ago."

Around the table, I heard the sharp intake of breath. Not all of them remembered The Vizier, but it was clear some of them did.

I had half a mind to get up and applaud Jamal's speech, but he was talking again. I listened as he spoke, marveling at how he held his audience captive by his words. His plan was simple. Start a publicity campaign to recruit people of magic to help us run the Kingdom.

I listened in awe as he set out a timeline of when he wanted everything done by. The advisors listened, and even more, they wrote down everything he said.

When the meeting was over, I waited until the advisors had left the room before speaking to him.

"You were magnificent!" I said. Next to him, Freya beamed with pride.

"It was Freya's idea," he said, glancing her way. I caught his smile as he looked at her.

"People around here have been fearful of magic for too long," she said. "But we can only fight magic if we have it. I don't know if anyone in Badalah has magic in the way you do, but there must be people like Jamal and I that are immune to what is going on. We need to build an army of people who remember the city, remember the kingdom, and remember how things used to be."

"We just need to convince people to come forward. Magic has been a taboo subject in Badalah for as long as I can remember. We might not get as many people as we would like." Jamal added.

"What are you going to do with all these people when you recruit them?"

Jamal took a deep breath and looked at Freya, who nodded her encouragement.

"We thought we'd send them out to the other towns and cities of Badalah and recruit more. The more people we have that remember the way things used to be, the more chance we have of getting it back that way."

I lowered my head, guilt weighing heavily on my shoulders. "I'm sorry. I should be doing more. I should have done more."

"No!" Freya said. "We purposely didn't come to you with this because you were doing the one thing only you could. We know this magic is something to do with you, and we think that only you can stop it. We can keep things going, but you are the only person that can end this. You need to figure out how to solve this while we do what we can here."

"But I don't know how. I know it's something to do with me, and it's something to do with The Vizier, but I don't know what. I think it's actually bigger than that too."

"Bigger than The Vizier?" Freya's eyes widened as though she could think of nothing worse than The Vizier.

I walked around the table, pushing in chairs. "A woman killed the midwife who was at my birth, not The Vizier. It's too much of a coincidence that she was murdered as this all started."

Jamal clicked his teeth. "But you don't know who the woman is. It could be anyone."

"I know," I admitted. "I need Genie's help to figure it all out, but his memory comes and goes like everyone else's. I need someone with his mind to help me figure out what's going on."

Jamal didn't even flinch when I mentioned Genie's name. I took it to be a good sign.

"I don't know how to help you get his mind back. If we could do that, we wouldn't be in this problem in the first place."

"Actually, I think there might be a way. I've been reading up on The Forge. They make potions there. There might be a potion for memory loss."

"Even magical memory loss?" Jamal asked.

I shrugged. "I don't know, but there is only one way to find out. I'm going to The Forge."

7TH JULY

A hard rapping on my door woke me from my slumber. Asher squawked as the knocking intensified, hammering persistently.

"What is it?" I replied, wiping the sleep from my eyes with the back of my fist as I pulled myself out of bed. I opened the door to find Jamal standing there, his eyes full of panic.

"Get dressed," he ordered, "We need you."

"What's the matter?" I asked, fear already churning in my stomach. Sparks began to fly from my skin, taking us both by surprise. I ignited my hand and let the magical fire burn to rid myself of the buildup of magical energy brought on by the sudden panic.

Jamal's eyes traveled to my hand, and I had to snap the fingers of my other hand to get his attention back.

"Jamal. What is happening?"

Before he had a chance to answer, a group of guards ran past us. I watched as they raced down the corridor and out of view.

"People are being recruited," he said, almost absentmindedly.

"I know. That was the plan, right?"

"Not by us," Jamal said, taking my hand in his as the other one flamed. "By The Vizier."

I felt weak, and the flame went out. "The Vizier? What do you mean he's recruiting people? He wants people of magic too?"

Jamal shook his head. "Get dressed and meet me in the entrance hall. I need to get the guards out. I'll see you in ten minutes."

With that, he took off down the hallway after the guards. I rushed to my wardrobe and threw on some pants and a shirt before running down to the entrance hall.

Freya stood by the open door as Jamal issued orders, sending the guards out to different parts of town.

"Anyone want to explain to me what is going on?" I asked as the last of the guards sprinted out of the door.

"He's after the lamp," Freya said, shutting the main doors. "The Vizier. He's looking for the lamp. He wants Genie."

My heart leapt into my throat at the thought of it. He'd tried and failed to get the lamp before. Getting it now would be disastrous. I was Genie's master because I was the first person to see him when he turned back into his magical self. I'd lose that right if someone rubbed the lamp.

I turned, ready to race to Genie, but Jamal grabbed my arm.

"You can't help him by being with him. We need to come up with a way to stop The Vizier from getting the lamp. I've got almost all the guards out looking for him, but so far there have been no sightings."

"Then how do you know?"

"We got word this morning that someone had been approached in a bar in one of the seedier parts of town. He was asked to go into the desert and into a secret cave to get a lamp."

"My father found the lamp in a secret cave. He didn't throw it back there."

"Gaia. The lamp is magic. Just because your father didn't go back to the cave himself, doesn't mean the lamp didn't return there. Without Genie living in it, it is free to return."

"You speak as though it's a sentient being. It's a lamp."

Freya walked over and placed her hand on my arm. "It's a magic lamp. You might have magic, but you don't know much about it. I've read the history of the lamp. It was a myth even eighteen years ago. No one really believed it was anything other than a story, but The Vizier did. That's why he spent his life searching for it. Your father freeing Genie would have stopped The Vizier from using Genie's magic to become all-powerful if you hadn't have stopped him first. I believe that the lamp is back in the cave where your father found it. Just like back then, The Vizier is recruiting people to go and find it."

"I need to free Genie!" I said, breaking away from both of them. "It's the only way."

I ran from them, my head spinning. I couldn't let The Vizier become Genie's master. There was no telling what havoc it would wreak, and if I lost my chance to free Genie, he would never get that chance again.

I ran into his room to find him drinking coffee at his desk. He stood when I barged in.

"Gaia, Whatever is the matter?" He pulled me into his arms as I began to shake.

"I need to free you. The Vizier is recruiting people to find the lamp."

Genie sucked in a breath and held me at arm's length. "The Vizier is here? In Kisbu? You're sure?"

"I think so," I answered, tears streaming down my face. "No one has seen him exactly, but someone saw a man trying to get people to go into the desert to find the lamp. It must be The Vizier. Who else could it be?"

The genie licked his lips and drummed his fingers on my arms, making his chains rattle.

"If The Vizier really is in town, then freeing me is the last thing you should do. I have powers now. They are limited without wishes, but I have them. Let me keep you safe, then if you do need to make that last wish, you can use it."

"No!" I cried out, frustration bubbling in my veins. "If he finds that lamp, it will be dangerous for us all. I won't have the last wish anymore. He'll have all the wishes, and he will use them against us."

Genie began to pace up and down the room. "He won't find it!"

"How could you possibly know that?" I cried out. "He found it before. He knows it's in the secret cave, and he knows where that cave is. Don't underestimate him. It is because of him you have these chains binding your wrists together. He is powerful enough to make you turn back into a genie."

Genie shook his head sadly. "And so if you use your last wish and make me a human, what is to stop him turning me into a genie again?"

I opened my mouth to answer, but the truth was horrifying. The Vizier was already powerful enough to make Genie a genie again. It didn't matter how many times I wished for him to be free. As long as The Vizier was alive, Genie would always be a slave.

"Then, we have to find the lamp before The Vizier does!"

"You don't even know where the cave is, Gaia. Even if you did, do you really think you'd be able to get the lamp out? Your father was incredibly lucky to survive. I can't put you in that danger."

I screamed in frustration. There was nothing I could do, and it was killing me. Genie held his hands up to my face and wiped the tears away with his thumbs. The chains hung down between us. I'd never felt more resentful of them as I did now. He lifted them and put his arms over my head then pulled me into a kiss. His lips were wet and tasted of salt, my own tears. With each new tear that fell, he kissed it away.

"We really can't stop this, huh?" I whispered.

"We can stop it, and we will. I just don't know how. We defeated The Vizier before, we'll do it again."

"I defeated him before," I reminded him, "but I don't know how. How can the birth of someone destroy someone else?"

Genie pulled the chains back over my head and went back to his desk where there was a huge stack of books, most of which were open.

"I don't know," he said, running his hands through his hair. "It takes a lot to stump me, but there are so many unknowns. The Vizier is more powerful now than he was before. I don't think he'd be able to turn me back into a Genie with only his own power. He must have someone helping him."

"A woman!" I said, perching on the edge of the desk. "The woman that killed the midwife. But we don't know who she is."

"No, we don't. Then there is the puzzle of how you defeated The Vizier. You and your siblings. We don't even know how many you have."

We had so many puzzle pieces that didn't fit together. "Can't you remember where the cave was? You lived there. Surely you could take us to the cave, and we could retrieve the lamp ourselves?"

Genie closed his eyes and placed his head in his hands. "I barely remember what I had for breakfast anymore. You are asking me to remember things, but my memory is gone. I don't know." He slammed his fist down on the table and shouted. "I don't know."

"I can't do this," I said, turning around and leaving his room. When I was outside, I leaned against his door and burst into tears.

Everything was hopeless. If Genie couldn't save us all, who could? Jamal and Freya were trying, but the odds against them were insurmountable. Even if they did find some people with latent magic and they were able to convince them to come to the palace, then what? Genie was once the most powerful person in the whole kingdom. I probably was the most powerful person in the kingdom now, but none of that helped me in my current situation. If The Vizier got the lamp, we were all doomed.

I wiped my eyes on the back of my hands and tried to pull myself together. If only Genie remembered everything, I was sure that he'd be able to figure all this out. He was a genius. He was just lost like the rest of us.

If he wasn't going to let me wish him free, I was going to free him another way. I strode down the corridor to my own room and quickly packed a bag of clothes.

"Where are you going?" Freya asked after walking into my room and catching me in the act.

I ignored her question. "I know you are not my maid anymore, but would you please run to the kitchen and ask them to pack me some food. I've not eaten today, and I'm starving."

She stood, her feet wide and her arms crossed. "Not unless you tell me where you are going. You are going to the desert, aren't you? You think you can find the lamp."

I pulled my bag over my shoulder and approached her. "Freya. I'm not going anywhere unsafe. I'm not going to the desert."

"So where then?"

"I told you already. I'm going to The Forge."

Her eyes opened wide in surprise. "I didn't expect you to go so soon. And for a potion? Surely they can't make enough for a whole kingdom?"

If it wasn't so serious, I would have laughed. "No. For Genie. He will figure all this out. You know how intelligent he is. He just needs to remember."

She nodded. "That's not a bad idea. I can't let you go alone, though. It's not safe."

"Genie's coming with me," I lied. I'd never lied to her before, but she and Jamal were busy enough without having to babysit me. Hopefully, by the time Freya realized that Genie was bound to the palace, I'd already be gone.

As Freya went to the kitchens, I went to say goodbye to my mother. She was sitting up in bed, staring at the wall opposite her. She didn't even acknowledge my presence as I kissed her cheek.

"I'm going to find a memory potion!" I whispered to her. "I'll bring some back for you and for father too."

She murmured an incoherent reply, almost breaking my heart in the process.

Freya caught up with me by the staff entrance. "When will you be home?" she asked tears in her eyes. I pulled her into a hug. "I'm not going to be gone long. I'll find the elixir and come straight home."

She nodded as she handed over the food. "I got enough for you and Genie."

"He's just outside," I lied. "I trust you and Jamal to keep the kingdom running. You two are doing a better job than I ever could."

She snorted a laugh between the tears. "I don't know about that. We are just doing our duty."

"When this is all over, I'll make sure the pair of you are recognized for your efforts."

"We need this to all be over first," Freya reminded me.

I gave her one last hug and slipped out of the door.

I hated that I was running away. Neither Genie nor Jamal knew that I was going. My plan was to get the first airship out, find the elixir, and come straight back. If things went to plan, I'd be two days, max.

I kept to the shadows as I ran through the backstreets to the Urbis Express station. I'd already checked the timetable. There was one due to leave for The Forge within the hour. I'd brought enough money with me to use the royal cabin if I had to, but I hoped there was enough space for me to travel in the main cabin.

I barely noticed the shadow that crossed my path, but the sudden thickness of the air squeezed my lungs. My whole body began to tingle with magical energy. I'd felt it once before in Kisbu, and it had turned out to be nothing.

I stood, darting my head around, quickly searching for the source of the magic. I already knew who it was. I could feel him, feel the malevolent force his magic generated, but it was only when he stepped out of the shadows that I stopped. The whole world suddenly seemed darker as though the sun had gone behind a cloud, and the ambient noises of the busy Kisbu streets had silenced. A chill invaded the air.

"What do you want?" I shouted out to The Vizier as he walked slowly to the middle of the alley about fifty feet from where I was standing.

"You know what I want, Gaia."

His voice was low, and yet, I could hear him even with the space between us. Even that was carried by magic. I looked around, hoping that someone would walk into the street, but it was unusually quiet, even for Kisbu's back streets.

"You want me. Why?"

"I believe I told you why when we were fortunate to cross paths in Urbis," he said, taking a slow step forward. With each step, he moved closer. I stumbled a step backward.

"You told me that my siblings and I defeated you. How do you know so much about me?"

"I know everything there is to know about you, Princess Gaia, you and your mother. It's an interesting story. It's a shame that you'll never get to know it."

He pulled his arm back and sent a jet of purple light in my direction. Instinct had me ducking just in time. I fell to the ground and rolled into a narrow alley. The second I was out of his view, I jumped to my feet and ran. I'd fought him before. I had no intention of doing it again. The alley took me into a residential district away from the airship station I'd been heading toward. Clothes hanging on lines crisscrossed the street forcing me to duck every few feet, slowing me down. I could no longer see The Vizier behind me, but his magic remained as strong as ever. At the end of the alley, I skirted a building and turned into a street I hoped would take me to one of Kisbu's main streets in the hope that he wouldn't follow me if there were witnesses.

After fifteen minutes of running, I stopped and allowed myself a rest. Taking a few deep breaths, I looked back. The Vizier was nowhere to be seen, but I knew he was behind me somewhere. The street I was on looked vaguely familiar. It was one of the ones I sometimes took on my nighttime rambles.

The spice market was close by. If I could get there, he'd never find me in the throng of shoppers. Not waiting for him to appear, I took off again, running this time on more familiar ground. Except when I got to the spice market, there was no one there. The spices and wares were covered over, closed for the day. Looking up, I saw that the evening had come quickly. Way too quickly. I'd left the palace in the afternoon. By my calculations, I'd been out just over half an hour. There was no way it could be evening, and yet the darkening of the sky told me it was. Had The Vizier altered time itself or had he messed with my mind in the way he'd messed with anyone else's. The thought of it scared me more than anything else. I was saved thinking about it too much by the bright colors of spices filling the air in an explosion of powder.

I took off again, winding through the alleys of the stalls, tears streaming down my face from the sting of the spices in my eyes and my lungs straining to breathe.

I ran, almost blindly through the market, feeling my way as the noise of stalls being hit by magic got closer and closer.

Each breath I inhaled burned at my lungs, but I didn't slow down. To slow down would be my inevitable demise, and yet, the pain of going forward almost had me falling to my knees.

Fighting fire with fire, literally, in this case, I shot out flames blindly behind me.

Everything, beyond the sound of the spice market going up in magic, was silent. Where were the people? This area of Kisbu was a hub, and even in the early evening would be full of people heading home from their work. Something was wrong, but without being able to see, I didn't know what.

I tripped over something, and fell forward. Holding my arms out in front of me to soften the fall, I was surprised to find myself plunging into water. Panic enveloped me as I tried to make sense of it. For a brief second, I thought I'd fallen into a river before sense prevailed, and I remembered that no rivers ran through Kisbu. As my face hit the water, the spices cleared from my eyes, and I was able to see. Sitting up in the knee-deep water, I found that I could see again. I'd fallen in a water trough meant for drinking water for horses and camels. I was soaking, but I was alive. The sun had fallen further in the sky. In front of the burning orb, the familiar silhouette of The Vizier appeared. I couldn't get out of the water quick enough. Water slopped out of the sides of the trough as I tried to move. The sun was entirely blocked out as The Vizier stepped closer.

I waited for the inevitable, but it never came. Instead, something happened that chilled me much more than my own death.

“You know, I think killing you right away would be a mistake,” The Vizier mused. “Your father found me the lamp all those years ago. How fitting it would be to use you to get it for me now.”

He leaned forward and grabbed the front of my shirt, pulling me from the water.

His menacing eyes glared at me as he held me up to his eye level, levitating me from the ground.

“You, my dear, are going to get Genie for me. You are going to help me bring about the downfall of Badalah.” And with that, he heaved me over his shoulder and began to carry me to the edge of town.

GODDESS OF FIRE

8TH JULY

Somewhere a clock struck midnight, waking me from sleep.

"We're closing, love. I'm sorry, but I'm going to have to ask you to leave."

I looked up into the kind eyes of the barman who'd served me coffee the previous evening. It obviously hadn't worked as I'd managed to fall asleep with my head on the table. The music had stopped, and the other patrons had left. Without the noise and hubbub, I felt suddenly exposed. My magical energy whirled beneath the surface, and I could feel the magic of The Vizier. Like an itch beneath the surface of my skin, his magic mingled with mine.

I'd managed to get away from the Vizier hours earlier when he'd hoisted me over his shoulder. Setting fire to the back of his outfit had been a stroke of genius on my part as he'd dropped me to the ground to put the fire out. I'd ran, but he'd chased me all over Kisbu before I'd finally lost him and hidden in a back street bar where the clientele were almost as scary as The Vizier. The same bar I was currently wiping drool from my face in.

The barman put down the cloth he was using to wipe the glasses and spoke to me. "Look, I don't want to come off as a creep, but you look a little lost. I live a five-minute walk from here. If you don't mind waiting for me to sweep up and lock up, you could crash at my place for the night." He held his hands up. "I'll sleep on the sofa."

My lips curled up at the sides as I stood. His offer was tempting, but in going to his house, I was putting him in danger.

"Thank you, but I'm good. I'm sorry for falling asleep on your table."

"Hey, It's not often I have a beautiful woman waking up next to me. You aren't my usual client type."

"I noticed," I said, picking up my coat. I ran my hand down his arm and then impulsively kissed his cheek. I wasn't in the habit of kissing strangers, but this guy had saved my life, even if he didn't know it.

Outside, the street was much quieter than when I'd walked in, but the underbelly of Kisbu didn't sleep. Strange people hustled past me as though they were going somewhere important. My heart pounded as I walked past each one, fearful that any one of them could be The Vizier. I pulled my hood further around my ears and continued walking through the maze of alleyways, sometimes having to step over the people who were sleeping rough. Had this part of Kisbu always been like this, and I'd just not noticed before? In all my nocturnal adventures, I'd not once ventured here. I'd always thought of myself as fearless for my nighttime escapades, but as I walked through this part of town with a powerful wizard out to kill me, I realized just how wrong I'd been. I'd not known it at the time, but I'd been protected before. Protected by walking through relatively safe streets near the palace. Tonight had shown me for what I really was. A spoiled rich kid who thought breaking the rules made her something special. The realization was sobering. I was scared. For the first time in my whole life, I was scared of Kisbu. It had always been my home, but now it was something malevolent with dark corners and strange people. I carried on walking, using the darkness as a cover as much as possible, unsure of which way to turn. Heading toward the palace would put me out in the open, and no doubt, The Vizier was waiting for me there. And yet, the palace was the only place I knew I'd be safe. I literally had nowhere to go.

A noise startled me. I turned on the spot and, without thinking, let off a fireball that streaked through the air. A cat shot down the alley with a squeal as my fireball fizzled out. I fell to the ground and let my head fall into my hands. I was twitchy and tired, and I'd used magic, which was the worst thing I could do. I was pretty sure The Vizier could sense my magic as I could sense his. Between that and the flash of light I'd produced, I may as well have painted a target on my ass and shouted come find me.

After a few deep breaths and a quick check to make sure I hadn't accidentally singed the cat, I stood up and ran, trying to get myself as far away from my burst of magic as possible. I found myself on the very edge of town next to the wall that surrounded it. The gates were all now open, thanks to my mother reducing the tax on farmers. It felt like a hundred years ago that we'd opened them, and yet, it was less than a week. I trailed my hand along the old wall, built way before my father's time when Kisbu was a young town and prone to attack. These walls had stood here since Genie was a child. They protected us through the dark days when all the kingdoms were attacking each other. The buildup of dark magic had been slow. So slow that no one really understood how bad everything was until the year I was born when everyone suddenly stopped fighting. I'd done that. Myself and my siblings. I didn't know how, and I didn't know why. I didn't even know how many there were of us, but I knew that our birth had brought about peace after years of darkness. Light had come back into the world again, but now it was fading. I never knew the dark times, but I'd heard enough about them to know that I didn't want them coming back. As one of the city gates came into view, something struck me. The Vizier had spent years trying to get control of Badalah and especially Kisbu, but this kind of thing had been happening everywhere. Eighteen years ago, The Vizier wasn't the only person with evil intent. There had been others. I didn't know much about Draconis, for example, but I did know that the queen had spent a hundred years in a deep enchanted sleep. Someone had done that to her, but who? An image sprung to mind. The woman who had killed the midwife. Could she have had something to do with the downfall of Draconis? Had she kidnapped Princess Azia? Worst of all, was she somehow connected to The Vizier? I brought a hand to my throat as I thought of how horrific it would be if those malevolent people who had wreaked havoc on the other kingdoms somehow came together. It was almost beyond comprehension, and the thought of it terrified me, but it made sense too. The Vizier wasn't powerful enough to make everyone in Kisbu lose their memories, but if he found others. Bad witches and wizards, and they had somehow come together...

I let out a moan, then threw up on the cold, dusty street. This was bigger than I had ever imagined. It was the only thing that fit.

After looking both ways to make sure I wasn't being followed, I slipped out of the town's boundaries and out into the desert.

People from outside Badalah always assume that the desert is devoid of life and searingly hot all year round, but that couldn't be further from the truth. Even on summer nights like this, I had to pull my sweater around myself to keep out the chill. On the very edge of the desert, life was abundant. Plants and wild grasses grew here, and many small animals scurried about. In the very far distance, the Badalah Mountains rose up from the dunes. In the daytime, it would be a riot of reds and yellows, but in the moonlight, both the dunes and the mountains shone blue. Somewhere out there, in the miles between me and the mountain peaks, was a cave, and in that cave, was the key to controlling Genie. Right now, as the wind blew tumbleweeds across my path, the desert was calm and peaceful. The feeling of The Vizier's magic had subsided a little. Wherever he was, it wasn't near me. He was probably waiting for me to return to the palace, which is why I was going to spend the rest of the night as far away from it as possible. I'd trek back there in the light of day, using the busiest main streets where he wouldn't dare to fight me.

I found a rock and sat, looking out past the large

cacti plants to the sea of sand. My father had told me once that the cave had risen up from the depths of the dunes by The Vizier's magic.

I stood up as a thought occurred to me. The Vizier wasn't the only one with magic; I was magic too. If I could find the lamp before The Vizier, I'd never have to worry about him gaining control of Genie. The moon hung high in the sky. A quick check of my watch told me it was just after half-past midnight. Only half an hour since I'd left the relative safety of the bar. I still had hours until sunrise. Without looking back, I stepped out onto the sand and began to run. My feet sank into the sand, slowing me down and making my calves burn, but with the moon on my back, I carried on, trying to sense the vibrations I'd come to know as magic. If The Vizier had found it by magic, it meant I could too.

But what I hadn't counted on was how exhausting it was. I'd barely slept all night. Half an hour with my head on a bar table didn't count for much against the harsh desert. Wind sent sand into my eyes, but with each step, a vibration beneath my feet became stronger. It felt different from the vibration of The Vizier's magic, less malevolent and thrumming at a different frequency. There was something almost joyful and exciting about it, and yet, looking around me, this part of the desert was the same as any other part. There was no marker here or at least no visual marker, and yet the magic swirling around me had all the hairs on my body standing on end. My own magic swirled around with it, mingling, pulling the fire right through me until I was an inferno. My fire twisted around me, gathering speed, lighting up the desert around me. I should have been more worried. The Vizier or anyone else that cared to look in this direction would see me a mile off. But the power I felt, surrounded as I was by all this magic, made me feel invincible. The tornado of fire flew upwards from my body, coming to land on the sand about twenty feet in front of me. Like a snake, it burrowed down into the sand, lighting it up like a torch and sending sand flying in all directions. I had to cower and hold my arm over my eyes as a stairwell deep into the sand appeared. Just as suddenly as it started, the magic stopped. The light show ended, and I was plunged into darkness with only the moon lighting my way. All I could see of the cave was a small opening in the sand with a set of steps leading down. Already exhausted by lack of sleep and the magic I'd used to open the cave, producing a flame on my fingertips took everything I had, but without it, I'd be descending into darkness.

My breathing increased as I descended the steps, each one taking me farther from the entrance. Genie had told me only the other day how dangerous this cave was, and it was all I could think about as the entrance above me got smaller and smaller.

Darkness surrounded me, both above and below, with the glow from my fingers only illuminating the roughly hewn walls around me, making shadows dance. With each step I took, my energy depleted, but to let my fingertips go out, would be madness. My body was reacting with fear enough without having to contend with pitch blackness. The hairs on my arms stood on end, and a sheen of sweat decorated my forehead. Despite the magical energy buzzing around me, there was something ominous about walking into the ground with tons of sand above my head, sand that was only being held up by magic and could cave in at any time.

Suddenly, there was light ahead of me. Light that

wasn't conjured by me. I blew on my fingers, and the small flame extinguished. Holding my hand to the wall, I walked slowly toward the light source, running my finger along the hard sand and feeling it come away in my fingers, reminding me just how precarious this whole place was. But as I got closer to the light and the magical buzzing increased, so did my confidence. As I reached the bottom step, a whole cavern shone out ahead of me.

My eyes widened at the sight before me. Gold filled the cavern both in bars and in coins. Treasure upon treasure twinkled at me. Rubies and diamonds and sapphires were piled high. There was enough wealth here to buy food for the whole of Badalah for years, maybe even centuries. How had this been under the desert all this time, and I'd not known about it? My father had known. This is where he'd found the lamp in the first place.

"The lamp!" I whispered. I scanned the gold and jewels and other treasures, desperately searching for the one thing I'd come down here for. Stepping out into the cavern, I found a small pathway through the mountains of gold coins and started to weave through it, careful not to disturb the precarious piles.

I looked this way and that trying to spot the lamp, but there was so much stuff down here that finding it could take me years. The cave was bigger than the palace and filled with so many antiquities that I feared I'd still be down here when morning came. If someone happened to look out into the desert, the cave opening would be easy to spot. I needed to grab the lamp and get out of here before anyone noticed, especially The Vizier. My foot nudged a coin, dislodging it from a pile that towered above me. That one coin rolled away then spun before it came to a complete stop about a meter away from where I was standing. The pile it had come from began to totter, making my heart race. If it came down, I'd be killed with the weight of it. I stood stock-still until the pile settled and quietened. If it had almost fallen with just one displaced coin, I didn't want to think about what would happen if I accidentally bumped against any more. I closed my eyes and took a deep breath, which I let out slowly. Any movement could send this whole place toppling down upon me. Thoughts of Genie flooded my mind. I was doing this for him. Tomorrow morning, Freya would tell him that I was on my way to The Forge. I wondered what would happen if the gold caved in, and I ended up down here forever. Would Genie send a search party out for me? Would Freya and Jamal travel to The Forge to find me? Would my parents ever get their memories back?

It was impossible to know, but I had a feeling that without me, The Vizier would take over. There was something that connected us. I might not know what, but I knew I was going to have to be the only one who stopped him. I'd done it before. I'd made him go away when I was only a babe in arms. This time, I'd make him go away for good. One of us was going to have to die. I just needed to get the lamp and get out of this gods-forsaken place before that person turned out to be me.

I carefully trod through the jewels, tiptoeing and keeping my hands to my side as I watched the path in front of me and only glancing up every so often to check for the lamp. I'd been searching for over half an hour when something had me paralyzed with fear. A voice boomed out, echoing off the walls and shaking the already precarious piles of gold and jewels. I spun on the spot to see The Vizier standing at the entrance to the cave at the base of the stairs.

"Well, you've made this very easy for me," he cackled. "If I'd have known you'd come here of your own volition, I'd have waited it out rather than chase you all over town."

Beside me, a pile of coins shuddered. "If I find the lamp, I'll use it to get out of here before I give it to you."

He laughed, an evil guffaw that bounced off the walls, reverberating through the cavern.

"No, you won't. I know you have feelings for the genie. Such a fool. You'll do as your father did and free him. He was a fool too."

"My father was no fool!" I shouted out and immediately regretted it as a few coins fell to my feet.

"Yes, yes, yes," he replied lazily. "That's why he's currently living on the streets instead of in the palace. He doesn't even know who he is."

I looked around, ignoring his sneers. I needed to find the lamp before he did. I'd have to use it. It meant that Genie would never be free, but at least, I'd have the lamp, and I'd be out of here. I'd find another way to free Genie. I'd destroy the lamp.

But as I turned to run away, a stack of gold came toppling down. A chain reaction started, bringing the gold crashing down around my ears.

"Damn you!" I heard The Vizier say above the noise of the gold. Presumably, he was running up the stairs to save himself as the ceiling began to rain sand down on me.

I ran, dodging falling sand and gold, but it was clear I wasn't going to make it. The entrance to the stairs was no longer there, and neither was The Vizier. My fears were coming to fruition. I was going to be crushed to death under the Badalah desert.

The noise was deafening as thousands of Rubees worth of gold crashed down around me. I'd not found the lamp. Not even seen it. Genie couldn't save me now. No one could. I scrambled through the falling debris, but it was too late. I tripped and felt myself falling. Before I hit the ground, someone scooped me up and pulled me into the air. The ground beneath me felt like it was moving, elevating me and the mysterious stranger upward. My hair flew out in front of my eyes, causing further disorientation, but a cool breeze hit me as we flew upward. For a second, my mind turned to Genie. Someone was gripping me tightly, someone who wanted to save me. One hand held onto him, fearful I'd somehow fall, but with the other, I dragged my hair from my eyes. My mouth fell open in surprise when I saw who had saved me and then again when I saw how.

"Fath...Aladdin. What are you doing here? Where did you get this...this...?" I looked down and saw it wasn't the ground coming up with us; it was a carpet. We were flying through the air on a carpet.

He grinned at me. "I don't know where it came from, but I feel like it knows me."

"It knows you?" I asked incredulously.

He shrugged as we swerved around a particularly large pile of gold. □I have déjà-vu about this place. It□s strange. I feel like I□ve been here before.□

"You have!" I replied as we ducked under a falling chest. "Do you remember how to get out?" I screamed as the whole place began to disintegrate around us.

"Nope, but I have a feeling the carpet does."

We flew higher and higher, dodging sand and gold, and then, as there was nowhere else to go, the carpet flew us right into the falling sand.

I clamped my eyes and mouth tightly together and held onto my father as sand closed in around us. The carpet began to falter. We were being crushed to death. And then when I thought I'd never breathe again, the carpet pulled free, and we were catapulted into the air.

I tumbled through the air, sucking in deep breaths. The world spun around beneath me, and I was aware that the first rays of sun were beginning to light up the sky. My trajectory changed, and I stopped flying upwards and began to fall. A scream was pulled from my lungs as I finally stopped tumbling end over end and saw the desert below me. For the second time in almost as many minutes, my father sent the carpet into a dive and grabbed me before I could fall any further.

"Are you alright?"

I shook my head, shaking the sand from it and pulled it back from my face. Below me, the sand was leveling out, and the cave was once again lost to the desert. In the far distance, a shock of purple smoke disappeared into the mountains. And where there's smoke, there's fire.

"The Vizier! He's gone that way. We need to get him."

The carpet lowered us softly to the sand. My father stepped off it.

"I'm not chasing that...thing. I don't know who he is, but there was something malignant about him. I felt it the moment he entered the cave."

"You were in the cave before he was? Why?"

"I saw you. You ran right past the tower when I was looking out of the window. I saw that man chasing you. You've done a lot for me, and it looked like you were in danger. I raced after you both, but you were so far ahead that I lost you both. With nothing else to do, I walked through the streets trying to find you. A couple of hours ago, I saw a small light in the desert. At first, I thought it was a firefly, but then I realized that it was too far away."

I lit up the tip of my finger to show him. He raised an eyebrow.

"Magic," I pointed out. "A bit like your flying carpet."

"It's not my flying carpet. I saw it in the cave and stood on it without thinking. I was as surprised as you to find it moving. I do feel like I know it, though."

"Maybe you do," I mused. He'd gotten out of the cave once before. Maybe the carpet had helped him then too. "So you followed me into the cave?"

He nodded. "I did. I thought it was pretty weird how there was an opening in the desert floor, but I'd seen you go down. I'd only been in there a few minutes when The Vizier entered. I knew he was bad news from the start. I could feel a coldness about him. I watched to see what he would do and when it became apparent that the whole place was caving in, I came to save you. And here we are."

"And here we are," I echoed. "We need to head to the mountains. I need to catch him."

My father looked over to where the mountains were burning brightly in the morning sun. He shook his head and then turned back to look at me.

"I don't understand what it is you are getting mixed up in, but I know evil when I see it."

"But..." The world began to spin around me as the heat blazed down. I'd barely slept all night, and apart from a beer in the inn, I'd not eaten or drunk anything in hours. "I don't feel so well."

Blackness pressed down on me, and I found myself falling. Once again, my father caught me. The last thing I remembered as I lost all consciousness was being whisked into the air.

9TH JULY

"Where am I?" I asked groggily as I opened my eyes. I rubbed the sleep from them and tried to sit up. Everything was dark. Panic filled me until a warm hand took mine.

"It's fine. You are here with me."

"Aladdin?"

"Yes. Here, take this." He passed me a cup filled with water. I swallowed it greedily.

"Where are we?" I looked around. In the dark, I could just about make out his silhouette.

"You are at my home in the bell tower. I was going to take you back to the palace, but you wouldn't wake up, and I didn't want to take you back in that state. Especially after..."

"After you stole my mother's purse?"

"Yes, after that. I thought they'd throw me in jail for hurting you. I figured I'd let you sleep and take you back when you woke."

"What time is it?" I asked.

"I don't have a watch, but the clock struck two a while back. You've been out all day."

I closed my eyes and let out a groan. I'd been gone too long. Freya thought I was in The Forge. I guessed the others did too.

"I should get back, I said, trying to stand. I wobbled and fell over."

My father passed me an old coat. "Lay down. Use this for a pillow and get a good night's rest. Finish the rest of this water. I'll take you up to the palace first thing tomorrow."

I wanted to argue, but my brain wasn't cooperating. I let the bliss of oblivion wash over me. My father was right. There was no point going to the palace in the middle of the night. It would only raise questions.

The smell of eggs woke me from my slumber. I opened my eyes to find a plate of food. The eggs were covered in spicy sauce, and a couple of sausages completed the meal. My father handed me over the plate and a cup of steaming hot coffee.

"Where did you get all this?" I asked, downing the coffee in one. My headache disappeared almost instantly.

"I know people. I do a bit of work for some of the restaurants, and sometimes they feed me. One of them owed me, and I thought you needed something to eat and drink more than I do."

I thanked him, then split the eggs in half. "We can share," I said with a smile.

I missed how easy it was to talk to my father. He

didn't remember himself, but the man I once knew was still there.

"Do you think that the queen will be too upset with me?" he asked, demolishing the last sausage.

"Come on," I said, standing up and taking his hand. "Let's see."

I was just about to head down the steps of the tower when my father tugged on my arm. "We have transportation, remember?" He pointed to the carpet.

"We can't possibly travel on that in broad daylight!" I said, but he pulled me toward him. The carpet took off, knocking me off my feet.

My long black hair flew out behind me as we flew over the streets of Kisbu. My heart raced with excitement as I took in the city below me. Most people didn't notice, but every so often, someone would look up at us in wonder.

"People will think they are going insane," I laughed as we flew over a group of children who were pointing up at us.

"Everyone is already insane," my father said. "Most don't remember who they are."

"I think you might remember when you see the palace."

He started to push the front of the carpet down to lower us to the palace gates, but I had other ideas.

"Let me steer this thing," I said, gripping the front of the carpet. I swerved it away from the guards and up to a certain window. The window was closed, but we were able to land on the terrace outside it.

My father peered out over the view of Kisbu. I watched him as he took it all in. This was the view he'd woken up to for the past eighteen years of his life. A flicker of recognition flickered briefly in his eyes. It gave me hope. I opened the door to his bedroom and ushered him in. The room was empty. Thankfully, my mother had gotten up and left the room at some point earlier. I pushed my father into the en-suite bathroom with the demand that he have a bath, and while he did that, I looked through his wardrobe to find a suitable outfit.

I passed the outfit through to him and stepped back out onto the terrace. In the far distance, I could just about see the peaks of the mountains where The Vizier was hiding. I knew roughly where he was now. I could send guards out into the desert to capture him.

I tapped my fingers on the railing, willing my father to hurry up. I missed Genie. I needed to let him know I was alright, but a part of me felt excitement at introducing my parents to one another. My father knew my mother was the Sultana, but it was unlikely that she'd remember him as the thief that stole her purse at the restaurant the other day. She'd barely seen him. I wasn't going to remind her of the fact either.

A tear came to my eye as my father joined me on the balcony. He looked like the man I'd grown up with. He held out his arm and gave me a grin as I linked my arm with his.

"I think it's about time you met The Sultana." I gave him a reassuring pat on the arm. "Just don't mention the purse. She'll never put two and two together."

It wasn't my mother, however, we stumbled upon first. Jamal walked around the corner and stopped in his tracks when he saw who was in the palace.

"Gaia...And The Sult..."

I shook my head and gave him a meaningful look.

"Aladdin. Mr. Aladdin, sir."

He walked forward confidently and held out his hand for my father to shake.

"Pleased to meet you."

There was something about the way my father shook hands with Jamal. He was so regal and yet jovial. The Aladdin that had grown up on the street and was now back on the streets was still there, but the eighteen years of training and leading a kingdom hadn't left him.

"I'm looking for Mother. Do you know where she is?"

Jamal's face lit up. "Actually I do. She's in the breakfast room. She's feeling well today," he added pointedly.

That boded well. My plan wouldn't work if she had one of the migraines that frequently plagued these days.

"Thank you, Jamal, we'll go and see her now. Mr. Aladdin saved my life the other night, and I'd like to introduce him."

Jamal's eyebrows shot skyward. "He was in The Forge?"

Aladdin looked between us with a great deal of curiosity.

"Not quite. I have news, but I think this is more important. I'll come to find you later. Can you make sure the guards are doing their jobs properly? I think we might need all the protection we can get."

Jamal hesitated. I could see he was torn between wanting to follow orders and curiosity about what was going on.

"I promise, we'll talk," I added. "Find Freya, and I'll come to talk to you both."

He didn't look particularly pleased, but he let us go on our way.

Outside the breakfast room, I made to open the door, but my father put his hand out to stop me.

"What's the matter?"

He shook his head. "I can't do this."

My first thought was to remind him that my mother

barely saw his face when he stole the purse, and it was unlikely that she'd remember him, but then I realized it was something else stopping him. He was nervous because he had a crush on her.

"Come on," I said, taking his hand in mine and trying to keep the grin from my face. "She'll love you."

At least, I hoped she would. I was pinning everything on it.

My mother's face lit up when she saw my father. I saw a hint of recognition in her eyes. It was fleeting, but it was definitely there.

"Mother, this is Aladdin. He saved my life the other day. Aladdin, this is Sultana Jawahir."

My father lowered himself into a deep bow as my mother smiled at me questioningly.

"A pleasure, Mr. Aladdin. You saved my daughter?" she turned to me. "Gaia, what happened?"

"It's a long story, but Aladdin saved me. I thought you'd like to meet him."

"Why, of course, please take a seat and join us as our guest for breakfast." She turned to one of the servants and ordered more food to be brought up from the kitchens.

I noticed that she looked back quickly, barely taking her eyes from my father. I picked up a bread roll and began to nibble on it.

"Tell me, Mr. Aladdin. Have we met before? You look very familiar to me."

My father shifted his weight and began to fiddle with the edge of the tablecloth. It was so unlike him to be nervous. It was cute.

He opened his mouth to speak, but a swift kick in the shin shut him up. He'd been just about to mention the restaurant where he'd stolen the purse.

“I don’t think so. He’s just a man from Kisbu,” I said before he could say otherwise. “He just happened to be in the right place at the right time.”

My mother reached across the table and put her hand on his. “Well, thank you. My daughter is everything I have. We are both lucky to have met you.”

I swear I saw the tips of my father’s ears go pink.

“I need to go and...er, speak to Jamal and Freya. You two enjoy your breakfast.” I picked up another bread roll and left them to it. The sparks were flying already. They didn’t need my help anymore.

I left the room, but instead of looking for Jamal and Freya, I headed to Genie’s room.

My hands shook as I pushed his door open. I’d lied to him and ended up falling into the trap Genie said I would. He’d tried keeping me safe, I’d set off for The Forge. I took a deep breath and pushed open the door.

He sat there, his face in a book. When he looked up, he stared at me blankly. My heart fell. His memory had left him again.

“Hello?”

I closed the door behind me and went to him. A sense of relief washed over me, knowing that his anger at me for leaving without telling him would not happen, but it was quickly replaced by a sense of loss. The sense of loss that could only happen when the person lost is sitting right there.

I took his hand in mine and pleaded with my eyes for him to remember me. The irony of it was not lost on me that the exact same scene was playing out with my parents in another part of the palace. The only difference was, they didn’t remember each other at all. I’d seen the spark of recognition in my mother. In Genie, there was nothing. I was completely gone to him.

"The Vizier is back," I said, but I could see there was no point. The sparkle in his eyes was dead. Despite my subterfuge, seeing Genie like this made me all the more determined to get to The Forge to see if they could help. I was willing to do anything it took to get Genie back, to get my parents back.

"I'll save you," I whispered through my tears.

He wiped them away with his thumb. Once upon a time, he'd kissed my tears away.

I put my hands up to his face. "Look at me."

He looked into my eyes.

"I love you."

He didn't say a word, just moved his eyes back down to his book.

I wanted him to remember me. Every part of me wanted to make him remember me, but I didn't know how. His memories flitted in and out. If only this infernal magical disease affected everyone the same, I'd know when to expect him to come back to me...to himself, but it affected everyone differently. I knew I had to prepare myself for him never coming back. The pain of that thought was almost too much to bear. I stood and kissed the top of his head.

If I couldn't speak to Genie, I'd go and do what I'd told my mother I was going to do.

I found Jamal and Freya in the conference room. The large table looked even bigger with only the two of them in there. They sat halfway down the rectangular table, far away from my parent's thrones. Today was not the day to point out that I was happy for them to use them. It didn't really matter anymore.

"Genie has forgotten me again," I said, taking a seat opposite them.

"Do you want to tell us what happened last night

and how you nearly died?" Jamal asked his jaw tight and his hands in fists.

I'd been so worried about Genie having a go at me for leaving that I'd not considered how Jamal would take this.

"The Vizier is back."

"Damn it!" Jamal said, slamming his fist down on the table. "I knew something like this was going to happen."

I braced myself for a tirade, but he merely looked down at the table and drew in a sharp breath. "Are you alright? Are you hurt?"

I shook my head. "My father saved me from the worst of it."

Jamal nodded slowly. "That's the main thing. I've... we've been worried. We've heard talk of something happening out in the desert, but when we sent guards out to investigate, there was nothing there."

"The cave is there. The cave with Genie's lamp. I saw it myself. The cave, not the lamp."

Jamal's eyes widened. "Wait, what? I thought you were going to The Forge. You mean to tell me The Vizier had you go into the cave?"

I sighed and took a bite of the bread roll I'd been holding since I left the breakfast room. It was more to calm my nerves than because I was hungry.

"I set off for The Forge. The Vizier got to me before I'd even got to the Urbis Express station. I'd barely left the palace."

Freya gulped and looked about her as though he'd suddenly appear. "He was near the palace?"

"Yes. Near enough. That's why I wanted you to make sure the guards were aware and doing their job. He's after me. I still don't understand why, but I know it's personal. I still want to go to The Forge and find a memory potion. I don't know what else to do."

Jamal drummed his hands on the table. "Gaia. I'm not your boss or your mentor. You are above me in every possible way. I know I can't demand that you stay here in the palace, and I know that you'd ignore me if I tried to demand that of you, but I hope I'm your friend."

"Of course you are. I think very highly of you."

"Then, as your friend, I'm asking that you don't run away again. We need to work as a team. This is bigger than anything else Badalah has ever seen, and we will not beat it if we are at odds with one another. I would never presume to try to run the kingdom. I have no desire to take over. I just want to help."

His words were worse than if he'd balled me out. I'd have deserved it if he had, but his quiet reaction pulled at my heart.

"I'm sorry. I shouldn't have taken off. I just want to fix this."

"We all do. Why don't you tell us exactly what happened and we'll work out a plan from there."

One of the servants brought us apple tea and pastries, and over the impromptu breakfast, I told them everything that had happened over the course of the last few days.

By the time I'd finished, Freya's mouth was so wide she could have fit a whole bread roll in it.

"Did you find the lamp?"

I shook my head. "I didn't even see it. The cave was huge. I could have searched for weeks and not stumbled upon it. I don't know how my father found it in the first place."

"Did you speak to him about it when he rescued you?" Jamal asked, taking a pastry. He rolled it around in his hands as he spoke.

I thought back to the time with my father this morning. "I didn't. I was just happy to have been saved. I'm hoping that now that he's speaking to my mother, they'll fall in love again."

"Even if they do, what do you want to come of it?" he asked, absentmindedly picking at the pastry, making a pile of flakes on the table in front of him.

I sighed. I didn't really know. It was my way of wanting things to go back to how they used to be. "You remember my father."

"Of course, I do," Jamal answered. "He is a brilliant leader. I know the man he is now isn't the man he was a few weeks back."

"Actually, I think you are wrong. He is the same man. He has the same ideals."

"He stole your mother's purse," Jamal pointed out.

"A momentary lapse in judgment. He did it as an excuse to meet my mother. He knows he loves her, he just doesn't remember why."

Jamal waved his hand. "So you want them to fall in love. Is your plan to have your mother so busy falling in love that we can get on with the job of ruling the kingdom without any more mishaps?"

Now it was my turn to be shocked. "No. That's not it at all. I want my father to rule the kingdom again. He knows how to. I figure that if he remembers my mother, he might remember his position."

Jamal sighed, putting down what was left of the pastry. "I think that's wishful thinking, Gaia. I want nothing more than your father to resume his role as sultan, but he thinks he's a street rat. He lives in a bell tower, and his bed is a pile of rags."

I brought my hands up to my temples and rubbed to

lessen the headache that was threatening.

"What do you suggest I do? Hide in the palace? For how long exactly? You know The Vizier is after me, but having me locked away from the people will give him what he wants anyway."

Jamal narrowed his eyes. "I'm not suggesting that you hide away. If anything, we need you to be more vocal. The kingdom has no clear leadership. Your mother makes good decisions then follows them up with bad. I'd love it if you took the reins, but most of the people in Kisbu don't even remember you and those that do think you are a freeloader. I don't even know how to deal with any of this."

"Neither do I," I sighed. "The only way out of this is to kill The Vizier, but even then, I'm not sure it will work. This thing is much bigger than him. He has people he's working with. If we kill him, we'll still have the others to deal with."

Jamal stood and began to pace up and down. "I wish we understood where all this was coming from. Freya has told me everything you've learned about your past, but it's like a jigsaw puzzle with half the pieces missing."

"That's exactly what it's like," I agreed, "And the bits that do fit together make no sense."

"Like the fact that you have six or more siblings," added Freya. "It's not possible. I went to see Genie when you were gone. I asked him what was the highest multiple live births in humans. He had to look it up, but he found out. Thirteen years ago in Enchantia, a woman gave birth to seven children. Three boys and four girls. All survived. They were extremely premature, and Genie thinks they only survived because of Enchantia's use of magic. Other than that, he says there have been a few cases of sextuplets, but it's really rare."

"Maybe the birth I witnessed wasn't my own then," I said, suddenly feeling sad about it. It was a stretch to think I had so many siblings.

"Who's to say that these princes and princesses were all born at the same time as you?" Jamal asked. "It's entirely plausible that you have brothers and sisters of different ages."

"They were all born around the same time," Freya and I said together.

"We were all born around the same time," I modified. "Thinking back to the birth, both babies I saw had lighter skin than me. I guess it was wishful thinking after all that it was me."

I felt tears prickle at the corners of my eyes again, but I held them back. I stood to leave. What else was there to talk about? I'd made it to the door when Jamal caught up with me. He brought me into a hug and held me as my body shook with sobs. I was just so tired of it all. "I hate that nothing makes sense. I hate that I don't know who I am."

Jamal lifted my chin and looked into my eyes. I'd forgotten how beautiful his were. "I know who you are," he said softly. "Freya knows who you are. Just because you don't know about your birth, it doesn't change who you are."

I nodded as Freya took hold of my hand. "We'll get through this. While you were gone, nothing bad happened. The Sultana wasn't feeling too well, but we managed. The residents of Kisbu have been relatively quiet, and the food is still coming in. Maybe you should talk to Genie and see if he knows why the thing you saw wasn't what you thought. Maybe he made a mistake?"

"I can't," I said sadly. "He doesn't remember me today. His wishes were legendary. There is no way he made a mistake. I saw my mother."

"So, we just need to figure out what that has to do with The Vizier and how we can use the information to stop him."

"I'll think on it," I said, feeling tired. "I need a nap first. I'm exhausted." I gave her a hug and said bye to both of them.

The palace seemed so empty, so far from how it was only a few weeks ago. I missed the hubbub of the palace, of the staff running from place to place. I walked aimlessly, not sure where to go and what to do. I wasn't as tired as I'd made out to Freya, but I needed time alone to think. The sound of laughing hit my ears. It had been so long since I'd heard laughter that I followed it to the main terrace. When I saw who it was, I hid behind one of the large potted plants and watched.

My mother's face was relaxed, and her beauty shone out. She laughed again at something my father said. Three or four weeks ago, this would have been a normal scene, but now it brought hope to my heart. I couldn't see my father's face from where I was standing, but I didn't need to. The expression on my mother's face said everything I needed to know. She was in love with him. She always had been. I left them to it and went back to find the man I loved.

"You again," Genie said as I walked into his room and shut the door behind me. I walked slowly over to where he was sitting and took the book he was reading from his hands. He didn't resist as I knelt at his feet.

"Genie. Do you know who I am?"

He shook his head slightly but didn't take his eyes from me.

"I'm Gaia. I love you."

He furrowed his brows as though he was trying to

place where he knew me from.

I leaned forward and kissed him lightly on the lips.

When I pulled back, I saw he was looking at me with curiosity. The kiss hadn't bothered him, but it hadn't made him remember me either.

I parted my lips and moved toward him again. This time, he yielded to me, and the kiss became something else. It became a kiss of lovers, not strangers. I'd found him again, and this time I wasn't going to let him go.

10TH JULY

My mother sang as she arranged flowers in a vase on the breakfast table. I'd left Genie sleeping and gone to find her via the kitchen for a cup of coffee.

"Good morning Gaia!" she sang, her eyes full of light and happiness. It had been a long time since I'd heard her sing. I'd forgotten what a beautiful voice she had.

"What's happening with you?" I asked, feeling the sides of my mouth curving into a grin. I had a feeling I already knew the answer.

"Nothing. The sun is shining. The flowers are blooming. It's a wonderful day." She walked around the table, a purple flower still in her hand, and gave me a kiss on the cheek.

"You look beautiful today, Gaia."

Now, I really knew something was up. I was wearing yesterday's clothes, having come straight from Genie's room. I'd not even showered yet.

"Did you have fun with Aladdin yesterday? He's nice, huh?" I wanted to say cute, but it felt weird saying such a thing about my own father. He was a handsome man, but she already knew that.

Her cheeks colored, and she swatted me away with her hand.

"Oh, Silly. We had a nice time, yes."

"What time did he leave?" I asked, picking up some baby's breath and handing it to her to add to her arrangement.

She paused, and a soppy look took over her features. "He did leave late. I quite forgot the time. You know, for a man that lived his entire life on the streets of Kisbu, he had some really good ideas about how to run the kingdom."

My ears pricked up. "He told you he'd lived on the streets his entire life?" Was that what he remembered?

"Well, he didn't exactly say that, but he had so many wonderful stories about his childhood. Some of it was spent in an orphanage, the rest on the streets. He told me that he was living in a bell tower now. Can you imagine it? Of course, I offered him a room here..."

I spat out the coffee I was holding, spraying the white roses with brown liquid.

My mother dabbed the table with a cloth and shook the roses, all the while giving me an exasperated look.

"You invited him to stay the night?"

"Not like that," she replied. "What do you take me for? We have plenty of guest rooms here. I thought he could use one. I didn't feel comfortable letting him go back to the bell tower. It just didn't seem right."

"So, is he here?" I asked, looking around, expecting him to walk through the door at any second.

"No. He said he didn't want to impose. I invited him for lunch, though, so go and get changed. I'd like you to look nice when he comes. If you see Jamal and Freya, would you ask them to come too? I know they've been awfully helpful around here during my illness, and I think they'd like to hear some of what Aladdin has to say."

For the first time in weeks, it felt like something was going right. Having my mother and father not only speaking to each other but actually liking each other was a start. Getting them to fall in love again would be easy because they were already in love with each other. They'd just forgotten. And while it started us on a road to recovery, it didn't solve the biggest problem of all. The Vizier. My parents had been an unstoppable team up until three or four weeks ago. It would take time for them to get to know each other again. In the meantime, I had to keep The Vizier at bay. Without being able to leave the palace, I didn't have the first clue how to do it.

"We need a plan!" I said to Jamal and Freya as I stepped out onto the terrace.

The two of them pulled apart quickly, and Freya's cheeks turned red in a similar fashion to my mother's only ten minutes earlier.

It was so obvious they'd been kissing and more so, now that they were so far apart that they were in danger of falling off each side of the bench they were sitting on.

"My father was here all day yesterday. My mother even invited him to stay."

Freya's eyes widened. "And did he?"

"No, but he is coming for lunch. My mother wants

us all there. She thinks he has some good ideas on how to rule the kingdom."

I couldn't keep the smile from my face as I said this.

Jamal jumped up. "That's great. I've been doing the best I can, but I'll be the first to admit I don't really know what I'm doing. If your father comes back and then your mother remembers things, it will be a huge relief."

Freya stood up and ran her hand down his arm, apparently forgetting they were hiding their relationship from me.

"You are too modest. The kingdom would have collapsed if it wasn't for you."

Now it was Jamal's turn to go red. It was almost like embarrassment was catching this morning.

"I didn't do a lot."

I walked toward him. "Freya is right. She seems to forget that she was half the team that kept this kingdom from falling apart completely, but you have done an amazing job. Both of you. However, as you said, having my father back will make a big difference. I'm hoping that the more time my parents spend together, the more they'll remember. I'm hoping it will cure them of this madness."

Freya looked toward Jamal then turned her eyes to me. "This won't cure them, Gaia. Even if they fall madly in love again, it will be like the first time for them. They won't get their memories of before back. Your father won't remember being at the palace before a couple of weeks ago, and your mother's memories flit in and out. It's possible that she'll fall in love with him again and then forget him again. We could keep doing this dance for eternity, and nothing will change until we stop the root cause."

I sighed. She was right. My mother's memory was functioning much the same way as Genie's. He'd remembered me again last night, but I could go back to his room right now and be a stranger to him.

I felt deflated. I'd put so much into my parents returning to normal that I'd put the real problem to the back of my mind.

"The Vizier is our main problem," I said pointlessly. They both already knew that.

Jamal stepped forward. "I have brought in all the guards we have. Most are protecting the palace. You are what he wants. I've got some of them stationed in the desert, so he'll struggle to get back to the cave to find the lamp. The rest are in town, doing what they can to find him. Just a word of warning, though. While they are looking for him, they are not doing their normal duties of keeping the peace among the citizens. Things are quiet at the moment, but you've seen how quickly things have been changing. People's memories are all being affected differently, so we can expect a lot of misunderstandings."

"I said we needed a plan," I said weakly.

"Have you convinced Genie that it would be better for all of us if he was free yet?"

I shook my head. I'd not brought it up with him for days.

"He thinks he can protect me better if I have a wish left."

Jamal stroked his chin. "If we can persuade him to give up that last wish, he's one less thing to worry about. I can take the guards away from the desert and bring them here. I'm afraid I'm not doing enough to protect you."

I bit my lip and considered his words. In theory, he

had a point, but there were things he hadn't considered.

"My father used his last wish to free Genie eighteen years ago. It lasted until The Vizier came back. My worry is that even if I do use that last wish to free him, The Vizier will be able to enslave him again."

"What if we find the lamp before he does?" Freya asked. "Maybe having the lamp itself is the key to this?"

I shrugged. I'd been through this so many times in my head, but it felt so much scarier when I put it into words.

"The Vizier managed to magic the manacles back onto Genie without the lamp. He can't control Genie without the lamp, but he seems to have the ability to control whether or not he is a Genie.

"Ok, so freeing Genie might be temporary, but if he owns the lamp, he'll never be able to be controlled. It's not ideal, but it's better than nothing while all this is going on.

"You're right!" I said, a little too quickly. My heart quickened its pace as I thought about what she had said. Until we caught The Vizier, the chance of him finding the lamp to control Genie was huge, but if we had the lamp, there was nothing he could do to Genie. Either the last wish would always be mine, or I'd use it to free Genie. Either way, he'd be safe."

"Hang on!" Jamal said, holding his hand out to the pair of us. "What exactly are you suggesting here? Didn't you say that you were almost killed when you went back into the cave, and you didn't even see the lamp."

"I don't know where the lamp is," I said excitedly, "but I know a man who does. And it just so happens he is coming to the palace for lunch!"

Jamal rolled his eyes, but he didn't have anything

to add. I was going to stay in the palace as promised, and it was an answer to one of our problems. It wasn't a permanent answer, but it was something.

"Now that we've figured out what to do about Genie, what are our plans to defeat The Vizier?"

Two pairs of eyes stared blankly back at me. For a second, I thought they'd succumbed to the sickness that was inflicting everyone else.

Freya shrugged and looked toward Jamal. Jamal held his hands up.

"I don't know. He's too powerful. Apart from you, we've had no sightings of him still."

"He's hiding in the mountains...wait. No one saw him the night he kidnapped me? He chased me all over town."

Jamal shook his head. "Nope. Not one sighting. I guess you must have kept to the back streets."

It didn't make sense. How had no one seen me being chased? "I was throwing fireballs at him for goodness sake."

Jamal looked uncomfortable. "People saw you. Just no one saw who was chasing you?"

I shifted my weight on my feet. "You think I made it up?"

"No," Jamal said, measuring his words. "I think that The Vizier is clever at not being spotted, even though we have people out looking for him."

"He's hiding in the mountains! I told you that. Have the guards looked there yet?"

"Yes. It's the first place I sent the guards to when you told me what happened, but the mountain range runs for hundreds of miles. There are caves and trees and a million places he could be hiding. We don't have the capacity to send too many guards there."

Freya marched between Jamal and me and raised her voice. “We can’t fight The Vizier now. We don’t know where he is, and if we did, we wouldn’t know how to defeat him. All we know is that this has something to do with Gaia and her birth and the other princes and princesses in the other kingdoms. Until we can figure that out, we will have to do what we can to stop too much damage. Arguing between ourselves isn’t going to help that.”

Both Jamal and I nodded, both of us looking contrite.

“Sorry,” I said. “I promised my mother I’d shower and change before my father comes. She wanted me to look nice when she introduced her daughter to Aladdin.”

Freya smirked at the irony of it.

“I was thinking of asking Genie to join us. It’s possible that seeing Aladdin will jog his memory too. He’s been hiding in his suite pretty much since this whole thing started.”

I waited for Jamal to say no, but to my surprise, he nodded and said it was a good idea.

“I’ll see you both in the dining hall at noon. Please can you make sure the guards know to let my father in when he arrives? I gave him some clean clothes yesterday, but after a night of him sleeping in the bell tower, they probably won’t look too smart.”

“Would you like me to make sure he has access to a shower and clean clothes when he arrives?” Jamal asked.

“Yes, but make it quick. My mother never liked tardiness.”

I left them to it. Maybe they’d go back to kissing with me out of the way. I found I didn’t mind. They were both so great and made a great couple. Maybe one day, they’d actually bring their relationship out in the open.

I looked at the clock. I had time to go and see Genie and invite him to dinner.

I wasn't sure if it was a good idea or not, but to have the trio together again would be wonderful. My mother and Genie were living in the same house, and yet, they'd not spoken to each other in weeks. They didn't even know who the other was.

I'd barely opened the door when Genie ran over and swept me off my feet. He greeted me with a kiss that took my breath away.

"I'm here to invite you to lunch," I laughed when I came up for air. "You've not eaten a meal with us for weeks."

He pulled away and turned his back to me, lowering his head.

"What's the matter?" I asked, putting my hand to his shoulder.

"There's a reason I've been eating here." He turned to me. "I know my memory is not as it was. Once upon a time, I know I was something. I have some memories. They are feelings rather than distinct memories, but I know I could once walk through these corridors and have people look up to me. Now I don't know who the people are. I don't know if they know me anymore."

"I know you."

He smiled and took my hand. "I know you do. Without you, this ordeal would have been too unutterably horrible to contemplate. I'm scared, Gaia. I'm scared that I'm lost. I've lost my past, and my present keeps being pulled out from beneath my feet."

I led him to the sofa and sat with him.

"Until a month ago, my mother and father ruled Badalah as the Sultan and Sultana. You were always there with them. Yesterday I introduced them to each other. They didn't remember each other, but the love they had was still there. My mother invited my father for lunch today, and I'm inviting you."

He wavered. "I don't know, Gaia."

I looked him in the eyes. "I've never known you to be scared, but I understand why you are."

"I'd go out and fight a dragon for you if you wanted me to."

I smiled. "I know you would, but I don't think it will come to that. I've not invited any dragons for lunch."

"Gaia."

"I'll be there with you. I'll be holding your hand the entire time," I insisted.

"You want to tell your parents about us?"

I leaned closer and kissed him. "It's not a secret. It's never been a secret."

"Besides, your parents don't even remember either of us," he smirked.

"That too." I returned his grin before he pulled me to him and kissed me.

"What time's lunch?" he asked.

I glanced at the clock. "I have to have a shower before lunch. I should go and change."

"Or you could just shower here in my suite," he replied with a wink. He wasn't the type of man that winked, which made it all the more amusing.

Later after a long slow shower that involved both of us, I dashed to my room and threw on a sundress. Genie stayed by my side the whole time, rushing me along the corridor to my room.

When it was time to leave, I saw his nerves in the way his hands shook and in the way he held himself. The Vizier had taken a big part of Genie by putting him in chains. He did his best to hide them as we walked to the dining room by putting one of his arms behind my back and the other under a robe. The length of the chains meant both his hands were to one side.

"Ready?" I asked as we came to the dining hall door. Genie took a deep breath and nodded. He knew he was there to meet my parents. He didn't know if he'd recognize them.

My mother stood and held her arms out to me as we entered. Genie dropped his hands to his side, taking one from my back. I grabbed it with my own hand.

"Gaia, darling. You remember Aladdin?" My father stood as I held out my hand to shake his. Beside him at the table, Freya almost choked, trying to contain a smirk.

"I do. Do you remember Genie, Mother?"

She paused, and the smile slipped from her face as her eyes turned his way. I saw recognition in them.

"You do seem awfully familiar. Gene, is it?"

She held out her hand to shake his. Beside me, I felt Genie relax.

"It's Genie. Pleased to meet you. And you, sir," he said to my father.

I watched as my mother's eyes flitted down to my hand. The hand that was holding Genie's. She raised an eyebrow and looked my way as Genie introduced himself to Freya and Jamal.

"Boyfriend?" she mouthed.

I nodded, feeling squirms in my stomach. I'd spent so long reassuring Genie about our relationship, that I'd quite forgotten to worry myself. Genie was my parents' best friend. My mother might not know that, but the age difference between Genie and I was difficult not to notice.

To my relief, she gave me a wide grin and held her

thumbs up.

Lunch was a strange affair. My mother and father flirted outrageously with one another much to the amusement of Freya, and if I was honest, of me too.

Genie barely said a word, which was unlike him. He wasn't one for small talk or waffle, but he could usually be relied upon to join in on affairs of the kingdom.

"The Badalah people outside Kisbu are still bringing food into the city," Jamal began. "I think they are only doing it because they are running out of money. Resentments are high between the city folk and the country folk, but as far as I can see, there have been no real problems for days. Obviously, Badalah cannot carry on like this, but for now, I'm taking every win I can. As you all know, the problems we are having stem from magic. The magic of the old vizier, who eighteen years ago tried to take over Badalah from Sultana Jawahir's father. I've got the palace guards and the town guards out looking for him both in town and in the desert. Freya has made up posters to recruit people of magic to help us in the fight against him, but so far, we've had little response. Years of fear and oppression against the magical folk have made recruitment difficult."

"Jamal is doing a marvelous job," my mother said, looking toward my father.

"I can see that. It sounds like you have everything in hand, young man."

Jamal smiled. "Only until our Sultan comes back. I'm trying to keep things steady until then."

My mother shot him a confused look, but she did not dispute him on it.

"Actually, there was something I wanted to ask Aladdin," I said. "The Vizier is after me, and he's after Genie. If he gets the lamp, he'll take control, and I believe his wishes will have severe repercussions on all of us. We know the lamp is in a cave protected by magic. I have the ability to make it open. I just need someone to go down there with me and get the lamp."

It was like all hell erupted around the table. I don't know who was shouting more, Jamal or Genie, but the gist of what they were saying was the same thing. Neither of them wanted me to go to the cave.

"Calm down, everyone," my mother said, standing up. "I can't hear myself think. Jamal, you first. What do you want to say?"

He glared at me then turned his attention to my mother. "Gaia promised me that she wouldn't leave the palace." he turned to me again. "You said Aladdin could do this."

"I know what I said, but then I remembered that Aladdin alone can't open the cave. He probably won't even be able to find it without me. It's only findable by magic."

"I can feel magic. I'll go with Aladdin," Jamal countered.

"You can feel it, but you can't use it. I can."

Jamal gritted his teeth.

"I don't agree to this," Genie said, butting in. "I'd rather be The Vizier's slave for eternity than put you in danger."

Jamal stood and held his hand out to Genie. "See. He doesn't want you to go either."

"It's not just me, though, is it? It's not about me, and it's not about Genie, it's about every single person in Badalah. What do you think will happen if The Vizier gets to Genie? He's already more powerful than he was eighteen years ago. Look what he's managed to do. No one knows who they are. Spouses are forgetting each other.

Parents are forgetting their children. He's managed to completely derail the whole of Badalah without being seen. Can you imagine the damage he will do if he has Genie's power too? It will be catastrophic. We need the lamp. We only know two people that can open the cave. Me and The Vizier. Who do you want to choose?"

"Why can't Genie go for the lamp? He's magic."

All eyes swiveled toward Genie.

"No!" I shouted out. "He's too valuable. I don't want The Vizier to get him even if he can't use his magic without the lamp. He'd lock him up until he could find the lamp."

"Don't you think you should let your boyfriend speak for himself?" Jamal spat out. "He's being awfully quiet about this whole thing."

Beside me, Genie sighed. "However much I wish it wasn't so, I cannot open the cave. There are certain caveats to me being a genie. I cannot escape the lamp, for example. Not unless someone frees me. I cannot give life, and I cannot interfere with people's free will. Opening the cave is one of those caveats."

The room became silent as everyone digested what he'd said.

Aladdin finally spoke. "It seems like we are at an impasse. I would be more than happy to do my duty and go into this cave of which you speak. It seems that young Gaia here will have to come with me. I will do everything in my power to protect her."

"So that's decided then," I said, folding my arms. "Tomorrow morning, we will go out and fetch the lamp. That should give you enough time to get the guards ready, right?"

Jamal nodded his head. His face paled, and he looked sick, but Aladdin had spoken, and whether my father knew it or not, he was still the Sultan of Badalah.

11TH JULY

Between the six of us, a plan had been put in place. The majority of the guards, both town and palace guards, had been pulled away from their duties and were due to meet at the palace before dawn. I'd wanted to make the trip out to the desert with just my father, me, and the magic carpet; but Jamal, my mother, and Genie had insisted on us having the guards with us.

The Vizier was probably out there watching everything from the outside, but I couldn't help but think that we might as well have a parade through town with a full orchestra announcing our plans.

I slept in Genie's room, but sleep was hard to come. Not even Genie's arms soothed me. He pretended to sleep, but each time I peeked through my eyelashes, he was staring at the ceiling.

In the morning, breakfast was a somber affair. My father did accept my mother's invitation of a bed for the night. He slept in our best guest room. No one had even asked him if he wanted to go to the cave. It was just assumed that he would. And yet he'd offered to go without question. If anything, I saw a glimmer of excitement in his eyes at the thought of the adventure. He was the only one around the table with any enthusiasm for the idea. But without any other ideas and no clue how to actually go about defeating The Vizier, it was all we had. It was only a stalling tactic, but anything that could buy us time was worth it. If it could stop The Vizier getting Genie, then it was definitely worth it.

As the sun peeked over the horizon, three hundred men and women began the short trek into the desert. We'd got so far without a problem, but I didn't expect it to last. There was no way The Vizier didn't know we were here, and it was not much of a leap for him to guess what we were doing.

Jamal took the lead on the back of a camel. He had a sword at his side and a bow on his back. He looked so dashing in one of my father's uniforms. My mother had loaned it to him so that he could show he was in charge if questioned. Behind him trotted a row of guards, also on camels. My father and I were on foot right in the middle of a hundred guards. The thought was that if the Vizier was to see us, he'd go for those on Camels first. I had ten guards to one side of me, my father on the other, and past him, another ten guards.

"Are you sure I've done this before?" My father whispered. "Before I rescued you, I mean."

Despite everything, the sides of my mouth curved into a smile. There was no one I'd feel safer going into a deadly cave with than my father.

"You did. You found Genie and saved the kingdom."

He furrowed his eyebrows then grinned. This was his greatest adventure.

The vibrations of magic strengthened. I shouted out the agreed command to stop. The guards feathered out, leaving a circle around my father and I. I closed my eyes and pulled on all my magic. Last time it had reverberated through my body, building up slowly. This time I'd been so consumed in conversation with my father that I'd not noticed.

"Stand back!" I shouted as my whole body erupted in flames.

Through the orange and yellow flames, I saw the look of shock on my father's face as he fell backward on the sand. I should have warned him. He began to stand, readying the carpet to throw at me to douse the flames, but Jamal jumped down from his camel and sprinted over to stop him. Presumably, he told him that me erupting in flames was normal and I was fine, but I couldn't hear a word because of the roaring in my ears.

The roaring abated as the wind whipped around my ears, pulling the flames from my body and diverting them to the sand. Just as before, an opening appeared in the desert floor. When it was fully open, everything became silent. I looked at my father. He cocked an eyebrow.

"Ready?"

I nodded

"The Vizier hasn't made an appearance. I think we are pretty safe," Jamal commented.

"He wouldn't make an appearance yet. I think the most dangerous time for all of us is when Aladdin and I go down there. That's when he'll strike. You'll need to keep the guards alert. Don't come down into the cave. I mean it. It's not safe."

Jamal nodded. As My father and I began the descent below the desert, I heard Jamal issuing orders to the guards.

His voice got quieter the further we went down.

"Does any of this look familiar to you?" I whispered, afraid that if I spoke up, the ceiling would cave in.

"Only from the other day. I don't know where the lamp is."

"I know, but I'm hoping that you will remember when we are down there."

At the bottom, things were exactly as they were before I'd knocked over the piles of gold when I was there before. They'd magically gone back into position as if this whole cave was some kind of magical booby trap. It probably was. Instead of stepping out onto the narrow pathway, we stepped onto the magic carpet and flew slowly over the gold and jewels.

"This is so much easier than the way I was doing it," I commented as we glided over towers of precarious piles of coins.

"Probably helps that we don't have a psychopath hot on our heels too."

"True, but I don't expect that to last. The quicker we find that lamp, the faster we can be out of here and heading home. Does any of this look familiar yet?"

Behind me, Aladdin sucked in a breath. "It's been eighteen years, Gaia. I'm not sure I'd remember even if I could...you know...remember."

"What does your intuition say?"

He looked around slowly, taking in the whole cave below us. "Try that way," he said, pointing at a dark corner of the cave.

I steered the carpet in the direction he'd pointed.

"Slow down!" he cried as we began hurtling toward the wall of the cave.

"I can't!" I cried, tugging on the front of the carpet. I closed my eyes and braced myself for impact, but we kept going. When I opened my eyes, I found we were shooting through a dark tunnel.

Ahead, a glimmer of light pierced the darkness. We shot over the lamp at high speed. I leaned so far over the edge of the carpet that my father had to hold onto my legs to stop me from falling off. I hooked the handle round my finger, scooping it up. The second the lamp was taken from the pedestal, the ceiling began to cave in like last time. I tried steering the carpet around, but it had taken on a mind of its own and was continuing its trajectory down the tunnel. We hurtled through the tunnel as sand poured in around us. Ahead, a hole opened up, and we shot upwards out into the open air about three hundred meters from the original entrance.

I shook the sand out of my hair and fell back on the carpet, laughing. We had the lamp, we'd escaped the cave, and The Vizier hadn't caught us.

My father patted my shoulder roughly. I looked his way, and he pointed to a point somewhere behind us.

I turned to follow his gaze. My stomach clenched, and bile rose to my throat as I took in the scene. The color red stained the desert floor. The guards that were still alive were frantically fighting The Vizier, but even at this distance, I could see it was a losing battle. He floated above them, shooting magic down, killing each one he hit instantly. In the middle, Jamal valiantly sent arrows up at The Vizier, but each one bounced off him as though he had some kind of invisible shield. I pulled my magic into myself and readied myself to shoot a ball of fire at him, but my father grabbed my arm.

"He doesn't know we are here, and he doesn't know we have the lamp," he said. "We can't save them all. We have three choices: Either leave before he sees us, grab Jamal and get out of here, or use the lamp."

"I can't use the lamp. It would bring Genie here."

"So? You wish for Genie to take us all home, and then I'll rub the lamp and wish for him to be free."

"You already used your three wishes! I'm not bringing Genie here. That's what The Vizier wants. I'm not leaving either!"

My father gritted his teeth. "Then we go in and get Jamal and hotfoot it out of here."

He made a motion to pass me on the carpet, but I stopped him. I couldn't leave the others to die.

"Oy!" I screamed out toward The Vizier.

"What are you doing?" my father screamed as I turned the carpet toward The Vizier.

"I'm saving everyone!" I screamed as The Vizier's attention turned my way.

He shot a bolt of magic toward us, which I blocked with fire. I was a much more evenly matched opponent. I had something the guards didn't. I had magic.

I swooped down as another bolt of magic headed our way. When the carpet skimmed the ground, I pushed my father. He fell, rolling in the sand as I shot back up into the air.

"Sorry!" I yelled down to him. "Get Jamal and the guards and get them all back to the palace! Don't take no for an answer. I'll meet you back there later. Make barricades. I'll fly in through the tower window."

I watched for a second as my father saluted me and began to run toward the mess of bodies. There weren't many guards standing, but if I could save some of them, this would all be worth it.

The Vizier flew toward me. Unlike me, he didn't have a carpet. He was defying gravity, and he was fast. Much faster than I anticipated.

"Come on!" I yelled, patting the carpet as though he was some kind of obedient pet. I steered it toward the mountains and away from the city. The Vizier followed. The only way to outpace him was to lie flat on the carpet while gripping the front. It made steering harder, but if it meant staying alive, I'd take it. The peaks of the mountains drew closer. This range bordered Draconis. No dragons lived in these mountains as far as I was aware, but it was a possibility. I darted around the mountains, weaving this way and that to avoid the magic being thrown my way. Every so often, I threw a bolt of fire behind me. My intention wasn't particularly to kill him. I knew I wasn't strong enough. My aim was to keep him from catching up and killing me. If I could keep him following my lead, I might be able to lose him in the mountains.

That was my theory, but in reality, he was too fast. Every time I dodged or swerved, he'd dodge and swerve behind me. Even at my fastest speed, he was still catching up.

"Come on," I murmured to myself, as I steered the carpet abruptly to the right.

In the distance, I saw a copse of trees. I flattened myself as low to the carpet as possible and willed it to go faster toward them.

A bolt of magic almost hit me, making my body sizzle uncomfortably. If I wasn't careful, I was going to go up in flames which wouldn't be good for the carpet. I flung a bolt of fire out behind me without looking, which eased the tension a little.

I could hear him behind me now. Even above the roar of the wind in my ears, the crackle of his magic was unmistakable. I could feel it more strongly than I'd felt it when I'd met him in Urbis. I pushed the thought to the back of my mind and pushed the carpet down into a forward motion toward the trees. As I passed under the canopy of the first tree, The Vizier hit it, making it creak, but by the time it fell, I was already halfway through the woods.

It wasn't thick enough for me to hide, but the evergreens afforded enough protection that he wouldn't be able to see me from above. He'd either have to wait it out on the outside or come in after me. I slowed the carpet to a hover and waited to see which option he would take.

Seconds later, I had my answer. The sound of magic filled the air, followed by the boom of falling trees.

"Come on, Carpet!"

I flew through the trees, confident that The Vizier was behind me. When I was in the thickest part of the woods, I pushed down, gently easing the carpet into a descent. As I came close to the ground, I rolled off the carpet, still clutching it, and pulled the both of us under a bush with the carpet lying on top of me.

I had to rely on the thickness of the canopy overhead to provide enough darkness. I held my breath as the crackling of magic became stronger, and the sound of magic hitting trees intensified.

The urge to set myself alight took hold as the vibrations of magic surged through my body. I'd still not mastered how to keep the magical energy at bay, but to set myself on fire would be like a beacon to The Vizier.

The pain became indescribable as The Vizier passed

overhead, but I held the fire inside, not moving.

When I was sure he had passed, I rolled back onto the carpet, and with flames flying out behind me, I took to the air and flew as fast as I could back to Kisbu and back to the palace.

Of course, It didn't take too long for The Vizier to figure out what had happened, but by the time he was on my tail again, I was already halfway across the desert.

His rage echoed through the air, caught up in his magic. Each vibration left me feeling sick to my stomach, but the magic he was firing at me was too far away to reach. With each minute that passed, he caught up a little ground, and each time I glanced over my shoulder, he was a little closer.

I hated that I was bringing him back to Kisbu, but the people of Kisbu weren't his main target. I was. I hoped that he would follow me to the palace and that the others would have had enough time to barricade the whole place up.

Instead of flying through the streets, I followed the outer wall for about half a mile before flying over it and heading right for the domes of the palace. Under the highest dome was a window just big enough for me to fly through. As I flew closer, I saw a face waiting for me. My father. The second I shot past him, he slammed the window shut. I crashed into the wall opposite the window, which sent me bouncing backward off the carpet. I fell to the floor, but before I hit it, I fell into a pair of strong arms.

"Gaia! Are you ok?"

The image swam around in front of my eyes, but I knew his voice, the feel of his arms, and his smell intimately.

“I think so,” I replied, rubbing my eyes.

Genie lowered me to the floor but held me steady as my vision cleared.

Jamal, my father, and Freya pushed old furniture in front of the window.

Genie took my hand and led me down the winding staircase to the lowest level in the whole palace. The basement. I was surprised to find it full of furniture and a great number of guards.

“Gaia!” My mother ran toward me and pulled me into a hug. Her whole body shook with sobs as my father, Freya, and Jamal joined us.

“You’ve cut your head!” my mother remarked as she pulled back. “Someone pass me a first aid kit!”

Within a second, someone handed her a box. She opened it and pulled out some ointment and cotton wool and began to dab my head.

“It must be where I hit the wall when I flew through the window,” I explained as she tried to wind a bandage around my whole head. I waved her off.

“It’s fine,” I assured her. “What now?”

“Now, we wait to see what he does,” Jamal said. “The whole palace is empty of people except for us down here. We’ve set the bells ringing in Kisbu, sounding the alarm so people will go inside.”

I nodded my head, which made my brain feel like it was thunking on the inside of my skull.

“The lamp!” I cried out, turning to Jamal. “Where is it?”

He pulled his shirt up and unhooked the lamp from his belt.

“You have one wish left,” he said, passing it to me.

“True,” Aladdin said, “but now we have the lamp. If you use the wish to make The Vizier go away, there are so many of us here that could free Genie later."

I looked around the sea of eager faces. Some of the guards were practically salivating at the prospect of getting their hands on the lamp.

There were only three people I trusted to use their wishes to free Genie, and my father had no more wishes left. That left my mother.

"Would you free Genie if I used my last wish to make The Vizier go away?"

She looked stunned that I would pick her out of all the people. She looked at Genie, confusion clouding her eyes. She wasn't fit to promise anything. She didn't even know who Genie was anymore. Even if she promised, there was no telling if she'd remember that promise.

I was still trying to find a workaround when the whole palace shook with an almighty boom.

The lamp fell to the floor with a clatter. I grabbed hold of Genie's arm to steady myself, but instead of flesh and blood, my hand passed through as though he was made of only air. While everyone else was looking fearfully around them trying to find the source of the boom, I watched in horror as Genie turned into smoke and was sucked back into the lamp.

Another bang echoed out, this time much closer, sending some of the guards near the outer wall flying to the floor. My father grabbed my mother's hand as Jamal took hold of Freya. As I was pushed toward the stairs leading up into the palace, I reached down, grabbing the lamp. The five of us dashed through the palace, with Jamal taking the lead. I followed blindly, not caring where he was taking us. Behind us, the sounds of screams pierced the silence.

It sounded as though The Vizier was managing to cut through the guards with little resistance.

We raced right to the center of the palace and into a corridor I'd never seen before.

Behind us, The Vizier had already caught up. I screamed as I sent a bolt of fire whizzing down the corridor behind me. He batted it away as though it was only a minor irritation and carried on toward us. I stopped running and turned to face him, throwing the lamp out behind me to my mother. There was no point running. He'd gotten through most of our guards with barely a pause. I pulled all my energy into myself and sent out a huge ball of flame, this one bigger than the last.

"Stay behind me!" I screamed to the others as I followed the fireball with more flames. The whole corridor was full of fire, obscuring my view of The Vizier, but I knew I wouldn't be able to stop him. This was a temporary fix. When the flames died down, I saw that I'd knocked him to the floor, at least. He rose slowly as I stepped back toward the others, edging away from him. He sent a bolt of magic hurtling toward me, but I blocked it, sending it ricocheting off the walls before it ebbed away.

My magic was waning. With each fireball I sent his way, my magic lessened. He was so much more powerful than me, and it was all I could do to keep him at bay. I used the last of my energy to block one of his spells then fell to the floor. I had nothing left in me to fight.

He rose up, walking slowly closer, a gleam in his eye as he stared down at me.

I vaguely heard Jamal shouting my name behind me, but I was too exhausted to move. As if in slow motion, The Vizier raised his hand to deliver the final shot. A flash of purple light lit up the corridor. There was a bang, and something soft and heavy landed on my legs.

Asher lay lifeless, his wings charred by magic. He'd flown in front of The Vizier's magic and saved my life.

"Come on!" Jamal shouted, taking my hand and pulling me to my feet. Asher's body fell to the floor with a soft thump. I resisted. I couldn't leave Asher, even though it was clear he was dead. My heart splintered into a thousand pieces as Jamal dragged me away from The Vizier and toward the others.

"This way!" Jamal ordered, opening a door. He held it open as we all dived through. Once I'd passed him, he pulled the door closed and jammed a piece of wood in the handle to stop it being opened from the other side.

"Where are we?" I asked. I thought I knew every nook and cranny of the palace, but I didn't know this room at all. Looking around, there were no clues. It was a bare room of about ten feet by eight feet with empty shelves along each side.

"It's the overflow pantry," Jamal answered. When parties are planned, this is usually full, but since we've had all these problems, it's barely been needed.

I wanted to ask him how he knew that, but now wasn't the time. Instead, I rubbed the lamp, freeing Genie.

"What happened?" he asked once he'd solidified back into himself.

"The Vizier is in the palace. I think he's killed most of the guards."

Genie nodded and crossed his arms, standing resolute. "Use me. Use my magic!"

Tears prickled at the corners of my eyes. "You have magic without my wishes. Can't you use that?"

He opened his mouth to speak, but before he said a word, everything went silent.

Jamal moved to open the door, but my father held

out a hand to stop him.

“Wait. It might be a trap.”

So we waited. And waited. And at some point, night time came.

12TH JULY

At first, we took it in turns to listen at the door, but none of us opened it. The thick door was the only thing between us and certain death.

"We need to go out!" I complained for the tenth time in an hour. Being cooped up was making me edgy. "Maybe he's gone. He could be running a rampage through Kisbu, and we are all stuck in here, hiding."

"I can hear something!" Freya said her ear to the door. "He's definitely out there."

I stood up and listened next to her.

"Someone is out there," I whispered. "What if it's one of the guards injured and looking for help?"

"And what if it's The Vizier waiting to pounce on us?" Jamal said, slipping between us.

I faced him. "We are the heads of this kingdom.

What kind of royals are we that we are hiding away like frightened animals at the worst possible time?"

"The kind that want to stay alive," Jamal retorted.

"We have a duty!" I said, knocking the wedged piece of wood, which turned out to be a doorstop, onto the floor. I tugged the handle, and as I did, a sharp shock ran up my arm.

"What is it?" Jamal asked his eyes wide as I pulled back my arm and gave it a rub.

"I couldn't open the door. The Vizier has put a spell on it. All that time arguing about whether we should get out and we couldn't even if we wanted to." I would have laughed if I didn't want to cry so much.

"What now?" Jamal asked, turning to the others. I looked at the expressions on their faces. My mother was lost again. Her eyes were blank. The change of scenery had made her lose her grip on reality, and I doubted it would come back anytime soon. I did notice my father holding her hand, which made me smile.

"Aladdin, what do you think?"

My father looked around him. "These shelving units are not bolted to the floor. We could use one to try and ram the door down."

Jamal made to grab the shelves, but Genie stopped him. "A ram won't get through magic. Only magic can do this."

Jamal stepped back to let him through. Genie put his hand to the door handle and gripped it in his fingers. Blue sparks filled the air causing the rest of us to take a step back. He contorted his face into a look of either concentration or pain. I didn't want to know which. The muscles of his arms bulged as he put his effort into opening the door. Color drained from his face as the blue sparks intensified. He let go and fell to the floor.

I ran to him, but he shrugged me off. "I'm fine."

His words said one thing, but the look on his face told a different story. I sat next to him and snuggled against his chest. His heartbeat was erratic, and his arms around me trembled slightly, but it was less than ten minutes before he stood up to try again.

Again and again, the same thing happened. He tried four times, each time falling to the floor. His skin paled considerably as he fell to the floor again.

"No more!" I demanded. "Look at you. It's going to kill you!"

"I'm stronger than that," he said, managing a weak smile. I stood and looked at the others.

"Genie is done. He can't open the door. We'll have to try to ram it like Jamal suggested." I made to pull the shelving unit away from the wall, but no one came to help.

"What?" I asked as five pairs of eyes stared at me.

"If Genie can't open the door, how can these flimsy shelves help?" Jamal asked softly.

"So what? We just stay here until we die? Is that your plan?"

Jamal shifted his weight from one foot to another and looked to Aladdin for help.

Aladdin shrugged, offering no help at all.

"There is one other way," Jamal offered. "You still have one wish left. Genie's wishes are much more powerful than his normal magic. You could just wish us all out."

"No! Not a chance."

"Why not? You've just said that we'll die if we stay in here."

The truth was I wasn't prepared to trade Genie's freedom for ours. "There must be another way!"

Jamal shook his head. "There isn't."

Anger swelled in my gut. Genie wasn't the only one who was magic. I had magic too. Yes, touching the door handle had hurt, but it had hurt Genie too, and he'd kept holding on until the pain got to be too much. I barrelled Jamal out of the way and grabbed the handle. Magic shot up my arm, but I held fast.

"Stand back!" I yelled as my body went up in flames. The magic running through me made my own magic uncontrollable. And yet, I held on as the others huddled in the far corner of the pantry for fear of getting burned. I pushed down on the handle, feeling a little give. It wasn't much, but there was some movement.

A hand joined mine. Genie screamed as my own flames licked up his arm. That, combined with the magic now pulsing through both of us, was an agony I couldn't bear. Not only was I in pain, I was hurting Genie. I tried to pull back, but Genie's hand on mine made that impossible. I had two choices. Either argue with him as he burned to death or put my energy into what we were both doing.

I yelled out as I pushed down, helped by the force of Genie's hand on mine.

Our screams mingled together as one as we pushed, and the handle finally went down, opening the door. Genie and I fell right through the door to the ground.

I closed my eyes as the sounds of chaos erupted around me. I heard the sound of water being splashed, but I was too exhausted to open my eyes. Something wet...a towel or something similar was thrown over my hand, which I realized was still holding onto Genie's. Or Genie was holding onto mine; I couldn't tell which. I didn't much care. The force of all the magic running through me, being expended by me, had all but knocked me out.

I felt someone cradle my head and try and force a few drops of water into my mouth. I thought it was Genie until I realized he couldn't possibly hold my hand and cradle me at the same time. I dragged my eyelids up and found Jamal looking down at me, a frown on his face.

"Thank all the gods. Here drink this."

I tried to sit up, but as I moved, the whole room seemed to spin around me. I had to let him drip the water into my mouth.

"The Vizier?" I mumbled when my lips were suitably wet enough to speak.

"He's not here. The corridor is a mess, and something smells of burning, but the palace is quiet."

I used my free hand to grab hold of Jamal's arm and pull myself up. The once white corridor was a mess of burn marks and rubble. I inhaled the sooty smell, which could have been left over from my fight with The Vizier.

Beside me, Genie groaned. I looked over to find my mother wiping his head with a cloth.

"Is he burned?" I asked, finally letting go of his hand. His skin wasn't blemished at all despite me making his arm go up in flames only moments before.

"I don't think so," my mother said her voice panicked, "but he's not waking up. I don't know what to do."

I'd never seen my mother panic. Not once in my entire life, but she wasn't the person I used to know.

I half crawled away from Jamal and to Genie as the others ran around the corner.

Genie's eyes flickered as I kissed his mouth lightly.

"Wake up, my love."

The corners of his mouth curled slowly into a half-smile. I gripped his hand again as he opened his eyes.

"The guards are dead," my father announced.

Behind him, Freya spoke. "Those that aren't dead are gone. The palace is empty, but it's a mess. The basement is full of bodies. Walls have been blasted through."

"Any sign of The Vizier?" Jamal asked, tension etched into his features.

"No."

"Let's do a proper search. Gaia, are you ok? Can you look after Genie while we search the palace?"

I nodded, too scared to speak. The Vizier could be anywhere, biding his time.

I heard Jamal issuing instructions all the way down the corridor. I held my breath as his voice became quieter and quieter.

"We can't let them go alone," Genie said, trying to pull himself up. Like I had, just moments before, he faltered and fell back. I picked up the cloth my mother had just been using and wiped the sweat from his brow.

"I nearly killed you back there," I remarked, trying to hold the tears back.

"I used magic to shield my skin as well as the magic to open the door. I'm fine. Look..."

He held his arm to show me. There was not a mark on it, but it was clear that he wasn't fine. His face was sheet white, and his eyes sunken into his head. His skin felt like paper, and though it wasn't burnt, I could see the blue veins beneath it.

"What is happening to you?"

He closed his eyes and sucked in a breath. I heard a rattle in his throat as he did.

"I'm dying, Gaia. My body is flesh and blood, but each time I use magic, it becomes less so. I told you that I was becoming more like a genie every day. A genie isn't human. I started off as human, and thanks to your father, I have had eighteen years of being a human again. But the transformation is almost complete. Once I become fully genie again, I'll not need to eat, to sleep. I won't be able to touch, to feel. The person you know will die. I'll still be here, but I'll be like a spirit. Everything I am will cease to exist."

Tears fell down my face. "I wish..." my voice cracked as I spoke.

"Not yet, Gaia. Not yet. Help me up."

"Why won't you let me free you? I can stop all this."

"You might be able to stop me from becoming a slave by making me human, but then what? The Vizier is still out there somewhere."

"Wrong!" A menacing voice echoed down the corridor. "I'm in here, but good guess. I've been waiting for this moment for a long time. I have the two of you right where I want you. The genie that has the power to grant me anything my heart desires and the girl who defeated me years ago. Where is it?"

He strode toward us and held out his hand. I looked up at him in confusion.

"Where is the lamp? I know you have control of the genie. I need the lamp."

My mind flickered to the last place I'd seen the lamp. It had been locked in the pantry with us, the door to which was only a couple of feet behind us.

"I'm not telling you," I said, standing up and staring The Vizier down. He looked so majestic from a distance, but up close, he had a sinister look in his eyes.

"Hmm," he replied, obviously not bothered in the slightest that I was standing up to him. He towered over me, and the way his eyes bored into mine sent shivers down my spine. "Your friends didn't have it on them, so one of you two has it."

He dragged his eyes up and down my body before landing them right back on my face.

"I still don't understand," he hissed. "Even knowing what I know about you, it seems inconceivable that a little girl such as yourself could beat me. A baby as you were then."

"What do you know about me?"

The Vizier laughed. "I know you are desperate to find out. I know everything. As soon as I saw you in Urbis, I guessed what you were up to. It was a coincidence, you know. Me being there at the same time as you. Connected, for certain, but imagine my surprise when I saw my little nemesis running around the streets looking for her history."

"It doesn't matter. If I defeated you before, it means I can do it again."

The Vizier narrowed his eyes at me. "You couldn't be more wrong. You have no idea who you are, and you have no idea why you defeated me the first time. I know how you did. I might not be able to really believe it, but I know how you were able to fell me all those years ago. I also know that you don't have the ability to do it again."

I wanted to slap the smug look off his face.

"Want to try me?" I said, pulling back my arm ready to shoot fire at him.

He had the audacity to laugh again.

"More fire? It's getting rather boring, don't you think? The others have much more interesting abilities."

It annoyed me that he was getting to me. I hated that he knew more about me than I did, but I couldn't let him know that. I needed to stop him from getting the lamp.

Pulling my energy in was so much harder than it had been before. I'd used so much just opening the door, but it was enough to send a small fireball his way. As I was so close, I was able to hit him right in the center of his face. He recoiled as his hair set on fire. He responded by sending jets of purple light toward me. I ducked as one narrowly missed me. A pair of strong arms wrapped around my waist and began pulling me back. Genie dragged me right past the pantry and into the huge kitchen.

"We need to go back!" I hissed as genie pulled me past the large ovens that cooked for the palace inhabitants and staff. "The lamp!"

"He won't go for the lamp. If there is a choice between you and me, he'd rather lose me. He wants you. He'll come after you, and when he gets you, he'll go back for the lamp."

Genie's words made no sense to me, but he was right. The Vizier stepped through the kitchen doors we'd just run through. He raised his arm and sent a jet of magic to the doors at the opposite end of the kitchen, sealing them shut. We were trapped. The only way out was the doorway directly behind The Vizier.

He walked slowly, deliberately toward us, a chilling smile on his face. He knew that we were trapped, and he knew we were both low on magic. He also had a good idea that the lamp was in the pantry down the corridor.

I pulled a pan from one of the stoves and threw it at him. He lifted his arm and deflected it with magic before it even got close. It hit the wall and crashed to the ground with a metallic clang. I backed up, pushing Genie backward with me.

"Wish us out!" Genie whispered in my ear.

I shook my head almost surreptitiously. "No."

"He'll kill you if you don't."

"So let him!" I replied, this time out loud. I grabbed a knife from a knife block and threw it at The Vizier, following it up with the rest of the knives.

He blocked every single one, and just like the pan had, they clattered to the ground.

I sent another fireball, but this one did no damage at all. And all the while, he was getting closer and closer. He had a gleam in his eye and a smirk on his face. He wasn't even attacking. Just deflecting my attacks. He didn't need to. He was literally backing us into a corner. We had nowhere to go.

"Wish us out of here!" Genie whispered again, this time more urgently. "I can't protect you unless you make a wish. I need you to wish it. I'm not strong enough without wishes."

"I'm not sending you back into that lamp!" I hissed, stepping back, further still.

The Vizier lifted his arm, almost lazily, readying himself to strike. Genie and I were like a couple of baby mice in the eyes of a hawk.

I tried pulling my energy in, but I was spent. There was nothing left. I desperately needed to recharge, but there was no time.

A flash of light flew past my left ear and hit The Vizier in the chest. He stumbled backward, clutching his chest, before tripping and falling backward. Genie grabbed my hand, and we jumped over The Vizier and back out into the corridor. Almost immediately, I felt a drag on my arm. I looked back to see Genie bent double. His breaths were coming in great heaves.

"Come on!" I encouraged, trying to pull him, but it was no use. Every bolt of magic he used brought him closer to death, and he'd just used everything he had to help us escape.

"Gaia!" I looked up to see Jamal at the other end of the corridor.

"The Vizier!" I wheezed. "He's in the kitchen. Help me move Genie. He's too exhausted to walk."

Jamal began to run toward us, but before he'd gotten anywhere close, a purple jet of light arced over Genie and me and hit Jamal, sending him flying backward down the corridor and into the wall at the end. After hitting the wall, he crumpled to the floor.

I looked behind me in a panic to see The Vizier. I threw everything I had at him as I dragged Genie down the corridor, but my fire was nothing more than tiny flames that he flicked away.

"Jamal!" wailed Freya as she rounded the corner.

"Go back!" I screamed at her as she fell to her knees beside Jamal's body.

It was too late. The Vizier repeated his action. Freya didn't have far to go, but she hit the wall and fell on Jamal. Neither of them moved.

"Stop it!" I screamed over my shoulder to The Vizier, only to be met with a cackle.

Genie pulled himself up and turned to face The Vizier.

"Let her go, Akeem," he said, pulling me behind him. "You can have me. The lamp is in there." He nodded to the open doorway of the pantry. "Take me and let her go."

"What are you doing?" I cried, trying to get past him. I wasn't about to let him give himself up. He wasn't as strong as he used to be, but he was quick enough to move to block me.

"You use my name, Genie," The Vizier said,

amusement in his voice. "It's been a long time since I last heard it. Eighteen years or so. The last eighteen years have been particularly bad for me, thanks to your girlfriend. Hand her over, Genie."

"No. You have me. You either get the lamp and enslave me or you fight me. There is no other option."

"Fight you?" The Vizier laughed. "You can barely stand. I could knock you over with my little finger."

As he spoke, we continued to back down the corridor toward Jamal and Freya. Each step we took backward, The Vizier took one forward. He paused outside the doorway to the pantry.

"Run!" Genie yelled, pushing me back. He dashed toward The Vizier and launched himself at him. The pair of them crashed to the floor. Genie laid his fists into The Vizier's face. He had the element of surprise on his side, but it wasn't just his magical strength that was waning. This was taking everything he had. I wavered for a second. Genie wanted me to run. He was literally laying his life down for me, but I couldn't leave him. I couldn't let him sacrifice himself just to save my life. I ran toward the brawling pair and aimed.

Neither noticed me as Genie pummelled The Vizier's face, turning it more purple than his robes.

The Vizier tried to pull himself out from under Genie. It was clear he was used to fighting with magic and not fists. I only had seconds to react. The second he got his hands free from under Genie, he'd be able to use his magic again, and with Genie being so close, it wouldn't take much to kill him.

I had the fire in my hand ready to throw, but in the chaos, I could just as easily hit Genie.

The little bit of energy I had left went out in a sputter. As The Vizier finally freed his hand, I lifted my leg and brought my foot down on it as hard as I could.

He screamed in pain as I put my full weight on it.

Genie jumped up and dragged me off The Vizier's hand. We raced down the corridor hand in hand. A flash of magic flew over our heads. I turned. The Vizier had risen up. This was it. Neither Genie or I had anything left. Genie had rallied in the last few minutes, but he was beginning to weigh me down again, and this time I could barely keep the pair of us up. I could only watch as The Vizier lifted his hand to strike.

Something flew over my head, but not from The Vizier. This came from behind and flew toward him. It landed on The Vizier's face.

Blood spurted from his face, and what followed was a scream so terrible, I'd never heard anything like it before.

"What's happening?" I whispered as Genie collapsed beside me. I fell to the floor with him. We both watched on in horror as The Vizier's face was mauled.

The thing turned around and flew back to us.

"Asher?" I whispered. "Genie, it's Asher. I thought he died!"

I could barely contain my excitement as my bird flew to me, something grotesque hanging in his beak. It was an eye.

I turned my attention to The Vizier. He was still screaming, holding his face as blood dripped to the floor.

As I watched, he disappeared, leaving only a puff of purple smoke in his wake.

"What happened?" I croaked. "Is he dead?"

"He'll come back," Genie whispered. I looked at him. His breathing was shallow, and his once muscular body looked emaciated. His skin was more translucent than ever. His eyes flickered and closed.

"I wish you to be free," I whispered. "I wish you to be human again."

A cold wind whipped around us as my wish, the only one of the three wishes I ever cared about came true.

13TH JULY

His body was warm. Warmer than I'd ever known it to be. All the while we'd been together, he'd slowly been turning into a genie. The change had been so gradual that I'd barely noticed, and it was only now that he was human again that the warmth of his flesh next to mine was noticeable.

I traced a finger over his bare chest, watching the steady rise and fall as he breathed softly. We'd fallen asleep in each other's arms, clutching onto each other for fear that one of us would somehow be taken away. It was our first time without chains lying between us. In the light of a new day, my fears hadn't completely receded. And yet, Genie was healthy. The pallor in his skin had gone, and the tone had returned to his muscles.

I leaned forward and kissed his cheek lightly, expecting him to wake, but he remained soundly asleep. Leaving him physically hurt, but the kingdom was a mess, and someone needed to sort it out.

Guilt tugged at me as I pulled on one of Genie's shirts. After everything that had happened yesterday, the two of us had gone straight to bed. I'd tried arguing, but I had been so tired that I'd acquiesced. In the cold light of day, the thought of the dead guards still lying in the basement, made my stomach churn.

The palace was deathly silent as I padded the corridors to my own room, barefoot. The guards that normally stood sentry were no longer there. The stench of fire and of death was everywhere, adding to the guilt I already felt. In my room, Asher came to greet me.

He landed on my hand and clucked as I stroked his downy head.

"I wouldn't be here if it wasn't for you," I said, giving him a quick kiss. He playfully nipped my finger, stretched his wings, and took flight out of the open window. I pulled on a pair of pants and headed back out into the corridor. I found my father sitting alone in the breakfast room.

"How are you, Gaia?" he asked as I walked in.

I nodded, unable to quell the churning in my stomach. I didn't trust myself to speak.

"The guards helped clean up last night. The injured have been taken to hospital. The families of the dead have been informed."

I nodded again, surprised that he'd taken so much action. My father, as he used to be, would have done that, but this wasn't my father anymore, or at least he didn't remember being...or did he?

"Do you know who I am?"

My father raised an eyebrow at the question. “Of course, Gaia. I greeted you when you walked in, remember?”

I sat down next to him. “I mean, do you remember me? Do you remember I’m your daughter? Do you remember living here?”

“I remember you once told me you were my daughter. I understand now that I’m not who I think I am. I remember growing up on the streets of Kisbu. I remember living in the bell tower. I don’t remember the bits between that. I’m sorry. I know that’s not what you want to hear. If it makes you feel any better, I believe you when you say you are my daughter.”

It confirmed to me what Genie had told me the night before. The Vizier wasn’t gone. Not really. He’d left the castle. Maybe he’d left Kisbu, but deep in my heart, I knew he would be back. This wasn’t over. The curse, or whatever it was, was still in effect. It would make everything so much harder. The six of us. My parents, Genie, Freya, Jamal, and I would have to pick up the pieces together, with three of the six having lost their memories.

My mother chose that moment to walk through the door. She came through the servant’s entrance, armed with a platter of food. I stood to help her put it all out on the table. There was no point asking why she was the one making breakfast. The staff were either dead or had run away.

I picked up an apple and rolled it in my hands.

“How many people died last night?” I asked, not really wanting to know the answer.

I’d put the question to my father, but it was my mother that answered.

“We had fifty-three fatalities and many more injured.

They have been dealt with and the families informed."

"Yes, Aladdin told me."

She looked at him, and I saw something pass between them. It looked a lot like love.

"We were planning on visiting the families later. I was going to ask if you wanted to join us."

"You are going...together?"

She smiled. "Yes. We stayed up half the night talking. Aladdin helped me a lot. We are going to visit the injured as well. I was going to ask Jamal and Freya if they wanted to come with us. They've been doing a marvelous job of helping me these past few weeks."

"Where are they?" I asked.

"I suspect they will come down soon. They both got nasty bumps last night. They need to rest."

"So did you come up with a plan last night? Apart from visiting people, I mean?"

"I'm not sure what we can do. We both know that things aren't right. My memories are fleeting, and I don't feel myself."

"That's the curse. I've been telling you for weeks."

"I know," she admitted. "It was only when Aladdin spoke of his own memories fading that I realized just how much was missing of my own memories. I'll need to rely on you, Gaia, to tell me when I'm missing things."

I wondered if my father had told her that he was the Sultan and that they'd been married for eighteen years. He might not remember it, but he remembered me telling him.

"What about the palace?" I asked.

"We did a walk through this morning before I went to the kitchen to make breakfast. It will take time to get back to how we were, but if we work together, we could clear the debris. We'll have to get people in to rebuild and repaint. It's mostly localized to the basement and the kitchen area, so it shouldn't be too much work."

"And Kisbu?"

My mother sighed. "I don't know. I've been concentrating on the palace as a way to not have to think of what is happening out there. I've not even dared to look outside the windows."

My father stood. "We need to round up the others and then go outside. The people out there will be hurting. We only know the damage that was caused in here, but I expect The Vizier created chaos out there too."

My mother looked up at him in awe. It was at that moment that Jamal and Freya walked in. I noticed that they were holding hands.

Freya gave a little wave as she sat beside me at the table. I filled her and Jamal in as they picked at the food.

"We can't go out as we are," Jamal stated.

I followed his gaze around the table. My mother was dressed in a plain sundress, but my father was still wearing the same clothes he'd worn the day before. Jamal was dressed in casual clothes, but Freya had done the same as me and put on a shirt.

Not one of us had dragged a comb through our hair.

"You want us to get dressed up?" My father asked.

"Aladdin. You are the Sultan. You may not remember. The people may not remember, but they will be looking for a leader. Her Majesty the Sultana too. We need to provide someone the people can look up to. I can arrange for you to give a talk from the balcony if you like. It won't take long to gather up the few guards we have left and get them to ring the town bells to get people to come and listen."

My father drummed his fingers on the table. "I think

you are right, but if I'm dressing up in royal attire then so should you."

"I'm not royal, sir," Jamal reminded him.

My father lifted his hand and clapped him on the shoulder.

"I've seen what you've done around here. I've heard from Jawahir how much you've helped. You may not be a sultan, but you've worked as one. The people don't remember me, but they remember you. If I go out on that balcony, I go with you. I go with you all. We are all the sultan. If this thing ever ends and we find a way to bring our memories back, I will take my place alongside Jawahir." He held his hand out on the table, and my mother took it, blushing as she did.

"We still have two guards on the main gate. If you don't mind asking them to do as you said, you can meet me in my bedroom in half an hour so you can borrow one of my royal uniforms....if that's alright with Jawahir?"

My mother blushed further. "Of course. I guess it is your room as well as mine. I shall wait and dress when you are finished."

"So it's settled then." he turned to me. "Gaia. Will Genie be joining us? I hear that he is just as big a part of running this kingdom as the rest of us."

"I'll go and fetch him," I said, standing up from the table. I still had the apple in my hand as I left the room.

Jamal caught up with me.

"Gaia. Are you ok? I've been worried about you. Freya barely slept last night. She kept asking me to come and check on you."

"You slept with her?"

His cheeks colored bright red. It was the first time I'd ever seen him embarrassed.

"I'm sorry," I said quickly. "It's none of my business."

"I love her if that's what you are asking."

I kissed his cheek, which made him turn red. "I'm happy for you, and I'm fine, by the way." I turned to leave, but he stopped me.

"Actually, I was hoping you'd come with me. I didn't want to mention it in there because your parents have been through so much, but we have a problem."

I cocked my head. After everything that had happened, I hated to think about what Jamal considered as a problem.

"Is The Vizier back?" I asked.

"No, not that. The town folk are protesting again. I saw them outside. Hundreds of them, lining the streets. I don't know how to handle this, Gaia. I know everyone is looking to me, but I'm not the Sultan. I've been helping where I can, but I'm not equipped to deal with this. Not now."

I took his hand in mine. "Come with me."

"Where are we going?" he asked, stunned.

"We are going to do what you promised my father you were going to do. We are going to speak to the guards, and after that, we will speak to the people."

"I'm not sure, Gaia. They have every right to be angry. We have almost no guards."

"Then we deal with it." I opened the front door of the palace. The scene before me took my breath away. Jamal hadn't successfully conveyed the sheer magnitude of the problem. He'd said hundreds, but there were thousands. It looked like the whole city had come out.

I ran to the front gates, which, thankfully, were closed.

A guard on the gate nodded his head to me.

"Please can you tell everyone that we will be giving a

speech in an hour from the balcony."

He gave me a look that quite clearly stated he thought I was insane. His mouth hung open.

"I'll head out the staff entrance and see if I can round up more guards!" I added, feeling flustered. "Just try and keep everyone under control. I know it's a huge job. I'm sorry."

"Your Highness. I don't think you understand," the guard began.

"I understand. I can see that we have a major problem. I'm trying to deal with it as best I can."

I felt Jamal tugging on my shirtsleeve as I spoke. I ignored him, but I couldn't ignore the people at the gate calling my name. No doubt, out for my blood for letting them down so badly.

"I think you should see this, Gaia," Jamal said, physically spinning me around so that I was looking straight at the people.

They had smiles on their faces. The ones at the front were pushing food and money through the bars.

"What's going on?" I whispered.

"That's what I've been trying to tell you," the guard said. "The people are here to support you. They all saw what was happening in the palace last night. They saw the bodies being brought out. At first, I thought they were coming to be nosy, but then they started asking what they could do to help. They started coming last night, but they kept coming."

A smile tugged on the corner of my lips. "They are here to help? They don't want to riot?"

"I believe that's the case, Your Highness."

"Then tell them we'll make a statement in an hour," I repeated. I took Jamal's hand and pulled him inside.

After a quick shower, I selected a dress that I'd worn

to a state occasion the previous year. It was beautiful. Three shades of pink with gold trim. It was by far my most favorite item of clothing, but it wasn't for me. I dressed in a green dress that I wore when we had guests and headed to Jamal's room. I knocked and waited. When he opened the door, his face turned to one of surprise.

"Gaia?"

"This is for Freya."

His cheeks colored again. He took the dress and thanked me before heading back inside.

Genie was up and awake when I got to his room. I threw him an apple as I entered. He strode across the room and brought me into a kiss that made my knees weak.

"I brought you an apple," I said, referring to the fruit I'd saved from breakfast.

He was dressed only in pants. The feel of his skin against mine had me wanting to go back to bed and never leave.

I ran my hand over his chest as he wrapped his arms around me.

"You feel different," I murmured, leaning down to kiss the skin below his collarbone. He was warm and smelled heavenly. I inhaled and took in hints of citrus and spice.

"Gaia," he said, pulling me back up. "I'm sorry you had to waste your last wish on me."

"I didn't have to," I whispered back. "I wanted to. I don't regret it."

"Not today, maybe."

"Never," I said, pulling him forward into a kiss.

His lips tasted of the apple he'd just taken a bite out of. I could have tasted him all day. "I want to get to know you," I said. "As you are now."

He stepped back. "I might be human, but I'm still not the man I once was. My memories are hazy."

There was a sadness in his eyes as he spoke. "I might never be the man you want me to be."

"You already are."

"For now. Akeem is still out there. This thing hasn't ended. We might have the lamp, but he has control. He's already shown once he can turn me into a genie. When he gets his strength back, he'll try again. We are running out of people who will free me from slavery."

"The lamp!" I cried out. It was still in the pantry.

"Get dressed!" I demanded. "Wear something regal. I'll meet you on the balcony in half an hour."

He looked at me questioningly, but I didn't stick around to answer. Instead, I raced out of his suite and back to the scene of the fight we'd had with The Vizier last night. In daylight, it looked worse than it had. I jumped over the rubble and ran into the pantry. In the far corner sat the lamp. I picked it up and held it to my chest.

Without this, the Vizier would never be able to command Genie. He could turn him into a genie as much as he liked, but he'd never control him. He'd never be his master. I gave the lamp a rub. Nothing happened. With a smile, I headed back out into the corridor. I wouldn't hide the lamp as my father had. I'd destroy it completely.

"What are you looking so smug about?" Freya commented as I headed up the main stairs to the balcony. She ran and caught up with me. She looked beautiful in the pink dress.

"That really suits you," I commented.

"Thank you for letting me borrow it."

"Borrow it? It's yours. You've helped me dress for years. I think it's about time you had something for your trouble."

"So, what is the smile on your face about?"

I held up the lamp. "Genie is free. Even if The Vizier manages to make him a genie again, he'll never be his master. I'm going to destroy the lamp."

Freya was quiet for a second.

"But you didn't have the lamp when you became his master," she pointed out.

"No, but I was there when he became a genie again. I was the first to make a wish when that happened. I was standing right next to him."

"So..." She sucked in a breath. "What if The Vizier captures him and turns him into a genie then? As long as he's the first to make a wish, the genie is his until he exhausts his wishes. He wouldn't even need the lamp."

In my excitement, I'd not thought of that, and yet it was so obvious. It hit me like a punch to the gut. The lamp was pointless. I couldn't stay with Genie and wait for him to turn back. I'd used up my wishes. I couldn't ever get them back. But what could I do? I could hardly ask anyone else to give up their lives to spend every second with him.

"We need to find The Vizier. We need to finish this."

Freya took my hand in hers. "I know we do, but he's gone. He's in hiding. I think the safest option would be to send Genie away. Send him to another kingdom where The Vizier can't find him."

"I can't be without him, Freya!" I croaked. "I love him."

"I never said he should go alone."

We walked the stairs together. My mind whirred with everything I had to do. Destroy the lamp, find The

Vizier, find my siblings, and stop the curse. But for now, my job was to be a leader. Or one of six leaders, for we were all in this together.

I thought the crowd outside had grown even bigger in the past hour, or it might have just appeared that way from the higher floor. I peeked out through the curtains at the cheering throng. Cheering! Not protesting, not complaining, but actively cheering. I still didn't really know what for. From my perspective, we'd spent the last couple of days in hiding, then fighting.

When the others turned up, I took Genie's hand in mine. On the other side, I took hold of my mom's hand. She did the same with my father, who took Freya's hand, who took Jamal's. With his one free hand, Genie opened the door to the balcony. As soon as we paraded out, the crowd went wild. Genie gripped my hand tightly. The noise was deafening.

As I looked out at the crowd, I was reminded what it was we were fighting for. The people of Badalah and especially Kisbu needed us

14TH JULY

I woke up from the best night's sleep I'd had in a month. It helped that I had genie's arms wrapped around me, and there were no chains between us. I watched him sleeping peacefully and gave him a light kiss before slipping out of bed to find my parents.

I found them in the breakfast room with Jamal and Freya. I hung back, not letting them know I was there so I could observe. My mother laughed over something Jamal said. From afar, it looked like everything was back to how it should be.

"Morning Gaia," my mother said, finally spotting me. She beckoned me in.

"How are you feeling today?" I asked as I took my place at the table.

"I'm feeling good. It's a good day today, thanks to

Aladdin and Freya and Jamal." There was something about her. The way her eyes shone and the way she spoke so animatedly. I could almost believe this was over. But it wasn't. This was merely a reprieve.

"The four of us have been having a discussion," she continued. "I've come to accept that I am ill, that the people of Badalah are also suffering from the same magical malady."

"A curse," Freya added.

"A curse, that's right. I know I've made some decisions that aren't in the best interests of Badalah. I can't even remember making them, but I trust that I did. I also trust that Aladdin and I are married. I don't remember, and I'm not going to jump into anything, but I believe that we have something... a connection if you will, that we can work on until there comes a time that our memories return." She held her hand out and placed it on my father's, who gazed at her with a rapt expression.

"As I am the Sultana and the only royal that everyone remembers, I'm going to act as a figurehead, but I've appointed Jamal to be my chief advisor until this is sorted out. He is now unofficially in charge, and every decision I make will run through him first."

I glanced over at Jamal, who sat with a shy grin on his face. Next to him, Freya's face held a more obvious grin.

"I think that's wonderful and very much deserved," I said, holding a cup of coffee up to him.

"Freya is going to bring magic back to Badalah," my mother continued. "She was a wonderful maid, but she never managed to keep you in check as your lady, so we've decided to start a new program, and she is in charge. Magic was never the problem, it was just the people that wielded it...Some of the people," she corrected herself.

"One person," Aladdin amended.

"Aladdin is going to help me rebuild. We both agree that Jamal will be in charge, but Aladdin has a lot of wonderful ideas on how we can make things better."

"I bet he does," I said, giving him a smile. "He always did."

He gave a slight tip of his head in response.

"What about me?" I asked. "Where do I figure in all this?"

The table went silent. My mother took her hand from my father's and held onto mine.

"You, my darling, have the hardest job of all. I can't ask you to do it, but I know that if I suggest it you will. I don't think I'd be able to stop you, even if I wanted to. You were always so strong-willed and adventurous. I knew about your nighttime walks around Kisbu, by the way. I always knew."

My cheeks reddened. I'd always thought I'd been so clever to sneak out, and my parents knew all along. It figured. My mother never missed a trick before she became ill.

"What job is it?" I asked, full of curiosity.

My mother glanced over at Jamal, who nodded. "You are the only one who can stop this. Our memories are still not what they once were, which tells us that The Vizier is still alive. He will return. Jamal has already put plans in place to recruit more guards. We've had thousands of applications already. The people want to fight. Freya is in charge of recruiting people of magic. We are going to build an army to protect Kisbu. You can't be here."

"What do you mean?"

"I mean, you should leave. The Vizier wants you. I'm not going to give him the opportunity to find you. I know that he only saw you by chance in Urbis. He can't find you if he doesn't know where you are. I want you to leave Badalah. I need you to leave Badalah. Go back to Urbis and find your birth mother if you must."

"You want me to leave you?"

She pulled me into a hug. "I don't want you to leave me at all. I want to wrap you up in cotton wool and barricade you in the palace, but I don't think you'd like that, would you?"

"No."

She ran her hand down my cheek. "You were always destined for great things, Gaia. I never expected saving Badalah from a magic curse would be one of them, but there you have it. I know that if anyone can save us all, it will be you."

I looked around the table at four expectant faces. I'd been wanting to leave for a long time, but not to go back to Urbis. Not yet, at least. There was somewhere I wanted to try first.

"I'll do it!" I said. If leaving meant keeping them safe, then so be it. "Freya, would you help me pack?" I stood up from the table. "There is someone I think I should tell, excuse me."

I ran to my room and picked up some of the newspaper articles I'd been keeping, before heading to see Genie.

He was sitting on the sofa in his office, nose deep in a book.

He looked up when I walked in. A smile spread across his lips. "You should have woken me up," he said, shuffling up to make space for me on the sofa. "I was thinking of joining you and your parents visiting the injured guards today. It is about time I got out of the palace."

"We can't stay here," I whispered to him.

Genie furrowed his brows. "The kingdom needs a leader, Gaia. It needs you more than ever. I'd forgotten how much until I stood out on the balcony with you."

"It has two," I pointed out. "It has four if you count Jamal and Freya. Did you know that Freya has been made leader of magical development in Badalah?"

Genie raised an eyebrow. "Your father still doesn't know who he is. He's doing a good job, but he's forgotten eighteen years of leadership experience."

"He didn't have eighteen years of leadership experience when he first came to the throne. He had my mother by his side. He still has that now."

Genie put the book to one side and looked at me thoughtfully. "You are serious, aren't you? Where do you want to go? Urbis again? You didn't find them the first time."

He was talking about my siblings.

"No, but they aren't there. They've not been there since we were all very young. I think that's where they are heading."

"What do you mean?"

"I looked at the newspapers again last night. I don't know why I hadn't noticed it before. I was so caught up in all the madness of curses and The Vizier that I didn't put two and two together."

"What did you find out?"

"My siblings...or who I think are my siblings have all left their kingdoms. Or at least some of them have. Some I'm not so sure about. I think they are heading out to search for each other."

"Think? Gaia, doesn't this all seem a little far-fetched?"

"Yes, it sounds utterly ridiculous, but until a month ago, my parents knew who I was, and we weren't sleeping together, and I didn't even know Jamal, and we didn't need a leader of magical development." I was babbling, and I knew it. Genie took my hand in his.

"I see. So if they are not where they are supposed to be, how do you propose to find them?"

"I'll have you to help me."

Genie arched a brow. "You want me to come with you."

I bit my lip. "Yes, I want you to come with me. I need you to be safe. If we leave tonight, The Vizier will not know where we have gone. We have to go soon before he comes back. He caught me on the way to the Urbis Express station before. I don't want to give him the chance to do it again."

"You want to leave the kingdom when there is a chance he will come back? Who will fight him?"

"You're not a genie anymore," I reminded him. "We had thousands of applications for the position of guards. Jamal is still sorting through them. My father made him the head of the guards. They will be fine. They can keep him at bay, but only I can stop him. I can't do that if I stay here, and I won't be able to do that if you stay here."

"You don't need me, Gaia. You never did."

"That's where you are wrong. I need you very much. Please come with me. You need to get away. I can't destroy the lamp. I don't know how. I can't keep you safe."

Genie laughed and pulled me onto his lap. "I thought I was the one who was supposed to keep you safe?"

I leaned into him and kissed him on the nose. "I think we are supposed to keep each other safe. Please come with me."

"Where are we going?"

"I was thinking of starting in The Forge. I was going to go there to find a memory potion, but I'd like to meet the daughters of the president. She has two. Twins called Ivy and Pearl. I don't know how they fit into all this, but I'd like to find out."

"And you think they are still there? You said that your siblings have all moved away from their kingdoms."

"I think so. There was a picture of them at some inventor's guild event in the paper a couple of days ago. I want to find them before they leave, too, before the curse finds them. Maybe I can warn them."

"You have this all figured out, don't you?"

"No. I have no clue what I'm doing, but I'd like to figure it out. I remembered something else yesterday when I was going through the papers. The people of Urbis knew me. They knew exactly who I was. They weren't affected by the curse. I think that if you leave Badalah, your memories will come back to normal."

"I'd certainly like that," he replied.

"So you'll come?"

He looked into my eyes. "Gaia, if you want me to, I'd travel all the kingdoms with you."

"That's good," I replied as he leaned forward to kiss me. "We might need to do just that."

And then his lips touched mine, and just for a moment, nothing else mattered.

MEET THE TEAM

The Kingdom of Fairytales Series was a team effort. Below are the people that made it possible:

EQP Management: Rhi Parkes & J.A. Armitage

Our authors: J.A. Armitage, Audrey Rich, B. Kristin McMichael, Emma Savant, Jennifer Ellision, Scarlett Kol, Rose Castro, Margo Ryerkerk, Zara Quentin, Laura Greenwood and Anne Stryker.

Our Editor
Rose Lipscomb

Our Beta Team
Nadine Peterse-Vrijhof
Diane Major
Kalli Bunch
Stephanie Woodwood

Our Proof Reader
Tina Merritt

And to all the wonderful people who loved the world we created and reviewed our stories.
Thank you

READING ORDER

SEASON ONE
SLEEPING BEAUTY
Queen of Dragons
Heiress of Embers
Throne of Fury
Goddess of Flames

SEASON TWO
LITTLE MERMAID
Queen of Mermaids
Heiress of the Sea
Throne of Change
Goddess of Water

SEASON THREE
RED RIDING HOOD
King of Wolves
Heir of the Curse
Throne of Night
God of Shifters

SEASON FOUR
RAPUNZEL
King of Devotion
Heir of Thorns
Throne of Enchantment
God of Loyalty

SEASON FIVE
RUMPELSTILTSKIN
Queen of Unicorns
Heiress of Gold
Throne of Sacrifice
Goddess of Loss

SEASON SIX
BEAUTY AND THE BEAST
King of Beasts
Heir of Beauty
Throne of Betrayal
God of Illusion

SEASON SEVEN
ALADDIN
Queen of the Sun
Heiress of Shadows
Throne of the Phoenix
Goddess of Fire

SEASON EIGHT
CINDERELLA
Queen of Song
Heiress of Melody
Throne of Symphony
Goddess of Harmony

SEASON NINE
ALICE IN WONDERLAND
Queen of Clockwork
Heiress of Delusion
Throne of Cards
Goddess of Hearts

SEASON TEN
WIZARD OF OZ
King of Traitors
Heir of Fugitives
Throne of Emeralds
God of Storms

SEASON ELEVEN
SNOW WHITE
Queen of Reflections
Heiress of Mirrors
Throne of Wands
Goddess of Magic

SEASON TWELVE
PETER PAN
Queen of Skies
Heiress of Stars
Throne of Feathers
Goddess of Air

SEASON THIRTEEN
URBIS

Kingdom of Royalty
Kingdom of Power
Kingdom of Fairytales
Kingdom of Ever After

BOXSETS

AZIA
BLAISE
CASTIEL
DEON
ELIANA
FALLON
GAIA
HALIA
IVY
JAKON
KELIS
LYRIC
URBIS

www.ingramcontent.com/pod-product-compliance
Lightning Source LLC
Chambersburg PA
CBHW020244030826
48979CB00030B/2617/J

9781989997598